The Invisible Thread

The Invisible Thread

MARIA STEFANIDIS

Publisher: Maria Stefanidis

First published in Australia 2023
This edition published 2023
Copyright © Maria Stefanidis 2023

Cover design, typesetting: WorkingType (www.workingtype.com.au)

Stefanidis, Maria
The Invisible Thread

ISBN-978-0-6456266-8-1

pp384

For my husband Michael
and daughter Chrissy.

CHAPTER ONE

Rizokarpaso

Despina had been fantasising about marrying the brown-eyed Muslim boy with the warm slippery tongue since she was six years old. She couldn't have possibly known that they were lovers before they were siblings. There was no page of any law book of God that would have conceded to such a union. Fate was unfair as it made its plans. It was said that a mother's fate is the dowry of a daughter. If her mother hadn't lost her mind at childbirth, and her other father hadn't become obsessed with the Turkish Armenian gypsy girl he'd hired as her milk-nurse, then none of it would have happened.

She came to the heavily Turkish populated village of Rizo, in the north of Cyprus in 1940. It was a time when Greek and Turkish Cypriots dwelled in discord as neighbours.

It was just after the biggest and final frost before spring she came riding through the marketplace on a splendid camel in a flowing, sheer robe of blue.

Her infant was cosy inside a basket of reed, a musical lute strung from the saddlecloth, and she at the reins chewing mastic.

Her eyes were like a dark forest with the sun hiding there. Her long, wavy hair that blew about her youthful face glistened with fiery red-mocha tones. The motion of her full-rounded hips synchronised with the cow's supple strides, incited the men into a frenzy. Though the gypsy was unaware of the clout she had on the men, this cheeky gesture seemed rehearsed to attract their attention.

Collectively the Greek Christian and Muslim women shook their heads and exchanged scornful glances.

'She's come to entertain us!' One woman exclaimed.

'Not us dear Muslim but the men! They are behaving like feverish wasps fighting over a nest!' Another woman tetchily censured as men wrangled their way through the disorderly gathering to get a closer look at the charismatic foreigner.

'They drool over the girl as if she were a hog on a spit to feed their starving bellies!' The voice of a third woman scathingly remarked.

Just then, a weary middle-aged woman in shapeless black rags and headscarf emerged in the marketplace. The woman was the village midwife. Though better known by some as Mana of Woes because of her unconventional and prehistoric approach to childbearing and remedial procedures. Awkwardly she side-stepped the overturned crates of squawking foul and produce. She shuffled to the forefront of the crowd and then stared up at the gypsy with dubious speculation as she rode past.

'Ah God behold! She has finally agreed to come!' she uttered.

Hastily she absconded the crowd to inform Spyros the Tobacco Merchant that she'd found a likely milk nurse for his newborn daughter Despina.

She was greeted at the door by a man built like a Trojan warrior with a frightful growth of black facial hair. And before she could pass on the news, he impatiently asked, 'do you think my wife's gone mad?'

'It's the terror, you see!' The midwife offered petulantly as she came through the door.

She then considered the woman cradling the unsettled newborn by the edge of the cot, and where an ashen-faced Ariana lay with her eyes rolling about the reed-thatched ceiling as if birds were flying there.

The woman whose name was Katina readily asked, 'Well, did you find someone?'

'Possibly. She's passing through the village on a camel ...'

'A camel! Then she must be a gypsy! Can't you find one of our own kind? Spyros complained.

The midwife became agitated by the idle talk. 'Now isn't the time for such intolerance. The importance here is not what one wants but what one needs.'

She adjusted the small knot of her headscarf and gave him a deliberate stare. 'If she agrees she will ask for para.'

'It's a milk nurse I'm in need of not a coffee reading! Spyros complained.

'You've come to your senses I see! Hopefully your wife will come to hers in due course by the mercy of God.' The midwife remarked.

Spyros restively scratched at his beard. 'You did say the birth cord will cure the gloom!'

'Nonsense! Katina exclaimed. 'You can't rely on such mythoi!

The midwife glared at her reproachfully. What would a servant know about midwifery! A wee ingestion of the placenta was a prophylactic for post-natal depression. She'd treated many women this way. Admittedly though she knew nothing about healing lunacy!

Madness was a destructive pestilence that could invade anyone's mind in the twink of an eye, or over the course of time for some genetic reason or other.

A strong and vigorous man might return from the war mentally unstuck after witnessing the horrors and devastation of carnage of that war. Or a refugee might become disoriented in his new homeland and consequently succumb to culture shock and lose their intellectual course in life. In the same way to that of a seventeen- year-old girl who'd been subjected to nine months of mistreatment by a brutal husband. It seemed that the unstable were many and the rational were few.

Now Katina returned the midwife a similar disdainful stare. 'Well! You must hurry before she leaves!' she urged.

'Very well, I'll be on my way.' The midwife expediently left and set out to find the girl. After much trudging she eventually found her in a field on the outskirts of the village.

The camel was harnessed to a carob tree and the girl sprawled on the ground with her back propped against its trunk. Nobody knew the girl's real name. However, because of the notable butterfly shaped birthmark at the hollow of her neck she'd become known by all as Pedaluda. Butterfly translated from Greek. Though it was a suitable name for someone as transitory and graceful.

'You decided to come Pedaluda!' The midwife said.

'Oh, it's you!' She gasped when she unexpectedly lifted her eyes from the infant at her breast to find the woman hovering over her.

'I'm sure you've made the right decision. What took you so long?'

'I waited for spring to arrive. How did you find me?'

'I saw you passing through the marketplace.' She explained, and then craftily set her weary eyes on the flimsy robe she had on, then added, 'your singing talent isn't the only thing that will attract attention. Your presence there caused disorder amongst the men to the disgust of their wives. You can't say that I didn't warn you!'

'I can't stop people from staring!' she brooded.

'A suitable dress would be a start koritsi-mou!' She lowered her eyes to the infant sucking at her breast. 'Mashalla, mashalla! Your daughter has grown healthy and strong.' Then upon thought added, 'though too young to give away just yet as she'll need its mother's milk.'

'What do you suggest I do in the meantime?'

'Don't despair. It seems things have worked out well for you. I wish I could say the same for the young mother whose infant I've just delivered. It was a difficult birth. She is very sick. She may not even live. Her newborn needs a milk mana. And you need the para, don't you?'

In the subsequent weeks, Pedaluda set up a crude tent and camped in the field. Her presence there attracted the attention of the men who made out they were on some errand in the vicinity, often hiding from view in order to listen to her lute playing and chanting Armenian folk songs. For the children, the novelty was the huge camel with its cavernous jaws munching on grass in the shadows of the carob tree.

Gradually, Ariana had no recollection of the past. Incongruously though she had not forgotten the trick of bestowing her gentle smile upon others, as if somewhere deep within the unintelligible faculty of her mind she sensed that it was what she was born to do.

There was a certain glow in her grey eyes whenever the girl in the flowing robe cradled the infant Despina in her arms.

Curiously she watched on as the girl slipped out her bosom to feed the infant where she sat under the olive tree. Ariana began to impersonate the girl's maternal gestures as if by some peculiar logic that this too was also what she was preordained to do.

Given that Spyros was theoretically a widower at the age of twenty-seven, he desired Pedaluda. There was a sensual aura about her presence that caused a fire and storm in his heart. One day she was in the lower yard and so he went there with the pretence of feeding the pigeons. Surreptitiously he peered from around the corner of the cage, watched the motion of her hips through the sheer gossamer of her robe, and listened to the melodious tone of her crooning as she paced up and down with the infant Despina in her arms.

Pedaluda blushed and voiced surprise when she noticed him which seemingly Spyros accepted that she was aware of his infatuation of her.

He flattered her with courteous gestures, made her *elliniko kafe* with plenty of froth, just the way she liked it, and offered her loukoumi and cool water from the clay jar.

He embraced a grooming routine which was carried out with meticulous detail early each morning.

He raked out the knots from his black curly hair and pruned his moustache so that it sat just right. Then rubbed lemon juice into his beard to remove the stale tobacco odour.

All which seemed silly gestures for a man who toiled in the dusty field all day.

Sometimes, on a whim after work he'd pull up by the side of the road and gather wild- flowers and red poppies from the field.

And each time a rosy-faced Pedaluda burst into squeals of delighted surprise which made Spyros feel like the protagonist who'd won the heart of his leading lady.

It was Sunday and they were peacefully reposed in the cool shade of the olive tree in the lower yard. The two infants, Despina and Zehra, asleep in separate wood cribs at their feet. 'I see you have become fond of Despina.' Spyros offered.

Pedaluda was turning the tiny cup in the palm of her hand with her eyes cast on the thick residue of coffee in order to read his fortune.

Offhandedly she replied *'mashalla*, Spyros bey your *kizim* is adorable. May Allah be kind and grant our children a happy life.' Then she raised the cup level with her eyes, her brows retracting by some momentous sighting.

'What do you see?' He asked amused, though unconvinced by such superstitious interpretations. He was the eyewitness of his own understanding of the truth and which he accepted was that his fate was already preordained. Difficult times lay ahead.

'Nothing that your eyes don't already reveal,' she said with empathy.

'And what might that be?'

'You are deeply troubled. Why?' Then added apologetically, 'pardon need I ask? The reason is obvious. Your wife has passed and with your sister the way she is how will you cope?'

'Life is what it is,' he heaved a sigh.

'What will become of your *kizim*? You know nothing about raising a child! She advised.

'True. It will be difficult.' He said, then readily added, 'you're welcome to stay on. I'd be forever grateful if you did.'

'Our *kizims* will bond like blood sisters. Both are of different seeds but will be watered and nurtured in the same soil,' she revealed.

He was impressed by her imaginative recitation and found her words reassuring. There's one question he'd been meaning to ask her. 'What about the father?'

'What about him?'

'Pardon my nosiness but I don't understand why a young woman with a child would want to lead a nomad's life in preference for a home and husband.'

'I had no choice. He was a young soldier who was discharged from the army by the time I found out I was carrying his child. I have no idea where he is. Anyway, what difference would it have made? I'm sure his parents would have disapproved. And he himself would have had other plans for his life besides marriage and being a father.'

Spyros wondered if she'd loved the young soldier but somehow found it easier on his spirit and conscience to dismiss the thought. Then another thought came to mind. 'What about parents, siblings?'

'None I'm afraid.' She told him her mother disappeared in the Syrian Desert. Her father died some years later in Syria. They were refugees.

She was of Armenian roots born in Ourfa Turkey.

The family were forced into exile in 1922 by the Turkish government when all foreigners were eventually kicked out after years of persecution and death and agonising loss.

Wars were a felonious ethnic cleansing of humanity, coerced by fundamental spiritual and militant leaders, dictators aiming to control the world for financial profit and democratic power. Their actions enforced world hostility set hurdles which deprived people of permanency and equality. The poisons of religious tyranny and patriotism contributed to the worst evil war crimes in history. Millions of people were caught up in this ethnic cleansing. Between 1821 and 1913 there was a horrific holocaust that most people care not to remember. To speak of the Russo-Turkish war, and the Greek war of Independence commanded by Kolokotronis for Greece's freedom. In 1821 between 26th March and Easter Sunday the southern Greek Christians massacred and tortured 15,000 Greek Muslim nationals, pillaged and charred their homes. Christians were dehumanising and crucifying Christians like Jesus. Young girls were raped and strung from the threshold and gutted, their blood spilling into trenches for the famished rats and dogs to drink.

'They speak of peace and freedom and internal life in the promised land and yet they slaughter millions of people. Devious charlatans and assassins! All of them!' Spyros proclaimed. 'It explains why you speak Turk.'

'I consider myself an Armenian Cypriot. Though I do speak three languages. I was tutored by a Syrian school teacher. Did you go to school?'

9

He told her school was just as ineffectual as religion. Only fools obeyed the rulebooks of haughty professors. Scholarly tyrants who wanted to disrobe the world of its ecological glory.

'Then I gather after being exiled from Turkey you took refuge in Syria? And your mother, you said she vanished in the Syrian Desert.'

'That's right! My father had worked closely with the military and so the Turkish army gave the family a cart filled with hay for us to hide. We were escorted by the Turkish soldiers until other Turkish soldiers stopped us. They speared the cart and then we were left to make our own way. We were led on a death march by foot across Turkey and into the Syrian Desert. My mother was just one of the many women that was raped and beaten and disappeared in the desert. We walked for endless days amongst the scattered dead bodies without food or water and eating grass whenever we could find it. I was too young to remember the journey.'

'A touching tale. How did you end up here?' he pressed.

'The Armenian refugee families that raised me in Syria found out that the Cyprus government was welcoming Armenians into the country. We came here on the boat.

They were performers so we travelled a lot and set up stage nearby to where we camped. So that's why I never had a home as such. I was taught to dance and sing and play the tambourine and lute. I helped the women with the making of costumes with material the men bought on the black market. And we did coffee readings for extra para.'

She couldn't have known that she'd just planted a rotten seed of distrust in her effendi's mind that would subsequently have a devastating impact in her life.

'You earned your bread this way?' He felt unduly slighted by her indiscreet boasting of self-exposure in the presence of men.

'We survived!' She offered serenely.

*   *   *

Their union flourished, and by spring of the following year Pedaluda bore him a son.

But it wasn't long before Spyros had begun to reveal his great obsession with his young mistress. And if she wasn't in the mood to submit to his desires at night then he suspected her of fornicating with the soldiers at the garrison and every other man besotted with her comeliness. The pain in his heart was so great he could no longer concentrate when in the field and he became a casualty of his own preposterous inventiveness. And if he didn't find her at home then he thought of every conceivable place to track her down. This proved not only exhausting but ineffective.

'If you didn't find me at the communal oven or the marketplace then I might have gone to fetch drinking water or was at the stream doing the washing.'

Pedaluda was frustrated by the constant interrogation. There was barely enough time in the day as it was with three toddles, let alone commit to indecencies.

Most of the time she had to rely on her friend Katina to mind the children on her day off from the mansion where she worked in order to do her chores. Though she'd been reluctant to ask her the favour again.

11

Not so long ago she had returned from the marketplace to find Spyros and Katina engaged in a heated argument. She was too afraid to go inside the house and so she'd waited outside. She'd only caught snippets of their dispute but could hear the children's frightened cries just the same.

One day, fuelled by alcohol and stoned on his turf-grown cannabis, Spyros tottered about the yard. 'Pedaludaaaaa! Where are you my spirited little desert moth?'

Pedaluda was squatted on the ground behind the storage shed in the lower yard and chanting an Armenian ballad as she cracked green olives with a stone thus had not heard him.

'Whore! I'll find you!'

This time she did and when she saw him appear from around the corner, standing there in his most gruesome form, her words sank with a melancholic plea. 'Must you be so unfair Spyros bey?'

'You take me for a man who'd allow a woman like you to tamper with his heart strings?' he barked.

'What kind of woman do you think I am?' she asserted weakly.

'You've already proved that! What about the boy? Who was the father this time?'

'It's you of course!' She offered incredulously. 'Who else's child could he be?

'Could be any man's child. When a chicken walks around all day it's bound to collect a lot of mud on its feet! And with those bouncy little hips of yours *kori* you could even arouse the piddle pipe of a flagging plough-horse!' he sniggered.

'I swear on my children I have done nothing wrong!' she appealed.

'You dare to swear your innocence on the bastard children of other men. At this rate you'll soon have you own clan of performers.'

Pedaluda might have reminded him of his own false play-acting. Hadn't he tried to woo her with insincere gestures to earn her admiration of him? How stupid of her to believe him.

She felt discouraged, robbed of her virtue and her eyes clouded over with unadulterated grief. Not even when she burst into tears did the Tobacco Merchant's heart soften to his young mistress.

'You might look a vision on a field stage kori but you bungle at acting.' He mocked, when all at once his eyes bolted to the restless motion of her hand by her side. 'What you got there! He unclenched her fist, and instantly his brow spiked up with mistrustful indignation when the stone she was holding fell to the ground. 'It should be me stoning you!'

Impulsively she crossed her arms over her head when he scooped it up. 'Don't harm me! I beg of you!' She implored through a tirade of blind tears but at once plunged to the ground when she felt the hard blow to her head.

Spyros stared down at his wounded and bleeding mistress with as much pity as one might have for a dying snake. He leaned over and tore away the apron at her waist, bound her arms, and then dragged her across the yard and into the shed.

Ariana who was squatted behind the palm tree and in the act of a momentous bowel evacuation, had witnessed this vicious attack. And when she saw him crossing the yard, she wiped her bum with a dry frond, sprung from the ground, and charged at him with her eyes spitting fire. 'Ooshoo! Ooshoo! *Skile mavro!*' she hissed.

Spyros caught her just in time! 'Don't tell me to piss off! Call me a black dog! And if you meddle with shit Ariana then you'll end up eating it! You're like a blood sucking mosquito on my skin that won't go away!'

Since Ariana was physically incapable of defending herself-because she was as weedy as a famished lizard- she haunted Spyros's psyche with infuriating gestures and damnable tongue.

'A man would be better off at a brothel!' He grumbled as he headed back to the house. Inside he retrieved the near empty bottle of zivania from the table, removed the lid and knocked it back in one go. At once the potent brew inflamed his nostrils, induced tears to his eyes. He retrieved another bottle from the kitchen cupboard and took a few swigs before he sat back down. 'A man without a dependable wife is like a king without a throne.' He rambled on incoherently, and before long he slumped over the table and lapsed into a state of impassiveness.

In the meantime, Pedaluda had aroused and when she looked around everything seemed distorted and lopsided. Why was she lying face down on the ground? Why were her hands tied! And why did her head throb! Then suddenly she recalled what had happened.

'Allah! He tried to kill me!' she gasped.

Then when her senses were jolted that the children were alone inside the house with Spyros she began to scream and plead. 'Let me go! Let me go! I swear I have done nothing wrong!'

At that moment her unrelenting wails roused Spyros from his intoxicated slumber.

Impetuously he leapt from the chair and with methodical malice grabbed an onion from inside an old sack under the sink. He ripped away the crisp brown paper, pounded it a few times to release the acrid juice, and then stormed out of the house for the shed.

When Pedaluda tried to get up she felt fastened to the ground, as if being held there under the weight of a heavy object.

'You are in pain, yes!' Spyros offered with his sturdy work boot pressed firmly on her spine. He then lifted his foot and prod at her side a few times. 'I prefer your singing my songbird. I find your wailing vulgar. It's given me an insufferable headache! I'll have to shut you up!' Then with a swift kick he flipped her over. As the hefty bulk of him shadowed over her a quivering Pedaluda stared up at him through a mouthful of dust. Then before she could scream Spyros was quick to silence her. Adulteress! Whore! I will make you confess even if I wait until hell freezes over!

CHAPTER TWO

Katina the Maimed was born with a disjointed hip, thus paced with a slight limp. Pushing aside this minor impairment she was moderately attractive with coiling brown hair. And there was always a sparkle in her brown eyes when she spoke. Now though a shadow had cast over them as she listened on to her friend's woeful tale.

'I'd rather he stoned me to death! At least I'd be spared of the ongoing misery!' Pedaluda murmured.

Katina stared at her patched brow. 'Five sutures, you said! *Diavolo!*' She scoffed.

'I thought he was going to kill me!'

'That wasn't his intention. Who'd look after those three children? Anyway, it should have been you stoning him. A girl must protect herself.'

'What hope would I have against such a strong man?'

'I see you easily lose your wits Pedaluda-mou!' Katina only had to think of that biblical hero David who'd managed to slay Goliath with a mere stone.

'A good one I'd say. When you think about it, that is. I mean a man would have to be delirious after consuming excessive amounts of alcohol. One would think his knees would be buckling under his feet on his way home late of a night from the *kafenio*. And one would also wonder how he'd even manage to get home at all without stumbling and cracking his skull open. You could hide behind the front gate.'

'What do you suppose I do there?'

'Slay him of course and make it look like an accident! What else would you do to man that tried to kill you?' Katina retorted.

'I could never do that!'

'Calm your wits kori! I'm only trying to help.'

'I won't do it! I won't!' Pedaluda argued.

'Alright. But if you'd rather let a brute attack than fight it off to spare your own life then you have no right to complain. If you ask me, there's a cliff before you and a hurricane behind you. Either you die or endeavour to survive. Understandably both are treacherous options,' Katina cautioned.

'It's a crime!'

'Isn't everything a crime. When you think about it, that is. To beg or steal or to love is a crime. Even remembering. What if he does kill you?'

Pedaluda burst into tears. 'You do it.'

'You have lost your mind! What alibi would I have?' Katina remarked twitchily.

'You did say it would look like an accident! Didn't you?' she reminded her.

'Yes, but I won't be the grieving widow left to raise three children on my own. My bet is the authorities will sympathise with a woman who puts up with a wife-beating drunk. They might even make you a cup of Tsai.' Katina offered with a shrewd sidelong stare.

'There's also a good chance they wouldn't believe me. I'd be imprisoned.' Pedaluda agonised.

'Then the coyote must flee before the lion wakes up,' Katina said.

'Where would I go? He will hunt me down.'

'A prairie wolf doesn't fear its predator once it has fled out of harm's way.'

'He has a firearm!' she disclosed.

'Even a man who presumes himself brave can lose his nerve when his finger is on the trigger!' Katina revealed, and then cast her eyes thoughtfully on the sun-browned woman having a discursive conversation with herself where she was squatted under the palm tree in the lower yard and with her hands clasped to her raised knees.

You can't always win first prize Ariana. Your calamity is a curse of God! She recalled the day Spyros almost killed her in the tobacco field shortly after they were married.

He worked Ariana to the bone and one day she'd swooned from heat and exhaustion and his field worker splashed water on her face and gave her a drink.

Spyros had been in the curing shed and when he came out, saw them huddled together amidst the dense harvest, he became suspicious and retrieved his firearm from the shed and threatened to kill them both. Then throughout Ariana's pregnancy he terrorised her proclaiming the infant would be dead before she heard its first cry. And since the fool had got it stuck in that thick cranium of his that his young wife was carrying his field workers child, then so be it.

Katina now said, 'If he has a gun then use it! And why didn't you tell

19

me this before? Would have made matters easier. You could have gone to the field and caught him unaware.'

'What would I know about firearms?' Pedaluda was shaken by her friend's steadfast plan.

'Well, it happens I know a thing or two about firearms. I used to go hunting with my uncle Stelios for *ampelopolia*. Songbirds. The idea is to strike your target with accuracy. The hand must be steady to stop the gun from swerving when firing otherwise the bullet will miss the crucial point intended, which most likely would be the heart, in your case,' Katina instructed.

* * *

By now the British forces were strengthened by six thousand volunteers. The British demanded the men learn to use all kinds of automatic weapons in resisting attack if the time came. And whatever reservations the Greek Cypriots had had towards British rule they'd become dependable supporters of the allied cause in World War II.

Guerrillas of the EOKA movement were steadfast on their long anti-British campaign for political union with Greece, or Enosis. The British were currently exercising A13 Cruiser MK 1V tanks on the island. Inhabitants of Rizo had attuned to the daily military drills of air raid sirens and droning of anti-aircraft that were launched from the British military base in Nicosia. Of the three hundred thousand inhabitants of the island more than thirty thousand would have served the British Forces by the end of the war. By 1946, the population had plummeted into further recession by the eruption of Greece's terrible civil war fought between the Communists and the government forces.

During this terrible war Communists gathered up and took as many as 25,000 children from their families to Communist countries in Eastern Europe and the Soviet Union.

Communist opponents claimed that the children were forcibly taken however the communists claimed that they were rescuing children from possible death during the dangerous constitutional war. Many of those children would never be reunited with their parents.

Two years into World War II, on the threshold of hopelessness and destitute, Pedaluda had not waited for the war to end.

One night when the roads had turned to swamps, she loaded her camel with provisions and rode off with Omer, the son Spyros had fathered. Forsaking Zehra.

And just as she'd forecast, her two-year-old daughter Zehra and her milk child Despina would blossom in the shadows of that soil where they'd been embedded side by side and would become as close as blood sisters.

CHAPTER THREE

Rizokarpaso — August 1946

The child sat on a rock in the palm scented shade, slapping the nuisance flies on her arms. Her brown eyes were aimed at the butterflies quivering around the jasmine vine and wild bushes near the sagging line.

Close by under the shade of a gnarled olive tree, a naked young woman was crouched on the ground and pouring water over her head from a clay jar.

Balding chooks and a stray dog were bickering over a morsel of corn-bread in the muddled yard, and where a cat roamed in search of its kittens, meowing plaintively.

The child slapped at another fly. The act prompted a misty image of an old man chanting a song. She missed Uncle Stelios.

The flies had been fat, like they were now when he died. She blinked away the tears that stung her eyes and let out a soft sigh. She was sad that he was no longer around to take her to watch the puppet show. As she sat there on the rock contriving indolent dreams the squeaking and creaking of a water wheel churning the sweet water of the mountains that crowned the wood scented plains resounded from afar.

She's inside the *kafenio*. Some of the children from her school are there too. And so is that little boy Rifat, son of Jusuf the Chair-Weaver.

Rifat does not attend Daskalo Panayiotis class because he is Muslim and so he attends Hodja Fajoula's class at the mosque.

They are huddled on a threadbare sheepskin rug in the corner of the room awaiting the puppet to appear from behind the red curtain of the makeshift booth.

Rifat squats beside her, and from the corner of her eye catches his brown eyes staring at her in as much the same way as the other children drooling over their cups of iced rose water.

The curtain draws and the string puppet drops and then breaks out into jaunty antics to a funny voice from behind the makeshift booth. Rifat bursts into loud laughter and he splutters iced rose water on her face, and when he licks it off with his warm slippery tongue, she giggles, and her tummy jumps all over the place it feels so nice.

The men retreat to a small room at the back. They smoke and drink ouzo and chew on dried pumpkin seeds, spitting the husks on the floor which is already outlandishly putrid with yellow cigarette butts and ash and newspapers with pictures of notorious diplomats, leftist factions and antagonistic militants.

When the puppet show is over the children's laughter subsides. One by one the men appear from behind the closed door of the adjoining room and collect their children and go home.

The puppet peddler he too has packed up his makeshift booth and left. Only she remains and a heavy silence disturbs the dusky room. Then a man with a mass of wrinkles draws near, and she returns him a smile and rises to her feet to greet him.

He offers her pasteli that is wrapped in brown crinkly paper like his hand that passes over her hand and then they leave.

Walking home the moon follows them and casts a faint glow along the dusty pathway, and in the jasmine and hay scented air the old man chants a song, as if he knows that songs are what a child likes to hear before bedtime.

Such was the child's concentration that she hardly stirred until she heard a voice calling.

'Despina! Despina!

Six-year-old Despina looked up to see Katina standing in the upper yard. She was fond of Katina. Her sister Zehra was sick again and so that's why she'd come to visit, she'd sensed.

If Zehra died, just like their mother, then she'd be lonelier than ever.

*   *   *

Zehra spews up the goat milk in the morning and Despina must mop up the stinking mess. She's mad at her father for giving it to her because he knows it makes her sick.

Zehra spends the day groaning with a belly ache in the single cot. Despina is lonely and bored and so she pretends to have friends inside her head like Bebek, her father's anathematised sister.

Bebek lives in a tiny nook under her father's house. She sleeps on a plank of wood and her pillow is a rounded stone. She only has one blue dress which is infrequently rinsed and flung over the buckled line. As she waits for it to dry Bebek sits naked on the rock in the yard sunning and chanting an unintelligible satanic jargon to God's adversary inside her head which is ludicrously strange to mankind but rational to the insane.

Bebek haunts Despina's imagination. It is impossible for her to decode her aunt's eruptions of blathering indecencies which transpire with a kind of malicious and bewildering pleasure.

But little Despina senses a maternal attraction to the sweet-faced woman and wants to befriend her, so she pretends to understand and imitates her words and pulsating actions. When Bebek beholds Despina's playacting she is convinced she belongs in her world.

They crouch inside the nook and Bebek allows Despina to comb her long brown hair with the pretty tortoise shell comb which has tiny sparkles on it. She shares with her the broad beans and crusts of cornbread with marmalade from the tin plate.

And when she slurps and licks it off from the cornbread her grey eyes gleam like cubes of ice, Despina giggles.

Nearby is a field of dry grass which has many fan-shaped carob trees and prickly bushes with purple flowers. Both are in the field and Bebek tilts her head and bursts a smile as she points to the black pods hanging from the tree as she likes to suck on the sweet pulp.

Despina scrambles up like a practised monkey. And when the pods smack the hard earth Bebek claps and then spreads her arms like the wings of a bird and runs all over the place with an angelic smile. They find a stone to rest and devour the pulp. After Despina watches Bebek raise her skirt, hunker down and defecate and then wipe her bum with sprigs of dry grass. Despina decides to do the same only there are thistles tangled in the grass and she lets out a deafening howl which blanches Bebek's face as she bolts off shrieking curses.

'Ooshoo! Ooshoo! *Skile mavro*. Piss off black dog! Despina fears Baba will punish her and so she remains in the field until dark. She peers up at the moon shining through the branches of the carob-tree and touches her cheeks and thinks of the brown-eyed Muslim boy with the warm slippery tongue. She knows she will marry him one day.

CHAPTER FOUR

Rizokarpaso

Spyros existed in a chasm of misery after Pedaluda ran off with their young son Omer. Even his concentration plunged into an abyss of forgetfulness and clarity that was analogous to that of a disconcerted scholar who failed to come up with the solution of a simple mathematical equation after years of familiarity and knowledge.

His newfound joy with his Armenian mistress had been as brief as a sudden downpour of summer rain that teased the baked earth before it could be quenched of its thirst.

Spyros was a self-admiring man, and the perception of rejection and betrayal did not sit well on his narcissistic conscience, thus Zehra became the recipient of his revenge. A young and confused Despina never understood the core of her father's antipathy towards her sister. Why he constantly aimed his criticism at Zehra when her only crime was a simple remark of hunger, or a common ailment like the cold or head lice.

Even her aptness and thoroughness infuriated him. Nothing ever made sense. And when she did cast doubt on his actions her questions were always left suspended in the air.

When her father did explain things to her in his own boozy way, even then, Despina never understood the concept behind the clarification. Like three days ago when she'd asked him why he'd locked Zehra inside the shed without food or water. He'd given her one of those, 'don't ask questions,' stares like he always did.

'Why did you? You're mean. I hate you! I'll tell Daskalos Panayiotis,' Despina argued.

'Some children don't deserve 'favours,'' he retorted.

Despina didn't know what the word 'favour,' meant. Though it had to be a horrible word given that he'd locked Zehra away because of it.

In their father's absence she's managed to break away a portion of an existing hole at the bottom of the timber door in order to nourish her sister so she wouldn't die. She'd sustained a nasty cut in the crease of her palm with the blade of the kitchen knife in her attempt to enlarge it to pass through the bits of cornbread. Young Despina had suffered a great deal of pain though she considered it minor compared to that of her sisters. She sat outside the door and read her stories just so she wouldn't feel sad and alone.

And when her father did let her out of the shed Zehra had become so malnourished that she'd taken on the appeal of a rag doll, empty of expression and energy.

Despina had to force feed her otherwise she really would die. At every opportunity she gave her pigeon broth and cornbread. She'd come to understand that goat milk made her sister throw up thus brewed chamomile tsai. Twice Daskalo Panayiotis came to the house to enquire about Zehra.

When he saw how emaciated she'd become, he implored of her father to summon the yiatro but he denounced the Daskalo for his intervention and chased him out of the yard. 'Don't come here preaching your dumb-headed thoughts!'

Their father prohibited the use of fuel until the last drop of light drained from the sky. It was harder in the winter months when it got dark so early. One kerosene lamp was shared between the three rooms of the house. It was impractical of a night to get to the outhouse in the lower yard and so the children made use of the chamber pot.

When Zehra had gained an ounce of weight, Despina read her stories and gave her coloured pencils and paper to draw pictures to paste on her school case.

Together they made wind-chimes by hanging forks and spoons on a circular wheel they made from old wire coat hangers. They even used the dried husks of snails. In order to remove the slimy snails from their husks, Despina put them in a pot of flour before cooking them with rice. They would drill tiny holes through the sun-parched husks with a needle and then join them with cotton thread. When strung from the branch of the olive tree collectively with the forks and spoons, a soft tinkling and clattering sound rung out in the breeze.

As a tobacco merchant, Spyros earned a modest income and ostracised the capitalists.

Chiefly, Yiannis Gapsalis who was a snobbish man. One often saw him strutting about the village collecting dues from leaseholders in a fine tailored suit with a maroon silk tie, hat and fat cigar at his fingertips, and he seemingly appeared content with the world. Others too might present themselves in a likewise manner if they'd been a manufacturer of illegal whisky during World War I.

Rumour was that his collaborator had been a British ambassador and a high-ranking Greek military officer who'd helped him smuggle the goods by ship to major European ports for consumption.

He'd capitalised by investing in the foreign market which empowered him to buy properties and acreages of land in the Kapasso Famagusta region for organic farming and fruit orchards. The orchards provided seasonal work for a quarter of the population in Rizo, many of whom had been financially impacted by World War II. The harvest was packed and stored in a warehouse before distribution to major retail outlets across the countryside.

With all this accumulated wealth, Yiannis had become the subject of enviable debate amongst the peasants inside the *kafenio*.

'I heard Yiannis is campaigning again for the next mayor of Famagusta. That megalomaniac doesn't like being the underdog. Couldn't stand his defeat eight years ago. You reckon he's got a chance this time in the upcoming elections?' One of the men remarked over a game of tavli.

'With his money he could buy his way into becoming the next president of this country!'

He's just bought himself another new vehicle. For that bachelor son of his I'm told,' his opponent revealed.

'Ah, yes one of them Benz vehicles. Imported from Germany I believe.' The first man clarified.

'Fuck that stiff nosed swindler and his mob of sour lemons!' Spyros interjected huffily through a haze of tobacco smoke from where he was seated at a nearby table. 'If I'd been bootlegging whisky and cooperated with the resistance then I too would be living and eating like an effendi! But instead, I eat charred pork liver and salted herring and pickles which cause me painful emptying of the bowels that aggravate my haemorrhoids. And I drive an old truck with the same digestive complaints.'

* * *

That winter Spyros caught Ariana standing naked on a ladder and sucking the incrustations of ice on the girders of the house. 'Get down now! Put a dress on! I've warned you!' he furiously howled.

When she refused to budge, he stepped up onto the ladder and tugged vigorously at her ankles. However, the ladder couldn't sustain them both, and all at once it tilted sideways, hurling them to the ground.

Quickly he untangled his body from the ladder atop of him and sprung to his feet, Ariana inelegantly ascending after him. 'Ooshoo, ooshoo. *Skile mavro!* she hissed.

'Anathema se! He exclaimed when he felt the warm splutter of froth smack his face. He seized her scrawny arm, hauled her across the mud-slick yard and into the storage shed then bolted the door behind him.

'I'll show you who's a black dog kori! Then abruptly his jaw locked when he observed Pater Christofis standing in the upper yard and appearing like a majestic spy clad in a black well-rounded hat and long woollen coat over his ecclesiastical robe. 'Looks like I've invoked the *diavolo!*' he uttered wryly.

The elderly cleric broke out into a fitful cough and simultaneously averted his eyes to the heavens as if seeking exoneration from God for having witnessed the naked flesh of someone else's wife. Or sister, whatever be the factual case. 'Pardon I'll come back at a more suitable time,' he offered.

Spyros joined him in the upper yard and reluctantly invited him into the house.

'Must be difficult!' The cleric offered stroking his long silver beard as Spyros indicated a chair by the table. The cleric reverently removed his hat and placed it in his lap, so the deep hollow provided a lodging place for the long crucifix at his neck.

'Now what be the reason for your visit Pater? I'm sure you didn't come here to discuss the Nazi surrender in 45'or what was left of Munich after their surrender!' Spyros offered wryly.

'Well, it concerns, shall I say your late wife.' The cleric offered with a nervous twitch of the neck. Even though realistically the situation didn't necessitate anxiety for he was aware that there'd never been a burial service for his wife. Besides, a lie was only a lie until it became the truth, the cleric mused, and opted to go along with the hypocrisy.

'I will be holding a service on the sixteenth of March which falls on the Saturday of souls. Despina might like to bring along koliva so I can bless and read the names of the departed. Also, Saint Theodore is celebrated on the day,' he added as an afterthought.

Spyros raised a critical brow, then turned and reached for the bottle of zivania from an upper shelf and then retrieved two small glasses and joined him. The cleric waved a hand as he was about to fill his glass. 'Thank you Christian but I only drink the blood of Christ.'

Spyros took a swig and then amusingly offered, 'if it's as mellow and palatable as red wine then I'd like to try it.'

'Then you might like to come to the service. It purifies the soul.' The cleric offered suitably.

'Like a good drop of zivania,' Spyros chortled.

'I wouldn't know about that Christian. What about your sister! A divine blessing of Christ's blood might help. Hmm!' The ceric offered, and then after a short interlude of coughing added, 'of course I suggest appropriate clothing for such cold conditions.'

'As you've seen she is beyond help! An animal is tamer! More civilised,' Spyros offered resolutely.

'May the Lord have mercy on her suffering soul,' he offered with a slight nod. Then added, 'what about an infirmary? When he caught Spyros's fierce stare the elderly cleric smiled back at him like his lips were attached to taught strings pegged to his ears.

'Only a thought Christian. Only a thought.'

'Now is there anything more you need to tell me? I have a toothache. And a light case of plugged sinus.'

'Then you must see the tooth yiatro,' he offered sensibly. 'Now since you asked, there is one more matter which concerns your daughters. Zehra and Despina. It appears there is no documentation of their baptism. Baptism is the beginning or induction of Christianity to become a citizen of Christ.'

'John the Baptist he too was a citizen of Christ. Where did that get him Pater? He was beheaded. His skull rests in a decrepit reliquary. Now like I said, I have a toothache of terrible sorts!'

'Of course. God be of assistance Christian! The cleric got up and left feeling out of sorts himself. And he had an irrepressible urge to piss.

He undid the buttons of his wool coat, slipped his hand through and drew up his long ecclesiastical robe and reached for the tool of God's creation and relieved himself against the wall of the Tobacco Merchant's house. Pater Christofis stepped out onto the cobbled road, his gaunt face revealed a puckered smile as he slowly made his way home, content that yet another day of God's work had been done.

CHAPTER FIVE

D
espina was brave beyond her years, and she had adjusted to the role of caring for her sister and tending to the daily necessities before and after school each day. Then there was also the burden of trying to make a meal from nothing.

Together she and Zehra went to the fields to gather dandelions and wild horta and whatever else edible thing they might find growing by the side of the road or within hand's reach inside a neighbour's fence. They went to fetch drinking water, and always inquisitive to watch the water wheel drawn by a donkey. Of a weekend they went to the stream to do the washing.

They descended through the rumpled cobbled roads and came into the market-place to find vendors negotiating their merchandise and hens screeching and beating their wings within the framework of their cages.

Pick-up trucks and vans were parked in the village square as drivers waited for peasants to arrive with produce on mule driven cats to be delivered to metropolitan regions for a fee.

Above the stone embankment was Mayor Neophytos's kafenio. Men were seated at tables under a canopy of grapes and drinking *eleniko kafe* over a game of tavli and cards.

Pater Christofis was there too, his hands moving in many directions as he talked. The road gradually declined, and spontaneously their footsteps quickened.

Reaching the end of the road the tall mosque came into view, its minaret looming over the rectangular, red-brown terracotta done of the Greek Orthodox Church.

The muezzin calls for prayer, but nobody seems to be heading to the mosque which is not surprising why the Greek Cypriots claim to be more religious than the Muslims. Because of their secularism their view that religion should not be introduced into public education or civil affairs.

Greek religious leaders, including Pater Christofis, denounced the Muslims and blamed them for almost everything.

Soon the Gapsalis mansion came into view. There it was standing on the hilltop in all its grandiose like a multi-tiered cake, and with its many terraces laced with railings. One could almost imagine its white-wash thawing under the scorching sun, and then washing over the foothills to purify the dusty pathways and mud-houses below.

'They must be rich to have servants,' Zehra offered, straining her neck.

'They'd have to be with so many workers.'

'Do you wish we were rich sister?' Zehra queried.

'Poor people wouldn't know what it's like. You think rich people wonder what it's like to be poor!' Despina revealed.

'Why do you think they don't?'

'Nobody wants to think about being miserable and hungry silly,' Despina offered.

When they reached the outskirts of the village the forest of red cedars came into view. They stopped to rest for a while amongst the many tombstones. Some of the headstones were leaning in a gesture of yellow grey age, similarly to the many skeletons beneath the earth.

The Muslim graves were distinguishable by the flowerbeds and small brass urns at the foot of the grave to pour 'water of the soul,' over the earth of the deceased.

'Do you think our mana is buried here?' Zehra queried.

'We'd never find her even if she were. We don't even know her name sister,' Despina revealed.

'Why do you think Baba never told us?'

'Probably because we never asked,' Despina said. 'Names are for the living, not the dead! When a person dies, they're only as good as the earth they're buried under.' Her father had once told her.

'Then why haven't you thought about it before? I wish she hadn't died,' Zehra offered glumly.

'People don't die unless you forget about them.'

'How can you remember someone you've never seen?' Zehra asked confused.

'Just try and paint a picture of mana in your mind and keep it under your pillow at night when you dream. Now we must hurry. We need to kindle the fire to boil water for Baba's bath. And he'll be mad if he finds the food cage empty.'

'He's always mad,' Zehra sulked.

'Don't worry I won't let him hurt you again.'

They continued walking and soon the mountain stream came into view, and beyond the foothills were the infertile plains.

At the stream one of the women remarked, '*Mashallah*. Look at those girls! They still have the taste of their mother's milk in their mouths and they're doing the chores of a betrothed woman.'

Another woman glowered over at them, 'one of them was raised on the milk of her father's gypsy mistress. And the other is the mistress's *bastardo*! Must they contaminate the water that we wash our clothes?'

Both girls were too young to make sense of the woman's racial and biased malice. On their way home Despina offered, 'if Maritsa with the seven moles causes trouble again, I'll push her into the stream.'

'What if she drowns?' Zehra implored.

'That's the whole idea stupid,' Despina chuckled.

'I say we go elsewhere!' Zehra offered timidly.

'Why should we? The stream doesn't belong to her.'

'I wish I was brave and smart like you sister! Zehra found it hard to keep pace with her sister's rapid steps. The basket was always heavier when it was laden with wet hand-wrung clothes.

However, it wasn't just this last burden that hampered Zehra's footsteps. Despina had stuffed cardboard inside her shoes to stop the stones from stabbing her feet.

'You get smart by going to school. And God makes a person brave! Despina offered.

'Baba says a person don't get a grain of corn more by going to school. And he doesn't believe in God.'

'That's why he's mean and stupid. He needs to be cleansed of his sins like Maritsa with the seven moles.'

By the time they arrived back at the village, their arms and legs ached. Then they had the chore of hanging the washing on the line when they got home.

They passed the procession of a Mohammedan wedding. The mullah held a Koran over the heavily veiled bride and whose arm was threaded through that of her husbands as guests bearing household gifts for the newly-weds followed on behind with a group of musicians.

They passed Jusuf the Chair-Weaver, looping strips of reed through the wood framework of a chair in the sunshine out front of his work-shop. Further ahead an old woman was weighing apples on a scale of stones. She looked up observant and inattentive until at last she offered a gummy smile.

The girls returned her greeting and trudged on and where they found under a roof of parched palm leaves Mustafa the potter.

His hands were moist with clay as he worked a fast-turning wheel of clay.

Outside the crude hut vases were baking in the sunshine on a make-shift table ready for glazing. Mustafa greeted the two young girls holding the washing basket with a broad smile. 'May your work be light.'

Amongst the great number of Turkish settlers, there were still many Greek Cypriots living in Rizo which was the last village on the Karpassa Peninsula bordering the coastline of the Mediterranean Sea.

Further beyond the peak of the Cape was the monastery of Apos-tolos Andreas where monks could be seen roaming about in their long robes in the imposing archways. During the religious festivities each year in late November people flocked there to pay homage to the saint and offerings were laid on a shelf inside the church.

Daskalos Panayiotis had organised a school bus excursion to the monastery before the school closed for summer vacation. He'd even endorsed Despina's request for Zehra to come along.

It was to be their first visit to the famed monastery. They lit candles in the sand pit and when they kissed the icon of Mary, mother of Jesus, holding her infant, they were overcome with an inexplicable sadness. A child orphaned of a mother was sensitive to the maternal affection of another woman towards her child. Many stalls were set up in the cloisters.

Pedlars sold pasteli, fruit conserves, nuts and strings of *shusouko*, a sweet made from grape- juice often stuffed with almonds.

Amongst other things Cyprus lace, commonly known as Lefkara lace, which was famous the world over, and sold by the proud women who crafted them in their village of Lefkara. And religious icons were on offer for those who wished.

At one of the stalls was a woman wearing a gaily coloured headscarf and selling a hodgepodge of souvenirs from the Near East. She smiled easily. '*Merhaba*! Hello.'

She sensed the children did not speak Turkish. She also perceived the hunger in their eyes as they stared at the pasteli on the bench of her stall. She passed them a slice each and when she accepted their unwillingness she walked around to their side of the stall. 'Don't be shy! I didn't ask for para!' She now spoke in Greek.

The woman accepted the children were unaccustomed to being spoilt and upon reflection turned and contemplated the knick-knacks on the bench of her stall.

She retrieved a couple of snow globes. Through the glass there were two figurines of a boy and a girl dressed in woolly clothes and scarf standing under a streetlamp, tiny specs of tinsel floating about gave the illusion of snow.

She handed them one each and felt similarly joyous when she acknowledged their excitement. 'Turn them over! They are musical. See, there's a little key at the bottom.' Then impulsively added, 'I have a camel! Look she's over there!' She pointed to the fawn camel prostrated in the shadows of a tall palm tree opposite the courtyard.

'Would you like to meet Cleopatra?'

The girls followed her to the cow. 'I must warn you not to touch her. Camels are known to spit on people!'

She explained it was a defence tactic when they felt threatened. She went on to tell them that camels like to greet each other by blowing in each other's faces.

The children giggled at the thought. 'They're interesting animals.' And she went on to tell them that a camel could run at twenty-five miles an hour and kick up speed at forty even when heavily burdened with merchandise.

'Don't they get tired and thirsty?' Despina asked.

'Of course! Look!' She pointed to the water skins straddled to the cow's back.

'Camels drink more water a day than we'd drink in a month.' She smiled. 'Between five to twenty gallons a day. And they can withstand all kinds of weather even in the hot desert. They also have a third eyelid to protect their eyes from sand.'

'What do they eat?' Zehra queried.

'Ah, you have a voice my shy one! Mostly grass and wood bark and leaves.'

Zehra screwed up her nose. Then the woman said, 'It's starting to rain. I must hurry back to my stall and your mother will be worried.'

'Our mother died. We came on the bus with Daskalos Panayiotis,' Despina revealed.

'Oh, my poor canims.' She stooped and gathered them both in her arms.

Her skin had an exotic scent and her breath smelt like rose-water. She erected herself then made a sweeping gesture with her arm. '*Hade!* May Allah be generous and protect you.' She was overcome with an inexplicable sadness as she watched them make their way back through the crowd for the past weighed heavily on her conscience. Simultaneously, a rush of tears welled in her eyes as sudden as the downpour of rain.

'Was that really my *kizim?* Daughter. My little Zehra!' she said with despondent yearning.

And then within her clouded eyes an image of a child appeared; her curly locks bouncing about her rose-bud cheeks as she fell into her mother's outstretched arms. *Well don't just stand here dithering in self-pity. Go after Zehra before it's too late.*

Pedaluda surged through the congregation, frantically looked around, but there was no sight of the children. Then she recalled the school bus and asked around when a withered old man pointed to a clearing beyond the courtyard. 'It's over there! I think it is leaving.'

'Allah! I'm too late. Forgive me Zehra,' she murmured.

She raised the scarf at her shoulders to cover her head and hurried down the cloisters of the Christian monastery. She passed through its imposing doors and then lit a candle inside to commend Apostolos Andreas for presenting her with the marvel that had come her way today. When she stepped outside the rain had stopped.

A rainbow appeared, producing a spectrum of colours through the fountains of blue air, and there was an aura of sanctity which provided Pedaluda with the faith that she would be reunited with Zehra again.

CHAPTER SIX

The birds had been smashing into the windowpane again. Despina rolled up the window and retrieved the injured sparrow from the ledge. She placed it in the palm of her hand and stroked its downy feathers. 'You poor thing,' she murmured. 'It's that sister of mine she keeps forgetting to open the window. Please forgive her. Her mind is all over the place these days.'

She hurried to the lower yard and where she'd strung a wicker cage from a small branch of the olive tree amidst the wind-chines. There she opened its door and placed the wounded sparrow in the company of two other maimed birds. She couldn't fix their broken wings but the least she could do was feed them. Though their deaths would be slow coming. She then went to the pigeon cage beside the storage shed.

She stood a while contemplating the lone bird. Once the cage had a dozen or more birds. Some her father had slaughtered for food and others had simply flown away. Despina told Zehra that if she told the bird her worries it would convey the message to the other birds and they would fly home. So far none had returned. 'You made it up!' Zehra had jeered at her sister's silly myth.

One day Despina was sweeping out the house when she found a tin of candy under the cot she shared with her sister. Painted on the tin was a picture of a cat with a long, curly tail.

'I didn't steal nothing!' Zehra protested.

'You're lying! And I don't like it! Pater Christofis says, "to ask is written but to take is stealing." You'd know this if you went to church!' Despina warned.

'It's the truth! What about your fib about the pigeon?' Zehra fled the house in tears.

'Do I have to chase after you all the time?' She complained when she caught up with her in the field of carob trees.

'Why do you? You don't have to!'

'You're my sister! I care about you! Despina took hold of her hand, but Zehra frowned and drew it away and said, 'more than that boy!'

'He's just a kid I see on my way to school. He goes to the mosque because he's Muslim.'

'Is that why Baba hates him? Because he's one of them?'

'You can't hate someone you don't know!' Despina chuckled.

'Baba's seen him. He called him a Muslim *kerata*. Rascal. 'He came to the house with a kitten. Said it was for you. It was that day you went to the bakali to buy Siva washing powder.'

'Well, what happened?' Despina's heart was battering.

'Baba gave him a good thrashing, that's what! Told him he'd send him back to his mana crawling on his knees if he ever came back. Told him he'd put a stop to it!'

'Did he just? I'll run away! Then who'll take care of him?' Despina brooded.

'What about me?' Zehra agonised.

'I'd take you with me. You know I'd never leave you. I'll always be holding your hand.'

'Where would we go?'

'To a shelter. Where else?'

'You think they'll let me take a bath and give me a clean dress?' Zehra probed quietly.

'I promise. Now come sit,' she pointed to a large boulder nearby. Then she removed a wedge of stale bread from her pocket and passed it to her.

'We could go find the camel lady if we knew where she lived! Baba must know her. He was asking about her.'

'Then you must have told him! Why did you Zehra?'

'I didn't sister. He caught me talking about her to Bebek.'

'You know she's not all there? I just pretended she understood when I was little. That's because I was lonely.'

'You had me to play with,' Zehra offered.

'Not when you were sick all the time. I had to take care of you. Now tell me what happened.'

'He shook me real hard. Bebek got mad with Baba.'

'Well good for her. He deserves to be kicked and spat at for trying to hurt you.'

'Yeah, but then he got nice and said he'd give me a tin of candy if I told him the truth about the camel lady. I swear sister I didn't want the candy. I was scared he'd lock me up again,' Zehra moped.

'Just let him try! I'll break a zivania bottle over his head. It must have been important to bribe you! What did he want to know?'

'Dumb things like if she had a mark on her neck. And if she had a boy with her. And what village she was from. If we knew we'd go and find her, wouldn't we sister? You think he really does know her?'

'Why else would he be asking after her?' Despina offered.

'I didn't see no mark on her neck. Or a boy. Did you sister?'

'You've got to have a reason to look for something silly. Like when we go to the fields for horta! Would we go there if we didn't know they grew there?' Despina revealed.

'Maybe it's a different camel lady. She spoke to us in Greek. You think she's one of us or one of them?'

'Our people are neighbours. Why wouldn't she speak Greek?'

'Do our people speak Turkish?' Zehra offered.

'You should know these things.'

'I'm not clever like you.'

'Nobody's stupid unless they're like Bebek. All you need is eyes and ears to figure things out,' Despina revealed.

'Then why can't auntie Bebek!'

'She hasn't got a brain silly.'

'Is it because she ate a green potato?' Zehra offered.

'Baba tell you that! Only believe in God and school sister.'

'He says books only make a person forget what they already know, then they become stupid,' Zehra explained.

'He must have read a lot of books then. He's so stupid he doesn't even remember your birthday sister. Or his own. He would if he wasn't drunk all the time or puffing on that bubbly 'snake pipe' that makes him act like his head is someplace else,' Despina scoffed.

'I wish we had a mother to take care of us sister,' Zehra voiced sadly.

'Haven't I promised to look after you? Now we'd better get moving before Baba comes looking for us.'

It was to be the first of the religious festivities leading up to the feast of the Panayia Evangelistria. Local merchants and peddlers had set up stall in the cloisters of the church. Earlier Despina had taken a bath and put on her best church dress.

'I wish I had a pretty dress,' Zehra told the pigeon as she pushed a scrap of bread through the buckled wire. Her dress had mismatched buttons and felt like the coarse fibres of hemp the village women weaved into rope.

Steadily her wet eyes traced over it, thought about the grit embedded in her belly button and under her fingernails, felt like a worm in the earth. She was neither clean nor pretty.

Then her eyes fell upon her bare toes poking through the gaping seams of her shoes. Just then she heard her sister's voice.

'What are you doing down here? Hurry or we'll be late.' Despina warned when she joined her in the lower yard.

'I've changed my mind. You go!' Zehra offered.

'I'm not going without you!' Despina sensed the odd transition in her sister's mood. 'You've been talking to the pigeon again.'

'My tummy hurts,' Zehra offered quietly.

'Come, I'll make you Tsai.' Despina took her sister's hand and led her back up to the house. Their father was drinking coffee at the table when they walked into the kitchen.

'You been giving Zehra goat milk again? You know it upsets her tummy and makes her throw up. And my sister needs a bath and a new dress. And a decent pair of shoes!

'She been causing trouble again. I'll teach her a lesson.' Spyros got up and snatched Zehra's arm and then shook and shook her until tears shone in her grey eyes.

'Leave my sister alone or I'll tell Daskalos Panayiotis!' Despina warned.

'Git, git you dirty rascal!' When he released her, Despina was quick to usher her sister to their room.

A tempestuous Spyros stormed off with malicious intent and headed for the niche recessed under the house and where he found a naked Ariana sitting cross-legged on the raised timber plank that was her mattress and combing her long brown hair.

He noticed that her hands were black from the fleshy hulls of the black walnuts that was used to dye hides and fibre. In Ariana's case she used the ink to tint her hair which on the face of it was a whacky and egoistic thing to do for a crazy person.

'Anathema se! Is this your revenge?'

Ariana stared up at him from under the alcove with an expression of perplexity.

'Ooshoo, Ooshoo *skile mavro!*' She hysterically hooted.

'Don't call me a black dog!' Spyros counteracted, 'And another thing, I forbid such indecent exposure! Put on your dress! I don't want any more bastards under my roof!'

His turbulent moods weren't entirely founded on Ariana's wild and irrepressible behaviour. He was angry at her for having forced him into sole parenthood.

Similarly, as his Armenian mistress for having ditched her bastard with him and ran off with their son Omer. He needed a trustworthy wife to relieve him of the pressures of fatherhood. Yesterday he'd met a peddler of hides inside Mayor Neophytos's kafenio.

Costas was a man in his early thirties with nerve grinding traits. When articulating he stretched his neck across the table and cocked his head in order to consider him more clearly. 'You've travelled a long way to find a wife,' Spyros offered over coffee.

'This is my first time to the north. They say a change of path means a change of luck,' Costas offered plainly, twirling his worry beads.

'I gather this tactic was unsuccessful,' Spyros said smugly, and with the thought that the chances of such a frightful looking man finding a wife was about the same as a scrounger finding a sack of gold. Though the tobacco merchant grudgingly accepted he'd underestimated the marketer's faculties.

'Unfortunately. I'll put in a good word for you just the same. But don't get your hopes up too high.'

'Because I'm a widower. But I am a man with reasonable collateral,' Spyros put forth.

'Don't mean a thing! Girls are absent minded and passionate creatures. And they have a high opinion. They walk with their chins in the air and bells tied to their girdles with the belief a young rich suitor will knock on their door. What chance do we have?' Costas chortled.

Spyros found his jocularity to be annoying. 'You don't say!'

'That's the way it is I'm afraid. Even though these girls don't see the rags on their backs or their mother's empty pot on the firewood.' He then offhandedly asked, 'you have daughters?'

'I have… two,' then as a postscript craftily added, 'one is young of course, though in a few years she will make a suitable wife for some lucky man.'

'Young, you say! How young?' Costas eagerly asked.

'Well, too young to bed, if you're wondering. Though, she will be useful in the meantime. Anyway, I believe the country isn't short of a brothel or two.'

Spyros himself patronised brothels when he went to hora. His pet was Lucilla, a young Africana girl with black saucy eyes and spongy plump lips and a broad rump. She was also prone to rowdy laughter and impish behaviour during erotic acts.

'It was really a wife I had in mind not a child, good Christian. Though I doubt very much if I'll ever have the pleasure of finding one. You said you have two daughters. And you want to give one away!'

'Regrettably of course. Though I'm content with just one.'

'What about grandparents that could relieve you?'

'None I'm afraid. Only a sick aunt. Why don't you drop by my house this evening and you can meet my daughter over a drink?

Spyros left the hide dealer, and as he made his way home, the thought that he'd be rid of Pedaluda's offspring once and for all rested auspiciously on his conscience.

* * *

'Wait here until I get back sister.' Despina urged and then hurried off to the kitchen and where she found her father munching on dried pumpkin seeds. She gave him a filthy stare as she passed him. She grabbed a clean dish towel from the drawer and then poured water from the clay jar into a plastic bowl.

Passing him on her way out she said, 'Stop treating my sister like she wasn't yours!' Spyros burst into hysterical laughter for her observation couldn't have been closer to the truth. 'You must have eaten a heart for breakfast *kori*! You're full of courage!'

Despina ignored his witty remark. Back inside her room she observed that her sister had yet to stop crying. She placed the plastic bowl of water on a low chair beside the cot. She wrung some of the moisture out of the dishtowel before she gently mopped Zehra's tear stained face.

'If you don't stop crying sister your eyes will look like beet bulbs!' Despina warned.

'I don't care if they do!' Zehra brooded.

'I care. I want you to look pretty!' Despina offered.

'I don't want you to care.'

'Who else have I to care about!' Despina pressed. 'You can wear my dress today. Shame on Baba! He could at least buy you a decent dress and a new pair of shoes. Instead, he spends it on himself. Now sit here,' she indicated the tiny wood stool before the shaft of stained mirror fixed to the wall. 'Let me brush your hair. A spider could happily nest there.' Despina chuckled, and then added, 'you know it's alright to tell me what you feel sister? You know I'd love you just the same.'

'You would?' Zehra murmured.

'Why wouldn't I? We're sisters.' Despina offered.

'He'll get angry if he finds out...'

'That you hate him? Let him! He doesn't deserve either of us! He's grumpy all the time because he's alone. Nobody cares about him. Mana wouldn't even put up with him if she were alive. Turn him into a frightened mouse, she would!' Both girls chuckled in unison. Zehra adored her sister.

One evening shortly after coming home from the field, Spyros was sprawled across the back porch with his back against the mud wall of the house when he overheard Zehra say to Despina, 'I'll see to Babas' bath and fetch clean clothes.'

When Zehra came through the open kitchen door and passed him on her way to kindle the fire in the lower yard Spyros looked up at her with intentional cunning. Why did she yield to him in such a susceptible way despite all his malice towards her? He might have been fond of the child had she not been Pedaluda's offspring, the sperm of an anonymous soldier.

With the child's grey eyes for all he knew she might have been fathered by a Frank or a Brit. He cursed his own idiocy for having been the dupe left to wash away someone else's sensual indulgence. He felt feverish, as if he'd been infected with an incurable disease that could only be cured when he'd purged himself of the child.

CHAPTER SEVEN

The old truck rattled and lurched as the engine rolled over, shifting into second gear with an ear-splitting screech at almost every tortuous turn, ascending at a snail's pace up a single dirt track flanked by mountainous cliffs. Spyros mused it was just as draining and disconcerting getting rid of the girl as it was keeping her. This was not a road trip for the fainthearted.

* * *

Olympus, (translated 'the snowy one,' at 1,952 metres is the highest point located in the Troodos Mountains of Cyprus at 6, 404 feet above sea level spanning most of the west of the island. In 1878, Cyprus was incorporated into the British Empire and found the need to move their administration from the hot plain of Nicosia to where it was located to the cool of the Troodos Mountains.

During the hot months the wives of the administrators would ride or drive into the fragrant pine forest and set up shops in Platres, a quaint village high up in the mountains. Winters at this altitude could be harsh and the snow could cover the ground for weeks. Families have been known to dig themselves out of two -metre -high snowdrifts piled up against the door of their homes. On a clear day one could see Turkey.

Driving on he passed alpine like villages and shortly was passing through the picturesque village of Kakopedria and where the houses were built on stilts and sat higgledy-piggledy over the sheer cliffs.

Some of the houses were built by the British administrators for their families over a decade ago, and even today their Victorian red brick villas complete with tin roofs and green painted shutters could be seen in numbers around the edge of the community lending it an old suburban feel. It had taken him almost three hours to get here from the Karpassa headland in the north.

About half a mile away at the end of the Marathassa Valley was the village of Pedhoulas which was built around a natural amphitheatre with views to Morphu Bay. On a clear day across the Mediterranean one could see the Taurus Mountains in Turkey. Hagia Triada (Holy Trinity) was a Byzantine church overlooked the bay.

During World War II, the church offered shelter for displaced children and families. Later an orphanage was attached to the church and was still functioning under the control of the nuns of the Holy Trinity. The government couldn't provide financial support and so the orphanage relied heavily on the more affluent population and charity organisations.

Spyros now rolled down his side of the window and picked a bunch of grapes growing from the vineyard out of the side of the mountain.

'It doesn't get any better than this *kori!*' he remarked.

Zehra appeared small and frail seated on the broken springs of her seat alongside her father. All she could see through the windshield and over the green bonnet was the tips of the green trees and patch of blue sky. Her small hand was firmly clutched to the cloth bag that was threaded across her body. The bag contained only a few bits and pieces; two sets of undergarments, a hairbrush, socks, one woollen cardigan and a dress.

There were also a few drawings that Despina had made for her. And that musical snow dome that the camel lady had given her.

The last time she'd gone on an excursion was a year ago when she'd gone on the bus with her sister to Apostolos Andreas. But she'd been happy that day because she'd been with Despina. Now she felt like a sparrow had lodged in her ribcage and she could taste the goat milk souring at the back of her throat. Despina had often warned her father not to give her milk because her stomach couldn't tolerate it.

'Why can't Despina come with me?'

'I've already told you *kori*!' Spyros mumbled through a mouthful of grapes.

'I want to stay with Despina. I don't want to go to a new home.'

'Who'll look after your Baba? Things might have been different if your mana hadn't died.'

'Why did she die?'

'She got sick. After she had you, that is. So at least you can do is repay her for her suffering to bring you into the world.'

'What do you mean?'

'Just like the Christian Jesus. Didn't he too die to save the world? Make it a better place.' Spyros wasn't surprised by the child's confusion for even he was baffled by his own sermon of self-sacrifice and world enhancement.

'Do I have to die for mana too?' Zehra was torn between pleasing her mana and losing Despina forever. How could the world be a better place without Despina? Zehra wanted to throw up.

'Don't be sick on me *kori*! Wait! I'll pull over!' Spyros cried as he made a sharp left turn of the wheel, but instantly the truck swerved off the road, and clipped the side of a tree before coming to a shuddering halt.

'Damn you! You nearly killed me!' He quickly climbed down from the driver's side to explore the outcome of the incident.

The truck was tilted to one side, dangling perilously over the cliff and sputtering clouds of smoke. 'That's all I need,' he exclaimed indignantly, then suddenly he saw the girl's side of the door open.

'Wait! Wait!' But it was too late for young Zehra. Spyros peered down into the gorge below, saw what appeared to be the child tangled amidst the undergrowth. It wasn't the outcome he'd expected. Perhaps it was better. Since he'd only come up here on a whim. And nobody could foresee an accident. He looked around, saw for the first time that the branches of the cedar trees had bowed from years of heavy snow.

And the air seemed more fragrant, and the heat was much lighter. His soul felt lighter now that he'd rid himself of the affliction that had plagued him over the years. What a remarkable and prolific day he'd had up here in the mountains.

*   *   *

Despina still had the nightmare dust in her eyes as she made her way to Katina's house. She passed Maritsa with the seven- moles house. Maritsa was seated out on the front porch selecting wheat from a round tray in her lap.

Further ahead was Pater Christofis's house and where alongside the door a dainty wicker cage of finches chirped. Close by the priestess was stringing beans for the evening meal before Vespers. Despina found Katina in her front garden. Her hat was drawn over her eyes as she cleared away twigs and leaves with a straw broom. The shuffle of footsteps along the stone path urged Katina to look up, and when she saw it was Despina there was a gleam of suspicion in her dark eyes in sensing the child was troubled. Shortly she was due to start work but she didn't mind the interruption for she'd known Despina since she was born thus it was only natural that she'd taken a maternal interest in the child's upbringing.

'No school today? Is Zehra sick again? She asked with dread, placing her broom on the ground.

'I don't know,' Despina offered glumly.

'Come sit over here.' She indicated the timber bench on the porch.

'Where could they be?' Despina sighed after she told her everything.

'I just want my sister to come home,' she brooded.

'She can't be too far away *koritsi-mou.*' Though she herself was just as perplexed. 'I made lemonade as there are plenty of lemons on the tree this time of year!' She went on cheerfully to dissuade the child's unease.

As Katina went inside to fetch the lemonade she tried to think of where they could be but couldn't think of anywhere.

In the meantime, young Despina was staring absentmindedly at a yellow and black butterfly quivering on the porch's ledge when at that moment the camel lady struck her infantile conscience. 'They've probably gone to see the camel lady.' She told Katina when she stepped back outside.

'This camel lady you speak of. Have you seen her?' Katina passed her the glass of lemonade and restlessly sat down beside her again.

After Despina told her the story Katina said, 'you met her at the monastery of Apostolos Andreas! About a year ago!'

'Her camel's name was...I can't remember.'

'Never mind,' Katina offered with a strained smile, then promptly added, 'tell me what makes you think your father knows her?'

'He was asking if she had a mark on her neck. And if she had a boy with her and if she told us where she lived.'

'And did she?' she anxiously asked.

'We didn't see a boy. And she didn't say where she lived. If we knew my sister wanted to go find her.' She told Katina about the snow dome she'd given them. 'We were going to run away. Baba was mean to Zehra. He used to beat her and lock her up in the shed for days without food or water. And made her work in the field.'

Of what help could an eight-year-old child be other than reap a few miserable crops. Katina pondered, then said, 'that poor child. Her place is at school, not in the field.'

'One day he left her outside in the rain. He told her to stand on one leg. Then he said if he came out and saw her standing on both legs then he'd cut them off and she'd never walk again.'

'Why that *diavolo*!' Katina hissed. 'Your sister is a very brave girl.'

'She said Baba and she played games in the field...'

'Games!' Katina interjected with alarm. 'Did she tell you what kind of games?'

'She wasn't allowed to say. She feared Baba would lock her up in the shed again. That's why she cried every night. She kept telling me she wished she was dead.'

Just then black anger rose from the pit of Katina's stomach. Her soul heavy with guilt. Young Zehra was just a string puppet to manipulate and appease the insatiable desires of a depraved psychopath.

It was obvious that Spyros' probing the children was to find out Pedaluda's whereabouts. He could cause extreme harm to anyone he considered to be his enemy, and Pedaluda was no exception, since she was his biggest adversary. Not only had he become unhinged that she'd been a disloyal mistress but more significantly she'd run off with the son he'd fathered.

She wouldn't have survived his beatings, or in the lesser case ended up as senseless as Ariana. She couldn't blame her for forsaking Zehra, it was a cruel admission on her part, though it was the truth just the same. An unmarried girl of twenty-one and with two toddlers journeying by camel across the harsh countryside amid a war and penniless and with only few provisions would be faced with catastrophic circumstances.

Pedaluda had been forced to make a conscientious and difficult decision. Sacrificing one child was better than two, thus chose to take her youngest born Omer. Though Despina said that she and her sister hadn't seen a boy with this woman that day. Was it possible that Omer had died? Though pitifully concluded that the infant mustn't have survived under such dire circumstances across the open and blustery terrain with minimal food and warm supplies.

'You'll have to come with me,' Katina said, then added, 'though you must be on your best behaviour.' Sofia, she knew, was a despotic and blustery woman that could inspire fear in a person with purposeful and quiet deliberation. Providing though, one respected her opinions and stuck to the orderly procedures of her domain she could be mildly tolerable.

The sun was blinding the skies where even the birds sought shelter, as they trudged up the incline towards the mansion. 'You walk up here every day?' Despina was panting with exhaustion.

'How else! I'd buy a pair of wings if they sold them! God didn't think things through *koritsi-mou*,' she complained.

When they arrived, Murat, Sofia's personal driver, was cleaning the vehicle out front.

Katina greeted him and he received her with a beaming smile, and then cast his eyes curiously on the young girl with her. Having passed through an impressive high wooden gate they both entered a spacious courtyard and where pigeons flew.

There was a pond and shelves of stone were set here and there and citrus trees provided shade.

The fragrance of scrambling jasmine and red roses fused with the herbs in clay pots. Attached to the mansion was a delightful cottage with gaping glass windows that overlooked the garden and pond below. This was Sofia's private retreat.

Two outer houses served as a larder and laundry room. 'Lovely, isn't it *koritsimou?'* Katina offered as they mounted the back steps and entered the downstairs foyer.

'Even more breath-taking inside, as you can see!' She added when she saw the child's enchantment. 'Think yourself fortunate to be here.'

'May I ask who the child is?' A voice queried.

Katina expectantly looked up to see a tall woman with coiffured red hair, angular cheeks that were glossed over with rouge and grey eyes that were shadowed with kohl. 'Kyria Sofia this is Despina. She's eight.'

Sofia came closer, took in the child's appearance with as much disdain as one might have for a mud frog reposed on their gleaming tiles. She offered the maid a sweet sickly smile. 'I can't see how a child in need of a bath and nourishment could be considered fortunate. Why is she here? After Katina explained the situation she said, 'the child has nowhere else to go.'

'This is not a refuge for the poor and homeless,' Sofia censured.

'It never crossed my mind,' she offered reticently, then added, 'she is well behaved, so you won't even notice she's here.'

'Very well I trust your discretion. However, as a maid you might have had the courtesy to seek my permission first.'

Katina wasn't the only one affronted by Sofia's reproach for young Despina was on the verge of tears as she tugged at her skirts. 'I want to go home. I don't like it here!'

'Why is that?' A man's voice asked, and just then Sofia diverted her eyes from the child to see her son approaching. 'Ah, Pandelis! The poor dear is troubled.' She patted the child's head for upshot and then passed on to him the information the maid had told her.

'Is that so? You said since last evening! What about the mother?'

'She has passed,' Katina's eyes were lowered not because she had lied but was mindful of the rush of warmth at her cheeks. It was silly of her, she knew, to even consider that such a charming and handsome and intelligent man could ever see her differently other than a simple and disabled maid. Though one looked upon such a gem with poverty in their eyes.

'May I ask who the child's father is?' Pandelis enquired.

'Spyros Manolas,' she revealed.

'She's the tobacco merchant's daughter?' He broke in officiously.

'You know him?' Katina asked.

'Only by reputation, that is!' he remarked with hidden disdain.

'How unfortunate for the child,' Sofia offered more candidly. Then derisively added, 'I don't see how a child of her age could be of any use in the field. Her place is at school.'

'I know the tobacco merchant's field. My father owns an apple orchard close by. I'll drive there myself and see if they're there. Then I'll have a word with mayor Neophytos. Someone might know something.

If not let me know in the morning if they haven't returned home. I'll drive to Lemnos and alert the authorities. They'll most likely organise a search party with the farmers. Please ensure the kitchen staff prepare some food for the child.'

'Most charitable of you Kyrie Pandelis,' Katina offered.

'I wouldn't expect anything less of my son,' Sofia curtly announced and then promptly dismissed the maid. Katina only got as far as the kitchen door when she heard her call out, 'Oh and don't forget my pills. And Tsai! I'll be in the drawing room upstairs.'

Katina mimicked her as she stepped into the kitchen. Perhaps an infusion of rue and pond- scum would be more beneficial.

When Despina tired of staring at her reflection rippling in the fish-pond, she sat on a nearby stone bench and considered all the nice food she'd been given to eat. It didn't seem fair that some people had so much food when others had none. Her sister would be starving by now wherever she was. She looked around, enchanted by what she saw. It was as if a rainbow had fallen from the skies and splashed everything with bright colours in the garden. Even the pigeons cooed and pranced around with an air of arrogance, and seemingly content with their abode.

She stared up at the white stone -washed mansion with its tiers of terraces and balustrades. And the heavy interwoven drapes within the spacious glass windows and where some had flower boxes on the ledge. She thought about the maids in their crisp white aprons and lapels strolling quietly and orderly in and out of corridors with feather dusters. And the beautiful wall tapestries and richly spun rugs on the polished floors. She wished Zehra were here with her to see how the rich people live.

Then she thought about the disorderly house she lived in with its mouldy walls and shabby furniture. The makeshift wardrobe of cables and plastic with its zip up door in her room.

The cigarette burns on the oilcloth on the kitchen table, the potato sack mats on the cement floors, and the clay jars of stream water beneath the stone wash trench. The scraping front wooden gate with its peeling blue paint. Despina wished she and Zehra could live in a proper home full of nice things. Though she sensed poor is what they'd always be.

Baba told her once that poor people had to scratch their own backs. Rich people had others scratch it for them. Shortly, the tall man that she'd seen earlier on with the grumpy woman came out into the garden.

'Mind if I join you?' He flashed her a smile that made young Despina feel incapable of responding for she was unfamiliar with sociable gestures.

He sat down on the bench beside her even though she hadn't wanted him to and then she heard him say, 'tell me young lady…'

'It's Despina,' she promptly offered.

'Pardon, Despina. Did you know your name means 'lady' in Greek?'

She shrugged.

'I gather you don't then.' He explained that it was common for a Greek to have been named after a saint. That's why almost every day was a festival of some saint. He now asked, 'do you like reading?'

'I guess I do.'

'I've bought you a book. Here,' he passed it over to her. 'As you can see it's called *The Little Matchstick Girl*. Have you read it?'

'At school.'

'Did you like the story?'

'I felt sorry for the girl,' Despina offered.

'Most stories have happy endings you know. What about the *Little Ash Girl* or *Cinderella*? 'She found a prince, didn't she?'

'It's not really true,' Despina frowned.

'That's what fairy tales are about. Children try to imagine it's them in the story. Didn't you wish you were the little ash girl?' he smiled.

Covertly he observed the child's attire: the frayed hem of her school tunic, the stains at the collar and pitted shoes. She also smelt of cooking lard. Everything seemed at variance with her youthfulness. Her appalling state was self-explanatory. Her father was the anathema of society. A waste of a man who'd kill a man for his gold tooth. Some years before Spyros had worked for one of the tenant farmers in a field that was owned by his father. When his father's elderly land tenant retired, Spyros hired another field worker and continued to sow the field but refused to pay his father dues.

Then when his father had wanted to bore in the field and channel water to an adjacent fruit orchard a bitter dispute erupted between the two men. A few months on his father told him the matter had been resolved. He'd also said that he suspected that the tobacco merchant had an accomplice in the Department of Land and Surveys who'd forged the original document. 'He's breaking the law!' Pandelis had censured.

'Let him sow his damned *nicotina* seedlings! I'm not going to cry over a bucket of toxic soil that's useless for organic farming!' His father had retorted.

'I guess I did.' Despina stared down at her old shoes, imagined the beautiful glass slippers on her feet.

'Now tell me pretty lady...'

'It's Despina,' she promptly corrected him again.

'Pardon. I've upset you. I'll leave if you like!' He stood up.

'I'm upset with my father.' Despina couldn't hold back her tears and he was quick to retrieve his handkerchief and pass it to her.

'It's clean.' He offered as a matter of courtesy. 'Keep it,' he smiled when she went to hand it back. 'Now can you let me see roses planted on your cheeks?'

Despina shyly smiled, amused at what he'd said.

'That's better, now may I ask why?' He sat back down again.

'Because he hasn't brought Zehra home yet! I don't care if he never comes home.'

'Who'd look after you? he hugged her.

'I can take care of myself. And Bebek! She's Baba's sister. She's dumb and naughty sometimes. That's because she hasn't got a proper brain like us.'

He smirked, and at the same time realised how carefree he felt in the company of the child. 'She's lucky to have you. Now tell me, do you like ponies?'

'I've never seen a real one. Only in books.'

'Would you like to go to my father's stables one day to see a real one?' Then he added, 'my father has taught me everything there is to know about breeding horses. I was an only child and I got lonely. I had to find things to amuse myself. Apart from horses, that is.' He offered thoughtfully.

'What did you do?'

'I'd write stories. Nothing that anybody would want to read, now that I think about it. I was just a smug kid. I thought I was better than what I really was,' he smiled.

'Aww, but I want to know'

'Well, there was this one story about a young girl.'

'What was her name?'

'I didn't think she needed one.' The question took him by surprise.

'Everyone has a name, even in stories,' Despina offered.

'You're right,' he grinned.

'You can still give her a name.'

'I doubt if I even have it. It was a long time ago. Twenty years, in fact. I must have been around your age.'

'Don't tell me you threw it away!' Despina brooded.

'Like I said, I wrote it a long time ago. Anyway, I found other things to amuse myself. I'd fly kites or I'd visit the 'wishing tree.'

'I've never seen a 'wishing tree.' Where is it?'

'It's a long walk I'm afraid. Past the forest of red cedars and beyond the ruins in a clearing near the sea cliff. It's surrounded by a crumbling stone wall.'

'What did you do there?'

'It was a good place to run my kite. Though most people went there to tie a ribbon or rag on the tree and make a wish. They believed that when the wind rustled the tree their wishes were carried to the Gods and spirit realm.'

Wishing trees were an Armenian tradition dating back to pagan times when certain trees were objects of veneration. Each rag represented a wish or prayer that the supplicant hoped to be granted. It was important to put all one's energy and intention as they tied the rag to the tree that they were connected to.

'Did you make a wish?'

'As a boy I never hoped for anything other than para to buy candy. Some folk left a penny under a pebble or at the foot of the tree, you see.

Anyway, there was a particular old man, a candy seller who pushed a glass-walled cart with spun candy and pistachio nuts. There was a wooden monkey on top of the cart and the old man would pull the strings and the monkey would screech and wave its arms and legs. When I didn't have money then I'd pull the strings to distract the old man and then slip a hand under the tray and steal candy.'

'It's wrong to steal. That's what pater Christofis says.'

'When you're just a kid you don't think of the wrongdoing, only the candy,' he grinned.

Pandelis glanced at his watch. 'Katina will be finishing work soon. She'll want to take you home. Wait here, I want to have a word with her before she goes. It was nice talking to you Despina.'

Earlier in the morning on his way back from the tobacco merchant's field he'd pulled up for gasoline. The owner of the depot, a plump, balding man with a bluish tinged nose had disclosed some unforeseen information. The owner he discovered was a gossipmonger. He'd lost patience with the man's frivolous talk. Pandelis wasn't interested in all the goings on in the village. The only time he came down was to collect dues from the leaseholders if his father was occupied.

'I'm in a hurry if you don't mind!'

The man grumpily threw his arms in the air. 'Seems everybody is in a hurry these days!'

'I have a meeting with my lawyer!' Pandelis offered frankly.

'Then I can understand the hurry! Early yesterday morning some screwball came thumping on my door just to fill a tin with gasoline. I wouldn't have opened the door if I'd known who it was.

Said he had a leaky fuel tank and didn't trust the truck to take him up to the mountains and back. As if I cared about that cracked brain's problems. Anyway, if that was the case then why didn't he leave the young one at home!' The man scowled.

'Young one. You mean a child?'

'That's right. She was sitting up front in that rusted heap of his.'

'Did he say why he was going to the mountains?'

'Didn't bother to ask. I'm not interested in that man's affairs. Can't be up to any good!'

Pandelis was sure who the customer was. It explained why he hadn't found Spyros in the field when he'd gone there earlier in the morning. And a trip up into the Troodos ranges and back was a matter of a couple of hours, three at the most, thus it didn't clarify why he'd been gone for two days. Even if the truck had broken down there must have been other means of transportation to return home. He had grave fears for the child. If they didn't return home by nightfall, then he'd alert the authorities at the station in the neighbouring village of Lemnos.

Katina had been hanging her apron up when Pandelis came into the kitchen. 'Make sure you prepare a basket of food before you leave...'

'Why that's kind of you but I have...' Despina will be hungry,' he interrupted. Then added, 'ensure there's plenty of everything. By the way, I'd like to ask a favour. I'd like to take her to the stables one weekend to show her the pony.'

'I'm afraid her father is a man of a different understanding,' Katina offered officiously.

'I'm aware she'll need permission. I was hoping you'd act as mediator.'

'Leave it with me. Oh, by the way, I've made fresh lemonade!' Katina offered in good spirit.

'Some other time. But thanks. You'll find Despina in the garden.'

Katina didn't need him to tell her where she was since she'd crossed the courtyard often enough to notice how he'd given the child his undivided attention.

Three times she'd passed through the courtyard in the hope she'd attract his attention and he'd ask her to join them. Once she'd gone to the pantry to fetch olives. Then it was to the laundry. Lastly, she'd gone out to pick lemons from the tree. The only way she would have attracted his attention was if she'd been a fly squatted on the tip of his nose. And he'd just declined her offer of lemonade. Katina felt feverishly agitated by the notion that she'd allowed herself to become a victim of her own illusions. Had she in her flurry of excitement forgotten momentarily to see herself through his eyes, to perceive what a common and disabled maid she was? She should have known that his only interest was that of a fraught and unhappy child. She'd always felt inferior around others because of her disability, even if it be a child.

'Where could Zehra be? Where could Baba have taken her?' Despina brooded when Katina took her home.

'She can't be too far.' Katina replied as she placed the basket atop the kitchen table.

'What's inside? Despina readily asked.

'I've managed some food. But you mustn't breathe a word.'

'Why did you have to steal? The man told me in the garden the food was for me.'

Katina felt slighted by the idea that the child would think Pandelis had granted her a special favour.

'You must have heard wrong. It's all this worry about your sister that's confused you. Now run along and see if you can find a change of clothes.

You can stay with me tonight. In the meantime, I'll go see to your… I mean Bebek. Your aunt must be so hungry she'll be chewing on stones by now.'

Katina felt unsettled by the near slip. She'd just have to be more prudent in the child's presence.

When she didn't find her inside the niche, she left food in the tin plate at the foot of the opening, replenished her pitcher with water and then hurried down to the lower yard. She wasn't there either and then Katina recalled the field of carob trees. There she found Bebek uttering indecencies, frothing at the mouth, and darting all over the place with her skirts raised, and her bare feet tangled with twigs and thorns. She observed this frightful display with intent contemplation. 'You never should have found me Ariana. But you left me no choice. I had to extinguish the fire before it spread.' She turned, crossed the dirt road, and then made her way back to collect Despina.

When they did eventually return home after two days Despina's grief was torrential, the ache inside of her worse than days of hunger. Or the pain when she'd slit her hand with the knife. She wished it was her inside that coffin in the booth of her father's truck. It seemed such a demeaning and hideous thing measured up to the naïve and sweet little girl inside there. Again, her sister had been incarcerated only this time it was too late to save her. Zehra was dead.

CHAPTER EIGHT

On the day of the funeral Pater Christofis escorted the departed body of her sister from the entrance of the church to the soleas, censing with the censor and chanting the: 'Holy God, Holy Mighty, Holy immortal' at a slow pace. 'Indeed, how awesome of our death is a mystery! How the soul is forcibly severed from its harmonious union with the body.'

The coffin was placed on a horse driven cart and Despina followed the small congregation of mourners to the forest of red cedars where Pater Christofis recited more prayers by the gravesite. 'What pleasure of life ever remains unmixed with grief? What glory endures immovable on earth? All are feebler than shadows, all are illusive than dreams. In a single moment all are supplanted by death.'

But. 'Like a flower it withers, and like a dream it vanishes and dissolves away human being. For you are the resurrection, the life and the repose of your departed servant Zehra.'

As the embalmed body was lifted from the casket and buried deep in the earth Pater Christofis recited the last prayer. 'Sprinkle me with hyssop and I shall be cleansed, wash me and I shall be whiter than snow.'

'Goodbye Zehra. I'll always be holding your hand.' Despina gulped back her tears and Katina gripped at her arm. 'Don't throw yourself into darkness *koritsi-mou.* I'll never be able to bring you back.'

Zehra's death provoked immeasurable outrage amongst both the Turkish and Greek population in Rizo. Some vented their fury in hushed tones, others more openly.

It was a calculated act of revenge, they deemed. At every corner and turn Spyros was confronted with reproachful and ominous stares. 'Miserable shirkers! Your government pays you fuck wits to occupy our land. Fuck our women! Go back to Turkey where you all belong!'

Mayor Neophytos had placed a noticeboard on the door of his *kafenio* that read; *Butchers and Traders of Fledglings Unwelcome!*

This blinkered pigeonholing on the mayor's part had enraged Spyros and a heated brawl ensued. The mayor's EOKA supporters they too became embroiled in the affray. In no time the room resembled a battlefield. Chairs became shields, men collided, and tables were bowled over and everything atop came crashing to the already squalid floor. At one point the mayor almost soiled himself mightily when Spyros brandished a pocketknife.

'Don't come back! You're like a flea-infested rat that causes a plague in this village!' A bruised and bloodied mayor warned.

Not even in the confinement of his own home could Spyros escape persecution. He sat in a creaking wicker chair by the flickering light of a stinking wink atop the table and binging on zivania to ditch his wrath.

'Wretched rebels! You dare attempt to bring down an innocent man? Next time your testicles will become fodder for the pigs!' Spyros incoherently grumbled. He then drew the spout of the *agele* to his mouth, drew in a few deep breaths and exhaled, the cool smoke clouding all around him, fusing with the stench of the kerosene lamp.

The effect was instantaneous. Drowsily he stretched out his legs, reclined back into the chair, but before long he was overcome by an undesirable panic by the voice inside his head.

'You're a condemned man! You didn't think you'd get away with it did you? Treacherous dog! You think a child's life is as valueless as a couple of lousy hides! Though you were right about one thing! The girl would have made a promising wife in a few years. I'm surprised you didn't keep her for yourself.'

'Enough! Enough! I should have pulled the trigger!'

'But you didn't! Coward! You don't even trust your own intuitions. You are like a pissed off bull with no horns!' The voice persisted.

'Don't test my courage *kori!*' Just then everything atop the table rattled, clinked and shook when his fist slammed down, causing the alcohol in his glass to wash over the oilcloth.

The thought that his lunatic wife could crush and defeat him at his own game reduced his brains to a grain of wheat. Then with a great sweep of his burly arm everything dispersed instantaneously, including the kerosene lamp, ignited the oil cloth. Spyros leapt from the chair and ran out into the yard yelping like a trodden livid dog.

'Below madness is pathetic. And you are pathetic Spyros Manolas!'

CHAPTER NINE

The roots of hatred between the Greek and Turkish Cypriots go as far back as the Ottoman Empire. As was the custom of the Ottoman at the time, after conquering Cyprus, they brought a big group of Turkish people from the mainland. The settlers were given houses and had started living on the island. While the Ottomans were fearless during times of war, they knew how valuable peace was too. To keep peace, they decided to give some representation in political decisions to the Greek Orthodox Church in Cyprus.

For three hundred years the Ottomans ruled Cyprus, and for three hundred years, the island experienced a period of relative peace. Turkish Cypriots and Greek Cypriots lived next door to each other, but also, without engaging with one another. Maybe this was when the first seed of distrust was sown, a feeling that became an idea-an idea that became a political agenda that became war. When the Ottoman Empire crumbled and the British took over Cyprus, they were aware of the tensions between Greek and Turkish Cypriots, and used them to their advantage, divide and conquer was a common façon de gouverner used by the British. British politics fuelled the hatred between the two groups while keeping the groups from directing their frustrations at the British rulers. By the 1950's the feelings of distrust between Greek and

Turkish Cypriots had formed into an idea, of 'us vs them.' One side there was 'us the Greek Cypriots, and them, the Turkish Cypriots that hate us.'

Despina was on her way to the communal oven when she spotted Rifat playing guerrilla warfare in the field with a group of boys.

When she saw him from the corner of her eye sprinting towards her, she picked up pace, almost dropped the basket of moist dough which had taken all morning to knead.

'What do you want?' She calmly asked when he caught up with her, and she felt a kind of mischievous pleasure when she noticed his confusion. Surreptitiously she observed his ridiculous attire which told her that he was play-acting a German soldier.

There was an emblem of a swastika at his arm made from a patch of white cloth with a red cross painted on it with the ends bent at right angles. A plastic rifle was in his hand.

A tumble of dark locks fell recklessly about his face from under a fawn military hat. A wide hemp belt secured the waist of an army shirt over baggy trousers that were tucked inside knee high rubber boots. The strangeness of it all, she thought.

'I was playing in the field when I saw you,' he offered uncharacteristically coyly. Then he asked how she was and if she was on her way to bake bread and if she needed help with the basket. Despina answered in monosyllables which befuddled him even more and then she said, 'I wouldn't want to hold you up from the battlefield. You might be needed.'

'Yok. No. The battles over. I managed to order the defence to the front line and capture and kill the enemy.' Rifat offered, hoping to impress her, which he did, yet Despina refused to praise his heroic efforts even if it were merely a stupid game.

'Well good for you,' she replied stiffly, then added, 'what's more the war ended long ago.' She picked up her basket and walked off, and Rifat stood there fluttering his lids in the beastly sun and at the same time considering what he'd said or done wrong. He turned and with his eyes cast to the ground made his way back to the field and with the odd sensation he'd just been wounded by his own plastic rifle.

Despina lifted the copper cezve off the blue -yellow flame, filled the small cup with coffee alongside the plate of semolina cake on the tray and then joined Katina in the lower yard. As they sat in the palm scented shade Despina listened on as Katina told her the story of her 'problem.'

'I was teased badly at school because of my "problem." My father was ashamed of me and feared there'd be no suitors. For as long as I can remember he kept telling me he'd work hard and save money for a doctor to fix my "problem." He wasn't a man of his word, as you can see child!'

Katina was raised in a small village on the fringes of the megalopolis of Famagusta in the Kapassa region. She understood the emptiness of being motherless.

'My mother, she too, rejected me because of my "problem." I was only seven when she walked out with my younger sister. Children sense favouritism. They bleed inside it hurts so bad. My father left me alone at night to go to the gambling houses. I remember I was so frightened that

I'd sit behind the door all night checking to make sure it was locked. At the age of fourteen he tried to marry me off to a man twice my age and at a time when I was still playing with dolls. I wanted to be a teacher. Through a friend I found out about a distant uncle living here in Rizo and so I came to live with him when I was fifteen. You might remember my uncle Stelios. When I mentioned how sad you were when Zehra was sick he'd come here to the house to pick you up and take you to watch the puppet show at Neophytos's *kefanio* to cheer you up. You must have been around five or six. He was eighty-five and died not long after those days. He might have lived to be a hundred if that useless and greedy orphaned dog of a field worker of his hadn't caused him so much misery. Never mind my rambling child.'

'It was summer I think,' Despina said. 'He would buy me iced rosewater and pasteli. And he used to sing to me on the way home.'

'Ah yes, Stelios was a good man. He adored children but had no desire to marry which is probably a good thing otherwise he might not have taken me in. My father made no attempt to persuade me into coming home which proved he didn't want me. He died of the 'white plague,' so you see *koritsi-mou* he was suitably punished. Nobody in this life is exonerated of wrongdoing.'

Cypriot customs were merely impractical misconceptions passed on by a primitive society and had no meaningful bearing on a woman's path in life. A woman's honour was invaluable. She should never be conditioned to believe she was just a domestic slave and child bearer to her spouse. Nor should she be regarded as a commodity, like an ornament on the shelf only to be admired by others. Arranged marriages were common practise regardless of how questionable or incongruous the affiliation. It would be fair to say child marriages became a matter of parental abuse in as much as the same way as the anomaly and brutalising marriage itself. A woman regardless of ethnicity was entitled to lead an independent life outside the unfeasible restrictions and sanctions of her motherland.

Without an education a woman's world was extremely narrowed. A woman had to commit to a peasant's existence of hard slog in the fields and shovelling dirt into potholes on roads while contemplating her chores at home and finding ways to make meals out of nothing and build dreams out of nothing.

Through her uncle's generosity Katina had finished school and furthered her education in London.

There she had lived with her aunt Kaliopi, Stelios's married sister, who'd migrated to the UK with scores of other Greek Cypriots seeking an unbiased life outside the warfare of their political divided country. London pre-World War Two was a city equipped with sophisticated amenities. There were theatres and trendy boutiques for the elite and fine restaurants. And department stores three or more stories high where one had to take a cage elevator to get to the floor levels above. And the women wore elaborate suits and hats with feathers almost as broad as the sidewalks.

'So, did you become a teacher?' Despina offered.

'Sure, but nobody wanted to give me a job. It was because of my 'problem,' you see, even though they'd never admit it. Bigots! All of them. They think the only place for a maimed woman is a nunnery or a domestic servant,' Katina scoffed.

'I wish I could be a teacher.'

Katina observed her piteously as she swallowed the last bit of semolina cake, and then averted her eyes to the sun browned woman wandering about the yard with unintentional purpose who happened to be the mother of Despina.

'You can if you want. But you must finish school first.' She went on to tell her that a good education reinforced a woman's status in life and earned the respect of others.

'And you get to choose who you want to marry.'

'Even a Muslim?' Despina asked the question as if it had been sitting on the tip of her tongue. Katina wasn't shocked by the observation.

Despina and Rifat were like two drops of water on a leaf.

Despina had an appealing quality about her which made other girls of the village look dull and uninteresting and so it was easy to understand why the Muslim boy had befriended her. Katina sensed that if she'd inherited her physiognomies and attributes, then even her 'problem' might have seemed superficial or disregarded by a suitor that might come her way.

Even though interbreeding had been around since the beginning of time the affiliation of a Muslim and Christian seemed a most unlikely combination to the majority of Greek and Turkish Cypriots. It was best they married their own kind.

'That's up to you!' Katina offered.

'Do you think I'm pretty?' Despina offered shyly.

'Rifat must think you as pretty as the Tulips of Istanbul.'

'You think he likes me?' She was encouraged by Katina's honesty.

'That's because he's sensed your fondness and curiosity of him.'

Attending Vespers of an evening granted Despina the opportunity to see Rifat on his way to the mosque for Friday prayers with his mother.

His family were just one of the many Turkish settlers in the village of Rizo. Although the minority of Greek Cypriots opposed the settlement of Turks on the soil which they claimed to be their own, thus a line of demarcation existed between the two factions.

The British started conscripting Turkish Cypriots into the police force, patrolling Cyprus to fight EOKA. EOKA targeted colonial authorities, including police, but George Grivas the leader of EOKA, did not initially wish to open a new front by fighting Turkish Cypriots and reassured them that EOKA would not harm their people.

Regardless of his assurance some Turkish Cypriot policemen were killed by EOKA members. This provoked some intercommunal violence in the spring and summer, but these attacks on policemen were not motivated by the fact that they were Turkish Cypriots. But in January 1957, Grivas changed his policy as his forces in the mountains became increasingly pressured by the British forces. In order to divert the attention of the British forces, EOKA members started to target Turkish Cypriot policemen on 19th January, when a power station was bombed, and the injury of three others, provoked three days of intercommunal violence in Nicosia. The two communities targeted each other in reprisals.

At least one Greek Cypriot was killed, and the army deployed in the streets. They burned the stores of Greek Cypriots and attacked their neighbourhoods.

The Greek Cypriot leadership spread propaganda following these attacks and suggested that the riots had been merely an act of Turkish aggression. Such events caused chaos and drove communities apart both in Cyprus and in Turkey.

Further to the north were the ruins of Agios Philon church, one of the few orthodox churches in Cyprus built in the Romanesque rather than the Byzantine style.

Standing in a cluster of palm trees the church is characterised by a profusion of arches and windows. Beside and around Agios Philon are the remains of Greco-Roman Karpassia and a fifth century AD cathedral built from stone plundered from it.

It was here in this great square of littered ruins set amongst thistle-downs and wildflowers that Despina and Rifat would come to be alone. By this time Despina was going on nineteen.

Rifat would ride his father's horse-drawn cart and they'd meet half-way in the forest of red cedars.

Today Despina had arrived early to visit her sister's grave. She frequented the grave once a week to tend to the flowerbed she'd made in honour of Zehra. It was the least she could do. After her death loneliness had become Despina's constant companion once again analogous to all those times when her sister got sick and couldn't play with her. Each night she'd cried herself to sleep inhaling the scent of her sister's pillow in the cot they'd once shared. It had taken her some time to wash it and store it away. She'd even refused to visit her grave for to go there meant acceptance. Though her feelings of self-blame and dejection were ever present to remind her of the one thing she'd promised Zehra. She'd failed to protect her.

Now Despina said, 'must you be buried under this earth? You don't like the darkness. You must be cold down there. Baba dishonoured you even in death, sister. Not even a tombstone. At least you have a grave with a name. It's more than he did for our mana. I was jealous at first knowing you'd be happy without me. But now I'm comforted by the acceptance that you are with our mana. You remember the young Muslim boy Rifat? Baba called him the kitten thief, remember! We've been secretly meeting here for a few years. He's such a fine-looking lad. And clever but of course I don't tell him this as a girl must withhold a touch of mystery about herself to keep a boy interested. I'm sure you'd approve of him Zehra! Oh, here he is now! I can feel frogs leaping inside of me.'

When Rifat joined her, they stayed a while to gather mushrooms. 'Why do you suppose they grow here in the cemetery?'

'It's all the rotting bones, your see,' Rifat dropped some of the fungi into the canvas bag he was holding. 'The bones nourish the soil. Make lots of worms.'

'What! My sister and mana are buried here!'

'You never visit your mana's grave.'

'What makes you think that I don't? Anyway, I don't believe what you said about the mushrooms!'

'I didn't think you would!' he grinned.

'Then why did you say it? Why don't you speak the truth?' she disputed.

'Alright! Well, you see here the mushrooms are sheltered from the wind! And the leaves and bark provide moisture which makes it a good place for them to grow. Some are poisonous. You can identify them if you know what you're looking for. Some are tinged yellow while others have a red skirt beneath the cup. My father nearly died once,' he offered soberly.

'Then why bother? And you might have warned me sooner,' Despina complained. 'What if I'd eaten one right now and died?'

'Well, you're in the right place Despinoulla!' He chuckled, and then on impulse added, 'want to play the memory game?

The idea was to reveal an object in order to take the lead and then trick the loser into forgetting to say the magical word, 'I remember,' when they pass them something at any given time.

'It's a child's game. Is that how you see me?'

'Yok. I just thought it would be fun. See if you can beat me,' he offered.

'You'll lose. What shall we bet on? What about a four-leaf clover!'

'This is a graveyard not a pasture silly. Besides, it's an unlucky place. If they grew here the dead would be asking your Christian Jesus to bring them back to life,' he laughed.

'What about your people?'

'Muslims are happy where they are!'

'I don't want to hear anymore daft stories.' Despina fled back to the cart and Rifat was quick to join her and take up the horse's reins. Riding out to the ruins a silence fell between them. Having reached there they sat on a bench of fractured stone.

Today Rifat had brought along his lute.

While he strummed up chords Despina raised her knees and rested her arms there and cast her eyes to the Mediterranean Sea which came into view through the windowless arches and pilasters of the ruins. Its blue glistening waters spun from the rays of the sun.

Far below the rugged cliffs before them was its sandy shoreline. After a while he placed the wood instrument in his lap and squinted over at her and quietly asked, 'are you still mad at me?'

'You could say that I am.' Despina offered and then curiously asked, 'who taught you to play that thing?

'This thing is called a lute. It's an old instrument that my father used to play back in Istanbul. But I taught myself by using a broomstick handle with strings attached to the peg box. I put a record on the gramophone and play along with the tune. I hope to write lyrics one day. Just for you.'

'What makes you think I'd even want you to?' She said with an upward gesture of the chin.

He strummed a couple of chords then peered up at her sideways, 'I thought you'd be pleased. But I was wrong.'

Despina felt weakened by the disenchantment in his dark eyes. Then he said, 'no need to go red. I can handle the insult,' he grinned.

'It's hot out here.' She fanned her face for effect.

'We can ride back to the forest. If you like?' he offered.

'I'd rather stay here.'

'Ah, the poisonous mushrooms!' He said soberly, squinting over at her.

'I should think your father was displeased after you nearly killed him,' Despina offered.

'Yok. He blamed himself for not warning me. I know better now. I avoid the ones with a red cap or white skirt on the stem. Though I believe some have yellow heads.'

'That's comforting,' Despina offered.

'Did you know that Jews were persecuted for being anti-Christian?'

'You read this?'

'Evet. Yes. They were forced to wear a 'badge of shame'. Two yellow strips of cloth on their sleeve. They were only allowed to remain in England if they served the king. They were compared to deadly fungi. People hated them so much they called them 'poisonous mushrooms.' That's why Adolf Hitler tried to get rid of them all. He sent them to a place called 'the family camp.'

But it was just a ploy to lure them there, you see. Once there his sympathisers sent them to the gas chamber. Some were tortured and burnt and buried alive. Even young children.'

Despina's hands flew to her mouth. 'You played a German soldier once. Remember! Why would you do that?'

'There must be opponents to fight a battle. Would you have preferred I'd been a Turkish soldier fighting against your people?'

'Of course not! I want our people to be friends. Why do you think our people hate each other so much?'

Despina said with her eyes on the menacing, squat brown lizards darting between their feet. 'Do you think it's because our religions are different. And because your people are Turkish Cypriot, and my people are Greek Cypriot? And why do they say that Hell if for Christians and Paradise is for Muslims? Pater Christofis says we all get to go to paradise if we believe in God. I don't understand any of it!'

Rifat pondered a while and then said, 'who knows how the idiots think. Allah is one. He is God. Only difference is we study the Koran and go to the mosque while your people read the bible and go to church. Most don't even understand what's written. How I see it is that their conviction to Allah is merely a subconscious delusion, a clutch to spare them from some unforeseen misfortune. It also gives them assurance of eternal life in paradise where they'll find rivers of honey and wine. And the men get to have fifty wives. They miss out if they go to hell!' Rifat laughed.

'Fifty wives!' Despina was dumbfounded although it somehow explained why he'd said that his people would be happy to stay where they were.

'It's what Hodja Fajoula says is written. Though I tend to listen with half an ear at such teachings. Anyway, the idiots wouldn't know who a real Cypriot is. There might not even be such a thing as a real Cypriot.'

'Do you know?' Despina asked, expecting he would, but she was wrong when he said, 'nobody does.'

'Then who do you suppose our people are?' she urged.

'Our people are the product of an assortment of fruit.'

'Did the Hodja also tell you this?'

'Yok. It's what I say, my own estimation after researching history books. Teachers keep their philosophies about ethnic and political affairs for the coffeehouses. You see the hatred between our people goes back a very long time. Nobody can lay claim to the land because nobody knows who it really belongs to. There's a list of rulers that are long as the tail of my father's horse.' And he was right.

Cyprus had been home to the Mycenaean Greeks, the Dorian Greeks, Syrian settlers, the Phoenicians, the Egyptians, the Persions, the Arabs, the Byzantines, the British Crusaders, the French, the Venetians, the Genoans, the Ottomons, the Greek and the Turk. And that the island had been subjugated, invaded, settled peacefully, traded and passed on as a gift from one Kingdom to another countless times.

'We'd be here all day. Your father will get suspicious.'

'I'm not afraid. Are you?'

'Yok. I'm not afraid of a donkey. With all respect.'

'You value a man who hates you! And Muslims!' she offered boldly.

'He's your father.'

'He never treats me as such.' Despina said, as if to herself.

'Then he doesn't deserve you. Just let me know if he ever hurts you!' He'd overheard his mother and neighbour talking over coffee one morning. He'd been in his room trying to finish an important thesis for his last term at high school.

Though he was distracted by their nattering that drifted down the hallway. He got up and listened on to their conversation from outside the door of his room.

'Your son likes the Christian girl. Despina, isn't it? She must be around Rifat's age. I hear she's bright and house trained. Mashalla there won't be a shortage of suitors but only one lucky one.'

'There are plenty of suitable Muslim girls in our village for our son.' His mother chided.

'Of course, of course. He's turned out a fine boy. I'm sure both you and Jusuf have had no regrets over the years.'

'Praise Allah! It would be inconceivable after all our efforts to raise the boy to hand him over to that Christian girl you speak of. Are you forgetting whose daughter she is? Why her father's a shaitan. They say he sent his wife mad. The woman should be in an asylum. Why he keeps her at home is beyond anyone's understanding. Perhaps it's God's way of reminding him of the evilness of his heart.' His mother castigated.

'Zenep canim, one can't choose their father.'

'Evet, but what about his mistress!'

'Ah the milk nurse! Armenian, wasn't she? Or was it Turk? What was her name again?'

'Pedaluda. A nomadic whore! Or whatever.'

'Come now Zenep. It was just hearsay amongst our people and Christian neighbours. People like to throw mud at a beautiful woman. Especially if she has a child out of wedlock. Maybe she lost her family and husband and is a refugee just like us. We must be more supportive of our neighbours.'

'Evet, but one can hardly empathise with a woman who forsakes her own child. Look what happened to her,' Zenep censured.

'The accident you mean! Up in the mountains, wasn't it!'

'Accident my ass! Some even said he sold the girl.'

'If he did then why bother about a coffin? A funeral!' The neighbour sneered.

'It was nothing more than a sham good Muslim. That viper tried to convince the villagers the girl was dead.'

'Then what was inside the coffin?' The neighbour asked.

'I heard it was the flayed carcass of a lamb wrapped in a white sheet. It's so horrifying it drains the blood from the body.'

'You don't say!' The neighbour uttered incredulously.

'It's what everyone says. Jusuf overhears everything in the coffeehouse.'

'Well, if you ask me the men in the coffeehouse like to embroider things to their own advantage. It makes them feel good by attracting the attention of others. Besides, who else have they got to listen to them while ploughing the field all day!'

Despina now said, 'why should you care about me?'

Rifat couldn't have been more aware of her existence or more protective of her if she were a fragile egg in the palm of his hand. 'You're different.'

'Because I'm a Greek Christian?'

'Yok. Would you think I'm different because I'm Muslim Turk?'

'You know I wouldn't.' Despina offered frankly. He was about to play the lute again when she said, 'you still haven't told me why?'

'You're curious about things that most girls couldn't care less about. The Muslim girls I know are so daft they wouldn't know a partridge from a rooster,' he chuckled.

'They must be pretty though.' She eluded his amused stare for she didn't want him to think she liked him enough to be jealous of other girls.

'Sure, but their mothers don't tell them that or else they get big headed. Propaganda. Judging by your stare you don't know what that word means. Well, it means when someone says the opposite to the truth. Muslim girls must obey the rules of the Prophet. Pride is considered a sin and so these girls are expected to be modest and righteous as your Christian nuns, so to speak. This way their mother gets to choose the groom. Even if he's as ugly and old as a plough horse. Then these girls become fungi growing in the shadows of a tree, just like the mushrooms in the graveyard,' he laughed.

'It seems our customs are similar. It's unfair if you ask me!'

'Evet, listen brown eyes, the key to being happy is having the ability to choose what to accept and what to let go. Even a girl with only half a brain would know that!'

'I'll keep it in mind. What about the men? How are they supposed to be?' Rifat gave her a knowing stare. 'The men are the boss of the household, so to speak.' He went on to explain. Unlike the women meekness is uncharacteristic of a Muslim man. Men are thought to be the ruler of the household, and of a woman. According to Islam law, and the Koran it is the woman who must be obedient towards her husband. A woman becomes a man's property once married, including the children. A man owns everything. A man can beat his wife if she deterred from the teachings of the Koran because it was said, 'he loves his wife, fears for his wife.' A woman has practically no rights to anything, apart from a Koran and prayer stone. They're just like *dohmbeh*. A bag of solid fat that hangs from beneath a sheep's tail.'

'Sounds awfully unfair,' Despina frowned.

'Anyway, you'll be pleased to know that the minority of men sidestep the laws of Muslim practices.'

'What about you? Would you treat a woman like this?'

'Yok. For me it's not about abiding to ancient customs and bylaws but acceptance from the people I care about the most.'

Despina thought him deeply philosophical for his age. 'You still haven't told me how we got to become who we are.'

Rifat plucked at the strings of his lute as he deliberated a while then said, 'try to imagine this country as a sole tree that over the years had been grafted with a multitude of fruits by various kingdoms. Understandably the tree would yield a hotchpotch of fruit that it would be impossible to distinguish the true origin of the tree. However, the doubt remains as to how a country with so many different identities became fixated on just two. Let's just say all the fruit had fallen from the tree save two. Let's say, a cherry and an apple. Take your pick brown eyes which would you like to be?'

'You choose,' she offered reticently.

'Taman. You said you like cherries! Then you can be the Greek Cypriot and I'll be the Turkish Cypriot apple.' Rifat was amused at his own whimsical insight, but Despina was to some extent hesitant by this prognostic observation.

'I thought you like figs!' she offered.

'Sure, only problem is that the birds like them too.'

'Now you are being unfair,' she complained. 'Now tell me who gets to claim the land!'

'It's complicated. You see, although neither of us can assert to be the true ancestors of the tree both of us claim to be the beneficiaries. That's why our descendants became embroiled in a religious war unified and reinforced by dissimilar revolutionary factions.'

A few weeks before Rifat was to be conscripted in the army they met in the ruins. It was the place where they'd held condemnation meetings against their parents. A place where they laughed and teased each other and planned for their future. Rifat hoped to be discharged within a couple of years. Though with the ongoing civilian and military constitution fighting in the country there was no telling when he'd be discharged.

They were huddled together with their hands joined on a stone bench and from where they had a view of the sea beyond the precipices.

'This place will never be the same. What will I do without you?' Despina murmured. He stroked her cheek. 'I'll never be far, brown eyes. Our hearts belong to each other. We'll be the pupils in the other's eyes so that we may see everything the other sees. We'll be like two birds in a cage!'

Then she watched him take something out of his pocket and she felt inwardly delighted and yet unsure about what was to happen.

He asked her to close her eyes. After he made a loop on her wedding finger with a thin strip of leather cord that stretched as far as his upper arm and where a gold ring was passed through the cord. He then asked her to open her eyes and when Despina saw the ring spiralling and slip neatly onto her finger she burst into giggles of rhapsody.

'It has my name engraved. I want you to keep it on your finger as testament of my love and promise to marry you after I'm discharged.'

'Oh, I wish it were true,' she sighed. He noticed that one strap of her dress had crept down her arm, and when he adjusted it back onto her shoulder Despina felt the prickling sensation of her skin.

'We will make it come true my cherry.' Rifat drew her closer and he allowed her to rest her head on his shoulder and Despina inhaled the pleasurable masculine odour of his skin.

Then she heard him say, 'I'll become a stonemason and build you a house with a nest on its roof so you can feed the birds. I shall plant a cherry and apple tree for you to water so that they may grow and bear the fruit we shall eat. I'll be the cure for your wounds and the mantle that warms you at night. I will be the father that brings home bread and plays with our children.'

'What makes you think that I'd even want children?' Despina offered impulsively.

He stared at her as though she'd just told him she had no uterus. 'Why would you want to deprive a child of a good mother?'

She returned him a similar astonishing stare for it was the nicest thing a boy could ever say to a girl. She adopted a face of defiance just the same and then said, 'how do you know that?'

'I sense these things. I will ask for your hand in marriage before I leave.'

'Oh, you mustn't! Baba will kill you!' she warned.

'I'm not afraid. I'd even die for you Despinoulla. Just like the sunflower in love with the sun. Did I tell you the tale? No. Well the sunflower was forbidden to face the sun. So, each day the sunflower silently worshiped the sun with its head bowed. At night though it peered up at the moon and imagined the sun there while the other sunflowers slept. This went on for some time until at last one day the sunflower bravely looked up at the sun and said, 'now that I have seen your face beloved I will gladly die.'

Despina sighed and when Rifat noticed the sentimental look in her eyes his brow contracted with remarkable speculation. 'We'll get married here in the ruins. I'll decorate the arches with laurel leaves and wildflowers. You'll wear a white dress. And I'll borrow a slice of the moon to adorn your hair. Just imagine how beautiful you will look.'

'What an imagination you have!' She removed the ring from her finger. 'Best I keep it around my neck.'

'Taman! If it makes you feel better. Here, let me help you,' he gathered up her long hair and fastened the cord to her nape.

Just then a strong sea breeze blew, skimmed over Despina's cotton dress, sent the fabric coiling and fluttering at her waist, exposing her nude thighs, but a few seconds was all it took for Rifat to notice the purplish-blue stain within her upper right thigh.

'Goodness! it's getting windy!' She remarked with burning cheeks as she tugged her dress back down before she quickly stood up. 'And it's getting dark. Baba will be suspicious.'

When they arrived on the outskirts of the village he jumped out of the cart and helped her down.

And as Despina clung to Rifat in that moment of parting neither could speak, and he allowed her to weep on his shoulder. He stroked her long hair ever so softly, smelt the familiar scent of wild herb soap. Then he raised her head to greet his face and when he saw the sorrow in her moist eyes he whispered, 'don't be sad brown eyes. I promise I'll write often.'

Despina found his words consoling, and then before she could speak felt the warmth of his mouth over hers and she was instantly aroused from the most inner depths of her womanhood. She was so spellbound by the sensual pleasure she felt at that moment that she didn't even notice that she'd slipped from his grip or hear him ride off for her eyes were still closed, as if afraid if she opened them, she would realise it had never happened at all.

CHAPTER TEN

T he howling wind and torrential rain caused similar havoc over the terrain that winter. Spyros worried that if the rain didn't stop the field would be too soggy to plant his tobacco seedlings. Fortunately, by the end of February he'd finished planting which would be ready for harvest in June. Once the tobacco was cured by the end of July it would be distributed to the cigarette companies. A good return would provide a substantial income for the months of respite ahead. One must work hard in the summer to live like an effendi in winter. By autumn he would cut lumber for fuel. But now with the planting of tobacco over Spyros ambled about the house doing the odd repair. Since the altercation with the mayor, he'd sought out different coffeehouses in the district to catch up on the gossip.

In Rizo the peasants discussed the plummeting economy and condemned reckless political leaders for the unrest of the country. While in nearby Turkish coffeehouses the Turkish Cypriots also had growing concerns and feared reprisal by their Greek neighbours and subsequently would be forced out of their homes and workshops and off their land. They complained of the deluge that had ruined their crops. Spyros grumbled over the price of aromatic seedlings for pipe tobacco imported from Turkey.

His main competitor was Syria.

A successful harvest meant a substantial profit in a few short months and would bring much needed economy boost to the Karpassa region. Some of the cooperative sales companies were producing fifty to sixty tonnes of tobacco annually. Others were producing up to ninety-three tons of tobacco which was shipped free of charge from Germany.

Spyros begrudged these capitalists for he could not compete with them with his few stretches of land. The men discussed the Electricity Authority of Cyprus. Presently there were twenty -eight companies serving six major towns and twenty-two smaller towns and villages. The Electricity Authority supplied consumers with electricity only in the evening. The Limassol Electric Light Company had its own power generator and launched a promotional campaign in which it provided free electricity for a trial period so people could see for themselves the benefits of this new form of power.

The peasants debated it was just another profit -making enterprise and they'd be hit with heavier taxes for the supply whilst conversely industrialists welcomed this modern convenience. It was said that wires ran through the walls of the house that were connected to a switch. A touch of the switch and at night one might assume it was still daylight.

Each afternoon Despina goes to mayor Neophytos's *kafenio* and waits for the mailbag to arrive from hora.

She does not read or write Turk thus relies on Mustafa the Potter to translate. 'What does he say?' She asks Mustafa in a rush of excitement where she sits on a low stool outside his shack where he has his potter's wheel and banks of clay.

'He starts by saying; 'my dearest cherry.' 'I assume this is you!

Mustafa asks with his brow raised inquisitively, and Despina senses the elderly man's awkwardness when reading the epithet 'my cherry.'

'It is because I'm Christian,' Despina explains red faced, but Mustafa grunts pensively and asks what a cherry has to do with religion.

She grins and says it is a 'special matter' between the two, and then Mustafa tries to reflect on this 'special matter,' but with no resolve. 'Go on,' she urges.

'He says, *'It brings me much relief that Mustafa the Potter has offered to read my letters to you. May Allah be generous and grant him a place in His paradise.'* The boy is sensible and modestly intelligent,' he paused to offer.

'Oh very much kyrie Mustafa.'

'No need for such gracious prefaces canim. Mustafa will do. Taman!'

'As you wish. Now what else does he write?'

'He says, *'I'm sitting under an olive tree writing this letter but am distracted by the army trucks patrolling along the dirt road ahead. You may smell the dust on the page of this letter '* 'The dust! Mustafa chortled, adjusted his spectacles and then continued reading.

'Where was I? Ah yes,' *'army life consists of mostly drills and doing nothing and so I play my lute and write songs just for you. You'll be pleased to know that I've learned of a recording artist in Turkey who might be interested in some of my lyrics. I have made a good friend here at the barracks who reads Greek. Yilmaz is from the nearby village of Lemnos and will be useful in reading your letters to me.*

During the evenings we both like to reminisce about our childhood and the girls closest to our heart. It is you my beautiful and brown-eyed girl that I talk of the most. You are the morning sun that lights up my day. And it's your smile that I behold everywhere. And your soft voice I hear in the tunes I play. I have missed you more than ever. I will write and let you know when I'm on leave so we can meet in the ruins. This thought brings me much relief. Until then may Allah always be present my beloved.'

From the heart Rifat.

Mustafa glanced over at Despina and asked, 'have your wings caught fire for this Muslim boy? Oh, you don't know the story! Well, the moth saw a bright light in the sky, you see. The brightness was like no other, brighter than a star. It flew up to the light and came to a window and looked in and saw a candle burning. It flew in through the open window and approached the flame and its wings caught fire. Then the moth flew away with the eternal flame of passion. From that tale there is a saying; 'moths won't fly to the flame and don't believe in love until their wings have caught fire."

'What a lovely tale,' Despina sighed, and then Mustafa added, 'pardon my prying but does your father approve of this lute playing soldier? The son of Jusuf the Chair-weaver?'

Despina was unsure what to say but the potter read the answer in her eyes and gave her a momentous stare. 'The heart wants what the heart wants canim.' He said sensibly, then added, 'the problem amongst our people is that they've been raised with their skulls scrambled by inflexible and legendary tales that don't belong in a society where people are obliged to live together. If both ethnic groups were more tolerant and accommodating towards each other then everybody would be happy, but instead they act like exasperated dogs snapping and growling at bees.' Mustafa burst a laugh, marvelling at his own silly irony as he wiped specs of clay from the lens of his glasses. After he passed the letter back to her, Despina scooped and retrieved a jar of glyko from the canvas bag at her feet. Glyko was a traditional sweet made from seasonal fruit that was eaten with a spoon from a tiny plate. It was offered with coffee by the female of the household to welcome guests.

'I almost forgot,' she offered as she handed it to him. 'It's quince. I made it myself. Tell me if you like. I've made several more jars that I hope to sell in the market this coming Saturday.'

'Mashalla,' he praised, then gave her a meaningful stare and added, 'it must be hard on your father. A dowry, that is. A useless article of trade if you ask me.'

'I don't want para!' Despina admonished when she saw his hand fumbling into the pocket of his work robe. 'It's the least I can do to repay you for your time and trouble.'

'Taman, but the pleasure is mine. Hade, may it be easy,' he offered with a smile that suggested he'd smiled many times over the years. Despina retrieved the bag and stood up to leave when he asked, 'by the way how old are you now?'

'Nineteen.'

'You think you'll go to college?'

'Not on Babas pittance.' Mustafa accepted her disappointment at having been disappointed because of the lost opportunity. 'Daskalos Panayiotis told me that he thought I would meet the requirements of a student scholarship. Though I imagine subsidies would be prohibitive since the government is trying to find cost effective ways to restore the country's economy. You know with all this civil rioting between ethnic groups. There'll be nothing left of this country soon. What then? Even an education would be useless.'

Mustafa thought the Christian girl highly learned. 'What would you have studied, given the chance, that is? Politics, perhaps?'

'Politics! What makes you think that?' she asked surprised.

'Just a hunch,' Mustafa offered indifferently.

'History. Or literature perhaps. Already I'm familiar with famous Greek novelists and poets of ancient Greece. I doubt if you've heard of Nikos Kazantzakis. He was one of the few authentic geniuses of modern Greece.'

'You said, 'was.' He must have died!

'Not so long ago. Before his seventy fifth birthday.'

'I'm afraid I wouldn't know about the scripts of such masterminds. I'm a man of the earth. Though I'd be curious to be enlightened.'

'I'd be happy to tell you more one day when I have time,' Despina smiled.

'Taman. Until next time then!' Mustafa then got back to work on his banks of clay.

Despina made her way back through the dusty pathway and came into the village square. Passing by the marketplace she noticed a smartly attired woman sporting an impressive beige suede hat with a black feather.

And a woman who presumably took pride in parading the copious volume of costly jewels that she displayed. Despina watched the woman approach a black, shiny automobile and where the chauffer opened the rear passenger door and waited for her to climb in before driving off. This eye-catching display of extravagance seemed absurdly inconsistent compared to the dismal hubbub of the marketplace. The woman Despina accepted was Sofia Gapsalis. She must have been around eight when she first met the austere red-haired woman with the sharply etched eyebrows. Having passed the marketplace she turned into a pathway wedged between high stone walls overgrown with cactus and where children dodged the chickens that pecked and squawked at their feet.

When the children trailed behind her Despina smirked knowingly. 'Oh, you want marbles! You might be lucky, let me see.' She dipped a hand into her bag and grabbed a handful and then tossed them over her shoulder teasingly, then peered back giggling with delight as she watched the children frantically scramble about to pick them up from the ground.

Above this noise she thought she heard a woman cry out and looked back over her shoulder to see Katina coming towards her and Despina paused to greet her. 'You are spoiling the children!' Katina remarked.

'It's a small price for such a gratifying reward, don't you think! Anyway, where are you coming from?' Despina asked.

'I might ask of you the same thing.'

'From Mustafa the potter. He was kind enough to translate Rifat's letter.'

'You've been writing to him for years. He should have been discharged from the army by now. Are you still serious about marrying him? You know how hostile your father is towards him.'

'Because he's a Muslim!' Despina interjected with annoyance.

'You should know his rage by now. I'd worry for that boy if I were you! You just never know what your father will do to him if he finds out you're still secretly seeing him. And you haven't forgotten what he did to you the last time he found out you were with him!' Katina warned.

'I'll never forget! But how could he have known I was with Rifat that day?'

'The evidence was right before his eyes. You came home with that gold band dangling at your neck as if it was your most cherished prize. What were you thinking? Did you think your father was going to rejoice that his daughter was marrying his most despised enemy?'

Despina had automatically come to think over the years that Katina was the only person she could depend on but now she had the propensity to doubt her way of thinking.

'I don't care what he thinks! What father treats his daughter this way? I told you he can't be my real father.'

'You're not going to start that nonsense again,' Katina scoffed.

'I'm sure Zehra would think the same if she were alive. No father in his right mind would do those things he did to Zehra. I might have believed his story about the accident when I was young but not anymore. You think that he suddenly had a conscience and that it was Zehra he had in mind that day?'

'Why else would he have gone if not for cherries?' Katina doubtfully asked.

'He's hiding something. But no secret goes to the grave with its keeper.'

'What could he be hiding?'

'The truth about our mother. Every child has the right to know its mother's name and where her grave is and touch the earth where she is buried. Don't you see how strange everything seems? What if our mother remarried after our real father died when we were young?'

'Then what happened to her? Or did she get struck by lightning? You might think I'm indifferent, but you can't go on tormenting yourself based on hunches and misgivings alone.'

'She probably got fed up with his constant abuse and ran away.'

'Then she must have been a self-regarding woman with no conscience. Even more merciless than your father. In my opinion she's not worth remembering.'

'You can't judge someone without knowing the truth. You never knew my mother. You said you were studying abroad. Surely someone in this village would know. What about Pater Christofis! Why didn't I think about it before! Or at least you might have thought of it.'

'Why should I?' Katina brooded.

'I thought you'd want to help!'

'It's just that I never took you seriously.'

'As a friend I'd take you seriously if you were in my position. Never mind I'll speak with pater myself,' Despina said earnestly.

'No. You mustn't!'

'Why not?'

'You'd be wasting your time. I mean there's nothing to say that she was from this village. Or even got married here. Maybe it was a proxy and the marriage had merely been a customary verbal agreement between the families. If so, then they'd be no evidence of a registration of the marriage. But if you like I can go have a word with pater in the morning. Why don't you come to my house for coffee after you've come back from the market?'

I should have some news by then. Now let's talk about something else. You were asking where I was coming from remember! I'm coming from the mansion. I asked to be excused with the pretence of a headache.'

'Is Sofia giving you a hard time again?' Despina queried.

'She's like a mule occupied by the soul of the damned!' Katina mocked. 'Nothing is ever good enough! The only time she is pleasant is when she's around her golden boy. That would be Pandelis, if you're wondering.'

'Well not even I would put up with it!' Despina condemned. 'I saw her near the marketplace earlier. She looked so out of place. Like a conceited peacock in a paddock of manure.' Despina burst a laugh then added, 'I can't imagine a woman of her prestige finding anything of use to her there.'

'She only goes to buy fabric. There's a merchant close by there who buys the fabric on the black market from the Near East. Some of the fabrics are exquisite,' Katina advised.

'I've been reading something that might interest you!'

'I hope it's more exciting than William Shakespeare was a thief!' Katina offered wittily.

'I've been reading about the women in Medieval Britain.'

'Oh, I didn't know you could read English!'

'The transcript was translated to Greek. Something I borrowed from the library in hora. Their personal grooming was impeccable. These Egyptian women used the secret potions passed onto them by the previous generation of prostitutes!'

'You mean they were whores? How did the women of England find out these secrets?'

'From the Third Crusaders when they returned from the Near East.'

'Well, whoever these men were my bet is they also passed on syphilis to these women!' Katina sneered. 'But go on.'

'They bathed in almond oil and goat milk and honey. And they made a brew of brown onion skins and tea leaves to give the effect of copper hues in their hair. And they made a wax of boiled sugar and lemon juice to apply to their body to achieve a hairless and smooth finish. They even clipped their pubic hair to produce heart and bird-shaped patterns...'

'Did they scatter rose and citrus petals in drawers to refresh their panties too?' Katina interjected mockingly. 'Just imagine Sofia reclined on a sofa in her room cropping herself down below! What if a maid walked in?'

'She'd probably ask her to do the job!' Despina teased.

'Why I'd refuse! I'd rather cut the toenails of a beggar!' Katina revealed.

'Can you imagine if her husband caught her in the act?' Despina went on humorously.

'Why he'd think his younger wife had completely lost her mind.' Katina laughed along.

'You never know! He might be thrilled!'

'He'd be revolted if you ask me. Probably tell her he's seen better at the zoo. The only time Sofia is nice to him is when she wants something. She's like a sugar-coated biscuit filled with anchovies. All sweet on the outside and bitter on the inside. Constantly she keeps him on his toes just like she does the maids. The other day she erupted over a minor adjustment her seamstress made to a gown. The poor woman left in tears. I doubt if she'll be back to even finish it. Anyway, it would be a minor loss to Sofia. She's got more outfits than the queen of England. Most of them she only wears once.'

'Why that ungrateful woman! What does she do with all those expensive clothes?'

'She donates them to her son's charity institute *Spitimas*.' Our House translated from Greek. 'She hires venues for these stage viewings and organises feasts and entertainment. All her high society friends and even diplomats attend these events. Monies raised goes to various shelters for homeless and orphaned children.'

'She doesn't strike me as the type of woman who'd have a conscience for the less fortunate,' Despina offered.

'Sofia's a pretentious boaster and thrives on these social gatherings. Unlike her son who gets personally involved with the children. Why he even makes sure the children get toys and Christmas tree they can decorate each year. Not to mention all the produce from his farming estate that is delivered to these shelters.'

'He sounds like a remarkable man.'

'Oh, he is!' Katina replied.

Despina sensed the dreaminess in her voice and inquisitively asked, 'how old is he?

'Maybe forty-two or three.'

'Is he married?'

'Not yet!'

'What is he waiting for!' Despina asked.

'Can't answer that.'

'I'm surprised Sofia hasn't arranged a proxy. What about all her rich friends? They must have suitable daughters.'

'Pandelis isn't the kind of man who'd be influenced by his mother.'

'It's unusual don't you think! A man of his status and age to be single. Maybe he's a womaniser. Is he as good looking as he is rich?'

'I've never thought about him that way. To me he's just the boss's son. I'm sure he'll get married when the right woman comes along.'

'What are you waiting for? Why haven't you tried to attract his attention? You're not still worried about your 'problem,' are you? You don't want to end up an old spinster, do you? There's a good chance you will if you don't take control of your life.'

Katina gave her an utterly disparaging stare that flushed Despina's cheeks. 'No need to get upset! I'm only trying to help!

'Well, I don't need your help! Or anybody's help, for that matter. Do you hear?' Katina said officiously. 'Now if you've finished counselling then I'll be on my way. And mind your own affairs in future.'

Despina stood there lost for words and at the same time wondering how well she knew her friend.

Clearly not well enough to understand why she'd reacted in such a hostile manner. Unless it was a spontaneous act of self-defence to lull any suspicions that she might have about her true feelings for Pandelis. Maybe she was in love with him but was consumed in self-loathe because she could only see the grim vision that she'd created of herself through his eyes as a pitiful and disabled maid.

Early Saturday morning Despina placed all the jars of conserves into a basket and left the house for the marketplace. Passing through the drab pathways she was greeted by hard working farmers browned by the sun, their mules laden with produce inside deep wicker- baskets.

As she entered the chaos of the marketplace there was the all- pervasive smells of fresh blood and open gutters and animal dung, and black flies and disembowelled animals. Despina ambled around in search of a stall.

She approached one of the merchants. 'I only have a few jars! The elderly man fingered his coiling moustache and then tetchily allowed her a tiny corner atop his bench. After having placed all jars there Despina nervously awaited customers but people only gave momentary glances and moved on. After an hour or so she reasoned that perhaps she'd been too optimistic of making a sale.

The making of fruit conserves was common practise amongst the women in the village. And the clamour of bartering merchants and throng of shoppers was deafening. Suddenly she saw Zenep, the mother of Rifat and his father Jusuf heading towards her.

'Look over there! Isn't that the Tobacco Merchant's daughter! She's mingling with the dirty panhandlers and hawkers to put food on the table.'

Despina sensed by her grimacing stare and the pitch in her voice that she'd been the subject of her slander. Conversely though she'd judged by the look on her husband's face, and the way in which he was yanking at her arm, to hurry along, he'd felt browbeaten by his wife's conduct. Rifat's mother wasn't the self-effacing woman who kowtowed to Muslim practises in the way he'd described. It was obvious who ruled the household. When she caught Jusuf's sheepish stare Despina returned him a half-hearted smile. Just then the village midwife emerged in the mayhem of the marketplace and a red-faced Despina inched back behind the merchant's stall to avoid her. She recalled that day she got home late after having spent time with Rifat in the ruins before he went into the army.

'If you've been with the kitten thief, that Muslim I'll have his throat!' Her father rebuked.

'Try and stop me! I'll run away!' Despina warned.

'You dare threaten your Baba? Has this boy touched you? A man's *poutso* has no conscience when it comes to a woman kori! Here let me see!'

Despina struggled as he tore away the upper part of her dress in search of the slightest evidence, a scratch, or bruise or whatever else would attest to his daughter was tarnished with carnal dishonour.

'What's this? Don't tell me you married this Muslim boy behind my back!'

Tempestuously he ripped the cord at her neck and curiously toyed with the ring in the palm of his hand before dropping it into his pocket.

'Give it back! I'll marry whoever I want! Give it back!' Despina wailed through a deluge of tears.

'I'll ask you again! Has this boy touched you? You haven't shamed me have you kori?'

'It's your own shame you must bear, not mine! Let go of my hair! I've done nothing wrong!'

'There's only one way to find out! I'll go fetch the midwife right now!'

'I swear he hasn't touched me. I won't allow it! I just won't!' she screamed.

* * *

'Everything is in good working order. Your daughter is as tidy as a letter sealed in an envelope.' The midwife informed her father when she came out from Despina's room and found him anxiously waiting outside the door.

Three weeks had passed since that day and Despina avoided her father whenever she could. And she deliberately attacked his dignity by responding to his requests with a strained grunt with her eyes turned away.

Now Despina's stomach churned by the thought that the old woman's hand had intruded her womanhood, explored that personal space between her thighs.

She hastily packed up and fled the marketplace, as if fleeing from the fury of her existence. 'I swear I'll throw a stone behind me and never come back to this awful village!' When she reached the road she saw a fan-shaped carob tree in a small clearing beneath Mayor Neophytos's *kafenio* thus decided to rest in the shade to compose herself.

Meanwhile a man was seated by a table under the arbour and reading a newspaper.

He finished his coffee, folded the newspaper, tucked it under his arm, stood up and glanced over the railing to behold a girl standing under a carob tree. And seemingly she was weeping because she was dabbing at her eyes with a handkerchief. He wondered the reason for her unhappiness.

At that moment an old woman paused by the side of the road to peek inside the girl's basket at her feet. She stooped and picked up a jar from inside, contemplated the portions of quince, then turned it a couple of times to review the consistency of the syrup. 'Bravo, health to your hands koritsi-mou. May your work by light.'

The man at the railing assessed the girl was selling conserves however she was far removed from the market. Perhaps she'd come from there and was now waiting to catch the bus to return to her village. He turned and entered the *kafenio* and approached one of the men competing in a game of tavli and asked him to accompany him outside.

'Are you a local?' he asked the farmer.

'Yes. Georgios is my name Kyrios.'

After both men exchanged greetings Pandelis said, 'pardon for intruding but this won't take long. There's a girl standing under a tree down below. She appears to be selling jam. I want you to buy all the jars.' He removed one lira from his wallet and handed it to him.

'I'll bring you the *resta*.' Change. Georgios offered.

'No need. Tell her it's your wife's favourite. Understood?'

The man stared at him tentatively and at the same time considering that it would take him four weeks of hard slog in the field to make this much para.

Though reasoned that since the man was the son of Yiannis Gapsalis then he could afford to squander his father's para. 'Leave it with me Kyrio!'

Pandelis waited until he was out of sight and then furtively glanced over the railing once again only to find that the girl had now stepped out onto the road. He watched his courier approach her and listened on to their conversation.

'You want to buy all of them? I was only hoping for a couple of *grocia* a jar. I'm afraid I don't have *resta*. You might like to try the *kafenio*,' she offered.

'Keep it! Quince is my wife's favourite. They say a happy wife means a happy life.' Georgios chortled.

'Then she is most deserving of you. Keep the basket,' Despina smiled.

Pandelis felt refreshed by the girl's apparent delight and waited expectantly for his courier to return.

'Nice girl,' Georgios remarked as he passed him the basket.

Pandelis gave a brief glance inside, set it atop a nearby table and then asked, 'have you seen her before? Do you know if she's from this village?'

Georgios was bewildered not only by his self-denial but also the abnormality of it all. He'd just assumed all these years that the son of Yiannis Gapsalis would have known who the girl really was. Clearly though he didn't. And he wasn't about to let on anything or otherwise he'd sorely regret it. 'Can't say that I have! Though I could be wrong.'

Pandelis gave him a bogus smile. A slipshod opportunist. He emptied his pocket of a few coins and slipped the money into his hand. 'Ah you've offended me! What are neighbours for?' Georgios feigned surprise yet readily deposited the money into the pocket of his shirt just the same.

'Now what can you tell me! I'm a busy man.' He was frustrated by the farmer's tactic.

'She came into the *kafenio* a few days ago. It was just after the village bus arrived from hora with the mailbag. They say it was a letter she'd come for. The girl's friendly with one of the Muslim boys in the village. He is the son of Jusuf the Chair-Weaver. His family are refugees. He's recently been conscripted in the Turkish army. It must have been from him. I can't imagine anybody would want to write to Spyros.'

'She's the tobacco merchant's daughter? Then why didn't you just say so?' Pandelis remarked with annoyance.

'It was only later I realised who she was,' Georgios offered.

'I also sense that you know her father.'

'Sure, I know that cabbage head.'

'Where do you know him from?

'I once worked for him. It was years ago. After your father fired me. It was just before he gave that field to that scum bag Spyros.'

'Spyros told you this?'

'Well, it wasn't exactly him that...'

'No need to go on!' he interrupted. 'The man's crazier than I thought. Why would my father endow him a field?'

'His daughter deserved to be fed. It was no fault of her own what happened.' Georgios informed.

Pandelis thought that the farmer had taken this issue with his father's land entirely out of pretext. He sounded as though his father owed Spyros a favour. Or his daughter, one or the other. Then he heard him say, 'shame about the other girl. Ah, you don't know the story! People assumed it was an accident. Some said the merchant sold the girl.'

'Sold her eh! Then who's buried in the forest? Pandelis asked.

'It's anybody's guess. Might be a butchered wild hog. Spyros must have caught it up in those mountains that day after he killed that little girl.'

'If you'll excuse me as I'm unaccustomed to the sun's glare.' He'd wearied of the farmer's blather for he was relaying the tale as if it was a contentious debate inside the kafenio. In as much the same way as the rumour about his father handing over his field to Spyros.

'Don't you want to hear the rest of the story? I thought you'd be interested.' Georgios offered disappointed.

He gave the farmer a pat on the back as if this gesture would restore his discomfiture. 'Listen good Christian. Boredom sometimes has a habit of making clowns out of people.

These men who supposedly entertain you in the *kafenio* oppose their own yarns. Then gloat when people believe them.

And what's more you don't have to describe the traits of an unbalanced man. But no matter how contemptible a man Spyros is he'd have to possess the soul of the devil to slay his own child. His own flesh and blood.'

'But that's what I've been trying to tell you. It was revenge. The girl wasn't ....'

'Pardon but I really must go.' Pandelis disrupted as he was due to meet his father's agriculturist at one of his fields to test the soil for organic farming. 'Thanks for your help.' He tipped his hat, retrieved the basket atop the table and left. Driving home in his late model Austin sedan he turned the radio on, then just as quickly turned it off. It had been a thought -provoking morning and now his thoughts were on the girl under the carob tree. The tobacco merchant's daughter. Many years had passed since that day he'd sat with her in his parent's garden.

Her shoes he recalled had been stuffed with cardboard. He'd felt a deep sense of self-depreciation and regret that day for his own inherited privileges in life. On the face of it, Despina was just as destitute and miserable as she'd been back then.

Perhaps it was a combination of paternalistic abuse and the death of her sister. Though they say life doesn't have to end after a loved one dies. Perhaps the soldier boy had resurrected her spirit. Driving on he stared out into the dry open fields shrieking with cicadas. After months of blistering heat, one yearned for the smell of autumn smoke and misty mornings. Suddenly he quivered when he felt the jolt of the sedan's wheels pass over a snake's vertebrae.

Then on a whim, as if drawn by an irresistible force, he diverted course and followed the dusty narrow path that led to the forest of red cedars. He parked the vehicle and climbed out and entered the forest.

He strolled aimlessly about the graveyard, pausing every so often to inspect the name and age of the deceased, as if by chance he would find what he was looking for. What was he looking for! What had goaded him to come here? Did he suppose he would find the grave of Despina's deceased sister? It was the most arbitrary and uncharacteristic thing he'd ever done. He continued walking amongst the rows of tombstones when he came across a patch of earth with a flowerbed.

The inscription on the leaning wooden crucifix which read; Zehra 1940 1948, was barely visible. Not even a family name, he mused, and at the same time was aroused with an overwhelming and interllectually deep sense of sorrow by the sight of the grave.

He stood there quietly, unable to move, as if with the belief nothing would be gained by disturbing the peaceful sleep of the young girl buried there. Then another atypical thing happened to him, something he'd never done before. He cried.

CHAPTER ELEVEN

On Monday morning, Sofia was in the upstairs drawing room having morning tea.

'Who made this quince conserve?' she remarked.

'I'm not sure,' Katina told Sofia cautiously as she considered all that Despina had told her when she'd called into the house on Saturday afternoon after she'd returned from the market. At first, she'd thought that she'd come to find out if she'd spoken to pater Christofis about her mother, though she'd completely overlooked the subject in her exhilaration.

'He bought all the jars, you said! And for one lira!' Katina was gobsmacked.

'I couldn't believe it Katina! He said it was his wife's favourite. And to think I didn't make a single sale at the marketplace. He insisted I take the para!'

Katina now informed Sofia, 'the other maids and I were wondering the same thing. We found numerous jars on the work bench in the kitchen when we arrived early this morning. We assumed you'd bought them and stored the remainder in the larder.'

Just then Pandelis came into the room and greeted them both. 'One of the village women was selling it at the market on Saturday.' He offered after overhearing their conversation.

'Why son, what business would you have there? I mean the stench of the place and all those nasty flies and paupers.'

'Eh, did you like it?' Pandelis queried perfunctorily.

'Well, if you hadn't mentioned where it came from son then I might have said I found it very flavoursome. In fact, I've never tasted better.'

'Good to hear. I'll be down at the orchard house if father needs me.'

When Sofia saw the maid expediently put down the teapot she was holding and trail after him she nodded intuitively. *You think you've blinded me with the fire in your eyes Katina? That fire will burn a hole in your soul. Love is sacred it can't nest in a dirty heart!*

'I've made fresh *bourek*.' Katina offered with breathless anticipation when she caught up with him in the downstairs foyer.

When she saw him reach for his hat on the clothes-rack she was quick to grab it for him. 'It'll only take a moment to wrap.' She went on as she handed it to him.

'No need to trouble yourself Katina.' He felt unduly uncomfortable by the maid's insistence to please him.

'It's no trouble. Now about the orchard house. It must need a good clean by now.'

He returned her a bland stare then said, 'I'll let you know if I need anything.' Then donned his hat and left through the back door. A couple of maids observed this incident from behind the open kitchen door. Lydia, the younger maid said, 'she fails to see what a pitiful spectacle she makes of herself in his eyes. She's relentless. But he's so handsome don't you think?

The elder maid, Thea gave her co-worker a derisive stare before she said, 'best you keep your heart and eyes dry over that man kori. Besides, he's too old for you. And if Katina wants to follow that fanatical illusion of hers then so be it.'

'What will she do if he becomes betrothed? She'll have to concede.'

'Bah! Love loves the impossible! My guess is she'll stop at nothing to end the relationship,' Thea scoffed.

'What could she possibly do?' Lydia asserted.

'Katina might be maimed but her mind is as sharp as that knife in your hand. And she has a treacherous soul. She can't be trusted,' the elder cautioned.

'Is that why Sofia treats her badly? Why doesn't she just fire her?'

'I can't answer that.' Then suddenly pressed a finger to her lips when she heard Katina's footsteps in the foyer on her way to the upstairs drawing room.

Sofia was turning the pages of a 50s mode magazine when she heard the maid rushing up the stairs. Then eyed her guardedly as she entered the room. 'You must take heed of those stairs Katina. You might break a limb. You don't want to end up completely debilitated, do you? End up in one of those hideous chairs on wheels and become reliant on some poor soul to push you around all the time! Then of course I'd have to replace you with a new maid, perhaps someone more dedicated and vigilant.'

'Pardon Kyria. I know how much your son likes to spend a lot of time at the orchard house and I thought.'

'You thought it's in need of a clean!' Sofia broke in touchily.

'That's right.'

127

'As a maid you have no right to amend the regulations of this mansion. Understood?'

Sofia had sullied Katina's mood for the rest of the day. Deliberately searching for the slightest excuse to fire her. She treated her as if she were a mutilated dog. And her bigoted remarks promoted Katina's own grim perception of herself which only powered her feelings of self-loathe.

She felt lonely even in the company of others and was drawn to those who were sub-standard as herself in order not to be judged and valued for who she was. She'd carried these feelings since early childhood. Her dreams were on fire and yet her spirit was in ruins.

Later that morning she was on her way to the laundry room when she felt a quickening within her chest when she noticed Pandelis come through the entrance gate.

'Oh, you're back Kyrio!' She uttered and when she saw him coming towards her the basket she was holding almost fell from her hands.

He politely tipped his hat and said, 'I'd like a few words with you.'

'With me! She pointed a finger at herself hesitantly. She wondered the reason for this unexpected beckoning. It could only be that Sofia had asked her son to fire her.

'Well, I don't see anyone else here! He casually looked around for upshot. 'We can sit by the pond.'

'I was on my way to do…'

'No need for concern,' he broke in punctually. 'You're with me now.'

She gave him an incredulous stare. *Has he finally agreed to marry me! Propose to me here in this splendid garden! O God my heart is racing so fast I think I might swoon!*

'Is something wrong? I only want to chat!'

'To chat,' she blinked and blinked again before nervously she accompanied him over to the pond. He indicated the bench beside him and when she sat down was shocked when he randomly asked, 'how's Despina?'

'Why do you ask?'

'She's your neighbour, isn't she?'

'That's right. I'm surprised you even remember her.'

'She must have finished school by now. What are her plans? College perhaps?'

Katina might have said that Despina's head was saturated with knowledge. Her room was full of history and literature books. And that she'd been asked to sit for the entrance exam at the University but instead she shrugged and casually replied, 'how would I know? Despina's like one of them fog clouds resting below a mountain that nobody knew what was hiding below. And one needs spades of para for those fancy colleges.'

He laughed. Then said, 'her father must make a reasonable income from the field!' Though he knew very well that he would rather squander his money on liquor and those whores he frequented in the brothels of hora than spend it wisely on his daughter.

'I wouldn't know about that either. Anyway, he doesn't believe in school. He'd be just as happy for his daughter to work in his tobacco field. Or sell jam for extra para. Your mother seemed to have liked it. You might have told her that Despina made it,' she offered purposefully.

'What makes you think I knew she made it? I wouldn't know Despina even if I saw her. But now that I know I'm glad,' he smiled.

129

'Oh, glad in what way? She asked with hidden displeasure.

'That I'd been of help in some small way. I must say she's grown into an attractive woman. Any suitors yet?'

She felt slighted that the topic of his conversation had been Despina over the past fifteen minutes. 'What makes you think she'd disclose such confidential matters with me? I'm only a neighbour, not her sister.'

'Speaking of her sister. How is she?'

'Sadly, Zehra's deceased. Accident up in the mountains.'

'My condolences. I'm surprised you never told me.'

'I must have thought it unimportant at the time. After all you never knew the girl.'

'Irrespective of whether I knew her or not, do you think that the death of a young girl to be of no great concern Katina? I might be a stranger, but I was concerned enough to want to alert the authorities if she didn't come home. The least you could have done was inform me of the tragic circumstances that day you approached me to tell me that Spyros had refused my invitation to take Despina to the stables.'

Katina was shocked to the core by this sudden admonishment. She lowered her eyes and just sat there flexing her hands back and forth and she found it was with great difficulty she could level her eyes to face him.

And when she began to weep Pandelis considered all her undue fussing in his presence and wondered if it wasn't just a self-seeking display of sympathy to attract his attention.

Stealthily he watched her raise her apron to her eyes, and when she stared up at him as she accepted his offer of his handkerchief, saw the pure pathos within her eyes, he realised that he'd been wrong in his assessment. 'It's clean if you're wondering.'

'It never passed my mind. But thanks. Forgive me, I don't know what come over me.'

'There's nothing to forgive. I might have said the same thing of myself. I had no reason to speak to you in such a manner. You get hard-pressed enough as it is from mother.'

'Never mind. I guess she has her days like everybody else.' Katina respected his openness about his mother's despotic manner.

'I'm not used to being around women. As you've just seen. I'm usually in the company of men each day.'

'No need to explain. It must be emotionally tiring having to make the right important decisions when dealing with corporate matters each day.'

Katina hoped that it was exactly what he wanted to hear and then to her delight she heard him say, 'an intelligent and insightful observation. If only others were as discerning and appreciative.'

'I guess some people find it hard to express their gratitude. Though you mustn't underestimate yourself Kyrio.'

'What about you! Do you undervalue yourself? he asked offhandedly.

Katina stared back at him with the awkward thought he was staring right through her, saw those long-suffering scars of self-abnegation there. It was her cursed 'problem,' she was sure. Fool! Say something! Now's your chance! Don't let your 'problem,' define who you are! But she knew purging the layers of one's self-induced emotional state wasn't as simple as turning a switch on and off. Then to her own displeasure she heard herself say, 'is it that obvious?

'Let's say that one's discomfort becomes evident after some time. A bit like walking around all day long in a tight pair of shoes. Mother should be more appreciative of her staff. I'll have a word with her.'

'No need. We're all different,' she offered sensibly.

'You're right. We can't change people's behaviour or way of thinking. As individuals we all have inbred traits.' Though he was inclined to think the maid had adopted her sentiments due to her handicap.

'You've been with us some years now. You've preserved your youthfulness well Katina.' He informally remarked, and when he saw her blush he added, 'pardon for my lack of clarity and expression. I meant it is a compliment, not to offend you.'

'I'm fair minded to such petty matters.' She advised with a weak smile. 'I started working for your family a few months after I'd graduated from college. That's partly why I remember.'

'You don't say! I'm surprised you've never mentioned it before today! That you went to college, that is!'

'No use boasting.'

'I respect your modesty. But you should be proud of such an achievement. More surprising that you chose to become…'

'A maid!' she broke in readily. 'I thought it was apparent. Nobody wanted to hire a teacher with an infirmity. Like it was infectious.'

'There's no place in society for such narrow-minded people. I'm sorry that you've been denied the opportunity,' he offered sensibly.

'Don't be. One learns to adjust to such intolerance. Like you said, we can't change people's behaviour. Nor their way of thinking.'

'Why didn't you make a complaint to the Department of Education?'

'One can't lift a heavy stone alone,' she modestly disclosed.

'Pity you hadn't spoken up years ago, I would have addressed the issue with the department myself.'

Katina expressed her gratitude with a smile when suddenly the vigour poured out of her when she caught a glimpse of Sofia staring down at them through the glass window of the cottage. She promptly stood up. 'Pardon I really must get back to work.' Then unexpectedly felt his hand on her arm as she turned to leave. 'I'd be offended. Please sit down.'

She did as he asked and then said, 'that's reassuring but I'm expected to follow the rules otherwise Sofia will fire me!'

'You're worrying needlessly.' He smirked, then added, 'now I want to ask you about Despina's mother.'

'Oh, what do you want to know?

'Do you know how she died?

'How would I know?

'I thought you said you've known Despina since she was born.'

'Yes, but it doesn't mean I know the truth about things,' she revealed.

'Truth. You mean nobody knows how she died?

'I'm merely speaking for myself. I just accepted that she'd died. It wasn't important that I knew how she died.'

'Spyros would have to know,' he urged.

'Clearly he would since it was his wife.'

'Do you think Despina knows?

'What makes you ask that? I mean why is it so important to you? Even if she did know, she'd never discuss it with me. I told you before she's very withdrawn. She's been this way ever since her sister died,' she advised.

133

'I see, well it's been nice talking to you. We'll catch up again some other time.' He stood up and tipped his head and Katina offered him a gracious smile. And as she followed him across the courtyard, she appeared like a woman with the attitude of perfect calm.

That night Katina endured hours of wakefulness reiterating in her mind all that Pandelis had said, as if searching for some tender word that would confirm what she'd longed for all these years.

She breathed into his handkerchief, stared at the sky through the crevices of the shutters, saw a star fall from the sky, and made a wish. She closed her eyes with the soothing thought that he really did care for her and fell asleep.

CHAPTER TWELVE

Pedhoulas village 1956

Jihan bey assessed the man in the mirror. What he saw was a man in his early fifties, rather slender and dressed in a three-piece grey suit, white shirt and maroon bowtie.

Though what he liked to think he saw was a young man of twenty-five, fresh out of medical school in Constantinopole in 1925. Jihan was a man who adhered to his own philosophies in life. His purpose was to follow a dependable path based on practicality and optimism, thus that course had led him to sail to Cyprus. Cyprus was under British rule. He'd found the British to be a jolly lot outside of their governmental duties. Many of these British administrators were former members of the Indian Civil Services. And evidently unaccustomed to the hot plain of Lefkosia-especially their wives- and so they had moved their administration to the cool of the Troodos Mountains. Over the years he'd become acquainted with many of the British bureaucrats both on a personal and professional level. He'd hosted many a dinner party in the glowing light of a kerosene lamp for there had been no electricity until 1930. When the power lines were finally extended from nearby Prothromus he'd paid for an electricity pole. Life up here in the mountains had been easier since then.

He was adequately comfortable in his Victorian brick villa that he'd purchased from a British diplomat.

Outside the late winter sun shifted above the apple tree, its luminosity suffused the room with the masculine odour of polished hide and cologne and hair balm.

Now as Jihan combed his hair he whistled and his heels tapped to the Turk ballad that came from the living room, arousing his patriotic emotions.

He donned a fine hat inlaid with satin, drew on his long woollen coat and curled a scarf at the fleecy collar and left for the kitchen to turn off his fish stew.

Then as an afterthought hurried back to his room to daub lemon cologne on his face, not too much, but just enough to charm Dilara hanim. Dilara lodged at the Hagia Triada -Holy Trinity in exchange for voluntary work.

He didn't want to smell like a fish monger in her presence. He burst a laugh, entertained by his own absurdity as he strode down the wide corridor. Midway he stopped outside Nilufer's room and quietly pushed open the door as not to disturb her from her nap.

He was compliant of the physical and emotional changes of an adolescent girl.

Nilufer was bussed to and from school each day which was altogether a twenty-mile trip to Lefkosia and back. He closed the door, reasoning he'd be back before she woke up. And if she did wake up before he returned from the orphanage there was plenty of her favourite fish stew. His Chinese housemaid Sui Lee, and whom had been with him for ten years, had the weekends off. He then proceeded down the corridor and paused outside an inner door. He removed a copious bunch of dangling keys from the pocket of his coat, slipped a key in the hole, turned it, and then pushed the door open and entered his clinic. The furniture compared to the rest of the fixtures in the two-storey residence was lacklustre and was used for the sole purpose of treating patients. A desk contained a hodgepodge of outmoded medical journals, a stethoscope, script pads an ink well and quill pen. These last things seemed to be there out of habitual fondness than of practical use.

Behind a folding screen of cloth was an examining bench. A glass cabinet contained numerous brown vials of medicines, tonics and peroxide for sterilizing hypodermic needles and rolls of gauze and surgical instruments, including a purgative rubber device to aid constipation.

Jihan grabbed his stethoscope from the desk, packed it into a satchel, secured the door behind him, stepped back into the corridor and left through the front door of the residence.

Outside, the snow had been lying around for weeks and wouldn't begin to thaw until early spring when the cherry trees would be dressed in their most virtuous glory on the slopes surrounding the valley.

He climbed into his Ford Consul parked in the driveway and drove at a slow pace along the slick road to consult his last patient for the day. He drove to the rear of the church and killed the engine.

He grabbed the leather satchel from the seat beside him and

climbed out of the car and trudged to the front door of the orphanage. It had been a long day of treating the ill, and even though he was depleted and hungry, he looked forward to his visit here as the sight of a child elevated his spirit irrespective of their status. The orphanage had been set up by the nuns at the Holy Trinity under the supervision of Sister Louisa in aid of the many displaced and homeless children by the devastation of war.

Some had been placed by a parent out of severe hardship or some other misfortune. His wife died due to a ruptured blood vessel after giving birth to a still born son.

Though the marriage had been short-lived, his wife had not only been a decent Muslim but had served him respectfully. When a person was grateful, then they didn't think of anything else. This gratefulness shone through when Dilara greeted him at the door.

He felt briefly humbled in her presence for she appeared remarkably admirable with her thick, brown curly hair tumbling over either side of her shoulders from under a green headscarf that had a fringing of russet and yellow daisies.

Jihan bey politely removed his hat which revealed much grey hair that was neatly undercut around the ears and nape by the village barber Themis.

Themis was a bit of a clown and who could come up with a joke at any given time. One day Themis told him the story of a self-regarding man with three strands of hair on his head.

'How may I help?' The barber asked the customer.

'A light trim with a side part.'

A month later the customer went back to the barber with only two strands of hair on his head. 'How may I help?'

'Cut it a little shorter with a centre part.'

A month later the customer went back to the barber with only a single hair left atop his head. 'How may I help?'

'No shear today. It's winter. I need some warmth.'

Confused, the barber asked, 'then why are you here?'

'Are you blind! Can't you see the wind has messed up my hair? Just tidy it up!'

'We've been expecting you doktoro bey.' Dilara announced, and then when she saw him considering his mud-damp shoes she added, 'don't worry we at the orphanage are unbiased to such minor matters. The floors get washed each day in any case. Come,' she revealed.

Jihan adjusted his bowtie and smoothed over his hair as he followed her down the hallway.

'These angels can be rather noisy when forced to stay indoors.' She continued when they passed a group of rowdy children. 'I'll be glad of spring. Here we are,' she pushed the door of the dormitory open and was about to leave when he deliberately arrested her departure.

'Sister Louisa tells me you have a natural ability with the children. She says you've taught them to sing and formed a choir and taught them to bake and sow vegetables. Also taught them to write Turk. A difficult task for children so young. Bravo Dilara hanim. You deserve an award.'

'Aww, come now no need for such praise. I try my best for these angels. God knows they deserve it. Who else have they got to lift their spirit when life fails them? Teaching them different skills from an early age is as essential as receiving affection. It boosts their confidence which gives them a sense of purpose and belonging in society. Otherwise, they'll become withdrawn and friendless. Don't you agree?'

He found her philanthropic, realistic and practical approach most inspiring. 'I couldn't agree more. The children couldn't be in better hands.'

'I might say the same thing of you doktoro. You've treated and cured countless children over the years.'

'I'm only doing my job,' he expressed mildly.

'Healing the sick isn't a job to be taken lightly,' she offered frankly.

'Sometimes God lends a helping hand!' He smiled, then added, 'now tell me has the diet I suggested for little Rosebud's diarrhoea helped?'

'I can't be sure. I mean with so many children to tend to each day it's impossible for me to keep track of these things. I'll have a word with Sister Louisa if you like. She's in the kitchen. I was on my way there when you knocked. You'll find the child in a corner alone somewhere. She gets frightened around other children.'

'Emotional stress can cause diarrhoea. Or it might be a case of stomach flu. Sometimes gastroenteritis or even food poisoning.'

'Food poisoning! Most of the produce is organically grown by the local farmers. Even the leftover produce Kyrio Lukas donates from the kitchen of his tavern. Hopefully by early summer the children's vegetable plot will be flourishing,' she went on readily.

'Good to hear. Ensure to boil the drinking water and wash vegetables thoroughly. Bacteria can be harmful and cause infection so to speak so toxins need to be expelled from the body. And you must keep up the fluids to prevent dehydration.'

'Oh, no need to worry doktoro. Sister Louisa is meticulous in such matters. However, I'll pass on this important information just the same. Now I must hurry. A mountain of work awaits me. As you know we are self-funded. The nuns are holding a fund raiser tomorrow in the cloisters. You're welcome to come along. The shelter is deficient of so many things.

And we are in desperate need of an outdoor over to cater for all the baking we do to feed these hungry angels. Like I said Sister Louisa is in the kitchen. I'm sure you'll want a word with her after you've seen Rosebud. I'll make you a cup of *elliniko kafe*. Or tsai if you like. But whatever you prefer is fine with me.'

'May the work be light Dilara hanim.' A jubilant smile marked his face as he watched her make her way back down through the hallway.

Even her unceasing blither tantalised his spirit. Dilara was an exceptional woman. Though there was a suggestion of mystery about her that he wanted to explore. What was she hiding? Where had she come from? Why was she lodging in an orphanage way up here in the mountains? She was articulate in both the Turk and Greek language.

Was she a refugee? A gypsy! He knew there had been a large migration from East India Armenia and Turkey to Cyprus. Perhaps her blood lineage had been a branch of this primitive migration. Not that any of it mattered. He couldn't silence his heart. Nor could he smother the flame burning there. Jihan bey heaved a sigh and shook his head reproachfully as he entered the dormitory. He'd come to examine the sick girl, not fulfil his amorous ambitions.

CHAPTER THIRTEEN

Lefkosia May 1962

It was a historical building probably dating back to Venetian times. And as Nilufer stood on the pavement, she imagined the establishment resonated with the despairing intonations of the emotionally disturbed. Even the two stone lions sprawled atop the pillars that flanked the bottom of the steps appeared sapped, she thought as she mounted them. The bronze plague alongside the door read; Professor Pavlos Lambros. Specialist Psychiatrist. She stared at it with diverse emotions. Questioned the anomaly of it all. Perhaps it was merely a subconscious delusion to accept that a mind doctor could bring her back from the darkness, help her discover the truth behind the shaded areas of her lost childhood. And she felt abashed to think that she was the subject of psychosis as an undergraduate in clinical psychology. How could she help others if she couldn't solve her own problems? Then again psychoanalysts weren't impervious to life's adversities. They were just like everybody else.

Nilufer had a distrustful approach to life and thought those around her had a morose sadness about them, but this bleak perspective of society was merely a reproduction of her gloomy self. If she wasn't happy, then neither was anyone else. In Nilufer's world everybody was on a par.

There was no line of demarcation between those who were normal and those who weren't. And most, like herself were insensible to their idiosyncrasies, thus were helpless to change the incongruity of their behaviour.

She pushed open the door to hear only a typewriter clicking away. She was greeted by an elderly woman dressed in a navy -blue suit which stood in stark contrast to her silver hair.

'My name is Nilufer Akalay. I have a ten o'clock appointment. I'm sorry I'm half an hour late. Will I have to wait long?'

The woman was astounded by the girl's insolence. Not only was she late, but she also necessitated immediate attention. She peered down at her diary then offered plainly, 'seems like you won't have to wait at all. You don't have an appointment.'

'I made the appointment for Wednesday the 16th at 10 a.m. So, there must be some mistake,' Nilufer offered.

'I'm afraid the mistake is yours.' She held up the appointment diary in front of her to validate the confusion. 'You're right it is Wednesday,' she added, 'but it's the 15th. Your appointment is scheduled for tomorrow which happens to be Thursday the 16th.'

'I've come a long way. I can wait.'

There was a sudden spark of amusement in the woman's eyes. Apparently, the girl also lacked sense, which she assumed explained why she was seeing a therapist.

Did she think that waiting to see a specialist physician was as normal as waiting at a bus stop to catch the next bus she'd just missed? 'I can fit you in tomorrow at the same time. Or alternatively reschedule your appointment.'

Nilufer reflected on her oversight. What had she been thinking when she woke up? Suddenly it all came back. The nightmare of the previous evening explained why she hadn't been her perkiest this morning.

The bad dream had become a familiar scenario over the years. It grasped her without warning or mercy. Sometimes she had the odd notion that an impalpable force was looming over her bed.

It was an indefinable hallucination, but the panic and terror Nilufer felt was real. She had aroused with the scream lodged in her throat and her heart beating at odds with the silence of the room. And endless nights of study and wakefulness had caught up with her.

She'd slept throughout the entire trip to Lefkosia. She'd only woken up as the bus pulled into the bus depot at Makarios Square. She'd absent-mindedly disembarked and instead of going to campus she'd ended up here. Just then she heard the woman ask, 'what would you like to do?'

'I've done nothing but waste my time!' She offered touchily, as if the mistake was entirely the receptionists and not hers. 'I'll just have to come back tomorrow.'

Professor Lambros was an old man, almost scoured to the bone, guarded smile, but his manner and voice suggested he was a man of great discernment, and who'd possibly spent most of his life with his head buried in intricate books. Her treating neurologist had told her that outside his private clinic he was a university lecturer in mental assessment at the Medical College in Zurich.

Nilufer's interest in the diminutive man rivalled that of the professor's own inquisitiveness of her.

'You have a reference?' His hands were entwined like a pile of twigs atop his broad desk. She got it out of her bag and passed it over to him.

He browsed over the referral from her treating physician which indicated his patient, Nilufer Akalay was twenty-two years old.

At nine years of age, she suffered from an unknown source of amnesia. A year or so later was diagnosed with a neurological disorder known as encephalitis.

Due to her illness, she was confined to a wheelchair and began to recover spontaneous movement and speech at the age of twelve. Over recent years, she has presented symptoms of depression, nightmares and isolated episodes of confusion.

He then looked up at her with clear authority and said, 'what kind of an impact did your childhood illness have on you?'

'It's rather a complicated story,' Nilufer said.

He shook his head knowingly. They all had a knotty story to tell. That's why they consulted him. His job was to try and make sense of their psychosomatic infirmity. 'I'd like to hear it.'

'Most of the time I was in terrible pain and slept a lot. My father hired a full-time nurse to care for me.'

'What about your mother?'

'She died when I was an infant.'

'Sorry to hear it. Has your father remarried?'

'No but he has a special friend. Miss Dilara helps him run his clinic a few days a week.'

'How do you feel about this?'

'I'm not unhappy, if that's what you're implying. They seem very respectful of each other. In fact. I've never seen father happier.'

'I'm sure he wants the same for you! Was she the nurse that cared for you?'

'I only met her a couple of years ago. She came to the house shortly after father's heart attack.'

'Good friends can be a great asset during a period of recovery.'

'I thought the same thing at first. But I was wrong. She's more than a friend.'

'What made you come to this assumption?' Some of his subjects were compulsive storytellers. And the elderly physician wanted to filter facts from fallacy.

'My confidence is not centred on theories doctor but facts,' she affirmed.

'Of course! He perfunctorily announced by the unexpected backlash. 'What can you tell me?'

'It never entered my mind that father would be in search of love again. I was so blind sighted that I never searched for the slightest variation in their behaviour when they were together.'

'You had no reason to. One doesn't intuitively look up at the blue sky on a clear sunny day in search of rain clouds, do they? What changed?'

'There was a certain aura that floated noiselessly between the two in a room. And I began to feel like an intruder. And their conversations led to other things outside their work at the Holy Trinity orphanage.'

'Dilara is a nun! A holy sister!' He remarked with rapid surprise.

'She lodges there as a volunteer worker. That's where father met her. As a physician he consulted sick children there. He's also well respected by the nuns for his charitable donations to the children over the years. As his daughter I wasn't exempt from his generosity. He told me once that I had an insatiable desire to want two of everything. He said that if he bought me something I'd always ask for one more. He said I told him it was because I wanted to save one for later.'

'What you describe is a phobia of being abandoned. It is common in young children. At least you recall something. Alright, let's move forward shall we. The nightmares, when did they start?'

'Over a year now. Sometimes I'm locked inside a dark and airless place where I can't escape. But I feel the presence of somebody else in this dream. I also sense I know this person. I try to scream but I'm paralysed with fear.'

The professor stared at her reflectively than said, 'I'm no expert at decoding dreams. Though it is understood that many phobias are often interpreted in dreams which indicates that in one's waking life they are discontented or faced with a dilemma in some way or other. The depression, how long have you been feeling like this?'

He knew from experience that each patient's situation differed. Some had had disastrous childhoods and were exposed to somatic and sexual abuse which usually contributed to feelings of isolation, social phobia and self-hate. Many had alcohol dependencies. Amongst other things acute shock, regret, shame and disappointment stimulated one's compulsive suffering.

But irrespective of an individual's condition, all hoped to be alleviated of their distress which often, remarkable as it may be, was merely a creation of their own mind. Or some simply slipped out of their existing world altogether and lived in a visionary world of their own making.

As Nilufer considered the question her eyes were curiously aimed on the miniature, ornamental glass birds dangling from synthetic string that was attached to the splayed branches of a small tree of sorts, and that sat on a globular brass bracket in a corner atop the physician's desk.

Somehow, she sensed a kind of momentous familiarity about those birds hanging there from the tree which prompted the onset of spasms within Nilufer's chest, and at the same time she was overcome by a deep sense of loss and sadness.

'A gift from a Japanese army commander. Lovely isn't it!' he remarked.

'Pardon!' She was abruptly drawn back to the conversation.

'The depression I mean, Miss Nilufer. A couple of years, a few weeks?'

'I can't be sure, but it feels like forever.'

He suspected that *forever* steered towards childhood. 'That's part of the problem.' Depression comes in many forms and most of the time never reveals itself until it's too late. The only word that comes to mind of chronic depression is Xilophagous.' Wood-Eaters translated from Greek.

'Those pests can destruct the internal wooden structures of a house for years unnoticed until one day nasty fractures appear on the exterior walls. One must try and exterminate those pests similarly to one's chronic depression.

Your condition I suspect is that of a psychological one and so you need to steer away from the problems you are faced with. You know, exterminate the pest.'

'I can't get rid of something I can't control,' Nilufer revealed clearly.

'I agree. But getting to the root of the problem often helps.'

'That's why I'm here. I want to find out who I am. I feel there are empty gaps in my life. And that my life is merely a falsehood. I can't distinguish what's real and what isn't.'

Nilufer retrieved mastic from her bag, and the elderly scholar watched her guardedly from within his diminutive glasses as she unwrapped the paper and slip it into her mouth.

'Can you tell me some of the things that might seem real? Like a place or thing or an event.'

'Strange but somehow I feel a connection to Miss Dilara.'

He produced a fitful cough. Everything seemed to revolve around Dilara. 'Can you describe what you feel?'

'There's something mysterious about her presence. The scent of her skin, her voice and smile all have a bizarre familiarity. It sounds silly I know.'

The Professor documented the details in his diary before he said, 'not at all. Sights, smells and sounds are all important aspects of remembering something of the past before someone has a lapse in memory. While your mind was idle at nine most girls at that age were doing all kinds of things. Think of your mind as a clock that has abruptly stopped and trapped the subject matter of your thoughts inside before materialising.

When the clock is recharged and starts ticking again so does the brain and so the aim is to try and make those thoughts reappear again. Perhaps this woman reminds you of a friend or a friend's mother. Or a teacher.'

'I sense I never went to school. Before my illness that is. My home tutor was an elderly man. A retired schoolteacher in the village.' Nilufer toiled with the long strands of her brown hair, her youthful face half-shadowed by the sunlight peeking through the window behind her, angling over one shoulder and settling onto the tiny flecks of dust on a corner of his solid wooden desk. Impulsively she inched forward and wiped it away with her hand, and the elderly scholar's brow contracted with remarkable speculation. There were those with subordinate compulsive disorders and there were those with extreme irrepressible disorders.

'Nothing like a clean desk. I never notice the dust until the sunlight reminds me it's in need of a clean. Now, where was I...ah yes, it's not uncommon for people to unconsciously associate somebody to someone they have lost. To fill in the void, so to speak. It gives them a sense of self being or self-preservation. Even a sense of identity. Perhaps Dilara has the characteristics of the sort of woman you'd envisioned your mother to be like. Let me ask, have you seen a picture of your mother. Your father must have one somewhere in the house. Or a photo album perhaps?'

'He might have put them away out of respect for Dilara. Though he might have considered my own feelings as his daughter.'

He wasn't surprised by this disclosure for it somehow confirmed

151

what he'd suspected all along. She disapproved of her father's relationship with Miss Dilara.

'You might like to suggest this to him. See what he has to say. Alright we'll conclude here. You've remembered something. Even if it be small. I'll arrange with my secretary to have you come back and see me in a couple of months.'

CHAPTER FOURTEEN

Pedhoulas July 1962

Jihan bey pushed back his chest and smiled at the man in the mirror. 'Everything is just delightful.' He said as he retrieved the small box from inside his coat pocket. He flipped the lid open and stared admiringly at the ring inside. He'd bought it a few days ago and he'd lost count of the number of times he'd looked at it since then, and each time his mood arose to peaks of ecstasy as he envisioned slipping it on Dilara hanim's finger. It was no random decision, he knew.

He pocketed the box and left the house whistling. He told her that he'd pick her up outside the orphanage at 12 a.m. She was two minutes late. Perhaps she couldn't come up with a reasonable excuse to present to Sister Louisa in order to take the afternoon off.

Then she appeared at the front gate, and when she saw him leaning on the bonnet of the sedan, she waved at him from across the road, and Jihan quietly nodded, but his heart triple churned by the sight of Dilara hanim.

'Isn't the view breathtaking?' she declared.

His eyes lit up, relishing her delight.

'I'm glad you like it here. I wanted to surprise you.' He knew it was a special place that she'd never seen before. They were standing on a mound that overlooked an amphitheatre far below. Some of the block sandstone benches and columns of the archaeological site had crumbled. Tall cedars skirted the auditorium flanked by gnarled trees, curved by centuries of tumultuous winds.

However, the parcels of flaming red poppies and wild yellow flowers growing amidst the dry overgrown grass offered a subtle quaintness.

'It has an aura of mystery and enchantment! Don't you think? Dilara announced. 'Who do you think built it?'

'Good question. Cyprus has had a succession of rulers. Romans, Venetians, Ottomans, Persians, to name a few. My guess is that it was probably built some twenty-five centuries ago by some great mathematical mind of that era.'

'I can just imagine the performers and musicians and famous Greek poets reciting there. Dressed in flowing robes of white belted with gold threads and their feet bound in leather sandals and crowns of olive branches.'

'Indeed, a descriptive observation Dilara hanim. You forgot to mention the protagonist who rescues the leading lady.'

'Who do you think they'd be?'

'There is a couple that come to mind.' He gave her a mischievous sidelong glance.

'Go away! She nudged his arm, and then asked, 'what's that water way down there?

'That's Morphu Bay, and beyond the Mediterranean Sea the Taurus Mountains in Turkey. Now, care to join me for lunch?'

They turned and made their way to the tavern and where a waiter with big ears greeted them before ushering them to a table by the window.

'How nice,' she remarked. He was pleased that she'd appreciated his effort. 'I asked for a table by the window when I made the reservation.'

He sat opposite her and ordered a bottle of champagne to celebrate the occasion.

'Ah, and a cold glass of lemonade for Dilara!' The waiter said readily, and Jihan frowned up at him. Big Ears returned a similar glare and then left without further ado.

'What is it? Is something wrong?' she asked.

'Do you know that man?'

'Why do you ask?' she queried surprised.

'A waiter doesn't address a lady by name if he doesn't know her! I made the reservation, remember? Why do you laugh?'

'I can't help it. You must have given him my name. Or he might have just assumed I was your wife!'

Momentarily the thought of what she had said appeased him immensely but just as quickly his mood turned sour.

'He also knew what you liked to drink!'

'Do I look like the type of woman who'd drink champagne? A modern woman?'

'It's only polite that he should ask before making such a hasty assumption just the same!' he brooded.

'Maybe a waiter has a knack of knowing what a woman likes to drink.

Who knows?' She remarked buoyantly and then added, 'let's not spoil our day over such petty matters.' Instantly Jihan bey's temperament softened by the sheer wholesomeness of her voice.

'You're right. You must think badly of my lack of character.' He offered apologetically, and when she noticed the restless motion of his hands on his bowtie she said, 'I wish you wouldn't do that!

'I'll try,' he offered with a strained smile.

Dilara accepted Jihan to be a gentle and self-doubting man which she found unusually intriguing.

Just then Big Ears emerged at the table. His presence had an unsettling vibe that set Jihan's fingers rapping irritably atop the table as he watched him crack the bottle open and fill his glass, and then stand over him with an air of menace with pad and pencil in hand.

After he ordered the food he said, 'you forgot the lemonade! And the bucket of ice! Proprietors of such establishments should know better than to hire useless waiters!

Big Ears clenched his teeth, glared at him with the apparent verdict he utterly disliked the rude customer. 'I'll get it immediately. With the ice…'

'Oh, no need! Champagne is fine with me!' Dilara informed, and then Big Ears strode off muttering. She turned to Jihan and said, 'why are you so rude to that man? And why do you insist on entertaining yourself with the bowtie? I wish you'd stop.'

'I'll try.'

'That's what you said before.'

'Forgive me for my mindless conduct.'

'What about the prayer beads?'

'You said they irritate you,' he said self-consciously.

'Oh, they do but I'd rather you did instead of that bowtie. You must treat it with respect or otherwise you'll ruin the delicate fibres.'

They'd consumed half the bottle before the food arrived and so Jihan ordered another.

'Why did your order more champagne? You're driving. You don't expect me to finish it on my own! Though I must admit I do like it! It has a delightful effect on me!'

'You go ahead, enjoy yourself,' he offered candidly.

Just then he felt the tip of her shoe nudge his ankle as she readjusted her hips on the chair, felt the burning sensation of his ears, as if the act insinuated her desire to attract his attention, and his bowtie became a crutch for his fingers once again, and Dilara unwittingly blushed by his habitual nervous gesture.

'I'm glad we became friends.' She raised her glass. 'Here's to an enduring friendship!'

'Friends sometimes become more than just companions.' He offered coyly as their glasses clinked but his heart was sprinting with the exhilaration of an athlete near the finishing line aiming for gold, hoping that she would affirm they were more than just friends. Impulsively he reached into his pocket as his thoughts were on the ring and marriage proposal. However, he guessed his timing had to be precise or otherwise Dilara hanim might come up with analytic excuses to snub his proposal. Maybe after she'd had a little more champagne since it had such an enchanting effect on her senses. But then again, the thought instantly subdued his mood for it defeated the authenticity of his purpose. It just wasn't right.

'I suppose they do but not always,' she offered demurely. Just then Big Ears arrived back at the table like a bothersome blow fly in his sight thus emptied his pocket of his hand. Impatiently he watched him set several small dishes of Middle Eastern and Cypriot meze atop the table from his tray.

'The food is delicious.' She offered when she'd finished eating.

'Then we should come here more often,' he suggested as he watched the delicate motion of her hand dab the corner of her mouth with the table napkin. 'My housemaid Sui Lee is Chinese. What about Chinese food one evening?'

'Chinese!' She uttered with surprise.

'You don't like the idea?'

'I can't dislike the idea of something I've never tried Jihan bey. Only problem is I've never eaten with sticks.'

'Sui Lee has tried to teach me, but I fail each time. It's a bit of a technique curling three fingers around a bone stick. We could try together if you like. Should be fun. Then when she saw his hand dip into his pocket she said, 'you're not thinking of smoking a cigar are you? Here in this restaurant!'

'Come now have you judged me to be a man short of respect in the presence of a lady?' He offered with a repertoire of facial expressions that were both ingenuously humorous to her. She laughed and Jihan bey reached over and took her hand, stared at her with meticulous observation. Imagined her bare of the dainty headscarf, her long brown hair trickling like fibres of silk through his fingers.

And the faultless shape of her brow that was raised probingly, or it might have been that she was staring at him with analogous awe. And the scent of her skin and rosy lips charged him with an irrepressible desire to kiss her.

'Ahh Dilara hanim you are the light of my eyes and the pulse of my heart.'

Dilara felt momentarily reduced by the charitable physician's confession of adoration. It never occurred to her that his feelings went beyond just a mutual friendship. 'I don't know what to say,' she murmured lowering her eyes.

'No need to say anything. It's only natural for vines to grow towards each other and intertwine.'

'As good friends, that is.'

'You see me as just a friend?' He instantly felt defeated by the invention of his own mind.

'I've never thought about you otherwise,' she offered sincerely.

'I thought the feelings were mutual?' he offered feebly.

'Pardon if I've misled you in some way. Let's not complicate matters.'

'But you are young. What about your own needs as a woman? A husband and home! A family!'

'I already have a family at the orphanage. What more could I wish for? Please may I be excused. I'm in need of some fresh air. The champagne has made me feel lightheaded.'

Just then the waiter returned as she was about to stand up and was quick to draw out her chair from under her, and Jihan bey felt the blood rush to his head by the polite gesture. Then as he watched him clear the table with thorough aptitude he asked, 'now tell me, is it true a waiter has a natural ability to know what a woman likes to drink?'

'I'm not sure what you mean.'

'Never mind. The woman I'm with have you served her before in this establishment?'

'Can't say that I have.' Big Ears gestured an arm around the tavern. 'I'm not the only one that works here.'

'You're right. But you knew her name!' Jihan pressed.

'Sure, but it doesn't mean I've served her.' Big Ears replied as he went about stacking plates on the tray.

'Don't mess with me boy! Tell me how you know her. Make it fast!'

'She comes here now and then.' The waiter was familiar with Dilara. She'd come in a couple of times to pick up leftover produce from the kitchen to take back to the orphanage. One of the farmers from the village of Kakopedria drove her here in his work van. But he wasn't obliged to give this rude customer the ins and outs of things.

'Is that right?' Jihan clamped his fist. 'Who was she with? Was it a man? Do you know his name?'

'I take people's orders not their names. But since he had a beard and moustache and wearing trousers then I'd say it was a man. Now if that will be all I have work to do.'

'Despicable! Allah give me patience.' He retrieved his prayer beads and thrashed them a few times across his knuckles but trying to smother his fury this way proved to be painful, and so he opted to just sit and take in the view outside until Dilara returned. She had been gone some time. Anxiously he searched all around but when she was nowhere in sight he was overcome with an undesirable panic.

Then a steady dimness poured into his eyes and an elusive vision of Dilara appeared with a man. They were in the auditorium and cosily seated on a bench and she was the soul of mischievous gestures which ruptured the core of Jihan's being. A stab of pain ripped at his chest, he felt nauseas and his face grew cold. Never had he felt so defenceless and afraid. Feebly he stood up, loosened his bowtie, removed his jacket and it tumbled to the floor. Then darkness trickled into his eyes again, and all his good intentions, this tavern, the scenery, the ring and marriage proposal and whatever life had existed was snuffed out.

CHAPTER FIFTEEN

Rizokarpaso August 1962

D espina stared at the mound of earth and where far beneath lay the skeletons that were once the breathing essence of Zehra. She averted her moist eyes to obliterate the thought, and at the same time wished she could just as easily wipe out her anguish with a mere curve of the eye. She removed the small bottle of oil from inside her canvas bag. She then kneeled and removed the tiny glass from inside the small wooden box resting on the earth at the head of the grave. She replenished the oil, lit the wick afloat there and placed it back inside the box before the icon of the Panagia. She retrieved the clay jar at her feet and poured water over the flowerbed that she'd upheld over the years.

At that moment she was startled by a man's voice.

'Hello Miss!'

Despina turned around and looked up at the tall and orderly attired man wearing a black hat.

'I didn't mean to frighten you! I came to pay my respects to my father. He died five months ago.'

'My condolences Kyrio.'

He expressed his gratitude and then said, 'I noticed there were lots of mushrooms growing here that day.'

'Well, it's a good place for them to grow,' she offered easily.

'Ah, yes after the rain.'

'And the soil is moist from the bark and leaves, and they're sheltered from the wind. Watch out for the poisonous ones. You can identify them if you know what you're looking for.'

'Sounds like you're an expert. I'd like to know.'

'Some are stained yellow while others have a red skirt beneath the cup.' Despina remembered everything Rifat had told her that day.

'Thanks for the advice. I know more about organic farming than I do mushrooms.'

'I know nothing about cultivation,' she revealed.

'There are benefits to be had in organic farming. Not only is the produce free of harmful pesticides but makes light work. Olive trees shed their fruit naturally and don't have to be tampered with at harvest time.'

'I have also learned something. Best I be heading off. May your grief by easy!'

'And yours Miss. Is the deceased a family member?'

'A sister. She is very dear to me,' Despina murmured.

'You miss her terribly eh! Sorrow is like a good cheese. It takes time to mellow.'

'I'd be mouldy by now if I were cheese!' She sighed.

He was drawn to her witticism. 'The garden plot is lovely. Bravo Miss. You are a tower of devotion. Your sister would be proud.'

'She was ever so precious. I can't believe she's gone.'

'I accept it must be hard.'

'Nobody can understand somebody else's pain when they can't see inside,' she offered subdued.

'If transparency existed then it would be an ideal world.' He offered in good spirit. 'Humans are complicated and biased creatures. They're often inclined to judge others superficially.'

'Nothing is as it seems. Even when we think we know someone so well we find out we never knew them at all.' Despina retrieved the clay jar once again. 'I better not forget it. I rely on water from the fountain in the village square.'

'Pardon I've held you up Miss. You must have other things to do than talk to me. I think I'll head up to the peninsula from here.'

'How nice. What do you do there?'

'This might sound silly but I'm a man who enjoys his own company. Particularly when taking in the fresh sea air and spectacular view.'

'It sounds like something even I would enjoy. If I had a spare pair of legs to get there, that is. I'm going to Lemnos from here.'

'Then you might need that spare pair of legs. Lemnos is a long walk from here. Allow me to drive you there!'

'It would be improper don't you think?'

'Come now Miss! There's nothing wrong with a man assisting a woman in need.'

'They'll gossip just the same. And you were going to the headland remember! I wouldn't want to spoil your day.'

'I can go another time. The scenery and fresh air won't go away!' He offered in good spirit. 'Part of the reason I go there is that it reminds me of my childhood. It used to be a good place to fly my kite. From there further inland is a 'wishing tree.' I'd go there in the hope of finding para to buy candy.'

'Don't tell me you are the son of Kyria Sofia! Pandelis!' she announced incredulously.

'How do you know me?' He feigned surprise.

'My name is Despina!'

'Why of course. Don't tell me the sister that was missing back then is buried here?' He kept up the pretence.

'That's right. Now I really must be going.' Just then he was quick to retrieve the clay jar from her hand. 'I insist. Now if you'll follow me.'

She accompanied him back through the forest and when he opened the passenger door of the vehicle she was touched by his politeness. Pandelis placed the clay jar on the back seat and then took up seat behind the wheel.

He drove for some time then broke the silence by asking, 'eh, tell me something about yourself. How old are you now?'

'I'm twenty-two.'

'Then it must be a few years since you finished school! What about a career? What would you like to do?'

'I don't have plans!' she responded curtly.

'Come now Miss, everybody has dreams.'

'What dreams could a poor girl have?' she voiced quietly.

'Dreams are for free.'

When he smiled over at her Despina averted her gaze and stared out the window before she said, 'I'm a realist not a fantasist. Optimism can be misleading. Only fools build dreams based on the meaningless words of a weak and unreliable society.'

He was moved by her astute observation while at the same time sensed she'd been betrayed in some way.

'Will you be visiting family in Lemnos?'

'My father is the only family I have.'

'I'm sorry to hear that life has treated you so unkindly Miss. Your mother, she must have been young? How did she die?'

'If I knew I'd tell you. My father refuses to speak about her.'

'Most children want to learn about a deceased parent when they are older.'

'I thought my friend Katina might have known.'

'Katina! Do I know her?'

'You must since she has worked for your family long enough.'

'Ah! That Katina. Friendly woman. But perhaps too dedicated at times. Always asking if I want this thing or the other. She has this thing with the orchard house. It's a charming house surrounded by orchards. She knows I like to spend time there.

Not a week goes by without her asking if I'd like her to go there and clean it. I can look after myself. I don't believe in human slavery!' he smirked.

'I'd hardly consider a paid employee as such! And it's not by choice she works as a domestic. She happens to be an educated woman.

And she's also self-conscious about her 'problem,' as she likes to put it. So, I'd be careful what you say around her. And if she wants to clean the house then let her do so if it pleases her.'

He was also amused by her resoluteness. 'It's a long walk to get there from our village. I don't see myself as a woman persecutor. If that makes sense. Besides, there is the matter of protecting one's reputation. You see the problem with the people in our village is they thrive on the opportunity to create a scandal to fulfil their wearisome lives. Most of what they say is unfounded. Let's just say some of my workers happened to be working in the orchard close by and saw a young maid regularly visiting the house. It would be reason enough to incite them with malicious gossip! I didn't have to tire you with such a long commentary but I'm a man who likes to clarify things Miss Despina. Now tell me, how did you and Katina become friends?'

'I'm not sure. Though it seems like she's been around forever.'

'Then she must know you well.'

'More than anyone. I don't know what I'd do without her.'

He reflected on Katina's own observation of her. *Despina's like one of them fog clouds resting below a mountain that nobody knew what was hiding beneath.*

'You also must know her well,' he deliberately went on.

'I can't say that I do! It's probably because she's never had to depend on me in the same way as I have of her. Though come to think of it she did tell me a few things about herself when I was younger.'

'What can you tell me?'

'Well, she said her mother abandoned her when she was young. She took her sister with her. She believed it was because of her 'problem.' Children sense favouritisms, she had said. Her father too, she believed was ashamed of her and feared there'd be no suitors and tried to marry her off at the age of fourteen to a man twice her age.'

'Sad story.' He shook his head. 'You said before she didn't know your mother.'

'She was studying to be a teacher in London at the time. Of mother's death, that is.'

'How could she have known that she even died if she didn't know her?'

'Perhaps Stelios told her when she came back. He's a distant uncle. He's deceased. He was very old I remember.'

'Where do you remember him from?'

'From my childhood days. They were sad days I recall because Zehra was sick all the time. I was also very lonely. I only had Bebek to play with.'

'Ah, Bebek. You told me back then that she was dumb and naughty,' he smiled.

'That's right. Poor thing. God only knows how she got that way.'

'Your father should know since she is his sister!'

'My father told Zehra that it was because she ate a green potato. Utter rubbish, if you ask me!'

'What is it about Stelios you remember? And you said Zehra was sick all the time?'

She told him how he'd come to pick her up and take her to see the puppet show. And how he'd buy her pasteli and sing her songs on their way home from the kafenio.

'I'd wait for him for what seemed hours when I knew he was coming. Such was my excitement. I have fond memories of those days. All the children of the village would sit on a rug on the floor and watch the puppet show with cups of iced-rose water. There was this little Muslim boy who'd always sit beside me. One time he laughed so much that his iced water splashed all over my face and he licked it off with his tongue.'

'This boy has left you with fond memories. Did you end up growing up with him?' he deliberately probed.

'Sure, but not in the way you're thinking?'

'Though you can't deny that it doesn't happen Miss. Though I would imagine such a friendship would be challenging since our Greek customs are different to that of our Turkish neighbours.'

'Why are you telling me all this? I'm old enough to make up my own mind!'

'You are right Miss. No woman should be denied autonomy or be controlled by ineffectual pre-historic customs. But girls have been known to be harshly persecuted if they oppose these customs,' he counselled. Then sensibly resumed to their prior conversation.

'What else did Katina tell you?'

Despina gave him a stare that might have readily prompted his face to redden had not his eyes been on the road ahead. What was his interest in Katina?

'She ran away from home and came to live with her uncle in Rizo.'

'What about her father and sister? Did she see them again?'

'I don't know about her sister. But her father died of the 'white plague.' She seemed unaffected by his death since he made no attempt to bring her home.'

'She never mentioned she was raised by her uncle.'

'That's because you never asked. Your parents should have at least known something about her over the years since they hired her,' Despina emphasised.

He might have just as easily said the same thing about her. 'At least now I know something about her.'

'You won't find out much more Kyrio, I can assure you.' Despina offered with fortitude, then spontaneously added, 'my existence depended on her as a child but now that I'm older I've discovered there's a different side to Katina. Often our opinions clash. And she can be burdensome and controlling. I can't do anything without her interfering.'

He sensed her distress at having mindlessly allowed Katina to weaken her fortitude. 'Sounds like she's taken over your life. Am I right?'

'Regrettably so Kyrio. Why I don't even know if I can trust her!'

'You can trust me Miss,' he openly confessed.

'Why should I? Even at the age of eight I realised you couldn't be trusted. You broke your promise, remember? After Zehra's death I waited for weeks, even months for you to show up at the house to take me to see the pony. And now fourteen years later you ask me to trust you? You take me for a fool! Now if you'll just pull over by the side of the road I'll walk from here!'

'I can explain the misunderstanding. I had Katina ask your father for permission. She told me a few days later that he refused my request.'

'You're lying! Wouldn't she have told me?'

'I have nothing to gain by lying. Perhaps it's Katina you should be questioning. I thought that day she would have told me about your sister's death. But she didn't. Perhaps in the same way as she ignored my request to let me know if your father and sister didn't come home by the following morning then I'd alert the authorities in Lemnos to organise a search party. Perhaps you were right when you said you can't trust her.'

'I've heard enough. I wished I hadn't said anything. Now pull over!' Despina felt a headache coming on.

'We've only reached the outskirts of Lemnos. It would take at least twenty minutes to get there. You might end up a blistered mess by the time you return home. If you return before dark that is. And you'd also be very hungry and thirsty by then. And your father will be worried,' he cautioned.

'Well, that's for me to worry about. Now do as I say!' Her head really was throbbing now.

He pulled over and killed the engine. And before she'd even opened the door he'd already arrived on her side, and when she saw him holding the door open for her to climb out Despina was infuriated even further. 'I said I'd walk! Do you always treat women this way? Do they have to beg you to leave them alone? It's no wonder you have yet to marry. How stupid of me to have passed you for a gentleman. Why you're nothing more than a distrustful womaniser. God only knows what really did happen in the orchard house. Well, you can't control me!'

He felt slighted by this unanticipated criticism. 'You have judged me wrongly Miss Despina.'

'The outcome of your conduct won't end well!' she retorted.

'Ah, the tobacco merchant! A devious and stupefied alcoholic I'm told to believe!' He announced petulantly, and just then when he saw her mortification he felt similarly chastened by his thoughtless and foolish actions. He lowered his eyes, scuffed the dirt with the tip of his shoe a few times before he looked up to face her again. Then before he could confess his remorse, Despina turned on her heels and stormed off.

And with the thought that it had been Katina he'd had in mind when he'd offered her a lift and not her. She wished she'd never laid eyes on Pandelis Gapsalis and hoped she never would again.

Pandelis stood there in the hot dry air and with his eyes firmly set on the girl as she headed up the dusty track ahead until she vanished from view, and at the same time wondering what her purpose was in Lemnos. It must have been important to want to go there, particularly on foot in the scorching midday heat.

He sensed she would sorely regret his offer of a lift. Conversely though she might not after he'd insulted her in such a harsh way.

He opened the door of the driver's side of the vehicle and was about to climb in when he noticed the clay jar resting on the back seat. He climbed in when he noticed her cloth bag poking out from under the seat beside him where she'd been sitting. He took hold of it when suddenly a few things tumbled out under the leg space. He noticed a half empty bottle of oil, a tab of matches, a tiny bag of wicks and what appeared to be a brown notepad. He leaned sideways and scooped them up and placed everything back inside the bag, save for the notebook. He turned it curiously over in his hand, opened a page, but just as hastily closed it again. Despina's personal affairs were her own. His hand struck the steering wheel with self-admonishment towards his unwavering interest in the tobacco merchant's daughter. His hand fell to the notepad on his lap once again. He skimmed through the pages, then paused on a page.

I write with the ink that drops from the heart. There are no colourful words to convey.

The red rose has been planted. It blossoms in the shade like an orphaned child.

Zehra has been long gone. I search for her everywhere. I see her face in the clouds. I hear her voice in the songbirds. I see her smile in the sunshine. I hear her lamenting in the stream. I hear the grind of her cardboard shoes on the pebbles. I hear her heart beating with mine.

There is darkness. Another day. Another day. All remains the same. It's hard to endue such a doomed fate. My spirit is in a place where the sun doesn't shine.

The migratory songbirds have returned from the south. The mother of the bereaving child never returns. The rose has blossomed in the shade again.

The doors have closed for the ones I love,
I live in a nightmare where no one can see,
How will I get rid of this evil curse?
Hoping He above will help me nurse,
Maybe when I'm down below,
There where my eyes will not see or fear,
I'll rest in memory of those I cherished so dear,
God grant my beloved peace and good cheer,
Always be near all through the years.

The sun awaits its beloved sunflower to raise its bowed head to declare its adoration.

The bridal shoes stand under the chair.

There is no father to place them on his daughter's feet.

And walk her down the path of happiness. And dance to the song in her heart.

The ink has dried up.

Pandelis closed the notepad and put it back inside the bag and at the same time deeply aroused by the poignant words of its author.

Clearly the girl had lost all faith in life. Just then he had an irrepressible urge to go after her. But what would he say? *How can I reach that disheartened place and it make it shine?*

The collar of his white shirt was saturated with sweat and so he removed his tie and undid the top button. After removed his jacket and placed them on the seat alongside of him. He would have been changed into something more casual by now if not for his chance meeting with the girl. She would have realised by now that she'd forgotten her things in his vehicle.

He started the engine and was about to turn and head back to Rizo when he saw a vague figure coming up the track towards him. It was her, Despina, and so he left the engine running and purposefully waited for her until she drew near before he climbed out.

'You're back!' he feigned surprise. 'You didn't find who you were looking for. Or did you realise that you'd forgotten your bag and jar in my vehicle?'

'I wasted my time,' Despina moped.

He considered her demeanour, the moisture at the bodice of her cotton dress, and the strings of hair that clung to her moist neck and forehead.

'If you'd like to tell me who it is you're looking for in Lemnos then I might be able to help.'

Despina considered the question and wondered if she could trust him. Though what other choice did she have? 'I'm looking for a boy called Yilmaz. He's a Muslim boy who's in the army with a boy I was betrothed to.'

'Have you broken up with this boy?'

'I don't know. I mean I haven't heard from him since I last saw him. That was a few months ago.'

'Three months is not long. I'm sure there's a reasonable explanation.'

'That's what Katina says. I don't know what to think.'

'Surely his parents would know. Why haven't you asked them?'

'I can't do that Kyrio! They oppose the friendship. It's because I'm Greek, otherwise I would have.'

'May I ask, this betrothed of yours, is he the Muslim boy you told me about from your childhood?'

'That's right.' Then when she recognised the reason for his broad grin she coyly added, 'well you did say it happens sometimes.'

'Now let me ask, if this boy Yilmaz is in the army with Rifat then what was your purpose of going to Lemnos?'

'I assumed that he must have been discharged. He reads Greek, you see. He'd read my letters to Rifat. Mustafa the Potter in our village has been kind enough to read Rifat's letters to me since I don't read and write Turk. That's why I went to Lemnos. Rifat also should have been discharged but with so much unrest and rioting going on in the country. I heard EOKA B bandits are everywhere. Up in the mountains and in the streets targeting anti-EOKA civilians and policemen. Slaughtering their own people. Even anti-EOKA Turkish Cypriots. What if he's been shot?'

'You mustn't think of the worse Miss. I'm sure there's a reasonable explanation. Anyway, you weren't gone long.'

'I decided to turn back.'

'Because you left your bag and jar?'

'I wasn't worried about the jar. It was too heavy to carry all the way to Lemnos. I meant to leave it at the cemetery. But I must have got distracted when you relieved me of it. It was more the bag I was worried about. Anyway, what would people think if they saw a girl asking around for a boy?' she unhappily explained.

'A smart girl like you might have thought about it sooner,' he offered wisely.

'What else can I do?' she sighed.

'I understand. Well, we can't stand here all day in this heat. Come,' he gestured an arm to his vehicle. 'I'll drive you as far as the first lemon grove near our village.'

'Do you remember my house?' He asked along the way.

'Of course. Why do you ask?'

'Your father I would imagine would take an offense to my turning up at his door to speak with his daughter. Call by the house late tomorrow afternoon. Hopefully I'll have some information.'

Despina let out an involuntary sigh by the prospect. Then she heard him say, 'though I can't promise. Call by just the same. By the way the house is a long walk and rugged climb from the village. I can always arrange for Murat the driver to pick you up from the last lemon grove on the outskirts of the village. You'll have to give me a time though.'

'There's no need. I don't mind the walk.'

He reached over and turned the radio on. 'Do you like music!

He drove on with the insightful notion that he and Despina were to become the best of friends.

CHAPTER SIXTEEN

Late the following afternoon, Despina found Murat the driver standing by the vehicle parked by the roadside out front of the Gapsalis mansion.

'I'm here to see Kyrio Pandelis!' she revealed.

Murat afforded her a smile before he unlocked the front gate and allowed her to pass through. When she stepped into the courtyard everything was just as she remembered it back then. Herbs in clay pots and redolent flowers of all variety and colour were in full bloom amidst the dainty clay figurines. The trees were heavily pregnant with citrus fruit and the fishpond with the sandstone bench around it at the rear of the garden was still there. How she'd longed to live in such a splendid house. What poor child wouldn't? She mounted the steps and tapped on the door.

As she stood there waiting to be acknowledged she looked up when she saw a tall, stylish and well coiffured, red-haired woman standing alongside the heavy brocade curtain and peering down at her through the wide glass window of the cottage. Despina accepted the woman to be Kyria Sophia.

Shortly a hefty woman with thick set grey braids and wearing a headscarf and full-length apron appeared unsmiling from behind the door. 'Who are you? And what do you want?'

'Good afternoon. My name is Despina Manolas. I'm here to see Kyrio Pandelis.'

The servant whose name was Thea observed her diligently, contemplated her polite manners before she asked, 'what is it about?'

'He'll know. He's expecting me.'

'Best you come inside then.' She promptly offered gesturing an arm into the entrance hall.

Despina followed her and noticed that even in this room was just as she remembered it as a child. The gleaming marble tiles, the lavish tapestries strung across the walls. The fine solid timber table in the centre of the room with its many porcelain and crystal vases, and the rich upholstered chairs.

'I'll let him know you are here,' Thea punctually announced, but as she passed the open kitchen door on her way to mount the staircase a voice from inside asked, 'who's at the door?' When Thea didn't respond, Katina moved away from the kitchen sink, wiped her hands on her apron and came out into the entrance hall to see who it was.

'Despina what are you doing here?' she asked.

'I've come to speak with your boss.'

Katina raised a brow. 'What for? You could have just as easily told me what it was about! You didn't have to trouble yourself by coming all the way up here!'

'I can do some things for myself!'

'I thought you'd appreciate my help,' Katina replied, insulted by the backlash.

'Ah Miss Despina! Glad you could come. I've been expecting you.'

Then Pandelis turned to Katina and said, 'my guest and I will be out in the garden. We'll both be wanting some cold lemonade. Thanks.'

Despina was unmindful of the ferocity in Katina's eyes set upon her as he escorted her through the door. Outside in the garden they both sat near the pond and where nearby an orange tree provided shade. 'Do you remember sitting here with me back then?' He asked.

'I've never forgotten that day. Nor this beautiful garden and fishpond. You cheered me up with all those stories you told me. You made me forget for a while that Zehra was missing.'

'I'm glad. Clearly you were unhappy.'

'Have you got any news about Rifat?' No sooner had she asked when Katina appeared with the glasses of lemonade on a tray.

'Here we are Kyrio. Your favourite drink.' Katina offered with a beaming smile, and the red tinge of his cheeks hadn't gone unnoticed by Despina and which she accepted was that of a discomfited and embarrassed man towards the foolish doting of a female member of his staff.

'Well, then I'll be off. I won't be far. I'll come back shortly to see if you need anything else!'

'Thanks Katina but that won't be necessary.'

'As you wish Kyrio,' she courteously replied and then turned on her heels and left.

'Now you know what I meant about her willingness to please!' He grinned; however, she thought it was his way of making light of the situation.

'I sense she makes you feel uncomfortable,' she offered sensibly.

Despina took a sip of lemonade, put her glass down on the bench alongside her and then frankly said, 'I find her annoying at times. Like I said, she thinks she can control my life. Just before she told me that I shouldn't have troubled myself by coming here. And that I could have just as easily told her what it was about. She thinks I'm obliged to inform her of my every move. I can't even post and pick up my own mail! She's been doing that too. Meddles in everything she does! Why are you staring at me like that? It's true!'

'I was just considering what you said about her meddling! I can understand how you must feel. After all you're a grown woman and you certainly don't need to rely on her in such personal matters. How long has she been acting as your mail courier?'

'A while now. Are you saying I shouldn't trust her?'

'You should ask yourself that question Miss.'

'Perhaps it's just me being distrustful again since my entire life seems to be a lie.'

'I see, well a lie is only a lie until it becomes the truth! And there's usually a cause for doubt Miss. I'd call it human instinct. That's my way of thinking.'

'You're right. You had every right to say those things you did about my father. I'm sorry I spoke to you rudely.'

'No need. Understandably a girl that must shoulder the disgrace of her own father in society would naturally feel ashamed to be the daughter of such a detested man.'

'I planted a tiny rose bush in the yard as a child. And I said to father, "look how beautiful it is! It will grow a red rose!" He kicked it and ripped it out, and that's when I decided he would never love me. I accepted that I didn't need his affection. All that mattered was that my sister loved me. A rose can be replanted but nothing can replace the love of a sister. He treated Zehra much worse. Acted as if he didn't own her and that's what hurt me the most,' Despina explained.

'What did that man do to her? If I may ask?'

'Nothing a real father would ever do. He'd beat her and lock her up in the shed for days unfed and without water. He forbad her to go to school and made her work in the field each day. She cried at night telling me she wished she were dead. He never bought her as much as a book or a pencil. And I'd have to stuff the inside of her shoes with cardboard to stop the stones from hurting her feet. I remember I asked him once why he was so cruel to my sister and he'd said, "some children don't deserve favours." I was very young myself and so I couldn't have understood the meaning of what he'd said. I told her we'd run away to an orphanage. Zehra was so kind and pure. All she could think to ask was if they'd let her take a bath and give her a clean dress in the orphanage. As if these were the most vital needs for her existence. She never thought to ask if she'd be loved and fed.'

Pandelis quietly pondered on this distressing tale then said, 'I can only express my heartfelt condolences. I wish there was something I could do. Tell me, about Zehra's death. Did your father explain how she died?'

'It was an accident, he said. Up in the mountains when he'd gone to visit a friend who owned a cheery orchard. I don't believe him,' Despina offered resolutely.

'What do you believe?' he curiously asked.

'I'd rather keep my opinion to myself.'

'I'd be interested in hearing it. I might be able to help,' he reassured calmly.

'I'm sure that you'd have the same opinion as Katina.'

'And what might that be if I may ask?'

'You'd think I'm exaggerating or just paranoid,' she offered self-consciously.

Pandelis recognised just how much influence Katina had over Despina. She had smothered Despina's emotions within her web of treachery.

'Not at all. You are entitled to your own beliefs. Regardless of what Katina or anyone else thinks.'

'And I'll stand by my beliefs. I happen to know my father threatened Zehra. She cried in bed each night. I couldn't have imagined why she did since I was only a child myself. But I know better now.'

'Why did she cry? And why did he threaten her?'

'I can't tell you that. I must respect my sister's honour.'

'You can't do that by withholding the truth. I'm sure your sister would want retribution. Don't you think?'

'You're right. It was because of those awful games father made her play in the field.'

'Don't tell me… God surely it can't be what I'm thinking!'

'Unfortunately, Kyrio it appears that way,' she offered solemnly. 'Father said he'd punish her rightly if she breathed a word of it to anyone. Told her he'd lock her up and starve her again. Only this time she would die.'

'Damn that son of a whore! Why I'll make him dig his own grave! I'll go down to that field that he stole from my father right now! If you'll pardon me Miss...'

'Please you mustn't! Despina urged as she quickly rose to her feet after him. 'Please I beg of you! No good will come of it!'

He accepted she was right! Nothing would be gained until justice prevailed. And he'd make sure of that one way or the other.

'As you wish Miss.' He sat back down and then she asked, 'you said he stole the field from your father!'

'That's right! It was many years ago. After I was discharged from the army.'

'Why there's no end to that man's crimes! Even the food he puts on the table is stolen!' Despina was revolted by the thought, it made her feel nauseated.

'One wouldn't expect less from such a man,' he mocked.

'Surely there must be a way you can rightfully reclaim the land!' she revealed.

He wondered what would become of her if he did reclaim the only source of income her father relied on to feed her. He observed her closely, as if seeing her through the eyes of the soldier boy. What he saw was a slender girl of medium height. Rosy-coloured skin, dark eyes and thick, feathered brows. A fall of loosely woven hair, the shade of rusted iron. Pandelis could easily see why the boy Rifat adored Despina. And her pleasant and unassuming disposition could make even a resilient man like him feel submissive in her presence. Something that he self-confessed no other woman had made him feel before.

185

Presently he said, 'I'm not concerned over a bit of earth. I'm just angry about what happened to Zehra. Now let me ask, this friend of your father's, the one that he said owned a cherry orchard. Had you seen him around before?'

'The first time I saw him was that night he came to the house.'

'Where were you when he came?'

'Zehra and I were in our room when father came in and took her by the hand and led her outside in her nightdress. I recall how confused I was because it was something he'd never done before. I was scared more than anything. I thought he was going to hurt her again or lock her up. I could hear voices coming from the kitchen and so I crept out of my room. I stood behind the door outside in the hallway and peered in through the gap between the hinges. That's when I saw the man seated at the table. Father joined him and sat Zehra in his lap and was smiling down at her and stroking her long hair. I heard the man ask him what her name was. And then the man stretched over and patted her hand. When I asked Zehra what it was all about she said that she knew Baba always said things he didn't mean when he smoked his 'snake pipe.' She said that she heard him tell the man how pretty her grey eyes were and how smart she was when she didn't even go to school.'

He needn't have guessed what had taken place that night. There weren't any words in any written language of a lexicon that could describe such a man. Trading an underage child was a heinous and unlawful crime. Spyros was a psychopath. Unfortunately, one couldn't cure the insanity of one's own mind. Nor could one protect a child that wasn't rightfully his.

'Do you think he handed my sister over to that man?'

'As much as I hate to believe it Miss but there's a good chance he did!'

'God Zehra was only a child. She was only eight!' There seemed no justice in what Despina felt at that moment.

'Even if that was the case it doesn't explain how she died,' he added.

'What if Zehra sensed he was going to give her away to that man on the day he took her up to the mountains. I'd say there's a good chance she got frightened and ran away.'

'Doesn't explain how she died!

'He must have been so angry with Zehra that he chased after her. What if he caught up with her and pushed her over the edge of the mountain! Then had everyone believe her death was an accident. And he already had an excuse for going up there in the first place.'

'Well, that's a good theory Miss Despina.'

He was impressed by her analytical discernment.

'Then again why would he? He wouldn't have traded your sister for nothing. A greedy man such as your father would want some form of payment, don't you think! To trade your sister, that is. And we can't altogether rule out that her death wasn't really an accident. I mean a frightened child in her desperation to escape wouldn't have been mindful of the hazards of her surroundings. It would have only taken a split second for the accident to occur. And before he even caught up with her. These are merely hypothetical theories until such time can be proven.'

'How on earth am I supposed to do that? I'd go look for the man myself if I knew who he was. At any cost. But where would I start looking?'

'Do you recall if this man in question came to your father's house on the night before he and your sister failed to return home?'

'I'm not sure. I was worried sick for Zehra. I thought how hungry and alone and frightened she must have been wherever she was! I never gave a thought about father.'

'Alright. Shall we get back to why I asked you here! I spoke to Yilmaz early this morning. He is the son of Mehmet the quilt-maker. I thought I'd tell you just in case you might need to speak to him in the future. He was discharged from the army a week ago. But it wouldn't have stopped this boy of yours from writing letters to you just the same. After all you did say this potter fellow read his letters to you. Yilmaz confirmed this. He told me that Rifat had sent many letters but never heard from you. He also sent you a ring.'

'A ring! Then why didn't I get it! It must have gotten lost. Just like his letters!'

'It would be most unlikely of such a coincidence.'

'Why didn't he just give it to me when he saw me last?'

'I put that question to Yilmaz myself. He said that Rifat had left it with a local jeweller close to the barracks to have it especially engraved. He wanted to surprise you!'

'He'll be so disappointed.' She told him about the gold band he'd given her in the ruins before he went into the army. And how he'd surprised her. 'He'd asked me to close my eyes and when I opened them the ring was twirling down the leather cord from under his arm and it slipped right onto my finger. It was the happiest day of my life. Until I got home that is and found father waiting for me in the yard.'

'Did he find out you were with him?'

'I was confused as to how he found out. I told him I was going to Katina's house to get her advice about the jam I was making. And told him not to expect me in the field because I'd be there most of the afternoon. As it turned out Katina scolded me for being so stupid for coming home with the ring at my neck. She told me the evidence was right in front of his eyes. The thing is he wouldn't have even seen it if he hadn't done what he did to me,' Despina complained.

'What did he do?' he suspiciously probed.

'I don't want to talk about it,' she murmured.

'It must have been something distressing. I was hoping you'd come to trust me by now. However, I won't insist.'

'He asked if the Muslim boy had touched me.' She now openly revealed. 'And if I'd shamed him. I swore that Rifat hadn't. I told him the truth Kyrio. Pureness was something I strongly believed in before marriage. But he stopped at nothing to prove me wrong. He summoned the midwife to carry out an internal examination. I'd never felt so humiliated. It was awful, just awful. I'll never forgive him!' Despina's head wilted with self-depreciation by the recollection of it all and couldn't hold back her tears.

'Here,' don't cry,' he implored, passing her his handkerchief.

'I'm sorry,' she sniffed.

'There's nothing to be sorry about. Rest assured that whatever you tell me will remain between the two of us. I promise.'

She peered up at him meekly and uttered, 'do you always have to rescue me?

He afforded her an amiable smile and said, 'well I haven't saved you yet! Though it would be a pleasant assumption if I could save you with a simple gesture of a handkerchief.'

'I washed the handkerchief you gave me as a child. Each time I open my drawer and see it there it reminds me of the day you gave it to me.'

He was touched by the gesture. 'Now tell me, have you heard the story about the frog and the scorpion! You haven't well. The frog asked the scorpion to help it cross the river, you see. The frog climbed onto the scorpion's back however midway the scorpion stung the frog and it fell into the river and drowned.'

'You still like telling stories,' she offered with a weak smile.

He sensed that she had not understood the moral of his story. Perhaps it was best he kept his thoughts to himself since he had yet to establish why her letters had gone missing. He now thought about all that Yilmaz had told him earlier in the morning.

'Rifat thought at least she would have written to thank him for the ring he sent her. Then a few weeks before I was discharged one did arrive. He wasn't feeling well that day so I collected it from the mailroom myself. I sensed that it brought bad news and so I decided to read the letter before I read it to him. And I was right.'

'What did the letter disclose?' Pandelis enquired of the gentle-eyed boy with the short cropped dark hair.

'Well, something in the lines that she'd fallen out of love with him. And that she'd been promised to a man of her own kind. And that he should forget her. But I was sure it wasn't Despina who wrote it because I was familiar with her handwriting. And there was this cute thing that

Rifat and she had going on between them, you know a nickname they both had for each other. Rifat called Despina his 'cherry,' and she called him her 'apple.'

'Then I assume that this pet name was omitted from the letter.'

'That's right! I've never known a man to love a woman so much. I knew he'd be heartbroken. I could have easily faked the words but decided it best he hear the news from somebody else. Just so I wouldn't have to witness his despair. I put the letter amongst his clothes in his locker hoping he wouldn't find it before I was discharged. I knew how wrong I was not to pass it on to him. May Allah forgive me!'

'You are a man of conscience good Muslim. One is a mountain behind a good friend's back. You just tried to stop the bullet that would stab his heart. Do you have any idea who could have sent the letter?'

'That dirt bag father of hers. Who else could it have been?' Yilmaz scowled.

'Then you must have known that he opposed his daughter's relationship with Rifat!'

'Sure! He hates Rifat because he's Muslim. He treats his daughter like a slave. As if she owed him her life. He even beats her. Our religion states that no man has the right to raise his hand to a woman. Rifat never stopped talking about how beautiful and intelligent Despina was. He said she'd wanted to study literature and Greek history. He mentioned something about her being eligible for a government scholarship. And she was expecting a letter from the university to sit for her entrance exam. I don't know what happened.

Maybe she never got the scholarship. You seem surprised. I thought you would have known since you said she was a good friend of yours.'

'She's a modest girl,' Pandelis offered.

He thanked him for the information and then headed back to Rizo to have a word with Mayor Neophytos. He'd ordered coffee and then sat at a table pretending to read the newspaper. 'Have you seen Spyros lately?'

'Haven't seen that sonofabitch since I kicked him out fourteen years ago.' The mayor scorned as he passed him his coffee.

'Why did you?' he probed.

'Don't want no fledgling slayer in here. I'm a respectful man, not an abettor to a crime!'

He was amused at the way in which the waning silver-haired man articulated his candid opinion on a felony that had yet to be attested. 'Hard to believe a man could kill his own daughter?'

'No man would! But that's just it! The girl wasn't his daughter! Anyone in this village will tell you the same thing!'

Pandelis took a sip of his coffee then casually asked, 'then if not his, whose was she?'

'Spyros had a mistress who had a daughter out of wedlock. That's the girl that died, if you're wondering,' he revealed.

'The mistress, where is she? Hmm!' He took another sip of his coffee.

'The whore ran away! He took his revenge out on the young girl!'

Pandelis thrust a hand under his hat and scratched at his head, as if trying to find some defensible reasoning behind the perverseness of it all. Then that man Georgios impinged on his conscience. He was the man he'd sent to buy the jam from Despina some time back. He'd told him things that day that he'd passed off as purely gossip.

But now everything seemed in line with the elderly's way of think-ing. A particular pattern of events had occurred that couldn't be just happenstance anymore. Or were they?

He readjusted his hat and said, 'I must say you get to hear more stories than I do.'

'The tobacco merchant should have been locked up years ago. Those police officers down at the station in Lemnos are a bunch of lazy scatter brains. Left that psychopath to be roaming wild like an uncontrollable plague amongst the people in this village. I don't mind that daughter of his coming here. She's a polite girl. Haven't seen her for a while.'

'To collect her letters, you mean!' He deliberately said, but when he caught the elderly's questioning stare he added, 'well, she wouldn't have any other business in a kafenio full of men.'

'Right you are.'

'If you haven't seen her then somebody else must have been collect-ing her mail.'

'I wouldn't know about that. My wife's been dispatching the mail for a few months now. It used to be my job to sort out the mailbag when it arrives of an evening from hora. But it's that mother of mine you see. She had a nasty fall. It's the arthritis you see.

She's been delivering babies all her life and now she's grumpy all the time because she can't do the things she did before. Forgive me good Chris-tian but why are you so concerned about the tobacco merchant's daughter.'

'It seems her mail has gone astray. For considerable months I'm told to believe.'

'Strange. I don't see how that could happen. I understand now why you asked if that father of hers has been in. I believe that nice daughter of his is betrothed. To a Muslim boy in this village. He wouldn't have been too happy about that. Maybe that air-brain has been sending somebody else.'

'You think it might have been Katina! She's a friend of his daughter's.'

'Ah, Katina the Maimed! I'll have a word with Erica. I myself haven't seen her since that sister of hers stopped writing. That was some more than twenty years ago.'

'Her sister wrote her letters!'

'Why would you be surprised? She's employed by you, isn't she?

'I must have forgotten she had a sister. Come to think of it she even told me where she lived but I seem to have forgotten that too. Perhaps you could tell me.' He kept up the charade.

'Hmm, I don't seem to be able to recall that myself.'

Pandelis left the kafenio. He hadn't solved the mystery of the missing letters. However, he had found out more than he'd anticipated just the same. He now drew his attention back to Despina. 'There's always a message to be learned in a tale. And most are true.' He offered with a side glance. 'I feel sorry for all that you've been through in life.

One requires enormous strength and courage to endue so much grief. Your mother would have been very proud of you Miss. Now about this boy of yours. I've been thinking about what you said. It could well be that he's been posted elsewhere. And if he has then I'm sure he'll write the moment he gets a chance.'

Despina sat pale-faced, trembling and confused. 'What if he really has been deployed to the streets? What if he's been killed?' She wept.

'Please try and stay calm.'

'How can I when my life has just ended! I can't breathe without Rifat! He's my everything. We've made so many dreams together. I'd rather die than live without him. I'll go see Yilmaz myself, talk to him. He'll know what's happened!' Hastily she stood up, felt unsteady and blurry-eyed, and then unexpectedly everything around her spun and she fell to the ground.

'Miss Despina! Despina! Are you alright? Clearly, she wasn't he reasoned and called out for help. He looked up to see the last person he wanted to see coming towards him.

Quickly he scooped her up in his arms and when Katina observed this intimate gesture she was enraged.

'Don't just stand there staring woman! Summon the doctor at once!' he shouted.

Katina felt utterly degraded by the sudden backlash, and she hoped with all her might that Despina would never recover to find herself swathed in the arms of the only man she'd ever adored.

When Sofia saw her son come into the entrance hall she asked, 'what happened? Who is this girl? And why is she here?'

'Now's not the time for questions!' He censured as he mounted the staircase for the guest room and where he placed the girl atop the bed.

'What happened?' Despina asked drowsily.

'It seems you fainted Miss. Doctor is on his way.' He was seated by the edge of the bed.

Shortly the doctor came through the door and Pandelis informed him what happened. Doctor Grigori Savva took the girl's pulse, monitored her respiratory function with the aid of a stethoscope, flashed a torch in her eyes and lastly checked her pulse.

'Her pulse is a bit low and she's somewhat pale and cold.'

'So, why has she fainted?'

'I can't be sure. Has she fainted before?'

'I don't know. Do you have any idea why?'

'I can't be sure. Her pulse is low which might indicate anaemia. Sometimes if the blood doesn't have enough healthy red blood cells it can reduce oxygen flow to the body's organs. Though she doesn't appear to be in any immediate danger. However, I'd like to carry out some blood tests. I'll write a referral for the pathology for you to pick up from my surgery in the morning. In the meantime, keep up the fluids to prevent dehydration. And she'll need to rest.' He moved away from the bed and then said, 'I'd like a few words with you outside before I go.'

Both men went out into the hallway and then doctor Savva asked, 'is the girl a staff member?

'Nothing like that Grigori. We became acquainted by chance. Why do you ask? Is something wrong?'

'I noticed some marks on her upper back and beneath the right arm. I'm familiar with this kind of bruising. Is the girl married?' He asserted solemnly.

'Betrothed to be married, you could say! Do you suspect she's been abused? Pandelis asked alarmed.

'Unfortunately, it appears that way! He must be a brutal man then!'

'Indeed not! The boy is very much devoted to Miss Despina. Though her father is a monstrous and inhuman man of the worst kind.'

'Well, if it was him that did this to his daughter then I'd have to agree.' Doctor Savva proclaimed. 'Undoubtedly it will be a problematic issue to be solved.'

'Don't be so sure Grigori. By the time I've dealt with that man he'll be crawling out of that hovel of his like a snail in search of the sun.'

The lean, grey-bearded physician found his friend's observation amusing however sternly advised, 'I accept your concern Pandelis. But the girl isn't a minor so you can't intervene. Only she has the right to make a complaint to the authorities. Though I doubt if she will. Sadly, many women exposed to such violence don't in fear of retaliation from a spouse or parent. If anything, they are liable to suffer even worse abuse. What about the girl's betrothed!'

Pandelis explained the situation then said, 'until such time she can stay here in the guest room.'

'Hmm, might be risky, don't you think?'

'She has nowhere else to go. To send her home would be like throwing her into a lion's den.'

'I understand, but if her father finds out that you're protecting his daughter he might retaliate. Things could get real nasty! I can't add much more to that! With the exception that all ends well. I'd imagine you have enough on your hands with your father gone. It was very sudden. The responsibility of managing a large corporation requires a sound and sharp mind. Though I'm sure with your experience in the field of economics and agriculture you'll be worthy of carrying on his legacy. I wish you success

Pandelis. Well, I guess I'll be off. I trust you won't forget that referral. I'll give you a call when I get the results back. It usually takes a few days.'

'Leave it with me! I'll see you out!'

'No need! He thrust out a hand. 'I know my way around by now!' Grigori Savva had established a close relationship with the Gapsalis family as their physician for over three decades. Pandelis was about to enter the guest room again when he saw his mother striding up the hallway towards him and uttering a volume of words under her breath.

'Is something wrong mother?'

'Don't tell me you're going to let that girl stay in this house! In the guest room!'

'Children aren't the only ones who need to be rescued and housed mother,' he condemned.

'This is not a shelter for the sick and poor son! I demand she leaves this house at once!' She stamped a foot.

'Perhaps I should reconsider your position as a member of the charity committee.'

'Why has this girl come to you? And who is she?'

'She's the tobacco merchant's daughter.'

'What! Sofia's jaw sunk. 'Have you lost your mind son? I won't stand for it! Resili! Disgrace.

'I'm only doing what any humanitarian would do! I suggest you do the same or otherwise you might end up as a disgraced fatality of your own actions.'

'You can't be serious!' She exclaimed with arms in the air, stunned by the anomaly of her son's actions. 'Do you really think that people will

applaud us for rescuing the daughter of the most despised and fraudulent man in our village? What about Katina? The girl can stay with her!'

'She's needed here!' He advised purposefully, though factually he
was of the same opinion as his mother.

'She's the last person I need here!' Sofia was infuriated by the sheer
thought that he could consider such a pitiful maid to be indispensable
in her household.

'Now Grigori has informed me that Miss Despina must rest and
take plenty of fluids. He's requested blood tests. And asked that I call
into his surgery in the morning to pick up the referral for the pathology
department at the Famagusta general hospital.'

'It'll take you two hours to drive there!' she disputed.

'You don't have to remind me. We own a hotel there and I drive there
frequently remember.'

Suspiciously she watched him open the door and peer into the room
to check on the girl. When he turned to face her again, to her astonish-
ment he said, 'in the meantime have the kitchen staff prepare food for
Miss Despina. And ensure she gets fresh fruit and water brought to her
room. And she'll need a robe and slippers after a bath. And a change of
clothes. I'm sure you'll find something new in your wardrobe.'

Sofia was unable to fathom what she was hearing. And the more her
son spoke in the girl's defence the more exasperated she became. And
he'd addressed her as 'Miss.' The latter alone intensified her hatred for
the girl even more. If that was even possible.

'You expect our staff to treat this girl as if she were a distinguished
guest in this house! The house your father established through many

years of hard sweat! Shame on you son! Your father would be outraged by your actions!'

'Just consider all the things you have to live for when others have nothing to live for.'

Without further ado he opened the door of the guestroom, walked in, and then slammed it shut in Sofia's face.

She turned and headed back down the staircase, clutching to the rail for support, fearing that at any moment she would succumb to the same fate as that despicable intruder lying atop the satin cover of the bed in the guestroom.

Feebly she crossed the entrance hall and entered the kitchen to find Thea and Lydia seated at the table and stuffing vine leaves. 'I can smell something bad!' Thea whispered, nudging Lydia's arm.

'Oh, my head is splitting! God what is my sin? My son has lost his mind! What misfortune has found me?' Sofia groaned as she slumped into a chair.

Just then Katina appeared through the door and asked guardedly, 'what is this misfortune you speak of?'

'Kyrio Pandelis has lost his mind!' Lydia revealed. Thea elbowed her again by her imprudent remark.

'Lost his mind! Why would he?' Katina asked.

Sofia gave her a foul stare and then said, 'you have twenty foxes inside your head. Ask one of them!'

'Is this how you perceive me? Katina uttered red-faced. 'As a sly headed maid! And one who merits to be insulted by your mockery! I won't stand for it!'

'Then get out of my house you scourge!' Sofia retorted. 'I'm the one who's had to put up with you all these years. And yet you have the nerve to stand before me with the opinion of self-importance! I would have thrown you out years ago! If not for my late husband.

Now git! And take that field girl with you! You are nothing more than a pathetic caterpillar that feeds in this earth!'

'You once crawled around in the red earth of your father's potato fields in Ayia Napa before you sweet talked your way into those plump pockets of your late husband's trousers. And don't blame me that Despina is here. I know as much as you do as to why she has come.'

'I'm not the fool you think I am! She's here for the same reason you've hung around like a curse in my home over the past twenty-three years! She's no more than a foolish young girl who thinks she can steal the heart of the main character. My son has a basket of beautiful kittens! All of whom are the daughters of wealthy and dignified families.'

'I'm sure he has! Though none can compare to that charming stray he's found.' Katina remarked, but just then flinched by what she thought was the slap of her own hand across her cheek by her unconstrained praise in Despina's defence.

Sofia instantly came to her feet and took firm grip of her arm. 'If you dare to throw another insult then not only will you be impaired of a leg but also a tongue! Understood? Now git!'

She gave her a forceful shove which only reinforced Katina's courage to even the score more with the woman who'd tormented her for years.

'More damning is that she happens to be the tobacco merchant's daughter. I'd hate to think what her father will do when he finds out your son is keeping her here. I'd say he'll come up here and hack the flesh off his bones with a scythe.

And I can assure you he has plenty of those lying around in his field. Or he might kill him! Such a man is capable of anything!' Katina removed her apron and tossed it at her feet.

'You might need this to mop up the mess!'

She marched out and as she passed through the front gate, Murat the driver acknowledged her respectfully. 'Nice evening Miss Katina!' When she atypically returned him a nasty stare the stocky man stood there curling his bushy moustache and wandering what he'd said or done wrong. Tempestuously she began to make her way down the slope when she heard a voice cry out.

'Katina Wait! Wait!'

'Damn you! How long must I wait Pandelis? I've waited half a lifetime for the chance to fall into your arms when it took Despina only a few minutes.

CHAPTER SEVENTEEN

Pedhoulas 3rd of December 1963

Dilara's rubber boots squelched in the snow and her warm breath vaporised in the frosty air as she panted uphill. She was relieved to find the bus hadn't left for Nicosia when she arrived in the village's square. She raised her knitted shawl over her head in order to conceal her identity by the local men boarding the bus.

She was known by some of the locals as Sister Dilara from the Holy Trinity orphanage. Others recognised her as Doctor Jihan's clinical assistant. Some even assumed her to be his mistress, though if it be known to Dilara she would have affirmed the accusations as untrue. She waited for the passengers to climb on board before she waved the bus driver down.

'*Kalimera*, Sister Dilara. What can I do for you?' The elderly driver was a friendly man with plump vigorous cheeks and an eye-catching rowdy grey moustache.

She returned his greeting and then said, 'I understand this bus pulls up at the bus depot at Makarios Square in Lefkosia! Is there a connecting bus service travelling to the Kapassa region in the north? To the village of Rizokarpaso to be precise.'

'Why I do believe there is. Why do you ask? Did you want a lift to Makarios Square?'

'No, but I need to ask a big favour of you! The matter is urgent.'

'It must be since you are here so early in the morning on such a miserable day. Now how can I assist you?'

'I have an important letter to be delivered to a good friend and it would take days or even weeks to arrive by post. I'd be most grateful if you would ask the bus driver travelling there to pass it on to my friend.'

'How will he know who this friend of yours is? Where will he find her?'

'Her name's written on the envelope,' she passed it to him.

'A last name would help!' he revealed.

'I don't know it.'

'I thought you said she was a good friend?'

'Never mind. Tell the bus driver when he arrives to ask for Katina the maid. She works at the Gapsalis residence!'

'Best I write it down on the envelope. What was the name again?' He was holding the pen from his pocket.

'Gapsalis residence! This matter is confidential. And it's very important I receive confirmation of its delivery.'

'Very well, leave it with me. Where's the best place to find you?'

'I prefer you come to the orphanage. If it's no trouble,' Dilara instructed wisely.

'I pass that way around six of an evening on my way back to the village,' he informed.

'Most grateful. Now I won't hold you up as there are men waiting to get to work.'

'If you'll be heading back to the orphanage then climb aboard and I'll give you a lift before you freeze.'

Dilara momentarily wondered if her presence on the bus would raise people's suspicions. Though she dismissed the thought for she had far more important things on her mind than to worry about other than what people might think, thus quickly climbed aboard.

'Come in Miss Dilara! Come!' Sister Louisa spoke with the sincere empathetic nature of a Christian nun and whose only purpose was to serve God and to others in need. The gesture of her small hands was just as placid as she indicated a wooden pew against the stone wall of the simple space of the room.

Dilara sneezed a few times for her office was just as chilly as the rest of the rooms of the orphanage.

'I hope you're not coming down with a cold! A hot cup of herb Tsai will do you good. I can fetch it for you now if you like?'

'No need Sister,' she efficiently offered.

'Have you considered Mr Jihan's marriage proposal yet?'

'An offer of marriage is not one to be taken lightly Sister. And there is my work here with the children.'

'Please Miss Dilara don't punish yourself. After all God sanctioned the unification between man and woman. The nuns and I feel indebted for your loyalty and support over the years. How old are you may I ask?'

'I'm forty-three, according to the Greek yearbook.'

'It only seems like yesterday you came through the gates of this orphanage on that camel of yours. You kept it harnessed under a tree at the rear of the yard. The animal brought much happiness to the children here at the time. When it died you cried as if it was your own child I remember.'

'It was the only family I had.' Dilara offered pensively, and then thought to ask, 'why do you ask how old I am?'

'It's only natural that I should ask! The nuns and I have had many conversations about you over the years. Nothing bad I can assure you! Besides it would be a sin to denounce one of God's servants. What I'm trying to say is that one doesn't have to be a man to be attracted to a self-confident, intelligent and attractive woman. Not forgetting your lute playing and singing talent. Even the nightingales would be jealous of your melodious voice. Oh, you don't have to blush Miss Dilara. It's the truth.'

'There isn't much to tell you except that I'm a refugee from Turkey and of Armenian roots. My family were kicked out of Turkey in 1922. After losing my parents I came here with a family of gypsies from Syria when the Cypriot government was welcoming Turkish Armenian refugees into the country.'

'My condolences for your loss.' Though her enquiry as to the real reason why she was here was unreciprocated. And she hadn't mentioned what happened to the family from Syria. 'Haven't you considered a family of your own?'

'At my age! I'd think not Sister. Besides the children are my family. This has been my home over the past fourteen years.'

'Just as it takes a special breed of women to commit themselves to God's work it takes a unique woman to devote herself to helping needy children. The children in the orphanage have no choice but you do. Mr Jihan has a comfortable house and earns a substantial income and could provide a most favourable life for you. Don't get me wrong I'm not trying to force you away by any means. Besides it would be our great loss. You've maintained a close relationship with him for some years now. Not only have you helped in his clinic you've also nursed him after suffering a couple of minor heart attacks. These aren't merely acts of charity Miss Dilara. They are endeavours of deep adoration and allegiance that a woman holds for a man close to her heart.'

'I can assure you we are just good friends. Besides, Jihan bey has family. And what would Nilufer think?'

'Nilufer is mature enough to understand the needs of her father!' Sister Louisa offered wisely.

'A marriage would only strain their relationship,' Dilara revealed.

'I don't see how! She has her own life to think about!'

'Things aren't what they seem. And I can assure you I'm the last person she wants her father to be with.'

'What gives you reason to think that?'

'I've been aware of Nilufer's behaviour when I'm around for some time now. A few years ago I'd gone into her room...'

'Why did you?' Sister Louisa was eager to ask.

'Sui-Lee the housemaid had forgotten Nilufer's bed linen that needed to go to the laundry. She asked me kindly if I'd go and fetch them for her. Anyway, in the bedroom I noticed a musical dome on the dresser. I was curious and asked her where she got it from when she got home. Well, it would have been better if I hadn't asked. She was furious. She told me I had no right snooping in her room. Or to be in her father's house. She told me to go back to that shelter where I belonged and never come back.'

'Sounds like she had a bad day. Maybe all that studying has caught up with her. Did you tell Mr Jihan?'

'Of course not! Nor did I tell him about that other time she accused me of trying to poison her when I offered her a bowl of rice custard. And it was only after Sui-Lee saw me in tears she told me that Nilufer was allergic to goat milk. How was I to have known! I thought that she'd appreciate my being around. I was wrong. But I guess no other woman can replace a child's biological mother. Do you know how her mother died Sister?'

'She died after giving birth to a still child. I think it was a ruptured blood vessel, or something of the sort,' Sister Louisa revealed.

'How is that even possible?' Dilara stressed.

'She wouldn't be the first unfortunate woman to have died under similar circumstances. Now let's get on with why you are here! I hope you haven't come to tell me one of our little doves is sick! Come down with a cold!

'What, is someone sick did you say?' Dilara asked absently.

'You seem a tad out of sorts yourself this morning. Is something bothering you?'

'Then it could only mean that Nilufer isn't his real daughter.'

'Clearly though he hasn't told you that either! Sister Louisa announced briskly. 'This I might add puts me in a difficult situation. If he wanted to tell you he would have by now.'

'I need to know more about the girl's past!'

'What is it you want to know? And more importantly why do you want to know?'

'Perhaps if I knew more about her then it might help me understand her better,' Dilara smiled.

The petite nun wasn't entirely convinced of her excuse but afforded her a smile just the same and said, 'I'm sure Nilufer is just as curious about you. Considering that I myself only just found out something about you. And that's after fourteen years. However, I'll provide you with the information based on your utmost caution in this matter.'

'I swear on your Christian bible I won't breathe a word to anybody,' she affirmed.

'Mr Jihan never remarried after his wife died. Nobody knew who the child was or where she came from. Or even knew her age. Though it was estimated she was around eight or nine.'

'Her name is Nilufer! Dilara was quick to affirm. 'The name means 'water lily,' in Turkish.

'It can only be that Mr Jihan named her after a family member. Perhaps it was his late wife's name. Or maybe it was the name that he and his wife chose if it was to be a girl before it was still born. Nilufer was found further up the slope of the valley near the orchard where one of the nuns had been picking cherries that day.

It was as though she'd dropped from the sky though more factually believed to have fallen from the edge of the mountaintop. At first the nun thought it was a mountain goat that had gone astray and got entangled in the brushwood. You can imagine her shock when she discovered it was a child.'

'How can anybody be sure it was an accident? What if someone pushed her?'

'One would have to be possessed by God's adversary to execute such a wrongdoing,' Sister Louisa asserted.

'People do drastic things in desperate situations. What if Nilufer was born out of wedlock! Perhaps she was a burden that imposed a threat to society, or someone.'

'There are shelters such as ours at the Holy Trinity for such unwanted children.'

'Were any of the child's belongings found?'

'You might like to check with Sister Charikla. Why do you ask?'

'I thought someone would have figured that out Sister. I mean if nobody knew who she was or where she came from then obviously the best place to start looking for clues would be an item of clothing. Or a toy or schoolbook with the child's name on it.'

'You're right, however one wouldn't consider such things when a child's life is at risk. It was fortunate that a local farmer working in a nearby orchard heard the nun's cries for help that day. He was quick to summon Mr Jihan and who in turn transported the child to the Limassol hospital with equal expediency and where doctors there treated her superficial wounds and suspected multiple broken bones. He made frequent trips to the hospital to see how she was progressing. Even sat by her bedside for most of the day in the hope she would recall who she was or where she came from.

He sacrificed a lot to raise her as his own daughter. Though her somatic injuries had healed over time it was her emotional state he was concerned about as she'd suffered a great deal of psychological trauma after the accident. And then she got an awful virus infection that left her paralysed. Then Mr Jihan had the difficult task of ensuring that Nilufer made a full recovery. And he had his clinic to run and was incapable of tending to her essential daily needs. He hired a full-time nurse to bathe, dress and feed her and assist her on the bedpan. Not to mention the medication and the rehabilitation process and the ongoing sessions with the neurologist.'

'What did he have to say about the paralysis?'

'He carried out tests which revealed it to be a disease known as encephalitis. Seemingly this disease also attacks the brain cells. You'll also appreciate that Nilufer lapsed in her schooling. Mr Jihan didn't compromise when it came to her education. He hired a private tutor. All these things add up to an enormous amount of money. I can entirely understand why he was resolved to claim the child if nobody else did.'

Sister Louisa paused to cast her eyes on the flurry of snowflakes through the window. The purity and whiteness of the fall prompted an image before her eyes. She saw a man coming through the gates of the orphanage just days after the child's accident. She diverted her eyes to regard her confidante once again, breathed heavily and then soberly disclosed, 'I have something to tell you. It's about Nilufer. I know that the Lord's clemency alone doesn't warrant my actions. I feel that it is time I must speak. Therefore, I must ask you once again that whatever I'm about to say will remain between us.'

'I swear on your Christian Virgin Mother,' Dilara assured.

'You see someone did come here looking for her. It was a man '

'A man! Dilara intercepted with alarm. 'What was his name? And how old was he? And what did he do for a living?

Sister Louisa readjusted her glasses then her small brown eyes afforded her colleague a dubious stare. 'Of what importance is the man's age! Or how he earned his bread. He came to tell me that he thought he knew who the girl was.'

'What made him think that?' Dilara was now seated on the edge of the pew.

'Perhaps if you didn't interrupt then you'll find out. His name was Costa. He was reluctant to give his name. He asked me if the matter had been reported to the authorities. I told him that I didn't know. He said he had something to tell me providing I didn't go to the authorities. I assured him that if the matter was other than that of a serious crime that I wouldn't. He said he thought he knew who the child was. You see some days before the girl was found he'd met a merchant inside the kafenio of the village he'd visited. He said this man told him he was a widower and in need of a wife. And asked him to be his proxy. Costas told him that he was also in need of a wife as he led a secluded life up in the mountains. The man invited him to his house that night for a drink and where he'd met his young daughter. The man told him he'd grown weary of raising the child on his own. His work was consumed in the field. Costa asked him if there were any grandparents that could relieve him. The man then told him that there was only a sick aunt. Had to take care of her as well. And said that he'd be willing to trade the girl for a couple of hides!'

Dilara placed a hand to her chest, let out an involuntary groan, as if at that moment she couldn't suppress the fright within there. 'I find it hard to accept that a father could consider his own young daughter as valueless as a couple of hides. Well, did he take the girl?' She expectantly asked.

'A futile question, don't you think? Or do I have to remind you that the girl in question happens to be Nilufer.'

'Why did this man come to you? And what made him think that the tobacco merchant's daughter was the same girl?' Then when she caught the force of the nun's questioning stare she asked, 'what is it?'

'I don't recall my telling you that he was a tobacco merchant Miss Dilara! What made you think that?' Sister Louisa remarked. And she had doubts about her confidante's arbitrary observations.

'I don't know. Maybe because tobacco growing has become a widespread source of income for farmers.' She replied artlessly, then added, 'well, what did he have to say?'

'He said that the day of the accident would have coincided about the time he met the merchant.'

'What he told you doesn't prove a thing! It was nothing more than a coincidence.'

'I see you are of strong mind Miss Dilara. And I also sense a kind of disavowal on your part for some odd reason by refusing to accept that what I'm telling you to be true. And I can assure you Costa had no intentions of making the young girl his wife. He swore on the Christian bible. He'd thought at the time she'd bring much joy to his lonely life.'

'Then what made him change his mind?'

'After the merchant told him he had another daughter he thought it would be a shame to separate the two young sisters. He said even if he'd agreed to take the girl, you know for the reason I already mention, he thought the girl would most likely fret for her sister and run away. What would he do then! He said he'd never forgive himself if she got lost or came to any serious harm. He said he'd left the merchant a couple of hides just the same as he felt sorry for him.'

'If he didn't take the girl then what was the point of telling you all of this? And there's no evidence to say that it was the same girl found in the orchard,' Dilara asserted.

'In his opinion he thought that the merchant had decided to come up here looking for him just the same. You know in the hope he could coax him into changing his mind. And if this was the case then the little girl must have sensed that she was going to be separated from her sister and had somehow managed to escape. Ran off. Did what he'd suspected all along. Then he decided to come down to the orphanage to see what he could find out. He said that he felt blameworthy in some way. He also said that if the girl did recover and the authorities established who she was then she'd be returned to her father. And mostly he'd try to give her away again. I told him that if by God's mercy she did recover then I'd place her here in the orphanage. You can guess the rest,' Sister affirmed.

'Did he tell you the girl's name?' She'd been bursting to ask this important question.

The holy nun threaded her hands and said, 'I can't see of what benefit it will be to you. Whatever her real name is has no bearing after all these long years. Nilufer's a grown woman.'

The name Nilufer seemed just as alien as the girl who'd come to adopt the title. 'Well, did he?' Dilara urged.

'I don't recall that he did. As we both know Nilufer has completed her studies and soon will take up employment with the state Health Department as a psychologist. Just imagine the impact it would have on her if she were to find out the truth. Not only would she feel betrayed and disheartened but also profoundly angry with her father for hiding the truth from her all these years. And what about Mr Jihan! He may not survive another heart attack!'

Despite of what the nun thought Dilara knew that Nilufer was seeing a psychiatrist. It somehow indicated that she might have been confused about her identity. Why else would she be seeing a psychiatrist? Sui-Lee the house maid had confided in her one day and said that she thought Nilufer was predisposed to depression. When deeply troubled she refused to eat and would often sit alone for hours inside her room or spend just as many hours in the pigeon house on the rooftop and talking to the pigeons as if the birds were the only ones who understood her problems.

Dilara now said, 'I'm sure that after everything you've told me that there's a space in Nilufer's mind that tells her she's not who she thinks she is. And she must be confused.'

'What makes you think that?'

'The past always returns to haunt one, Sister,' she revealed pensively.

'Does your past haunt you Miss Dilara?' She sensed that for some unfathomable reason she knew more about Nilufer than she was prepared to say. Would you like to share your burden with me in God's trust?'

'What can I say? Other than I haven't been honest with you,' Dilara finally confessed with quiet self-shame.

Sister Louisa afforded her a gracious smile and said, 'I've already established that. Everybody has a past. Without a past there is no present. Because the past is often the foundation that maps one's life, or who they become. And if you should choose to open your heart to me it should be of your own free will. Let me ask you something, would I be right in sensing that the chapel and this shelter was your way of atonement all these years?'

'It has been a place where I could hide. Somewhere I could forget my unhappy past. The open fields had become my home for many years. The family that raised me were performers,' she revealed.

'Then it explains the talent! Do go on,' Sister Louisa urged.

'We travelled around the countryside and performed wherever we camped. Also, coffee readings for extra para. I was not yet nineteen at the time I met a young soldier. He was stationed at the barracks opposite the field where we were camped. There he was this dashing and tall young boy dressed in military uniform. I was attracted to him the moment I laid eyes on him. His smile alone made my heart flap. I'm sure he noticed how self-conscious I was of his presence. And that he was just as attracted to me as I of him.'

'Did a romantic relationship ensue?' Sister Louisa enquired.

'Not for long, but long enough for me to fall pregnant just the same.'

'You had a child? Have a child!' Sister Louisa corrected herself.

'That's right!' Dilara murmured.

'Then where is it? With the father? The soldier boy?'

'He was discharged before I could tell him.'

'Then you must have left the child with the refugee family you were with?'

'I was too afraid and ashamed to tell them. Though I reasoned that with each passing month they'd realise my condition and so I decided to part with them. It was a difficult decision. One that I'd come to bitterly regret,' Dilara said pensively.

'I can only imagine. You said you regretted leaving the family. What did you decide to do? Where did you go?'

'I made the mistake of trying to find him. I didn't even know where he was from. I drifted around the countryside on my camel in the hope that I would. I was young and foolish Sister. And fearless. It never crossed my mind that I'd endanger the life of my unborn.'

'And that of your own! An unborn infant thrives off his mother's nourishment! Otherwise, it could be stillborn! How did you manage to exist?'

'My musical talent kept me going for a while. I played wherever I thought there'd be an audience. A religious fair or near a marketplace. Not enough to survive on just the same. Anyway, one day I came to a village called Lemnos in the north. I was squatted by the roadside and singing an Armenian folk song. A group of men from a nearby *kafenio* had gathered. When they'd left a woman came over to me and praised my voice. She asked if I was Turkish. I told her that I was Turkish

Armenian. She then went on to tell me that it wasn't right for a young and unwed girl to be making such a spectacle of herself. I burst into tears and told her it wasn't by choice but a matter of survival.

She was sympathetic of my situation but warned that in my condition I needed a safe place to lodge until my baby was born. Otherwise, the outcome would be bleak.'

'What did she propose for you to do since you had nowhere to go?' Sister Louisa asked.

'She knew of a Turkish Cypriot family in the village who'd be willing to take me in. And went on to tell me that she lived in the neighbouring village of Rizo which was about a mile or so from Lemnos.'

'I hope you agreed,' Sister Louisa counselled.

'What choice did I have?'

'Then I gather this charitable midwife delivered the infant!'

'Some six weeks later. Then a few days later she came back to visit me in Lemnos.'

'Oh, did she have post -natal concerns?'

'She came to try and persuade me into giving the infant away. And she knew of a childless Muslim couple from her village that would welcome a child that was one of their own kind and could offer it a good life.'

'God always finds the answer when we our lost.'

'Not always Sister.'

'You mean you didn't give the child away? Why not?'

'The day I went looking for the midwife everything changed. I did what she asked.'

'What did she ask Miss Dilara?'

'To become a milk mana for the infant that she'd delivered only hours before.'

'What about the infant's mother?'

'The midwife said she hadn't recovered after the birth. It was a strange case like none she'd seen before. Thought she'd lost her mind.'

Just then a fear-provoking thought impinged on Dilara's conscience that set her mind searching for the smallest defence that would tell her she was wrong. But there was no doubt in her mind that she was right.

'Allah!' She voiced by the awakening. 'That girl under the house wasn't that man's sister! It was his wife! And I believed him! How stupid I was!'

'What man? Whose sister? And whose wife?' Sister Louisa enquired confused.

'The man who'd employed me as his infant's milk mana. He was a sadistic narcissist. And a jealous and manipulating man that no woman should ever have the misfortune of meeting. I wasn't yet twenty. And a destitute and homeless single mother without family or a home. Not only was I desperate but also very raw to the deceitful traits of mankind. And it was easy for me to surrender to all his acts of kindness. By this stage I'd moved into his house.'

'The girl under the house! Are you saying she was his wife? And he told you it was his sister? And you realised this just now?' The midwife had forewarned you what had happened and yet you failed to see the interconnection linked to that of his mad wife and that of the fabricated story that she was his sister.

But what amazes me the most is that neither the midwife nor this man had confirmed that the woman who'd succumbed to infirmity at childbirth had died and yet you went on imprudently assuming she had,' Louisa rightfully lectured.

'Allah forgive me for not figuring things out for myself!'

'I can only sympathise with you as I'm sure this man was gloating when he accepted your helplessness and naivety while bullying you,' Louisa asserted.

'It's all coming back to me now. He called his wife Bebek. And despite her irrational behaviour she really did have the angelic face of a child. You know I think she understood that it was her own infant I was nurturing. She'd gently stroke the infant in my arms with such longing in her eyes. Pretty grey eyes they were. The tortoise shell comb she wore in her hair reminded me of the one I once had. Her bed was a timber board and a pillow of flat stone,' Dilara revealed.

'Why wasn't she in an asylum? What a vile man! May the Lord rightly punish him for all his wrongdoings!' Sister Louisa settled with fortitude.

'When under the influence of alcohol and cannabis he turned into an even worse monster. He broke out into a delirious frenzy. I can just imagine what he did to his young wife. He must have accused her of adultery. And persecuted and beat her like he did me. I was on the brink of despair. I even thought about taking my own life.'

Sister Louisa averted her eyes again to the falling snow simultaneously comparing its calmness and cleanliness compared to that of the turmoil and adversities one was confronted with in this life.

'I might have if it wasn't for those three children,' Dilara went on despondently.

'Three children! Don't tell me you had a child with this man?' Sister Louisa exclaimed, turning to face her, then instantly felt the breath sucked out of her when she announced, 'I had a son.'

'Then where is he? Did you leave him with this man? His father?'

'He's with the Muslim family the midwife told me about.'

'And your other child? Where is it?'

'I left my daughter Zehra with him,' Dilara confessed regretfully.

'I don't believe what I'm hearing! You forfeited your daughter to be shepherded by God's antagonist! Did you think she would remain a child forever? A man is prone to lust Miss Dilara. Especially towards a daughter that is not of his own blood.'

At that moment a deluge of tears soaked Dilara's cheeks and Sister Louisa carefully watched her dip a hand under her shawl and remove a handkerchief from inside her coat pocket and then swipe at her eyes. 'May Allah punish him if he lay hand on my daughter!' Dilara sniffed.

'It is written in the Christian bible; "when lust is conceived it bringeth forth sin and when sin is finished it bringeth forth death." Do forgive me for my forthrightness. It wasn't my intention to upset or frighten you. I was merely expressing the facts. Undoubtedly though given the serious-ness of your circumstances at the time it must have been an extremely difficult decision.'

'Harder than anyone could imagine. He would have killed me if I'd stayed. Those three children would have been orphaned. It was two years into the war. It was either see the children perish or entrust them to God. Omer was my youngest born.

I never would have become his mistress if I'd known what type of a man he was! Had his child! I'd bonded with my milk child as if she were my own daughter. Despina was a sweet-natured child with grey eyes.'

'If this man lied to you then he must have sold the same story to those children. And they wouldn't have known that the sick aunt was really their biological mother. In very much the same way as not knowing they weren't real sisters. And they'll probably never find out! If he'd never confessed the truth, that is. It's a heartbreaking thought.'

'I can never make up for the great injustice I've caused those children,' she informed despondently.

'May the Lord be pardoning of your transgressions and be accepting of your predicament Miss Dilara.' Then upon reflection added, 'that man must have become enraged after you abducted the son he'd fathered. And forced him to raise a daughter that wasn't his. I doubt very much if he could have coped on his own caring for two toddlers. Almost impossible. Weren't you scared he'd come looking for you! Seek revenge!'

'I had nightmares for a long time. I'm still frightened even after twenty years. You know, always expecting him to appear from behind some shadow or corner.' She raised the handkerchief in her hand and dabbed at her tears.

All this mournful talk had weakened the small holy nun and she sensed a foreboding presence in the room, and at once briskly rubbed at her arms when she felt an icy tremor seep her fragile bones. She got up and walked over to the timber closet alongside her desk, opened it, stared at the bottle of whisky there, ignored it, and withdrew an old grey military blanket from inside. 'You might like one for yourself to warm your legs.'

When she declined her offer the nun acknowledged her confidante with a slight nod before she sat down behind her desk.

She covered her legs with the blanket, laced her hands and then expediently said, 'hadn't you ever thought about the seriousness of the outcome if this man found out in some way or another that the boy was being raised by this family in his village?'

'All I could think about at the time was running for my life before he discovered I was gone and had taken the boy with me. I'd managed to secretly meet up with the midwife the previous day to arrange a meeting place on the eve of my escape. The weather I remember was treacherous. It had rained so hard that winter that the roads had turned to swamps. I'd left with very few provisions in the dead of night. And I had to wait until he passed out drunk and the children were asleep before I could leave the house. That was the last time I saw them.' Just then yet another downpour of tears washed over her face.

'May the Lord Jesus ease your grief and give you strength.' The holy nun offered nodding meditatively, and then asked, 'you must have given the boy a name!'

'Omer. I named him after my late father. He'd be going on twenty-two now,' Dilara offered with silent reflection.

'Then I gather the two girls wouldn't have been much older when you abandoned them. And they would have grown into young women themselves. Did you ever think of a way to see them again? Or contact them? What about a friend that you could have kept in touch with?' Sister Louisa offered sensibly.

'I had one friend. Her name is Katina. In fact, only this morning I sent her a letter to enquire about them.'

'Why now after twenty years?'

'I've been having bad dreams lately.'

'I find it hard to believe that it was the reason that encouraged you to write Miss Dilara. And this friend of yours might think the same thing if you'd given her the same excuse. Why didn't you write sooner?'

'I should have but fear prevailed. If Katina told him where I was then he'd surely come after me.'

'I thought you said she was your friend! Forgive my confusion but I sense that with the exclusion of your fear of this man there is something else that concerns you. Do you think Katina might be related to this man in some way?'

'That's right.'

'In what way?'

'I think he might be her brother-in-law. And that his wife is Katina's sister.'

'Then that would mean your milk child Despina is Katina's niece Miss Dilara?'

'You're right! I probably wouldn't have figured it out if I hadn't had this conversation with you today. But it's all coming back now. I overheard her one day calling her sister by the name of Anna... no it was Ariana, that's right. Then there was that awful argument I overheard between that man and whom we can assume is her brother -in- law. A quarrel would be a mild assertion. It almost turned into bloodshed '

'Good Lord! The nun broke in restlessly. 'It must have been a serious matter. Well, did you find out what it was all about?'

'It was over that field of his. He got all fired up and said, "you think a dowry of a few stretches of land to sow a handful of miserable seeds would be enough to compensate me for a contract of marriage!"' Dilara revealed.

'Sounds like Katina used the field as bait and Ariana was the unsuspecting pawn. Obviously though this brother-in-law of hers wasn't satisfied. He must have felt cheated at having received the burnt end of the stick,' Sister Louisa said.

'Why should he? Dilara forcefully asserted. 'He must have known from the start what the agreement was. Even if it be just a few stretches of land. It was enough to put bread in his mouth. What more did he want?'

Sister Louisa considered everything then said, 'probably nothing until that poor wife of his lost her mind. He hadn't negotiated for a useless wife that he couldn't bed or breed. Or cook and wash and clean.'

'Don't you think you've overlooked the real issue. Ariana wasn't useless when he wed her. He was the perpetrator! I can imagine he must have done the most unimaginable and insufferable things to his poor wife. Anyway, I somehow sense there's more to it. Katina must be hiding something.'

'Well, you'll never find out. Just as you'll never find out what Katina's motive was.'

'I'd say it would have to be out of some devious convenience to satisfy her own needs. Who knows what those needs were! But I guess important enough for her to want to free herself of Ariana. And she was even more desperate to get rid of the brother-in-law since she tried to convince me to kill him. Now that I think about it! And at my expense. She'd even plotted a motive to make it look like an accident.

She made out that it was me she was protecting from her brother-in-law's physical abuse when all along it was to cover her own back. You know, just so she wouldn't be held accountable. And I'd be the accused and imprisoned.'

'She wanted you to commit a crime! That's treacherous. Some friend Katina turned out to be!' Sister Louisa remarked. 'These are rather remarkable revelations Miss Dilara.

You certainly got yourself into a dangerous situation. So, I can entirely understand your fear now for not writing to her. Wait! What about a forwarding address?'

'Allah! What have I done?' Dilara said with quiet alarm. 'Do you think she'll tell him?

'That's a question you should be asking yourself. She'd have to be of the same mind and heart as that brother-in-law of hers if she does. Unless you can think of some small reason why she would! What about a personal grudge!'

'Nothing that I can think of. Unless she was angry with me for abandoning the children. Though why should she! After all I was her niece's milk mana. And surrogate mana for her sick sister's child! Even risked my own life! And the feud between her and the brother-in-law has got nothing to do with me! I'd even clung to the idea that she might have returned the favour and cared for Zehra in my absence. How wrong I'd been. Look what happened!' Dilara revealed thoughtlessly.

'What did happen?'

After some time of silence Sister Louisa expectantly urged, 'well?'

'I mustn't be thinking clearly Sister,' Dilara offered coyly.

'I'm not at all surprised.' The elderly nun afforded her a weak smile even though she was unconvinced of the pretence. She was determined to get to the truth just the same.

'What about your son Omer! Did you tell her you left him with the Muslim family in Rizo?'

'I never told her of my plans.'

'Thankfully you did something right! The woman can't be trusted. What will you do if she does tell him?'

'What can I do? There's nowhere else to hide!'

'You might consider Mr Jihan's marriage proposal.'

'I could never do that!'

'You mustn't disregard a blessing that comes your way.'

'Why Sister did you take me for an opportunistic and self-regarding woman who'd marry a man merely out of convenience?'

'Umm, I see. Then clearly your heart still yearns for the soldier boy. Had you lived in the hope that he would find you again?'

'Of course not! You think he'd been thinking about me all these years? Why he's probably married with children by now. Besides, how would he have found me way up here in these mountains?'

'Only mountains never merge. People do!' she smiled.

'If I'd had this conversation with you earlier then I wouldn't have given the letter to the village bus driver,' Dilara offered bleakly.

'Why did you do that?'

Dilara explained that she'd thought it would save time. And she'd given instructions for the letter to be delivered to the Gapsalis mansion where Katina worked. The pious nun sensed the name Gapsalis was associated with the orphanage in some way but failed to make the connection at that moment. She now asked, 'how old do you think Katina would be now?'

'I can't be sure. Perhaps a few years older than me. Why do you ask?'

'She may no longer work there. Or she may have married and moved on. Does she have family living in Rizo?'

'She was living with an uncle. He was very old I understood.'

'Why was she living with him? What about the parents? Somebody must have given her that field.'

'You're right. Let me think. Somehow things don't make sense. Katina only spoke of having one younger sister. Her mother ran out on her father when she was fourteen and took her sister with her. And I doubt very much if she's married.'

'What makes you think that?'

'She was born with a defect, a slight limp, so to speak. I sensed she was very self-conscious that she was different. And it wasn't by choice she became a maid. She's a qualified teacher. She thought that nobody would employ her because of her 'problem,' as she called it. She was convinced her mother was ashamed of her because of it. Her father tried to marry her off to a man twice her age. That's why she ran away and ended up living with this uncle I told you about.

Anyway, my point is that if she was estranged from Ariana then it doesn't explain how she ended up living in Rizo. Unless she had another sister that I never knew about.'

Sister Louisa pursed her lips as she considered everything, then said, 'well I don't think you'll find that out Miss Dilara. And you can only go on the assumption that she'd perhaps inherited the land from her uncle. Though in my opinion there were many reasons why Katina would feel envious of Ariana. Jealousy is one of the immoral tribulations of mankind. Resentment isn't an inherited trait but something one unconsciously acquires due to the situations they are confronted with which makes them feel imperfect or threatened in some way. And it certainly sounds as though Katina had enough discontentment to fill her belly with sinful misdeeds. Naturally she'd felt inferior and bitter knowing that Ariana had been their mother's favourite. And her parents had cast her aside. And another contributing factor for her disillusionment was that she couldn't pursue a teaching career because of her disability,' Sister Louisa announced sagely.

'Perhaps they are all substantial reasons but there's one other reason that I can think of,' Dilara revealed. 'What if both siblings were in love with the same man?'

'Katina obviously knew she couldn't compete with Ariana,' Sister agreed.

'And she must have been furious when she'd found out that her sister had won the heart of the man she loved. Then she'd have good reason to avenge Ariana and so she forced her to marry a treacherous man,' Dilara offered.

'Your theory certainly supports Katina's actions. And despite all her ill will towards her sister she was probably perfectly content just knowing that she'd ruined Ariana's chance at love and happiness. It was a case of 'if I can't have him then neither can you! But I guess you'll never find out how Ariana ended up in Rizo.'

'Well, she couldn't have been estranged for too long. Ariana was a young girl I remember. Probably no older than sixteen or seventeen,' Dilara revealed.

'Alright! Let's get back to the important issue that concerns us. We were talking about Nilufer.'

The pious nun had summed up all the evidence over the past hour. And she'd noticed her confidante's agitation when she'd briefed her on Costa's account of the story. She had good reason to believe that the girl found in the orchard fourteen years ago was her daughter Zehra. Everything couldn't be just a coincidence.

Then without further ado she asked, 'do you think she is your daughter Zehra?'

'Are you serious! What makes you think that? Dilara replied with disguised alarm.

Just then a burst of red colour marked Sister Louisa's sallow face, and her small eyes almost engulfed the lens of her oval specs, as she dubiously glared over at her, felt slighted by her confidante's charade. Perhaps she'd underestimated the charitable and unassuming woman whom she'd come to greatly admire.

'You were this tobacco merchant's mistress, weren't you? And you did saddle him with a daughter that wasn't his. And you did abduct the son he'd fathered! It might have been best if he had found out that his son had been residing in the same village. For your own sake! Surely, he would have wanted to avenge you for your actions.

And even now there's nothing to say that he won't! If he finds you that is! Your only defence is that he'd maltreated and traded your daughter. I mean you yourself said somebody must have pushed her off the edge of the mountain. And you did say that the child must have been an unwanted burden. Wasn't Zehra just that to this tobacco merchant? Isn't it the reason why he wanted to give her away to Costa?'

Over the past few months, Dilara had deliberately come to doubt her own reasoning behind her suspicions. However now, based on her intuition and findings, she realised that she'd been right all along. And that what had transpired was a case of mistaken identity, a misconception of a perverted man's mind. And that the child Spyros had been so intent on giving away to Costa wasn't Zehra but his own daughter Despina.

CHAPTER EIGHTEEN

Rizokarpaso — August 1963

As Katina trudged home from the mansion late that afternoon her eyes were still stamped with the scorching image of Despina in Pandelis's arms. And she'd recited endless profanities after her fight with Sofia. Her hands were shaking so much that the key she was holding fell into the pot of geraniums before she could unlock the front door.

'Hope you yield to an incurable disease witch!' She voiced in a muttering splutter, slamming the door behind her. It was all Despina's fault.

She wouldn't have lost her job if she hadn't turned up at the mansion. She had no right coming there without consulting her first. But why did she come? Katina instantly smacked her head. *Stupid! Why you'd heard it with your own ears! She's here for the same reason as you. She's no more than a foolish young girl in love who thinks she can steal the heart of the protagonist.*

Katina accepted now that Despina's fainting had been cleverly staged so she could end up in his arms. *You ignorant fool! It might have been you in his arms if you'd thought of the same tactic!*

All that reading had turned Despina into an intellectual genius. And without even having set a foot inside the university door! She might have had she received that letter from the administration department a few years back. And if she'd passed the entrance exam at the University of Lefkosia she might have ended up as President Makarios's private secretary. But instead, she'd been peddling jam in the foulness of the marketplace and toiling in the tobacco field.

'Serves you right! *You can't have everything Despina!*' She begrudged. Directly, Katina felt affronted by her own unwitting admission when she realised that perhaps she hadn't wanted anything more than Pandelis. She'd set her sights on him long ago and without her even knowing it. It was apparent they'd formed a close relationship. Perhaps they were lovers. This last thought incited Katina's wrath even further. She searched for the smallest scenario that could justify to where they could have met. Yes! That had to be it! Pandelis had bought her jam. Despina's head had been in the clouds that day she'd told her that a stranger had bought all the jars. She'd had good reason to be ecstatic since she'd earned an outrageous profit.

At the time Katina had accepted that what she'd told her to be true until that Monday morning when she'd gone to work when she'd heard him tell his mother he'd bought the jam from a woman at the market-place. And he'd deliberately lied to protect Despina's reputation from his mother's nasty backlash if he told her the truth. Then of course there was that day she'd ran into Despina on her way home from work with the pretence of a headache. Hadn't she asked her how old Pandelis was. And if he'd married yet. And if he was as good looking as he was rich!

At the time Katina had thought she was merely curious given her adoration for Rifat. But now she was seeing things from a different perspective. She hadn't received correspondence from Rifat in months and so this alone confirmed her suspicions that she'd broken off her engagement. And she didn't have to guess why! She must have realised the serious hurdles she'd be faced with by marrying a Muslim boy and whose religion was that of a different God.

And even if they eloped from the discriminating eyes of society, she couldn't survive on Rifat's sentimental vows alone when measured up to that of a wealthy entrepreneur that could transform her from a peasant girl into a Minoan princess and reside in a mansion. All these things were solid reasons to renounce Rifat.

Yet she'd cleverly kept up the subterfuge to distract her from her real intentions to pursue Pandelis. And when no letter arrived from Rifat she acted as though her life was about to end and said she'd die if she couldn't marry him. Then she had the cheek to take her ploy even further by insinuating that the mayoress wasn't doing her job properly at sorting out the mail in her husband's absence. And that she'd either misplaced her letters and forgotten about them on a shelf of the kafenio or she'd carelessly redirected them to somebody else.

She would have pointed the finger at her in the end since she had nobody else to blame. *You are an ungrateful and treacherous niece! And if I'd known what you were up to then I never would have offered to be your mail courier! You and that sister of mine are two of a kind.* She'd been grooming Despina about the truths of life since the age of ten and at her own shortfall just to become a puppet for her to manipulate and mock.

Those beauty secrets she'd told her about had been a deliberate ploy to mess around with her innermost feelings of being rejected by society because of her 'problem.'

She'd even said that if she didn't hurry up and make a move with Pandelis she'd end up an old spinster.

Katina felt so disheartened and miserable that a deluge of tears flooded her face.

You fool Katina! You really think he meant it when he'd said you'd preserved yourself well! Or when he told you not to worry and that you were with him now! He was taking pity on your 'problem,' just like everyone else! Well, you can go to hell Despina!

'I'd tell you to go to anathema too Ariana if you weren't already there!' she voiced aloud.

You stole my school drawing and won first prize. And you stole my only friend Dimitris! And you even stole my mother. Then after she died you came and found me and stole my job at the orchard house. Then you tried to steal Pandelis from me too! Did you think I was going to allow you to win first prize again Ariana?

You tried to hide those blood-stained panties in the trash bin. And then you coughed up your bowels on that poisonous rue you drank when you tried to abort the child! Though you did give that fool headed husband of yours the benefit of the doubt. With that field worker of his. You made a big mess of things just the same. Look what's happened? But how could you know! Your minds been scrambled for the past twenty-three years. Anathema se!

You certainly didn't live up to your name. 'Most holy! The sham of it all.

The name would serve a whore more justice Ariana. Now I'm left to solve a situation that's become as big as the Cyprus problem. There never will be a peaceful resolution! Unless I tell the truth! But I could never do that? Pandelis would surely spit in my face.

Katina went to her room and removed her work clothes and dressed into her house gown. She was about to leave when she found herself standing before the mirror. She studied herself carefully, as if searching for some aspect that would be appealing.

She removed the pins from her upswept hair, let it fall to her shoulders and imagined it glistening with shades of copper.

She moved back and unbuttoned her gown, let it fall to the floor and removed her undergarments. She stared at her naked body through the mirror, noticed at the age of forty -four that her nipples were taut and erect on her full breasts. Gradually she lowered her eyes to discover for the first time that dark and scruffy place in her lower groin, blushed by the spontaneous image of a heart or bird shape there. She opened the top drawer of the dresser and took out a tiny pair of scissors.

Seated on the edge of the bed she spread her legs apart and began to clip and clip, allowing the trimmings to fall to the floor, when abruptly her cheeks burned, as if somebody else was seeing her through her eyes. Coyly she put her gown back on, stared around in a conscious effort to reassure herself nobody else was in the room. Then shook her head in wondering if there wasn't a tiny corner of absurdity within the logic of her own mind.

Did you think this artistry alone in such an inconspicuous place would help stupid woman! She'd just have to stick to a more sensible approach to revamp herself she concluded as she left the room for the kitchen.

She removed the brown skin of four onions and dropped them into a pot of water with some black tea leaves. She then left the pot on the gas burner to simmer for a while to release the liquid before she went outside to the washing shed to kindle the fire to boil water in the cauldron. After she went to another shed and removed the galvanised bathtub from the hook on the mud-hay wall and placed it in on the ground.

Then she returned to the kitchen and lifted the pot off the gas burner and placed it on the sink for the liquid to cool. She then rinsed, towelled dried her hair, hurried off to her room, and turned on the light switch. 'Why it gleams like my polished copper cezve!' She squealed with delight where she stood before the mirror under the incandescent light. Back in the kitchen again she poured a good helping of honey into a bowl of goat milk and stirred it well. By this time Katina had begun to feel itchy down below. Back in the outhouse after relishing in the warm bath of honey and milk she no longer assumed herself to be that pathetic caterpillar that feeds in the earth. *Yes, now he'll notice the beautiful, white lotus flower, not just the unsightly swamp.*

CHAPTER NINETEEN

Mayor Neophytos rapped on the door of Jusuf the Chair Weaver's workshop. He twiddled his thumbs impatiently as he waited to be acknowledged by his Turkish neighbour. Shortly a heavily whiskered man of slim build with longish, greying hair appeared from behind the door. Jusuf regarded the elderly mayor before greeting him with a slight bow of the head. 'Come in! Once he'd stepped inside Jusuf stretched his head out into the lane way and cast a furtive look around before he quickly shut the door behind him.

'Tsai!' Jusuf curtly asked.

'I make it all day long. But thanks just the same.' The mayor offered pleasantly as he breathed in the wood-dust of the room. He then considered the many different tools along the bench, and the sheaves of reed stacked against the wall, and the timber shavings that carpeted the floor amidst the many partially constructed chairs. Then upon reflection reasoned that making tsai and coffee all day wasn't so bad after all.

'Eh, what can you tell me?' Jusuf expectantly asked.

'You know Pandelis Gapsalis?'

'Everybody knows the wealthiest man in this village! What about him?'

'He's been asking about that girl Despina. Wanted to know if that father of hers has been collecting her letters,' He revealed.

'Strange. What made him think that? And how would he know the girl?' Jusuf doubtfully enquired.

'Good question. He must know her just the same. At least well enough to be curious as to why she hasn't received correspondence from that son of yours.'

'You'd think that man would have more important things to do than waste his time enquiring about the tobacco merchant's daughter!'

'May I ask why you've never intervened before now?'

'I thought my son would forget the girl once he was enlisted in the army. Though I was wrong. He's been saving para for years to finish that cottage on the land I gave him.'

'A soldier can't save para in the army good Muslim,' he offered wryly.

'True. Though he's managed to sell a few of his lyrics to recording artists back home that he'd found out about through friends of his in the army. He tells me they've already been recorded. My ears have been tuned in to the Ankara radio station.'

'You don't say. Bravo! He's a talented boy!'

'Has been since a child when he first noticed me strumming the lute. I learned to play back in the old country of Constantinople,' Jusuf revealed.

'And the chair weaving!'

'Something I learned from my father. He told me to learn a trade and then hang it up on the wall. He wasn't wrong. Playing the lute wasn't going to put bread on the table.'

'What about your son! What are his plans once he's discharged?' The mayor offered cautiously.

'None, other than marry the girl! They've been like a needle and thread since childhood. Growing up Rifat was more interested in writing songs and letters to her instead of doing his homework. Come take a look!' Jusuf pointed to his workbench. The mayor followed him over and then watched him remove a shoe carton from beneath.

Curiously he watched him open it to reveal countless folded white pages from a schoolbook. 'I've had to hide them from my wife all these years.'

'Why did you take them?' the elderly probed.

'It was like I sensed this rotten smell in his room that I needed to eradicate. The air became more and more polluted as if breathing it would rot my soul.

It's a problematic and grave situation. My son can't marry the girl! There is no page in the book of Allah's law that consents to a marriage between two siblings. It's incest! An immoral transgression. This matter must be resolved as quickly and quietly as possible,' Jusuf restlessly disclosed.

Mayor Neophytos accepted that the small man appeared weighed down by the intensity of his anguish and wished there was more he could do to alleviate his Muslim neighbour's dilemma. But he knew there was nothing he or anybody could do to rectify the ill-fated circumstances that had transpired by the union of two people whose love for each other had surpassed both ethnic tradition and the sacred law of God. 'It's a terrible situation.' Then he thought to ask, 'as a matter of interest, has the real mother of the boy ever tried to contact you since she left the village?'

'Praise Allah she hasn't!' Jusuf was quick to reply. 'My wife doesn't know who the boy's real parents are. She never would have agreed to raise the tobacco merchant and his mistress's son. In my eyes a child is a child regardless of where it came from.'

'Was Rifat the boy's name when you got him?'

'It was Omer. My wife and I chose the name. I couldn't risk the boy growing up in the same village with his real father. For years he'd wanted to avenge his mistress with the belief she'd run off with his son. Why he'd have our head if he found out the boy had been breathing right under his nose all these years. And found out that the boy who wants to marry his daughter is his own flesh and blood. And his daughter's half sibling,' Jusuf revealed anxiously.

'If you ask me the mistress made a bad decision. We can't blame her for running away from that man. But her biggest mistake was that she chose to leave her daughter with Spyros and not the son he'd fathered. She should have left the daughter to be fostered,' he revealed.

'That was the plan, well according to your mother,' Jusuf offered.

'Then why didn't she? What made her change her mind?'

'Your mother first came to see me and my wife to tell us that she'd met this unwed and pregnant girl in Lemnos. She said that once she'd delivered the infant the girl had agreed to give it away. Though we'd lost all hope when we hadn't heard from her...'

'What happened?' the mayor eagerly broke in.

'Well, I was getting to that part!' Jusuf remarked with the same impatience.

'The girl came to the village some months later with the promise she'd made to your mother. It just so happened that it was the day your mother had delivered the merchant's wife's infant hours before. As you may well know his wife completely lost her mind at childbirth. It was for this reason that the merchant asked your mother if she could seek out a milk nurse for his infant.'

'I presume the infant to be Despina!'

'That's right. Then your mother told us that since the circumstances were as such we'd have to wait until both infants were off the breast. But as it turned out the girl stayed on, became the merchant's mistress and bore him a son. That would be Omer, or Rifat the boy I've raised.'

'Well, things certainly did take a turn in the most unexpected and complicated way. Though the matter isn't entirely irresolvable good Muslim.' The mayor offered empathetically.

'How do you suggest I do that?' Jusuf probed, then just as quickly added, 'you're not implying I tell Rifat the truth! You want me to tear his heart out!'

'My guess is he'll find out sooner or later! And you can't dissolve an enduring relationship between two lovers by simply withholding correspondence. That won't solve the situation. And you might like to reflect on your own mistake by hiding the truth from your wife. A woman has a special way of dealing with such sensitive matters and there might have been a good chance of preventing this grim situation. Anyway, I must be heading off and in the meantime you decide. I'll be in touch.'

'May God be pleased with you good Christian,' Jusuf said escorting him to the door.

Mayor Neophytos stepped out onto the cobbled path, lit his pipe,

243

and the glow of the matchstick produced an unsightly web of wrinkles across his thin face. He took a few puffs of the aromatic tobacco then thoughtfully shook his head. He failed to understand why Jusuf the Chair Weaver couldn't solve a simple domestic issue. Why was he suffocating in the stench of his own making? The elderly rambled on with a sequence of hand gestures, and then voiced a reedy falsetto as he trudged back to his trouble-free life of brewing coffee in the kafenio.

CHAPTER TWENTY

Pandelis had awakened Despina very early the following morning to avoid a nasty confrontation with his mother. He'd frequently made the long drive to Famagusta on business trips and yet the trip seemed never ending this morning. Most people living in the north had to rely on public transport to get there which was an inconvenience for those who merely required blood tests. Or even for those whose medical conditions necessitated the service of the hospital on a regular basis.

After Despina's blood tests she'd been feeling faint and nauseated so Pandelis had taken her to a nearby outdoor café and ordered fruit juice while he drank coffee. In a day or so he would take her to consult Doctor Grigori for the results.

'I've put you to a great deal of trouble driving me all this way Kyrio!'

'It's no trouble. The health system I'm afraid is failing to open medical clinics in rural regions due to insufficient funding. Something needs to be done without imposing too high taxes on the public servants and rural farmers.'

'Our government would rather spend money on its political administration and defence forces than open rural hospitals and pathology clinics. While raising the hopes of needy people with false political propaganda!' she criticised.

He was caught by surprise by her wise observation. 'You'd do well in government legislation. Are you feeling better?' He asked with a side-glance from where he sat behind the steering wheel as he drove back to Rizo. 'I hope you're not still worried! About your father, that is!'

'I can't help it. He'll be furious! I bet he's been out all night searching for me,' she sighed.

'You need to calm down Miss!' Though he knew she wasn't wrong in her assumption.

The merchant had come hollering and bashing on the mansion's gate with a sledgehammer in the early hours of the morning. It was a good thing she'd slept through the tumultuous racket.

'You are a philandering sonofabitch! I'll bury you alive for abducting my daughter Gapsalis! You're just like that thieving father of yours! I'll have the police arrest you if my daughter isn't home by morning. You'll rot in jail!'

Pandelis had been of the same mind for beating his daughter. The bruising on Despina's body that the physician had seen was evidence enough to hold him accountable. The only problem was that it would have to be Despina who made the complaint to the police. Though he doubted very much that she would. Just like his friend Grigori had said. However, he would do whatever it took to seek justice on Despina's behalf. Even if it meant convincing Grigori Savva to provide police with a formal medical report which would enforce them to investigate. Though he doubted if his statement alone would be sufficient evidence to liberate Despina from the brutal oppression of her father.

'The first person he'd think to ask is Katina!' she continued.

'Ah, Katina!' he remarked dryly. *The scorpion who stung the frog!*

'I knew I couldn't trust her. I'm not even sure if I want to see her again.'

'Mother fired her yesterday. There's been a lot of animosity between her and mother over the years. So, it seemed an inevitable retribution on my mother's part.'

'I wonder what she'll do now! She'll be miserable!' she deliberately said.

'Why would she?'

'She won't be around you. I've sensed she's been in love with you for a long time,' she revealed unashamedly.

'I've never regarded Katina in that way.'

'Strange you should say that because she once said the same thing of you! I wasn't convinced. Why do you think she wanted to clean the orchard house! Because it gave her a chance to be spend time alone with you. I mean why else would she be attracted to the house?'

'You'll see for yourself soon,' he said.

'What do you mean? Wait! You're not taking me to the orchard house now, are you? I need to go home right away or…'

'Or what? Your father will beat you again!' he interjected critically. 'Doctor Savva told me about the bruising on your body!' He suddenly swerved over to the side of the road and killed the engine.

'Why have you stopped? And why are you staring at me like that?' She squinted over at him with fluttering lashes, as if in a subconscious effort to shelter her eyes from his penetrating and questioning stare.

'Would you like to talk about it?' he asked directly.

'Talk about what!'

'You must be so terrified of him because you're too afraid to speak! I'm sorry I had to bring it up.'

'Take me home or I'll walk,' she demanded.

'Well, if you faint along the way then I won't be around to save you Miss!'

'What a big-headed man you are! I'm not Katina! I can survive without you!' She opened the door and fled.

'Wait! I'll take you home if that's what you want!' He shouted after her in order to calm her.

'Then why didn't you agree in the first place!' She exclaimed when he caught up with her. 'Why do you interfere in everything I do?'

'I'm concerned about you.'

'Well, don't be! Worry about your own affairs!' she retorted.

'Your father's a vile man!' he warned.

'I'm a grown woman! Not a child! You're no different to Katina. You both suffocate and irritate me! Now go find yourself another victim to antagonise!' she exclaimed.

He felt improperly affronted by this defiant and derogatory counterattack. 'I'm sorry if I make you feel this way.' He intuitively expected another back lash, but instead she abruptly turned and reeled to the side of the road and threw up. 'Are you alright?'

'If you'd leave me alone then I would be!' She uttered as she tried to catch her breath.

'I'm sorry I didn't think my behaviour would make you this sick. Seriously, though are you alright?'

'It must have been the orange juice!' Despina said sheepishly as she composed herself. He regarded her closely, noticed her own confusion by this unexpected incident. 'Clearly you're unwell.' He retrieved his handkerchief and passed it to her. 'Here, it's clean!' He watched her self-consciously turn her back to him and wipe the dribble from her mouth.

He waited for her to face him again and then motioned an arm towards his parked vehicle. 'Please! You need to rest.'

'Only if you agree to take me home!' she warned.

'As you wish. Come!' He helped her back into the vehicle and drove off.

About a mile west from the outer edge of the village Despina noticed he was driving through an unfamiliar trail and was enchanted by the beauty of the landscape that came into view.

She stared out at the endless stretches of orderly rows of citrus trees to one side of the road, and on the other side, the vineyards were just as methodical. 'I wonder who owns all these beautiful groves?'

'They are part of my family's estate,' he revealed.

'How fortunate you are Kyrio.'

'Perhaps,' he said offhandedly.

'You don't seem too pleased about your family's prosperity.'
'I'm not ungrateful. But it doesn't necessarily mean I'm content either. Wealth is just an advantage one inherits.' He was now driving through a wide-gate and into a circular driveway before pulling up outside the front door. The orchard house was reminiscent of a provincial Mediterranean villa.

'Why have you brought me here? You promised to take me home,' she pressed.

'In good time,' he smiled, 'now best you climb out.'

Just then Thea came through the door and approached them in the driveway.

She respectfully greeted him and then regarded the woman at his side. 'Welcome! Are you feeling better?'

'Thea! Please be respectful and address our guest as 'Miss Despina.'

'Pardon. As you wish Kyrio. Now I've cleaned the house and restocked the pantry. I've also put fresh linen on the bed in the spare room. Have you got a bag Miss? I'll help you unpack.'

'Unpack! Spare room! I can't stay here!' she protested.

'I'm sure you'll find the environment peaceful,' he smiled, then added, 'and you'll also find a collection of contemporary and historical books if you wish to read.'

'You sound like I'll be here on vacation.'

'I'd hoped you would consider it as such! Nobody will bother you here!'

'Why do you insist on keeping me here?' she disputed.

Thea was of the same mind. Though whatever the reason was she was just glad that Pandelis had assigned her to the orchard house and where she was far removed from Sofia's endless ranting.

'You take me for a man who'd allow himself to put a defenceless woman's life at risk!

Have you forgotten about going to Lemnos for the results of your blood tests! I doubt very much if your father will drive you there!'

'I'll go in a couple of days by bus. Doctor Grigori's clinic shouldn't be too hard to find! And I'm impatient to speak with Katina.'

'That would be foolish. You don't think she'll confess that she's betrayed you by keeping your letters do you!'

'Why the gall of that woman!' Thea mumbled.

'Leave it with me! I'll sort things out. Now if you'll both excuse me much work awaits me at the office. Thea, I trust you'll make our guest feel at home.'

Once inside Despina was struck with unimaginable awe. 'What a charming house!'

'As you can see it's unlike the mansion. You know with all those bulky pieces of outdated furniture Sofia collects. Antiques as she calls them. They'd make good firewood if you ask me! And those chandeliers that I'm forever cleaning from top to bottom. On a ladder, mind you! Pardon for my frankness Miss!' she announced.

'The truth always speaks for itself!' Despina disclosed and the densely braided woman took delight by her admission.

'Then I sense we'll get along. Here you can move about easily and sit anywhere you like.'

Despina sat down on the sofa and then closely observed the spacious room.

On either side of the room sandstone columns flared up to a domed ceiling of thatched reed supported by sturdy wood beams. The sturdy grey sofas were of thick woven cotton, punctuated by cushions in warm autumn shades.

Many Cypriot artifacts were displayed on the shelves. And there were paintings on the white-washed walls which Despina recognised to be of historical Cypriot landmarks she'd seen photos of in books at high school. And the large fireplace with photos on the mantel was an additional feature of the room. And alongside this she could see many books inside a sturdy timber case that Pandelis had mentioned earlier on for her to read.

'The landscapes have they been painted by local artists?' she probed.

'Pandelis has a natural talent. He has a small studio at the back of the house. You can see it if you wish after refreshments. Now what would you like to drink?'

'Water will be fine, thanks.' She considered the maid as she shuffled about the kitchen then added, 'one could easily forget the outside world in a place like this.'

'That's why he likes to spend time alone here. I don't blame him. His mother's constant bleating grinds on the nerves after a while. Even churchgoers would get tired of hearing a priest's constant recitations of Kyrie eleison. During Eucharist!' Thea snickered in a manner which suggested she was pleased that someone would listen to her yarns. Then added, 'the blind man asked for one eye but instead got two.

Sofia got more than she'd hoped for when she married her late hus- band. Even God must have realised his mistake and retaliated for her extravagance and ingratitude. She doesn't seem to be in grieving just the same. Here we are Miss. I'll put the glass of water on this side table beside you. Now can I get you anything else before I start cooking?'

'Why don't you sit down so we can chat,' Despina urged.

'As you wish!' Thea sat opposite her.

'What about the army?' She asked, then took a sip of water as her mouth was dry.

'He did his time. Probably wished he hadn't been discharged with all the drama going on at the time. One of his father's land tenants refused to pay his dues and even refused to budge from his field. A gold hunter, so to speak,' Thea huffed.

'Was the matter resolved?' Despina had already found out who this land tenant was.

'Hard to say. Though rumour was that Yiannis gave him the land. Probably for the sake of peace. Though nobody got much of that, peace that is, after that new maid started working at the mansion.'

'What happened, if I may ask?'

'Best that you don't know Miss.' She remarked with a wave of the arm, which on the face of it was just a charade so her guest wouldn't think her a gossipmonger, but Despina had already guessed that she took delight in bringing up the private matters of her employers.

'Then it must have had something to do with what happened here in the orchard house!'

'Then you must have heard something!' Thea readily asserted.

'You might say that I did.' Despina kept up the pretence to find out all she could.

'I'm surprised that the rumour is floating around after so many years. Proves that people have nothing more to do than dig up the past to keep themselves amused. It was Katina who started it all! Because of the new maid I told you about. Forgive me but I couldn't help overhearing what you said outside. You said something about her withholding your letters. Who were they from, if I may ask?'

'My betrothed. He's in the army and I haven't heard from him for some time.'

'There's no need to go on Miss! I know what that woman's been up to again. She's trying to break you up with that boy of yours,' Thea warned.

'Why would she? What would she gain?' she asked.

'Nothing from a logical point of view. Her only purpose was to deny you the chance at love and happiness. It's in her sour nature. The soul joins what the mind detaches Miss. You can smell the stench of Katina's soul on her breath even at a distant. It's like the bird pecked grapes rotting on the vine in the sun,' Thea asserted

Despina placed a hand to her chest, felt a whine there that wanted to scream. It was an alarming description of the only person she'd trusted and relied on since childhood. And to think she'd been the ultimate cause of her misery without her even being aware of it.

She only had to think about how she'd come up with all kinds of arbitrary justifications in order to delude her- from what now Despina considered-from finding out the truth about how her mother had died. She'd even denied ever having known her mother. She even told her that she was paranoid for believing Spyros wasn't her real father.

She probably did know that he wasn't but wanted her to believe he was. Only Despina and God alone knew of the terrifying ordeal she'd endured at the hands of such an evil man. The thought of him now churned her stomach again, felt like the sickness had opened a dark pit in her soul.

Despina now said, 'what an indecent human she is! Who was this new maid?'

'I don't seem to remember. I'd never seen her before she came to the mansion, and nor had anyone else. Katina must have known her just the same.'

'What makes you think that?

'From the very first day the girl arrived on the job Katina bullied her like she had every right to do so. She got jealous when she found out that it had been Pandelis who'd asked his father to put her on at the mansion. That scorpion would get in the way of anyone in a dress that caught his attention.'

'How did you find out about all of this?'

'I was like a fly on the wall of every room in the mansion Miss. I knew the ins and outs of what was going on each day. His father had hired the girl as a seasonal harvester. She'd been working in the apple orchard across the road. It was said that she'd wandered into the front yard. She was thirsty and when Pandelis saw her at the water pump he suggested she sit under the porch and rest a while out of the hot sun.'

'Nothing wrong in what he did. He must have felt sorry for her otherwise he wouldn't have asked his father to give her a more suitable job.'

'I agree but the girl became the thorn in Katina's bosom. She did everything in her power to have her fired! Once she put one of Sofia's diamond rings in her apron pocket. After she went straight to Sofia and told her that she saw the new maid go into her room and steal it. Then gloated when she saw the girl down on her knees sobbing before Sofia and pleading her innocence.'

'What a dishonourable and mean thing to do! Did she have it her way in the end! Did they fire her?' Despina probed.

'Sofia would have if her husband hadn't acted in the girl's defence. That's another thing Katina got mad about. Then all hell let loose when she found out that the girl had been assigned to take over her place here at the orchard house a couple of days a week. Katina was at her happiest when around Pandelis, you see! Then she got it stuck in her head that the girl was seducing him when she came here to clean.'

'Really?' Despina was astounded by the deviance of Katina's way of thinking. 'Go on.'

'Her soul became enflamed all over a hair clip he'd given the girl. I'm telling you the woman's not in her right mind! It was only a tiny thing and yet Katina made out that he'd given the girl his heart. Fool that she is! It was a lovely hair clip just the same. The upper half was curved with specs of crystals, or something of that description. I'd judged the maid to be a shy and mannerly girl and not the type that would flirt with men.

I wasn't surprised when she told me why he'd let her keep it after she found it amongst those frames he uses for his paintings while cleaning his studio. Her hair was always hanging over her eye, you see, and so he told her that they were too lovely to conceal.'

'What a nice compliment a man can give a girl?' Despina smiled.

'I don't think I ever saw her without it in her hair after that day. Which was probably an unwanted curse for the poor girl just the same,' Thea scoffed, then added, 'why Kyrio wouldn't have given that young maid a second glance even if she'd thrown herself at him. His heart was already busy.'

'Busy! Oh, his paintings you mean!'

'They too were a distraction between other things at the time,' Thea said.

'I can't understand why this maid would even tell Katina after all her malice towards her. I mean don't you think she would have kept it to herself!' Despina said.

'In my opinion that girl had no choice.'

'What do you mean?'

'Well, Katina must have forced it out of her because she didn't believe her.

The idea he'd given the girl a gift didn't rest too well on her conscience, even if it be such a tiny thing. So, her only defence was to slander the girl again by reporting to Sofia that she'd been stealing again to have her fired,' Thea uttered petulantly.

'Why there's no end to that woman's malice!' Despina said angrily. Then thought to ask, 'in any case what was he doing with a woman's hair clip! Strange thing for a man to have in the house don't you think! Unless he had a lady friend here.'

'I'd say he found it elsewhere and decided it was too nice to throw away,' Thea had to come up with some excuse.

'Do you think he might have had feelings for the maid?' Despina urged even after Thea assured her that he hadn't.

'I'd have to be just as unbalanced as Katina to think that!'

'Nobody really knows the inner thoughts of others,' Despina said.

'He wasn't interested in other girls,' Thea revealed.

'Then he already had a sweetheart!'

'He was a handsome and tall boy of twenty-two back then. And an eye-catching sight in his army uniform. Even I would have fallen for him if I'd been many years younger,' Thea said wittily.

257

'Then where is this girl?'

'He lost track of her after he was discharged. I'd never seen a man so heartbroken. Sadly, he's never gotten over her. The heart never mends koritsi-mou,' Thea said soberly.

'It explains why he's never married. Pity he's never taken the chance at love again.'

'She'd have to be a special woman. He's never brought a woman here.'

'As you know it's not by choice that I'm here.' She reminded her when she caught her probing stare. 'Then it's clear he had no feelings for the girl. Why do you think Katina was never fired?'

'I sensed she had control over the family in some way! She strutted about as if she were the queen bee in the mansion,' Thea said.

'The Gapsalis family are the most influential and important people in this village and you're telling me they were afraid of a domestic maid!'

'At least Sofia was up until her husband's death, that is! Now she's as fearless as a mountain lion! Yesterday she finally threw that scorpion out of the mansion.'

'Pity she waited until her husband died. And I bet Katina didn't see it coming. Anyway, I was there yesterday! When did this happen?'

'You were upstairs in the guest room. Might have been a good thing that you were. It was nothing short of a slanderous squabbling racket. It was as if all the ill-feelings they felt for each other had been tightly sealed inside a bottle. Then boom! The cork suddenly burst open!'

Despina indulged the mature woman with amusement, took a sip of her water, placed the glass down, and then asked 'how did the argument start?' Though I did sense Katina was in a bad mood when she saw me at the mansion yesterday.'

'She wouldn't have been pleased to hear a beautiful woman tell her that the man she adored had requested to see her! Or watch him carry her back to the house in his arms after she fainted.'

'He did! Despina blushed.

'That's right. My guess is that she might have put poison in your lemonade had she known that was about to happen,' Thea chortled.

'I sense I was the reason for their argument.'

'It was expected.' The maid waved a hand. 'Sofia hurled all kinds of insults at Katina. Told her that she'd hung around like an unwanted scourge in her household all these years. For her son, of course. She was right! But the best insult she left until last when she told Katina she was nothing more than a pathetic caterpillar that feeds in the earth.'

'I couldn't imagine a more demeaning attack. It must have been very hurtful for her.'

'Maybe now we'll get some peace in the mansion.' Thea leaned into the sofa and sighed, and what Despina saw etched in the mature woman's eyes was an interpretation of someone who'd seen and heard much in their lifetime. She wanted to explore her psyche to find out all that she knew. She wasted no time to ask, 'what happened to the girl?'

Thea drew herself forward and concisely said, 'how would I know?'

Despina sensed that this curt response was merely to avoid any blame against her if she talked about what she knew.

'You worked with her, didn't you? And you did say you knew the ins and outs of what was going on. And you were like a fly on the wall in every room of the mansion! You knew everything,' she revealed.

'Just about! Except for what happened to the girl. You probably know as much as I do since you said you'd heard the rumour,' she explained.

'I'd rather hear it from you. People interpret things differently. You never know what the truth is,' Despina urged, hoping she could persuade her to talk.

'That depends on who started the rumour. If one's smart they'll only believe the word of an honest person. Otherwise, it's bound to be a lie.'

'What do you believe?'

'I'll be the judge of that! Then impetuously added, 'besides, my son wouldn't lie to me!'

'Then he must have told you something. And you know the truth!'

'You're wrong. But he did say something on the night before the girl didn't show up for work at the mansion on the Thursday of the following morning. But it doesn't mean to say that it was her screams that he and some of the other men heard coming from this house when they'd been working in the orchard across the road.'

'Who else could it have been! She was the only one that worked here. Well! Did they come over to find out what was going on?' Despina asked.

'She was out the door before they could. Running for her life, he'd said. And screaming her lungs out.'

'After that, where did she go?'

'Well, that's a good question. She was last seen heading down the road. In the opposite direction of the village, he'd said. By the time they got up to the road she'd already vanished. In the orchard, they'd thought.'

'She wouldn't have been so petrified if she'd seen a snake at her feet. Wait! Katina came down here and scared the life out of the girl. You know, warned her to stay away from Pandelis.'

'Why would she even bother? She was already pushing her around at the mansion!' Thea asserted.

'That's all she could do there! But here she could do anything. Especially, in a jealous rage.'

'Katina was at the mansion that morning.'

'Maybe she'd found an excuse to leave. Or she might have left without anyone even noticing. Clearly though at some point in time the girl must have taken her seriously. She vanished, didn't she! Then again, what if Katina was right?'

'What could she ever be right about?' Thea grumbled. 'But go on.' She shifted her buttocks on the sofa, feeling jaded by all the theories and presumptions.

'Right about the girl seducing Pandelis. Don't you think she would have come down here to find out what was really going on when she came here to clean the house? What if she'd caught them kissing or even worse caught them in a carnal act! I'd say her eyes blackened with rage. She would have done anything to get rid of the girl once and for all. But all this is guesswork on my part. It could have been the other way around. What if he did have feelings for this young maid?'

'My ass, he did! Are you trying to force me to confess to something that never existed between him and the girl? And even if there was, don't go jumping to conclusions Miss. It was a load of pig shit! Troublemakers all of them! I would have told those fruit pickers who started that rumour myself that he wasn't even here that morning. Shut them all up once and for all!' Thea said hot faced.

'Forgive me, if I'd known I wouldn't have brought it up.' Then she bravely asked just the same, 'are you sure?'

'I wouldn't have said so if I wasn't! He'd come up to the mansion early that morning to pick up some document, ah yes it was his old passport. He was going abroad the following week for his studies. I heard him tell his parents that he was going into hora to renew it. He'd also said he was going to catch up with one of his ex-army comrades while he was there! So, you see, he wasn't anywhere near the house that morning. I've known Pandelis since he was a young boy. I've never met a more selfless and decent man. He has a big responsibility managing his late father's estate. And even more to his credit he set up a charity foundation after World War Two in support of homeless children. Does this sound like a man who'd purposely molest a young and needy harmless girl? Thea voiced with annoyance.

'Of course not! I'd really like to find out what happened to her.'

'I can see that! But why are you so concerned about all this?'

'I've become extremely sensitive towards somebody else's loss. It reminds me of my own loss when my young sister vanished. A few days later father brought Zehra home dead inside a box. I'll never get over it. Occasionally I make koliva and hold a private memorial service at her burial site in the forest of red cedars. I go there each Sunday to refill the oil in the icon box. I've planted a flowerbed there. The forest is also the place where Rifat and I would spend time alone during our adolescent years. Now it has become a place where I find solace just being alone with Zehra.' Tears welled in her eyes.

'My condolences Miss. And may God be comforting of your loss. Forgive me I'd forgotten about it until you mentioned it. You were only eight years old when Katina brought you to the mansion. Kyrios Pandelis sat with you by the fishpond that afternoon in the courtyard.'

'You have a good memory. I was so sad that day and remember how hard he tried to cheer me up. Recalling his childhood and about all the naughty and wonderful things he did. He even offered to take me to the stables to see the new pony. He made me feel special that day. He still does, although between you and I he'd never believe it since I give him such a hard time.'

'Fate certainly has a way of surprising us all. I sense he still enjoys being in your company Miss Despina. Forgive me for asking, but I believe your mother is also dead!'

'From what I've been told. Her death is just as much a mystery as this girl we speak of. Nobody knows how my mother died or even knew her name. Though I would have thought somebody would have reported the girl missing. Or at least known her name. Even you don't remember.'

'If this brain of mine gets a push on then I'll let you know.' Thea said, then added, 'maybe the girl had a pet name. Nothing unusual about that. People acquired such titles from their childhood. It usually stuck with them into adulthood. These days they want to know who your father and great grandfather was to find out if you've got Turkish, Armenian, or Greek blood. They try to act civilised but it's just a diplomatic way of hiding their bigotry.'

Despina was impressed by Thea's understanding of worldly affairs. 'One would hope not. Though times have changed and so people's views change accordingly.'

Thea smiled compliantly then said, 'you might like to ask Katina. She'd have to know the girl's name.'

It would be like asking a fox where it's hidden its prey. Despina quietly mused, then said, 'the orchard house is a long walk from the mansion. Even further from the village square. What if somebody had given her a lift here that morning. And then followed her into the house. Or it might have even been one of the men working in the orchard who knew she'd be alone inside.'

'If only those empty -headed peasants in this village had of thought of it before causing a scandal for Pandelis. That father of his never spoke to him after he returned from abroad.'

'Are you serious? Why do you think he'd do such thing to his own son?' Despina asked suspiciously.

'I work for the man not read his mind,' Thea shrugged.

'You must have some idea!'

'Well, I don't.'

'You're the one who should know everything.' She accepted Thea's willingness to talk had softened, thus gave her more reason to believe she was hiding something.

Thea leaned forward again, raised her chin, gave a furtive glance through the window opposite her, in a manner evocative of an informer who was about to disclose secret information and was afraid of getting caught.

'You can trust me,' Despina pledged accepting her unease.

'His late father was an ambitious and greedy man, Miss. And he wasn't short of arrogance either. At the time there'd been talks of him campaigning for the next mayor elections in Famagusta. Of course, that didn't happen until some years after the war. Though there was nothing out of the ordinary for Yiannis senior to come over to the house from time to time whilst supervising his workers in the orchard across the road. You know what I'm getting at! A scandal such as this at the time would have ruined his chances of becoming mayor.'

'You mean his father had intentionally forfeited the reputation of his son in order to spare his own honour in the eyes of society? And his marriage? Has he no conscience!' Despina scolded.

'Another thing he lacks!' She grunted, then offered judiciously, 'sometimes one must sacrifice the most beautiful of grapes to save the rest in the basket Miss. But if he did touch that girl then may the fire of my mana's curse burn forever in his rotten soul and his bones never turn to cold ashes in that hell where he's gone!'

She knows Yiannis is guilty. 'What else can you tell me?'

'He'd been talking all week about coming down to the house to fix a faucet in the kitchen that was leaking. Though it doesn't prove anything.'

'Let me ask, did he know his son was going into town that morning?'

'I was serving him and that prissy wife of his breakfast in the dining room when their son came in to inform them of his plans. You think he might have come down here after his son left?' Thea asked with solemn reflection.

'He had the perfect excuse, didn't he? And the girl wouldn't have thought anything unusual about her boss calling in to fix the faucet. She'd probably let him in and gone on about her business without the slightest idea what he was about to do to her! And he wouldn't have been stupid enough to hang around and wait to be caught. He wasn't going to risk his reputation or go to jail. He accused his son, didn't he? That says it all about the man!'

'He must have been very scared otherwise he wouldn't have fired my son and those men,' Thea said.

'Did your son tell you why?'

'His excuse was that he'd bought some fancy machinery that could do the harvesting much quicker than his manual workers. He was cutting his costs, so to speak. But I'd say his guilt got the better of him. He couldn't confront his workers with a clear conscience each day. Katina knew his dirty secret just the same.'

'How would she have found out?'

'I'd say from the girl herself! How else would she have known? When you think about it, that is.'

'Then you were right! She must have known the girl!'

'Ah, I'm never wrong, Miss. And that scorpion probably knew where she'd gone. Probably even knows where she is today. And she must have told Yiannis that she knew what he'd done to the girl.'

'What makes you think that?'

'You see, some weeks after the girl vanished—or what I'd believed to be the case at the time-Katina's relationship with Yiannis seemed more of a close friendship than that of an employee. Twice I saw her go into his office without even knocking, like she was in control of whatever was going on between them. It was characteristic of her conduct after the girl became extinct. And there was that time I saw them huddled together behind the hedges in the garden.'

'Really? Where was his wife?' Despina was becoming even more intrigued.

'Murat, the driver, had taken her into town to have lunch with those high-society friends of hers. Sofia loves nothing more than getting dolled up and shopping in those swanky boutiques. Splurging her husband's money. Being civilised, as she calls it! Sometimes one gets bored of dwelling in a mansion. They can't purify the animal manure in the air, nor erase the images of destitution that surrounds them each day and which constantly reminds them of the reality of their existence. Hah! She forgets where she came from. It's a case of the bottle that rolled and found its cap,' Thea mocked. 'Anyway, back to what I was saying. I'd gone out to pick herbs that afternoon. And when Yiannis peered over the hedge and realised that I'd seen them he waved me over to tell me he was organising a surprise birthday party for his wife that following week. He'd asked Katina if she didn't mind working that evening as he'd hired extra staff and wanted her to supervise the catering. Even more strange was that he'd asked her what she thought would make a nice gift for Sofia. Fool that he was must have thought an unschooled maid like me would buy his hog shit story. Why I'd never seen a man so insensitive towards a wife. He'd never bought Sofia as much as a bar of chocolate let alone give her a surprise birthday party. It was a load of hog shit Miss.'

'What do you think was really going on?' Despina asked.

'My guess is she must have bribed Yiannis. You know, told him that she'd reveal his secret if he didn't do as she asked,' Thea said.

'Para!'

Thea burst a laugh, then said, 'all the money in the world couldn't buy what that scorpion's heart desired. It was more like she was trying to persuade him to get his son to marry her. Did she think she could win a man's adoration by bartering as if his heart was a kilo of apples at the marketplace? I'd say if Yiannis was culpable then he would have been desperate to shut her up in fear of a catastrophic scandal. He probably convinced the sentimental fool that she really would eventually marry his son.'

'He used his own son as collateral in exchange for his own self-protection and freedom. What a disgusting man he is,' Despina said, then thought to ask, 'do you think Sofia suspected or knew of her husband's dirty secret?'

'Sofia was the snake forced to swallow its own poison,' Thea revealed.

'Even so, don't you think she took a risk by firing Katina. After her husband died, that is. There was no guarantee she wouldn't talk,' Despina said.

'I'd say Sofia had nothing to lose anymore. Logic would have told her that Katina's hopes of marrying her son were buried under the earth with her late husband. And the authorities couldn't arrest a dead man. She wanted to defy Katina. She'd had enough of her impudence and reign over her household.'

'Everything is based on your own beliefs about what happened. You just assumed Katina knew the girl and where she'd gone or was. Or even that Sofia knew about Yiannis secret.' Despina said.

'I'm never wrong!' Thea objected.

'Somehow it doesn't make sense why the girl never reported the assault at the time. And how did Katina get involved?'

'My guess is she probably forced her to keep her mouth shut. Threatened her in some way. Like she was doing all along.' Thea said.

'You could be right. It was the perfect opportunity for Katina to bribe Yiannis. Her only chance with Pandelis. Then she must have known the girl, and most likely knew where she'd gone after she vanished.' Despina concluded.

Just then Thea stood up and said, 'best I show you around. You might like to freshen up. No need to worry about a change of clothes and toiletries. I've taken care of everything Miss. Courtesy of myself, not Sofia.' She purposefully informed.

'Most kind of you Thea. But first I'd like to see the studio.'

Despina followed her down a corridor to the rear of the house. 'Here we are!' She pushed open a door that led into a sunlit room that smelt of paint and oil of turpentine.

'Kyrios hasn't been in here for a while.'

An easel with an unfinished landscape stood to one side of the room. A bench exhibited a palette with polychromatic knobs of parched paint and a variety of brushes standing upright in a clay jar.

'But his talent hasn't gone wasted, as you can see!'

'The landscapes are most appealing. And I recognise the architecture in some are of the Byzantine era. Oh, who is this girl?' Despina took a step forward, directed her eyes up at the lifelike portrait that had suddenly captured her attention.

'She's beautiful!' She considered the thick sweeping brows, the dark oval eyes, the rosy cheek bones within the pear-shaped face. The girl emanated a spiritual and intimate energy. She stared at the lavish tumble of brown-red wavy hair that draped one side of the girl's bare shoulder.

The other side was swept up, fastened with a curved shaped comb just above the ear. *Could this be the same comb as the one Pandelis had given to the young maid?*

And was this the girl that had warmed his heart like a winter's sun and then left it to solidify like a block of ice preventing him from finding love again? From having a family and from living the blissful life he deserved.

Despina turned to ask Thea, but strangely enough she had *left the room. Had her move been deliberate? To avoid any uncomfortable questions that she may ask! She wondered what else she was hiding.*

She made her way to the door, when impulsively as if by some cosmic force, she was drawn back to the portrait once more. *Who are you? Who are you?* She didn't know it now but the girl she was staring at was her mother. Dilara.

CHAPTER TWENTY-ONE

21st December 1963 — Lefkosia

As Nilufer hurried through the tangle of dirt patched pathways the sound of gunfire could be heard within the old Venetian walls of the city. She paused to catch her breathe but momentarily couldn't remember where she was going. *I've exhausted my brain.*

Just then the metallic odour in the frosty air jolted her senses and she picked up pace again. *It's not safe on the streets. I must hurry before the last bus leaves.*

But first I must get to Nikos. By this time only few people were on the street when a short while ago there'd been chaos and confusion. Vendors had rolled down the awnings of their shops and gone home. It seemed the military factions of both the Turkish resistance and Greek Cypriot National Guards had at last obeyed their president's appeal for calm and a ceasefire had ensured.

Only a few days before Christmas and people were getting massacred. Would there be no end of hatred and bloodshed between the Greek and Turkish Cypriots! Now Nilufer was caught up in this intercommunal strife. Posters of the extremist movement of EOKA (National Organisation of Cypriot Fighters) were displayed on electric poles and shop fronts; some were torn with edges flapping in the wind. Further ahead at the fork of the intersection was a church. An elderly long-bearded priest in black ecclesiastical robe emerged like a secret spy from its doors and then rapidly vanished within the cloisters. Or was it merely an illusion? Just then she saw a group of armed paramilitaries appear from around the corner and she receded behind an awning of a closed shop.

However, the bottom half of her dress and shoes were exposed and one of the soldiers ordered her to come out.

Nilufer noticed he was not of the Cypriot National Guard. Ethniki Froura. There had been speculation that the British had commissioned Turkish police and armed forces of the Turkish resistance to partake in the insurgency.

Her father had once said; 'you must always know the language of your enemy to know what they are thinking.' Thus, she told the soldier that she was British. The soldier impetuously asked to see her identification papers in a dense English accent.

'They're at the hotel. On Ledra Street. Over there!' She pointed in the opposite direction of the hotel which aroused the soldier's suspicions.

'I'm in a hurry,' she side-stepped him to leave when he caught her arm, drew her back, then smirked at her thoughtless move.

He stared at her leeringly, raised a hand to her ear, his fingers tinkered with the gold loop there, and when Nilufer lurched back, expressed her repulsion, the soldier grinned, gratified by her annoyance.

Allah, help me. I must get to Nikos. As a clinical psychologist she had come to recognise the torture and inhuman degradation some of the juveniles received in detention centres by police after being arrested and convicted for stealing.

Though it was thirteen-year-old Nikos's case that was of interest to her the most. She wasn't sure why. Maybe she was intrigued by the complexity of his nature. Or his life story. Or perhaps it was the interrogating stare of his brown eyes when contemplating the answer to her question.

Or maybe it was the sympathy she felt when staring at the unsightly imperfection of a missing ear lobe. Or merely just the anomaly of him being a Syrian boy with a Greek name.

The soldier now considered the idiocy of her fabricated tale.

Perhaps she was one of those foreign maids who were often on the run from a repressive or molesting Cypriot employer. Or a foreign whore on the run from her pimp. Not even this line of thought derailed his interest. Enticing, if anything.

Teasingly he ran a finger under her chin, drew it up the side of her cheek and when Nilufer felt his other hand slip through the opening of her dress, grip her bosom, she slapped his face, and the soldier returned her a slap equally as hard, if not harder. '*Sharmuta*! Whore,' he snarled.

'I'm not a *putana*!' She impulsively reverted from English to Greek.

'Did you hear brothers? She speaks Greek! She is one of *them*!' The knowledge somehow amplified the soldier's interest in the fugitive. He clenched her chin, held it tightly in his fist, and when he caught the glare of wrath in her grey eyes, his eyes searched there as if probing for the truth behind the lies. 'But you are a liar.'

'I'll call the police!' She screamed, but the soldier burst a laugh by the deviation of what she'd said.

'What can those motherfuckers do? They'll fuck you like they did their mother and sisters!' His words came out in a mangled fashion of Greek.

Nilufer glared at him with utter loathe, simultaneously anguished at having been caught up in this interracial and bigotry crossfire. 'Your vice president Kucuk has appealed for calm and yet you ignore his warnings. You seek impartiality but you slaughter us like lambs!'

'*Our president!*' He derided by her governmental slip-up. Not only do you lie but you listen to 'them' as well.

Go tell your leader Makarios he's a clown for believing he can rely on a bunch of infidel revolutionists to help him achieve enosis with Greece. At once he drew the pistol from the holster of his girdle and aimed at her head.

'Come!' Forcibly he grabbed her arm.

'Let go of me! Help! Help!' She tried to fight him off. *Perhaps the United Nations Peace Keeping Forces or Greek Cypriot militants are patrolling the area and come to my aid.*

'You are strong!' When the feverish soldier felt the biting stab of her teeth clamp down on his hand as he fought her resistance, the pistol fell from his hand.

All the other men laughed in unison at their comrade's plight with the woman as they watched him pick it up off the ground. Erratically he pointed the pistol at her head again and then barked an order to his men and they dispersed into the street like a flock of frightened birds from a tree.

'God help your people! Even the women and children would take up firearms if they knew they were under the command of lunatics!'

'You are also foul-mouthed!' he shouted.

Nilufer spat in his face, and on reflex, the soldier's fist struck the side of her jaw causing her lip to bleed.

'Do as I ask! Or I'll kill you! Understand?'

'You maniac! Go on! She challenged. *Allah help me!*'

'You dare me ah!' He was quick to angle the pistol at her temple. He then gave a furtive glance around before he hauled her by the hair off the sidewalk and into a nearby deserted alley. There he ordered her to bend over and place her hands against the stone wall and where a torn poster of EOKA rustled in the wind above her head.

Allah help me. He's going to rape me. He will kill me if I try to run. Leaning there, terror blanched her face and her stomach throbbed.

Tears gathered in her eyes, fell, clung to her lashes as if they too were clinging for their life. Then a scuffle followed by a single gunshot and a terrified Nilufer sucked in her breath, as if it were her last, awaited to fall, but she was standing and breathing. *Allah I'm still alive.* Slowly she let her hands fall from the wall, and nervously turned around to see her antagonist stooped at her feet, his trousers rumpled at his calves, saw the blood oozing from the bullet wound in his upper arm. Bewildered, she looked up at the tall man dressed in heavy Turkish military uniform standing before her. And despite the expression of gentleness in his brown eyes as he stared back at her Nilufer felt weakened, mortified in his presence.

'Merhaba!' she breathed quietly.

'You speak Turkish!' he smiled.

'*Evet!* Yes. I panicked and tried to have him believe I was British. It was a mistake. He might have left me alone had I spoke in Turk.'

'It wouldn't have made no difference. The opium makes them crazy.' The junior Lieutenant offered, then removed his pistol from the holster at his belt beneath his heavy military jacket.

He then aimed it at the wounded soldier groaning at his feet. 'See to this delirious idiot before I finish him off.' He commanded his soldiers huddled in a semi-circle on the sidewalk ahead of him. The men were quick to obey his orders before heading back to the streets.

He then turned back to the woman and said, 'they like to think they are brave soldiers when they behave like reckless outlaws after a thrill. I'm extremely sorry for your ordeal. Rest assured I will deal with the matter. Are you alright?'

'Evet, evet,' she nodded.

'Forgive me. It was a stupid question. Cleary you aren't because you are trembling.' When Nilufer saw him about to remove his military jacket she said, 'please, no need. I'm alright.'

He retrieved his handkerchief from the pocket and passed it to her. 'Here, your lip is bleeding.'

When he saw her staring at the initials embroidered at one corner he said, 'the R is for Rifat if you're wondering. I have a meticulous mother. She insists on labelling everything since I joined the military. Even my socks,' he smirked.

'You have a kind and sensible mother,' she said. Shyly she wiped her mouth and was about to hand it back when she thought better of it.

'I will wash it and put it aside. But I can't promise you'll get it back. You almost killed that man. And for me. I can't thank you enough! You saved my life.'

He considered the observation then said, 'I'm not a rebel but a soldier of duty. Whatever the case may be.'

He preferred to keep his opinion to himself even though it was evident that this recent outburst of conflict was activated by EOKA revolutionaries.

Turkish militants of the resistance were responding to the slaughter of the previous evening of Greek-Cypriot police rebels of EOKA after having raided the home of a Turkish military doctor within the old Venetian walls.

His wife and three children were brutally murdered by automatic gunfire and the four had been found in a bathtub after having sought shelter in the bathroom.

In years to come the house where the massacre took place will become the 'Museum of Greek Barbarism.' By dawn two Turkish Cypriots were dead and eight others, both Greek and Turkish Cypriots were wounded. And word had spread that the Turkish Cypriots were retaliating and patrolling the streets, and that armed Turkish Cypriot gendarmes had attempted to storm the Greek Cypriot police headquarters in Famagusta.

Fighting was also reported at Kyrenia. Two hundred and seventy of Turkish Cypriots mosques, shrines, and other places of worship were desecrated and vandalised.

'My name is Nilufer,' she reticently offered.

'Nilufer! I like that name. It's a beautiful flower! And it floats on top,' he smiled.

'I never thought of my name as such. Thanks for informing me.' Not even her father had explained the meaning behind her name.

'There is so much unrest and animosity amongst our people. It's not safe on the street. As you have just experienced for yourself some soldiers are desensitised of human emotions, even more so when it comes to a woman. I need to see your identification papers.' The request was that of curiosity, not duty. He had no reason to suspect she was involved in the revolt between opposing military factions. However, he did wonder what she was doing out on the streets. The reason must have been important, he mused, or otherwise she'd be at home with her family by the fire.

'Taman! Oh, my bag, I seem...'

'It's over there!' He said indicating the wall where she'd been leaning. 'Are these shopping bags yours too!?

She nodded, and then watched him collect them off the ground.

And as he passed them over to her, Nilufer felt abashed at having drawn so much attention to herself in the presence of the young and handsome Lieutenant and a rush of colour spread to her cheeks.

After she opened her handbag she said, 'it's not here. I must have left it in my other bag at home.'

'Well, it's no good to you there. Never mind. Where are you from?'

'Pedhoulas is my village.'

'Nice place. I believe it produces the best cherries in the world. And it's a long way.'

'I'm accustomed to the travel.'

'Then you must work in Lefkosia!'

'Yes, at the hospital.'

'Ahh, a nurse.'

'No, I don't have the stomach for it. I'm a clinical psychologist. I have a consulting room there.'

'Then you treat those who are emotionally disturbed.'

'You could say that. Sometimes I consult adolescent refugees held in detention centres after being arrested for felonies. Most of them are traumatised by the ill treatment they receive at the hands of the prison officers.'

'Human violation is a crime. Something must be done,' he said.

'You're right. I'm working on it. Now I must hurry before I miss the last bus. I was on my way to Makarios Square when I was apprehended by your soldiers. Thanks once again. I don't know how I'll ever be able to repay you. *Gurusuruz.*'

'Take care Nilufer hanim.'

Just as she was about to leave gunfire resounded from an inner street.

'Quickly! You are in danger.' He snatched her arm and ushered her to a patrol jeep parked across the road. He opened the door and a frightened Nilufer climbed in. Affixed to the passenger side of the windshield was the familiar red Turkish flag featuring a white star and crescent moon.

He turned for the central district of town but after a few minutes of driving she said, 'you can drop me off here!'

'Are you sure? I thought you were going to Makarios Square.'

'I was, I mean I am, but first I need to drop off these groceries to a friend. She lives just up the street.'

'I'll accompany you, then drive you.'

'I might be held up. Thanks for the offer.'

'Are you sure?' he asked again.

'Evet, evet,' she impatiently said as he pulled over by the curb.

'Take care!' he pressed.

'No need to worry Lieutenant.'

He quietly nodded, considered what an unusual girl she was as he watched her make her way down the pedestrian street. Though doubtful of her move just the same.

The district was known for its brothels and bars where young military recruits gathered, and nationals lobbied Russian, Thai and Armenian sex workers who'd come to Cyprus on working visas posing as domestic servants. It wasn't exactly the kind of neighbourhood a woman of her academic status would come to see a friend. After the recent intercommunal violence between Greek and Turkish Cypriots, by 1964 the UN would send peace keeping forces to the island to establish a buffer zone between the north and south to prevent further fighting.

Now when the Lieutenant saw her enter the Artemis Inn further ahead, he was aroused with further suspicion. Was this friend a prostitute? Without further ado he climbed out of the jeep and proceeded towards the inn. The street was deserted, save for a Russian prostitute smoking a cigarette in the doorway of an empty and dimly lit tavern. The only unlikely customer was a scrawny ginger cat meowing and curling at her feet in search of food. Or perhaps company.

When Nilufer stepped into the foyer the inn keeper, a short burly man with a nose like a turnip bulb, was reading the Cyprus Times behind his desk.

There was an article about a Syrian boy aged thirteen who'd escaped from the juvenile detention centre in Strovolos. He was wanted by police over the attempted stabbing of a prison guard. When he heard the shuffle of steps he expectantly looked up.

'Ah, you're back!'

Nilufer removed two liras from inside her handbag and passed it over to him.

Satisfied she'd kept her word he secured the money in the register. She turned and proceeded down a sunless corridor inlaid with a faded yellow carpet and where overhead a fly specked lightbulb hung from the mouldy ceiling.

Meanwhile, the anomaly of this brief negotiation between the woman and the inn keeper prompted the Lieutenant to come out from behind the door of the lobby where he'd been hiding.

'The woman that just came in, why is she here?'

'Woman…' The inn keeper appeared a smaller version of himself.

'Yes, the one you were talking to a minute ago. Why is she here?'

'This is an inn, so what other reason would she be here for other than to sleep.'

'When did she check in?' The Lieutenant sensed his nervousness as he fumbled to close the newspaper he'd been reading and thrust it aside.

'Must have been late yesterday afternoon.'

'Why did she pay you? She hasn't checked out yet.'

'A deposit is required. Said she'd pay me the following day.'

'Did she leave a passport? As security?'

'I trusted this one because she was alone, you know unlike the friendly couples who want a room for a few hours and then bolt before I can sniff them out.' The inn keeper spoke but his eyes were restively focused on the front door.

'Are you expecting someone?'

'Customers! Who else? You could say times are tough!'

'Did she say when she's leaving?'

'I didn't ask, but why do you ask?'

'A matter of precaution. There's a revolution going on outside. People are getting killed. I'm surprised you're still open for business!'

'Customers are my main priority. Excuse me but there's much work to be done.'

'Then I won't hold you up.'

Just as he turned to leave, two Greek police officers strutted through the front door.

'Ah, paying customers!' He said wryly, but when the inn keeper saw the officers draw their pistols by the sight of the Turkish Lieutenant he exclaimed, 'please, please officers. In the name of God. We are all neighbours! The Lieutenant is not here to make trouble! He was just paying for his room. His lady friend left a minute ago.'

'Is this right?' One of the officers asked him grim-faced.

'You heard! I'll be on my way! He saluted with the pretence of respect, turned, and then took unhurried steps towards the lobby when he overheard the officer say to the keeper, 'when you rang you said a woman brought him in. Are you sure it's the boy we're looking for?

He retrieved a spare key from off the board behind him and passed it over to the Greek officer. 'See for yourself. But first we have some business to settle.'

'We haven't arrested the fugitive yet,' the first officer said dismissively.

'Alright, alright. Room five. I'll be waiting.'

The Lieutenant now made his way out of the inn, passing the Russian prostitute as he made his way back through the pedestrian street.

He sat in the patrol jeep and waited for the officers to emerge from the inn, unsure of what to expect next. He tried to make sense of the anomaly of it all. Shortly, they filed out onto the sidewalk with the girl and boy handcuffed. One of the officers ushered them both into the back seat of the police vehicle while his colleague took up seat in the front.

The woman was in serious trouble, he thought. He climbed out of the jeep and headed back to the inn. He snuck quietly into the lobby, withdrew the pistol from its holster, and then crept up to the desk. A single bullet to the head was all it took to remove the look of terror from the inn keeper's face.

'You've just seen your last paying customer traitor!'

CHAPTER TWENTY-TWO

Pandelis paced the corridor as he waited for the doctor to come out of the emergency ward. It had been over an hour since they'd arrived at the general Famagusta hospital. Wearily he sunk into a chair, his eyes were dull, his mind drifted someplace else, a place far removed from the dismal environment of sterility, beeping pages, and masked, white robed doctors pacing in and out of wards and corridors. Momentarily, Pandelis envisioned he was seated beside eight-year-old Despina by the fishpond in the tranquil surroundings of the mansion's garden. She was unhappy because it was the day her sister Zehra was missing.

'Now tell me pretty lady'

'Despina is my name!' She promptly corrected him.

'Pardon, I've upset you.'

'I'm upset with Baba because he hasn't brought my sister home. I only have Bebek to play with. She's Baba's sister. She's naughty and dumb because she hasn't got a brain like us' Despina said.

'As a boy I'd go up to the wishing tree.'

'What did you do there? Despina asked.

'I went in the hope of finding a coin to buy candy. I'd steal candy if I didn't find a coin.' He'd told her.

'*It's wrong to steal.*'

'*When you're just a kid you don't think of the wrongdoing, just the candy.*'

'*What was the girl's name in the story?* Despina asked.

'*I don't think I gave her a name.*'

'*Everybody has a name. You can still give her one.*'

'Here comes the doctor now!' Thea said.

'Kyrio!' She shook his arm.

'Doctor! What?' he stirred from his reverie.

'He's here!' They rose to their feet and expectantly observed the short, balding man in white coat. 'I'm doctor Vassilis. My condolences! She has lost the baby!

'Baby! Despina was pregnant!' He said absent-mindedly. *He asked if the Muslim boy had touched me. I swore he hadn't! God is my witness.*

'You are her husband, aren't you?' Doctor Vassilis asked.

'Despina's fiancé doctor!' Thea was quick to reply. This was followed by a spell of coughing in a deliberate bid to avoid Pandelis's confounded stare.

All that she had told him when she'd rung from the orchard house was that Despina was in terrible pain. Only a woman understood another woman's emotions and somatic pain whilst enduring a miscarriage. More importantly a woman that wasn't in her most virtuous state when she married was considered a used and abused dust-cloth. A useless commodity.

'I'd like to see Despina!' Pandelis said.

'She's sedated. After the anaesthetic, that is.' He explained that he'd performed a curette to clear the uterine of any remaining placenta.

'To prevent infection, so to speak. Let me ask, is this your fiancés first miscarriage?'

'Why I....'

'Yes, doctor,' Thea interrupted.

Doctor Vassilis frowned at the elderly woman's incessant interference.

'May I ask what your relationship is to Miss Despina?'

'She's a close friend. Why do you ask?'

Doctor Vassilis disregarded her enquiry and went on to explain to Pandelis that his fiancée was confused by the miscarriage. Even more so by the pregnancy itself. 'That's why I ask.'

'Understandably she would be!' He uttered, as if to himself.

He tore away the top half of my dress. He stopped at nothing to prove me wrong. I'll never forgive him.

'It's after 3 a.m., and I'm about to go off duty. If Despina makes a full recovery she will be discharged tomorrow. Call by the hospital sometime before midday.'

They left for the Asteria hotel in town where they could both get a few hours of sleep.

The Asteria hotel was part of Pandelis's late father's estate. The hotel was conveniently located in the business district of Famagusta. Up until his father's death five months ago he'd been the municipal's mayor. He'd never been as ambitious as him. Managing the family's industrial estate with almost two hundred employees and his charity work kept him busy enough.

His father would have regarded the former things as leisurely hobbies just the same. And would have viewed his lack of interest to succeed on a wider scale as an indication of character weakness, a disabling attribute which would result in failure.

As Pandelis drove along the east coastline the Mediterranean Sea provided the ideal canvass for the silvery moon to cast its translucent glow upon its dark waters.

In a few hours it would give way to the sun to emit its own portrait of golden brilliance upon the ocean and earth. Tourists would then flock to its sandy beach to bask and swim.

As he breathed in the sea air through the open window his thoughts were on Despina. He was so distracted that he was unmindful of the maid seated beside him.

Thea was glad of it because she wasn't in the mood to respond to his questioning. Inevitably, though she would have to take accountability for her lies to doctor Vassilis. And she was right.

'Why did you tell the doctor I was Despina's fiancé? You also told him that she'd never miscarried before. I must say I found your behaviour strange. Unlike you Thea! Speak up!'

'What if she never hears from her fiancée again?

'And you used me as a substitute.'

'Well, there's nothing wrong in it. She doesn't deserve to be humiliated.'

'I agree, but my pretending to be her fiancée won't solve anything. And if word leaks out, just imagine her embarrassment. Even worse if her fiancée hears the rumour. She's very much in love with Rifat. She's heartbroken by what has happened. And I sincerely worry about her future if things don't work out between them.'

'It's all Katina's fault! She's an expert at ruining relationships. She's just as jealous of Despina as she was the maid that worked for your family years ago.'

'What maid?'

'Come now Kyrio it doesn't befit a smart man like you to act naïve.'

'I can assure you there was nothing going on between us. Besides, I wasn't even at the orchard house that day!'

'You don't have to convince me. I know you were in town most of the day. To renew your passport. But somebody else was there! Knew the girl would be alone in the house.'

'The question is who? I can't think of anyone! Can you?'

'I might say that I can.' Thea reasoned that her days of working at the mansion were nearly over. She felt compelled to speak the truth.

She pursed her lips, waited expectantly for his next question, hoping it would be the right one that would relieve his conscience of the undue shame that has plagued him for years.

'Who do you think it was? I'll bury the bastard alive!'

'You won't have to Kyrio. He's already buried!'

'How do you know that?'

'I was at his funeral. And so were you. And so was your mother!'

'Are you saying we all knew this man?' His pulse quickened.

'Since you were born. He's your father.'

He shook his head empathetically by the disclosure. The prospect of absent-mindedness, misperception and silly prattling in old age scared him. Even physical exhaustion could drain one's mind of all logic.

'You've been with us a long time. How old are you Thea, if I may ask?'

'Stop using my age as an excuse to fire me!' She chided.

'Why would I do that?' He grinned.

'Because you think I'm senile. Well, I'm not! I know very well what I'm saying. You must know the truth. Whether you like it or not! And don't expect me to make koliva for the memorial service. I'd rather spit on that man's grave.'

God, she's serious! Just then, even he had the urge to spit out the window, as if this action would abort his abhorrence. Up ahead he could see the blue neon sign of the Asteria hotel. But deliberately pulled into a nearby clearing with a bench by the side of the road.

'Why have you stopped here! I'm too old for this romantic stuff, don't you think?'

'I want you to get some fresh air Thea, not stargaze. It's been a long day and I want you to clear your head.'

'My brain is clear as water! And my legs are just as sound,' she mumbled under her breath when he offered to help her out.

When they'd settled on the bench he said, 'I'd like you to tell me everything you know. Convince me of my father's guilt.'

He stared out over the ocean as far as his eyes could see, and concurrently as he heard his life unfold into a shroud of lies and betrayal, he imagined himself drowning in its bottomless depths.

'I don't know what to say! I'm in shock. Why didn't you tell me all this before I went abroad? Why now after all these years?'

'You can say it's my way of atonement before my final days on earth. I wanted to discharge you of the unnecessary humiliation you've endured all these years Kyrio. You had to know the truth.'

'I'm grateful for your honesty Thea. Did Katina really believe that she could bribe my father into my marrying her in exchange for her silence? And what about mother? She should have thrown her out of the mansion. And had father arrested. Instead, she shut up to elude the scandal so she could uphold her lavish and carefree lifestyle. Not even father's remoteness towards me bothered her. What a spineless and self-centred woman she is!'

'You don't have to tell me what a boneless woman Sofia is Kyrio. She controlled your life whilst protecting you under the wings of her poison. And your father saddled you with self-shame. Now he's buried and you are free to move forward with your life.'

'You're a wise woman for figuring out everything by yourself. Katina must have threatened the maid not to go to the police to report the rape. She used that poor girl's misadventure for her own advantage.

To blackmail father. And you'd said that she hadn't left the mansion on the day of the incident. So, you were right. She must have known the maid. And I have the odd feeling she's hiding more than Despina's letters from her fiancée.

You see, Despina doesn't believe her mother is dead. Nor does she believe Spyros is her real father. Why Katina is hiding the truth from her is a mystery. Let me ask, did she ever mention she had a sister?'

'Hmm, let me think. Oh, that's right. She lived abroad.'

'Did she say where? Not that it matters. What matters is the fact she had a sister!'

'Where would her sister fit into all of this?'

'I'm not sure. I'm just trying to figure out where she would have known this maid from.'

'You think it could have been her sister!'

'Did she ever mention her mother? Or if she lived abroad?'

'She must have. Her sister mentioned a stepfather in a letter to Katina.'

'Interesting. Do you remember why she brought it up?'

'She was like a grape with no juice that day. She was like that when you weren't around to put stars in her eyes. Anyway, like I said, she received a letter from her sister. She'd written to tell her that the stepfather was giving her a hard time. Abusing her, or something of the sort. She said she wanted to run away.'

'Then that might explain why she ended up in Rizo. And how it came about that father employed her as a seasonal worker in the orchard. Before she worked as a maid at the mansion.'

'That's when the problems started. And they're still ongoing. Now you have Despina's father to worry about.'

'Despina's a grown woman. The police can't charge me for her abduction. If anything, I'm protecting her.'

'I just hope he doesn't come after you with a scythe like Katina said he would!'

'Let him! By the time I've finished with him not even the dogs will be able to find his pieces.'

'I never passed you for a savage man.'

'That's because I'm not, Thea. But the man's a sociopath!'

'Let's just hope it won't be your pieces those dogs will be looking for!'

'Let's get some sleep, shall we? The sun will be up in a few hours.'

CHAPTER TWENTY-THREE

'I've come to talk about your son and Despina,' Pandelis told Jusuf the Chair-Weaver as he stood on the threshold of his workshop.

'My son broke off with the girl months ago!' he said irritably.

'How do you know that?'

'I'm his father.'

'Did he say the reason?'

'A man can come to his senses, can't he? Both are from different backgrounds. And one must abide by the rituals of their ancestors. Not by the foolish emotions of the heart.'

'You are merely speaking from your own perspective, and not that of your son's. Rifat and Despina are deeply devoted and plan to marry.'

'They can't marry! Now git!' Pandelis caught the door before it closed in his face, inched sideways, and passed through into the chaos of his workshop.

'That wasn't a neighbourly thing to do good Muslim. I'm not here to make trouble. When was the last time you saw your son?'

'That's none of your business!' Jusuf scowled.

'You're right! Miss Despina has a right to know where her fiancée is, and why he's stopped writing.'

'That's the logical thing to do, isn't it? When someone breaks up.'

'Not when Despina is pregnant with his child! Why are you shocked? It's a natural and physical act that occurs between couples.'

Not even this tactic worked to make him talk. Instead, his revelation was met with further protest and hostility.

'There's nothing normal about their relationship! Do you understand? And who are you to come here and defend the daughter of that sonofabitch Spyros? I don't want to hear your miserable lies! Don't come here again!'

'Then I'll find Rifat myself! Remind him of his responsibility!'

'Are you threatening me Gapsalis? He snatched a piece of shaved timber near his workbench and brandished it in the air. 'Now git! Git before I break your skull!'

Pandelis found the small man's behaviour remarkably strange and sensed his son's and Despina's backgrounds were just an implausible excuse. There had to be some other fundamental reason for trying to break them up.

'As a neighbour I've come in peace good Muslim and yet you treat me like an offender.'

'I've warned you! Now git!' Jusuf scowled.

Just then his wife came through the door bearing an oval tray with tiny glasses of Tsai. 'What's going on Jusuf?' Zenep asked uneasily.

'Zenep honey, be a dutiful wife and go back to the house. I'll drink Tsai later.'

'I'll do no such thing!' She retorted as she placed the tray atop a chair. She turned and asked, 'well! Why are you shouting at the customer!

'Your husband is cross because I've come to talk about your son and Miss Despina.'

'Did you hear that Jusuf? That whore has suddenly become a lady!' Zenep mocked.

'You have no right to attack the dignity of a woman you don't even know! I'm sure Rifat would also disapprove of your actions. And I don't believe he's broken up with her. Her pregnancy confirms their commitment to each other.'

'Pregnancy! You see Jusuf? Not only is that woman a whore in body but also in soul! That cheap run around whose been chasing our son for years is trying to trick him into marrying her by making him believe that bastard in her belly is his! What will she come up with next to try and snare him?'

Jusuf paced the floor with his hands pressed to his ears. 'Blocking your ears won't make things right Jusuf!'

'Enough! Despina has done nothing wrong. She's just as much a victim in all of this as our son!'

'What are you saying?' she cried.

'Once I've explained, you'll understand that things aren't what they seem. Despina and Rifat are siblings!'

'Siblings! Zenep shrieked!'

'Rifat is the tobacco merchant's son.'

Pandelis now understood the underlying reason for his Muslim neighbour's erratic behaviour. And he was shocked to the core by the disclosure.

'You mean his mother is that dirty scoundrel's crazy wife? Please tell me this is a joke! Or I swear I'll divorce you Jusuf!' Zenep cried tempestuously.

'Are you saying Spyros's wife is alive?' Pandelis asked.

'Well physically she is but her brain's dead. She lost her mind at childbirth. Strange case,' Jusuf said.

'What? Then where has she been all these years?'

'At home. Where else would one's wife be?' Jusuf asserted.

'If you could call a hole under the house as such!' Zenep said wryly.

'Are you serious? Despina thinks her mother is dead. And she never spoke of a brother. Only a sister. Zehra. She's also dead.'

'Why I'll put my spit right here if that girl's dead! Spyros, that cholera sold her and then had people believe it was an accident up in the mountains. He even staged the funeral.'

Pandelis thought the narrative got more and more bizarre with each disclosure.

'You mean there's a chance Zehra is still alive?'

'Well, whoever the fraudulent man was that bought her must have forced the girl to marry him. Though it's anybody's guess where on earth she is.'

'Where does Rifat fit into all of this?'

'His mistress bore him a son. Omer. My wife and I changed his name to Rifat. After the midwife brought him to us,' Jusuf said.

'The midwife. Isn't she the mother of mayor Neophytos? How did she become involved in this outrageous conspiracy?' Pandelis urged.

'Like myself she was concerned about Rifat's and Despina's association. We discussed the situation many times between ourselves. We came to an arrangement, you see, she would have her son the mayor pass on Rifat's letters to her so she could forward them on to me. I've had them for a few months now.'

'Then it explains things! Though sadly Despina will never know.'

'I can only express my sympathy. Though it's best we keep it to ourselves,' Jusuf urged.

'What choice do we have? I'm surprised that you and the midwife didn't intervene sooner before things got out of hand. Then I'm assuming the mayor knows about this!'

Pandelis recalled how the mayor tried to throw his questions off course about Despina's letters going astray.

'I'm surprised the old woman didn't. I brought it up recently when he came to see me. I guess I'd been shouldering this burden for so long on my own that I just wanted to get things off my chest. Perhaps it was my subconscious way of asking for help. I must say I felt instantly relieved good Christian.'

Pandelis tried to evaluate everything but there were still pieces of the puzzle missing. He turned to Jusuf and asked, 'do you know if the midwife delivered all three children? Rifat, Despina and Zehra? I ask because you said Spyros's wife got sick after she gave birth to Despina. And if you say he fathered a son, Omer, or Rifat as he is now called, with his mistress, then where does Zehra fit in to all of this? Who's the mother?

And why would Spyros and this anonymous mistress of his willingly give away their son to somebody else to raise?'

After Jusuf explained everything Pandelis said, 'if the mistress ran off with the son Spyros had fathered and left her illegitimate daughter with him then it explains why he wanted to get rid of poor Zehra! It was an inhumanly act of revenge! The man's unhinged! Though clearly the mistress made a disastrous decision to leave her daughter with this lunatic. She should have given her child away to be fostered and left the boy with his father. This way Omer, or Rifat as he is now called, would have grown up with Despina as her sibling. And this sinful affair between the two wouldn't have developed, could have been prevented.'

Jusuf nodded soberly, then turned to his wife and said, 'forgive me Zenep. You never would have agreed to raise the boy if you'd known the truth. That's why the midwife and I agreed not to tell you. Believe me I did everything to try and prevent it.'

'How Jusuf? Do you think by hiding our son's letters from the girl it would end? All you had to do was tell me the truth. A mother has a special way of dealing with things. Now what are we supposed to do? How are we going to amend this miserable disaster without hurting our boy?' Zenep wept inconsolably.

'It's a love story that has ended in a great tragedy.' Pandelis announced. 'Despina and Rifat have been chasing sunsets since childhood when all along they were siblings. They made dreams together. Planned to marry and have children. How does one make sense of such a thing. Even more absurd is that Spyros's son had been living right under his nose all these years. A boy whom I believe he utterly despised.

However, we must all take pity on Miss Despina. She believes the girl buried in the forest of red cedars is her sister and that there's a good chance that Zehra's somewhere out there alive. Even if it be her real sister or not, the thing is they both shared a childhood together.' He concluded.

'Allah! I just remembered! You said Despina's pregnant! What now?' Zenep asserted panic-stricken.

'She's lost the baby. She's had an overnight stay in hospital.'

'I'd pass on my condolences but clearly I can't,' she said regretfully, but relieved just the same. 'Everything happens for a reason.'

'Perhaps it's God's empathetic way of accepting the graveness of the situation,' Pandelis reinforced.

'Where is she now? Does her father know?' Jusuf fearfully asked.

'I can't answer that! I haven't had a chance to talk to Despina yet. She's resting at my orchard house. I intent to keep her there where she'll be safe. Her father has been beating her.'

'Why the man's even more sick of mind than that wife of his. They should both be in an infirmary. You see Jusuf, Allah sees everything. It was His wish that we raise the boy!'

'Zenep honey be kind! Allah also hears everything. And like you said, everything happens for a reason. Now, if you both don't mind much work awaits me. A man can't earn para by wasting his precious time trying to resolve the neurotic minds and merciless actions of others. I'll see you to the door. Please keep in touch.'

Pandelis departed appearing ghostly pale and expressionless. How was he ever going to explain everything to Despina? He couldn't.

'Of all the women my son could have he gets the dregs of this village thrown in his lap!' Sofia moaned as she paced the floor of her upstairs retreat. The ringing tone of the phone momentarily apprehended her temper. Though when she answered, it wasn't the call she'd been expecting.

'Thea it's you! I thought it was my son. Has that field girl left yet! Or do I have to come down there and throw her out?'

Thea lowered the receiver and rubbed her ear.

'Did you hear, or have you gone deaf?'

'I heard you!' Thea replied.

'Then answer when I speak to you! And you must respectfully address me as Kyria! Understood?'

'Yes, Kyria.'

'What was wrong with her? You said it was urgent when you rang last night! I hope it was food poisoning!'

'Oh, nothing like that Kyria,' she assured.

'That's a shame! Just another scheming game of hers with my son. I'll have Murat drive me down there now! Throw her out myself!'

'Miss Despina has left!' She lied. She was resting in the guest room with a severe case of the gloom. However, just to insult her further, Thea might have told her that Despina was outside planting the rose bush that her son had bought for her from a roadside plant market on their way home from Famagusta.

'Then why didn't you just say so and spared me the agony? And I insist you stop referring to that rustic as Miss! You sound utterly ridiculous.'

'How else should I address a polite and educated woman? But when a woman likes to think herself as a lady and demands to be addressed as such when she's not, seems even more silly!'

'What is this brash nonsense? Tell my son I want to speak to him. Now!'

'He's not here either.' This bit was true as he'd left the house shortly after they'd arrived home to go and speak with Jusuf the Chair Weaver. Thea didn't have a clue as to why! From there he said he was going to Lemnos to speak to Doctor Grigori.

'Then where is he?' Sofia urged feverishly.

'I can't tell you that either!' she replied calmly.

'Are you refusing to obey me?'

'I'm your son's and Miss Despina's housekeeper. My duty is to obey their requests, not yours!'

'You dare to attack my dignity with the bread I put in your mouth for years! And boast of your loyalty towards a girl from the slums!'

'Despina might seem as such in your dim eyes but if you could see her through that of your son's then you'd realise why he's attracted to her. And it's about time you climbed down from that high throne of yours and come down to earth. Face the reality that you're a nobody in the eyes of decent and sensible people.'

Thea was so fired up to crush Sofia's self-image that all she thought about was her subsequent line of assault, thus was entirely insensible to everything else around her.

'Why you impertinent mindless old woman! You're fired! Fired! Did you hear?' Her tempestuous voice almost ruptured Thea's eardrum.

'What makes you think I'd even care? You're the stupid one! I mean for being conceited enough to think that I'd stress over a loathsome and selfish woman who covered her husband's crime just to save face before her high society friends. And whose grief never touched her bones when he died. I wonder if General Pappas's wife knows about her best friend's longstanding affair with her husband! And that his mistress bore him a son. You were short of two months. Then you duped your husband into thinking the infant was born prematurely. How do I know! Well, I was like a fly on the wall in the mansion. Nothing ever passed my sight or hearing. What a naughty and sinful woman you are Sofia. That's another thing I'll have to tell your son. About Yiannis not being his real father. Not that he'd give a damn about that snotty narcissist since they never got along.'

'Enough of your outrageous lies!' Sofia was so wound up by the elderly maid's malicious defamation that the sweat was pouring out of her now. Not even the tiny fan she was fluttering wildly at her face could cool her wrath.

'What a hypocrite you are! Your son had to know the truth about his father raping that young maid. We both know your son never laid a finger on that girl. And yet you heartlessly watched him suffer in undue self-shame. Who else did Yiannis have to blame? He wasn't going to risk shaming his reputation at a time when he was running to become the next mayor of Famagusta. Power and wealth and prestige meant everything to him. And now that I think about it, you and that late husband of yours were both cut from the same cloth. Both turned a blind eye to the other's indiscretions for your own devious convenience.'

Thea expected she would have slammed the phone down in her face by now. But guessed the only reasoned why she'd persisted to stay on the line was to find out just how much more she really knew.

There was a long silence. 'Well, if you have something to say then just say it! She defiantly continued, then added, 'or has that foul tongue of yours that runs on a battery all day long run out of energy! I can tell you mine is fully charged!' Thea felt a kind of bewildering pleasure by the thought that she'd defeated her antagonist. Just then she cringed when Sofia's exasperated voice resounded in her ears.

'Shut up! You scourge! I've heard enough of your imaginary stories! I want you out of the house now! You hear? And you can take that peasant girl with you before she pollutes the air!'

'You haven't got the authority to throw us out! You don't own the title deeds. Neither does your son. A great shame I might add because it's a glorious villa. I guess that's just another bit of unfortunate news I'll have to tell him before I retire!' Thea warned.

'Shut up you scatter brain! You don't know what you're saying!'

'I guess that pathetic caterpillar that feeds in the earth was lavishly compensated even though she never did get to live in this house with the man of her dreams. You see, she couldn't afford to waste time in finding a husband for that pregnant maid before it all came out in the open. That was the sealed deal between her and that late husband of yours.'

Thea held her breath for the predicable, uncontrolled backlash but all she heard was a succession of throaty gasps. Then a deafening turbulence which sounded like glass breaking and shattering in the room. Curiously, she pressed her ear against the receiver and now all she heard was a low humming noise through the line.

She hung up. 'Hmm, I wonder if Sofia had a heart attack!' She mused with a spontaneous tug of a silver braid. *Guess there's more bad news I'll have to tell Pandelis.*

But she didn't have to tell Pandelis anything because he'd overheard every word she'd said from where he'd stood in the entrance hall. And he just hoped that the maid had been right in her hypothetical forecast. And that the woman who'd raised him under the poison of her wings would never recover.

CHAPTER TWENTY-FOUR

Lefkosia- September 1964

Everything seemed unsurprising when Nilufer stepped into the waiting room of Professor Lambros' psychiatric clinic. The rude matronly woman was clicking away at the typewriter behind her desk, glasses resting on the tip of her nose with a turquoise peacock brooch at the lapel of her tweed jacket. The leaves of the shrub in its pot on the small magazine table was withered, spotted yellow, and in need of revival. Even the sofa where she sat sagged and creaked. It was as if time had stood still, nothing ever changed compared to the everchanging pace of her problematic and indefinable existence.

'Miss Nilufer you can come in now,' Professor Lambros announced.

She stared up at him responsively, then thoughtlessly before she recognised the fragile man standing in the doorway of his consulting room.

When she entered, he indicated the chair in front of his desk.

'I know my place,' she said curtly.

'It's been a while. I'm surprised you came to see me today Nilufer.'

'I'd appreciate it if you didn't call me by that name!' She said as she sat down.

Momentarily he stood by the door wondering what could have prompted this weird announcement. He closed the door and took up seat behind his desk and then asked, 'I sense you're angry. Has something happened since you last saw me? You want to talk about it? Is it Miss Dilara again?'

'That's another name I don't want to hear again. I've got more important things to think about other than a woman who played with my father's heart as if it were a toy. Then threw it back to him before she left!' she retorted.

'You mean she's gone? Has she left the orphanage?'

'Good riddance to the woman I knew she couldn't be trusted.'

He leaned back in his chair, folded his arms and stared at her with cryptic scepticism and simultaneously tried to understand the real reason for her anger. Was she angry with herself? Or with Dilara?

'I thought you would have at least taken my advice the last time we spoke. However, I see you haven't. Would you like to tell me why?'

'How could I decide I wanted to be happy in life as a child when I don't know who that child was? Or even know if that child had ever experienced happiness. Though it is my understanding that it would have been impossible for that child to have even come close to knowing what joy was.'

'Why have you come to this assumption? I mean is there something identifiable or specific that has encouraged you to believe this?'

'Presentiment.'

'People often do construct their beliefs on instinct. If you linked these hunches to characterise someone then who do you think this person might be? Or more specifically, the child you've been searching for.'

'Zehra!'

'Zehra! Did you say?' he remarked ambiguously. 'Who is she?' He wondered if this Zehra might be one of her patients. But even this hypothesis seemed farfetched.

The elderly Professor unfolded his arms as he watched her open her bag for mastic, a habit of hers when she was nervous.

'Oh, I must have changed my bag again,' she uttered with annoyance.

He took out a packet from a drawer and passed it to her. 'I keep a supply for my patients.' He smiled, then waited for her to pop some into her mouth before adding, 'well, who is she Nilufer?'

'Don't call me that name again. It gives me the shivers. Haunts my conscience.'

'My name's Zehra. And I was supposed to have been sold when I was eight!'

He was even more shocked by this extraordinary disclosure. 'Hmm, interesting,' he uttered taking notes. He then looked up at her and said, 'I sense you're angry at being Nilufer. A name is just a name. We don't decide we dislike somebody just because we don't like their name. A name doesn't demonstrate who we really are. As individuals it's our genetic traits that define who we are! However, if it makes you happy to be called Zehra then it's ok by me. Here.' He reached over again and passed her the box of tissues from off his desk.

'You're crying like you've suddenly remembered how to! It's a good sign. It means you are finally letting go of your emotions.' He waited for her to compose herself before he asked the crucial question he'd been wanting to ask. 'I'm curious as to where you got this information.'

'Never mind. I shouldn't have come! I need to see Nikos. I want to make sure he's alright!'

'You got yourself into a lot of trouble with the law because of that escapee. Even got yourself a prison sentence. Don't you think it's beyond your professional duty to harbour juveniles from criminal activities? You can't look after the world. You have your own life to think about! You never mentioned anything about Zehra the last time you were here. You spoke about your near rape and your arrest. You also said you'd been seeing the young lieutenant since your release from prison.'

'As a friend Professor.'

'I think the word 'friend,' would be too modest a word to describe a man who saved your life and took the time to reach out to you in prison to ensure you were alright. He brought you books and sweets and a wool cardigan, you'd said. Other women would regard this military lieutenant their knight in shining armour, their hero so to speak.'

'I never read my name in his eyes Professor. His heart belongs to Despina.' She said impassively, though he accepted her disappointment which told him it was a setback to her relationship moving forward with the lieutenant.

'What makes you think this?'

'He never stops talking about Zehra's sister.'

'Wait!' he broke in. 'Is this the same Zehra that you've come to convince yourself to be her?

'I didn't need convincing Professor. You see, Rifat had overheard his mother talking to their neighbour in his final year at high school. He said he'd kept it a secret from Despina. He thought it would only confuse her more and she'd be heartbroken. Anyway, after everything he told me and according to my calculations of things, then yes Despina is my sister. Or more factually, I assumed she was when I was a child.'

The Professor tapped his pen on his desk a few times, paused to ponder, then shook his head by the fleeting notion that perhaps it was *he* who needed counselling.

'Remarkable! You said you were sold when you were eight. I'd like to know the reason why Rifat brought all this up?'

'Like I said, he never stopped talking about Despina. She and Rifat were childhood sweethearts, you see. And he said that Despina's father opposed his relationship with his daughter because he was Muslim. They were engaged to be married shortly before he joined the Turkish resistance against EOKA.'

'I'm not interested in his military status, just the story he told you,' He interrupted. 'That's what you're here for isn't it? Let's not waste each other's time.'

Just then the tissue box in her lap fell onto the floor and when she got up to put it back on his desk he punctually said, 'keep it!'

He knew some epic sob story was coming, there always was. Though he was doubtful that what she was telling him was entirely true. Patients were known to fabricate mindboggling tales to block out the trauma of their past existence.

'What else can you tell me about Zehra and Despina?'

309

'You think I'm making this all up, don't you?' She announced assuredly.

He smirked and said, 'I like your analytical skills. I'm only doing my job. And I can only do that by trying to identify fact from fiction. Please go on.'

'The more Rifat spoke of Despina and all the things she'd told him about her and her sister Zehra's childhood, my conscience was awakened. Everything came flooding back to haunt me as if I were reliving every event. Like I'd come out from behind a foggy cloud and saw the light.'

'Can you tell me some of the things you recalled?' he asked taking notes.

'Despina and I made windchimes with old wire hangers. We'd hang forks and spoons. And once she gave me her clean dress to wear because I cried that mine was dirty. And gave me her good shoes in exchange for my old cardboard stuffed ones. I even remember the story she told me about the pigeons. Now I understand why I was drawn to the pigeon house on the rooftop of my father's house. Or the man whom I thought to be my real father all these years.'

'What was it about the pigeons that attracted you?'

'The house where I grew up with Despina had a pigeon coop in the yard. I remember it only had one pigeon in it. She said if I told the pigeon my problems, then it would convey the message and the other pigeons would fly home again.'

'And did they?' he asked.

'Of course not. She made it up. She tried to cheer me up like she always did. She even suggested we run away to an orphanage.'

'You never mentioned the man's wife. Despina's mother!'

'We both believed she was dead!'

'Did Despina's father have you believe this?'

'Despina and I must have been very young and so it was easy to believe everything we were told.'

'Had you ever suspected you were adopted prior to learning what you know now?'

'Naturally, I wondered why I'd never seen a photo of my mother or of me as a child before I suffered amnesia. I think I told you this when I first came to see you about my awful nightmares. I'd always felt there were missing parts of my life I couldn't piece together. Now it's clear that I was adopted. Probably from the Holy Trinity orphanage where my adoptive father consulted sick children. And where he met Dilara. He's probably told her and yet he failed to tell me!' she criticised.

'Why do you think he would tell Dilara?'

'Because he was in love with the woman! He wanted to marry her. And I was a part of his family that he wanted to share with her. And yet she shared nothing of her own life with him.'

'The emotions of the heart often overshadow one's logic.'

'Why the woman denied him of all reasoning. He was obsessed with her. He'd never thought to question himself as to where she came from or why she'd taken up refuge in an orphanage. And she left him without even as much as a note of explanation. Don't you find that strange?'

'It is strange though she must have had a good reason just the same. And in my opinion your father wasn't concerned about Dilara's past. It's not unusual for a man to want a woman's company after their wife dies.

And he'd fulfilled his duty in raising and educating you and it was time to think of his own needs. Furthermore, I think that if he knew how much you hated Dilara he'd probably discreetly think you selfish. And disappointed that you didn't approve of her.'

'Well, he can think what he likes. It's not going to change my opinion. There's something creepy about her. She was like a snake waiting to bite me.'

'Why do you really hate this woman so much?' he shrewdly asked.

'She's weird and she makes me feel uneasy around her.'

'Then there must be something she's said or done to make you feel this way, that is? Is there anything in specific you want to talk about?'

'Sui Lee our housekeeper told me that she'd been asking questions about me.'

'What kind of questions?'

'Well, for one she wanted to find out about my childhood illness and amnesia and how I got that way. Then she asked her where I got that snow dome from in my room! Why the nerve of that woman! She'd already asked me the same question one day when I'd caught her snooping around in my room. And yet she'd asked Sui Lee the same thing. What is she trying to prove?'

'Where did you get the snow dome from? It's something that an adult would give a child. Did your father give it to you?'

'I don't remember. Anyway, what difference does it make who gave it to me? Even though his patient thought the question to be irrelevant he on the other hand thought Dilara's interest in the snow dome wasn't merely out of curiosity.

'I had one myself as a child. My mother bought it from a street market stall.'

'Stall! That's right!' She broke in by the recollection. 'It was the camel lady!'

'Camel lady, you said!' he uttered questionably.

'That's right! Despina and I saw her at a festival we went to once. It was far because we went on the school bus and there was this monastery with lots of stalls and crowds of people there.' She went on to explain that this woman had shown them her camel and given them both pasteli and a snow dome each.

'That time Despina said we'd run away to an orphanage I told if we knew where the camel lady was then we could go find her.'

'Why was it that you were drawn to this woman so much?'

'She was kind and beautiful. She was anxious I remember because she thought our mother would be looking for us. And when Despina told her that she'd died, she swept us both in her arms. I remember how good I felt and realised for the first time what it was like to have a woman embrace me so caringly.'

'Did you wish this woman was your mother?'

'Yes, I longed for her day and night.'

The elderly scholar stared at her with silent reflection as he thought about the time his patient had once told him she'd sensed a familiarity about Dilara.

'Did you ever have the same thoughts about Dilara?' he asked.

'Are you kidding me Professor? She's the last person I'd want as a mother! Sui Lee told me that she'd overheard Dilara say to my father that I'd accused her of trying to poison me!'

The elderly scholar chortled by this disclosure as he took notes. He would have thought it would have been the other way around. That his patient would want to poison Dilara.

'What's so funny Professor!' She asked somewhat annoyed.

He looked up and forced a straight face, coughed then said, 'why do you think she'd say something like this?'

'She must have known rice custard makes me very sick. That was her whole intention.'

'Then you must be lactose intolerant. But how would Dilara have known? Don't you think it might be possible that you're looking for excuses to retaliate by hurting her feelings and make her look like the villain in your father's eyes?'

'Of course not! I'm not the one prying into her life. Why she even had the nerve to ask Sui Lee if I had a birthmark. Of all the strangest things to ask! Why in her state of mind anyone would think she'd escaped from an institution for the insane. Probably explains why she ended up at that orphanage because she had nowhere else to hide.'

The elderly scholar adjusted his spectacles and at the same time considered the incredibility of what she'd said.

And even though the latter seemed an unlikely scenario he did however have doubts about the question of the birthmark. It seemed to signify that Dilara was searching for even more clues that might link her to his patient.

'Well, have you got a birthmark?'

'Even if I did it's none of her business.'

'Moving forward, would you like to tell me what else Rifat told you that he'd overheard his mother tell their neighbour!'

'Well, I was getting to that part. I'm supposed to be the unlawful child of a Turkish Armenian gypsy. This woman also happened to be Despina's father's mistress. They had a child together. A boy. She ran off with him!'

'Then that would make this boy wherever he might be and Despina half-siblings. If my estimation of things is correct.'

'Strange now that I think about it. You know, to have been so disillusioned into thinking my mother was dead when all along my real mother was still alive somewhere.'

He jotted down more notes and at the same time pondered on the intriguing story she'd presented him. Then asked, 'how do you feel about what you discovered?'

'If there's any truth in it then the woman's a heartless whore! I hate her!' She burst out angrily. Then sadly added, 'not only was I born out of wedlock, but she also went on to have another child with her lover. And she didn't think twice to run off with the boy. It's obvious she loved the boy more than she did me otherwise she would have taken me with her.' She miserably wept.

'Can I get you a glass of water?'

'I'm alright, thank you!' she sniffled.

'Understandably, you are very disappointed at having been deserted at such a tender age. Though you're reacting purely on the speculation of what Rifat overheard his mother tell their neighbour. Maybe he misunderstood things or what he heard was unrelated to what he assumed to be the case. And you can't judge people simple on the theories of others without knowing the truth. I'm assuming your natural mother must have been young when she had you and you don't know the circumstances of her life. Maybe your biological father abandoned her when she was pregnant. Maybe he met another woman or got killed. Perhaps in the second war. There are many theories about what could or might have happened.'

'It doesn't justify why she deserted me. She could have also taken me with her. Those reoccurring dreams I was having about being trapped inside a dark place where I was frightened and alone. And how I'd wake up frozen with fear and unable to scream!'

'Is there something you've become mindful of that you can connect with this dream?'

'That haunting illusion of someone standing over my bed was Despina's father. I remember him as an evil man. He locked me up inside the shed and what would seem like forever to a young child. Despina opened a small hole at the bottom of the wooden door so she could pass me bread. Then she sat outside the door reading me storybooks so I wouldn't feel alone and scared. This man beat and starved me and forbad me to go to school. Not even a colouring book or pencils.'

'But you did say you went to the monastery on the school bus?'

'Despina told me she'd gotten permission from the teacher.'

'Did you stay home alone while she was at school?'

'He made me work in the field each day.'

'What did you do there? You couldn't have been much help at such a young age.'

'I'd help him sow seeds. I think it was during the wet season. Because by summer the harvest had grown way above my head. And he'd hang it up in the shed to dry. Sometimes he'd smoke it.'

'Ah, tobacco?'

'What difference does it make what he grew? The thing is I didn't want to be there with that horrible man.'

'Did something happen in the field that you remember that's made you angry? Or would you rather forget because it's too painful to talk about?'

He needn't have waited for an answer as he'd already guessed that she'd been subjected to sexual abuse. He now stared at her guardedly as he considered the inhumanness of it all. Amongst other things he'd even began to suspect this Dilara woman to be her biological mother. There was a particular pattern taking place that wasn't merely coincidental anymore. The missing parts of Zehra's life were starting to slot into place. Though the question remained as to how she ended up with the man who'd adopted her. Had he adopted her from the orphanage as she'd suspected, or had he found her someplace else?'

'Never mind. He seemed like a sadistic and heartless man. Undoubtedly, you've been traumatised now that all of this has resurfaced. Let, me ask, have you told Rifat that you've concluded you're Zehra?'

'Why do you ask?'

'Don't you want to see Despina?'

'I'm not sure. I mean I don't know. It's been so long.'

'I thought you'd be overwhelmed with joy. I'm sure Despina would feel the same. Especially, to know you're alive.' Then as an afterthought asked, 'do you think you've betrayed her in some way?'

'What kind of a question is that?' she laughed.

However, the elderly scholar knew it was the kind of spontaneous laugh one expresses when trying to cover their guilt. A misdeed was a prison for one's conscience.

Despina was the real heroine in Zehra's story because she'd loved her unconditionally. Zehra would never have betrayed Despina and Nilufer's rejection towards her given name wasn't in as much as the name itself, but instead, was a disturbing reminder of her disloyalty for allowing herself to fall in love with the only man Despina had ever loved since childhood.

Professor Lambros could only hope that Zehra would find it in her heart to revoke her sentimental feelings towards Rifat to conserve Despina's enduring love and adoration.

CHAPTER TWENTY-FIVE

Pedhoulas — July 1964

Sister Louisa regarded the fragile man seated in front of her desk. His fine three-piece suit and bowtie suggested he was mindful of his academic status, while at the same time defenceless to contest old age.

'Like I told you over the phone Professor I'm not sure if I can help you! Miss Dilara left the orphanage several months ago. Shame we had to lose her. She was the soul of this orphanage. The children will miss her terribly.'

'How long was she here for?'

'Some fifteen-years.'

'Do you know why she took up residency in a nunnery and why she left?'

'It's not my business to pry into the personal lives of others Professor. That's your job, not mine. And I don't know what initiated your interest in Dilara. Is there something important I need to know?'

'I wouldn't be here if it wasn't. And without sounding biased I think you're being dishonest.'

'Are you implying that I'm lying?' Sister Louisa said hot-faced.

'I'd hoped not given that you're a nun of the holy order. I'd also like to add that as a professional it's unethical to get involved with patients outside of consulting hours however I feel this is an exceptional case that must be investigated.'

'I fail to see how Dilara has anything to do with this.'

'My patient's father was in a relationship with this woman.'

'I'd hardly consider it a relationship. Dilara's association with the doctor was that of a platonic friendship. She helped him run his clinic up in the village a few days a week.'

'Nilufer said her father wanted to marry her. And she's angry that she left without an explanation.'

'She's always been mistrustful of Dilara's intentions towards her father. Even towards her, I might add. Mr Jihan isn't the type of man who'd put his own interests before that of his daughter. She has no right to discredit the woman after all she's done for her father.'

The Professor was taken aback by her reproach towards Nilufer while at the same time was unsurprised at her attempt to exonerate Dilara of any wrongdoing. Therefore, seemingly it affirmed she was withholding Dilara's secrets.

'People come to me in the hope they'll be cured of their phobias. Often these emotional fears arise from a traumatic childhood. A child regards its mother as their protector. They need to be reassured of their mother's adoration, guidance and trust. A mother needs to heal her child's wounds in some way. Otherwise, they grow up to be mistrustful of others because they've been deprived of a stable and happy family.

Sometimes it takes years before any progress is made. Often there's slim or no progress made at all. And even when progress is made even then the cure can be worse than the ailment.'

'Mr Jihan raised his daughter in the best possible way.'

'Then his daughter would have approved of his relationship with this woman. And wouldn't have doubted her integrity but the woman was probing into her personal life behind her back.'

'I'm sure Dilara had more things to do with her time than to stick her nose where it doesn't belong Professor. Though I've suddenly realised where you're coming from,' she readily remarked. Then added, 'in my opinion it was all a misunderstanding. I mean with that rice pudding thing. How was Dilara to know Nilufer had an intolerance to milk? And to say that she tried to poison her is rather overblown, don't you think? It was the housekeeper who'd asked her to go into Nilufer's room to fetch the dirty linen. Otherwise, Dilara never would have gone there and there's no big deal about someone asking where they got a child's figurine from. It's a question that anybody might have asked someone. No wonder she needs a psychiatrist! I'm doubtful if she'll have a successful career as a psychologist if she is predisposed to discriminate.'

'I'm sure this matter goes beyond an allergy and a child's trinket. And it wasn't I who updated you about all the things you mentioned. Seemingly, though it was Dilara herself who told you.'

'Who else did she have to confide in? She wasn't the kind of woman who'd deliberately hurt someone's feelings.'

'I'm sorry I had to bring this all up. Though due to the complicated issues that have arisen I've come to you in the hope I'll get some answers.

And I must say the coincidences of events are almost inconceivable as they are problematic. I'm hoping after hearing what I have to say you might change your mind.'

'Then enlighten me Professor.'

He explained about Nilufer's encounter with Rifat, the lieutenant who'd rescued her from being raped by one of his Turkish militant squadrons during the Cyprus conflict last Christmas and how she'd been arrested for harbouring a juvenile delinquent. His visits to see her during her time in jail.'

'Why that's frightful. It's a wonder Mr Jihan didn't have a fatal heart attack! He's made a few visits to the orphanage since then and even attended our annual charity raising fete and he didn't mention anything to me. Then again, he's a humble and self-sacrificing man who'd rather keep things to himself rather than burden others with his problems.' Then inadvertently added, 'he was rather lost after Dilara left. Like he'd had all the life sucked out of him.'

'What you describe is suggestive of a broken-hearted man who was deeply in love. Not of a man who'd just lost a good friend. I'm sure you'll agree.'

'Hmm, very well Professor.' Then without further ado asked, 'now is there something else important that I need to know?'

He went on to elucidate further about the significant things Nilufer found out from Rifat.

Sister Louisa sat quietly and attentively at first, then stared at the flowers in the window box, as if this was a pleasant distraction from all the disquieting things she was hearing.

She now stared back at him sad-eyed, breathed heavily before she said, 'and you said Rifat found out what he assumed to be the truth when he'd overheard his mother and their neighbour talking in his final year at high school. And he and Despina are childhood sweethearts. And he never told her what he'd found out before he went into the army! It seems cruel, don't you think?'

'People are known to take radical measures in order to protect those they care about the most. And it must have pressed heavily on Rifat's conscience to let her go on believing Zehra was her real sister and that she'd continue to grieve for her eight-year-old sister believing she'd died fifteen years ago.'

Sister Louisa compressed her small hands firmly together on the desk in front of her as she considered the happenstance of the events that had transpired.

'It's heart-shattering. How does one cope when they find out they've been disrobed of their identity? And to know they have lived their life as somebody else when their life has unexpectedly been reversed in the most irrevocable way!' She offered woefully.

Professor Lambros reflected on the exactness of the nun's wise observation then announced, 'the reason why Nilufer consulted me in the first place was to try and find out the missing parts of her childhood before her amnesia. She might not have even remembered anything if she hadn't crossed paths with this lieutenant that day. Sometimes finding out the truth can be unkinder and harder than knowing the truth. The cure sometimes is worse than the ailment, as people often say. Perhaps history is best left untouched. But we can't ignore the situation just as Nilufer can't ignore that she's really Zehra.

Or that she was born out of wedlock and her biological mother was Despina's father's mistress! And that her mother had a boy with this man. Then ditched her and run off with their son.'

Sister Louisa's eyes lit up with tears for she'd already heard from Dilara herself most of the things he'd told her. 'You're right Professor.' She disclosed quietly with concealed self-shame.

'I didn't come here today so you could prove me wrong after years of diagnostic research.' He officiously remarked, then added, 'I'm sure you and Dilara had had many private discussions during her long stay here. Now, can you tell me if I'm right in believing this woman Dilara who'd spent half her life dwelling in a nunnery is the real mother of Zehra? That abused and forsaken child who'd been starved of maternal protection.'

The nun dried her eyes, then submissively said, 'the Lord sees all, and He won't pardon this man for all his evilness towards a harmless and innocent child. And God's law has taught us that lying is the gravest of sins. Therefore, I'll tell you the truth. However, it's with great effort and pain that I speak of my honourable colleague's life.'

'I'm also a fair-minded man who's come in good faith. Not to persecute or pass judgement on people caught up in the fateful events of their lives.'

'May I get you Tsai or coffee.' She casually asked, and when he declined her offer added, 'I have a something a little stronger in my cupboard if you like.' She afforded him a playful grin and the elderly scholar stared back at her with burning cheeks while at the same time had the odd notion that the holy nun was flirting with him.

'You mean liquor?' he asked unsteadily.

'It helps calm the nerves.'

'You're right! Though I would have thought...'

'Forbidden?' She broke in with a smile. 'What about the blood of Christ? Though I do enjoy a good drop of malt occasionally.'

'Guess I'm not always right!' He chuckled while he tampered with his bowtie. 'Perhaps some other time. I have a long drive ahead of me. And I'm anxious to hear what you have to say!'

She went on to tell him what Dilara had confessed to her early on that winter's morning just before last Christmas. After she'd given the letter to the bus driver in the village to forward onto Katina in Rizo, in the north.

'Dilara described this man Spyros as a merciless man who persecuted and humiliated her in the worst possible way. Provided her with barely enough provisions for her and the children to survive.'

'What about Zehra's biological father?' he interrupted. 'What happened to him?

'He was a young Greek soldier by the name of Pandelis. She adored him and said she'd read her future in his eyes the moment she'd met him. He was discharged before she could tell him she was pregnant.'

'That's most misfortunate. What about the barracks where he was posted? Some of his army comrades would have known where he'd gone. Or at least known where he lived.'

'I can't comment on that Professor. Only Dilara knew her situation at the time.'

'Alright, let's move forward, shall we. You said Spyros persecuted Dilara.'

'She claims that most of the time it was his foolish obsession with her that contributed to his erratic and violent behaviour. He accused her of being unfaithful. She was fed up with his questioning as to her every move throughout the day when he came home from the field. He was so suspicious that he even began calling into the house at any given time just to make sure she was there.'

'The man must be an utter screwball! Where would she have found the time for such promiscuousness with three toddlers to care for?' He remarked incredulously. 'Go on.'

'This day Dilara had been cracking green olives in the yard when he came over to her and began to interrogate her again. Her constant denials of infidelity infuriated him and so he pulled her up by the hair and then struck her head with the stone she'd been using. She said she'd collapsed to the ground and briefly passed out. Then he tied her wrists up with her apron strings and dragged her across the yard and into the shed. After he tied her ankles up with rope and left her there lying on the ground. We can only assume it was the same shed where he'd locked up poor Zehra. Dilara said all she could think about was the three children inside the house as they were only toddlers at the time. She feared he would take his anger out on them after consuming alcohol and cannabis. Then he became aggravated by her continual screaming and claimed it was giving him an insufferable headache, Dilara had said, and so he shoved a raw onion in her mouth just to shut her up. Left her there until she almost suffocated.'

'The man's an absolute psychopath! If Dilara was powerless to defend herself against this brute, what hope would a young child have?'

'True, true,' she sighed, then added, 'hard to imagine how any woman could fall for such a man.'

'From experience I'd say it would be easy. On the face of it, socio-paths appear charming and kind and are usually smart. And they praise people with the things they want to hear which are all typical traits of a psychopath so they can easily deceive one's perception of the real person they are.'

'That's why she trusted him. Dilara had the purest of souls. And she had all the wonderful qualities that any man could wish for in a life partner. She was bright and generous, gifted and funny and even mischievous at times. She played the lute and sang so beautifully that one could easily get lost in her folktales.'

'I wouldn't mind a wife like that myself Sister,' the elderly chortled. 'Though we can't reverse the inevitable! And one mustn't complain when granted liberties others are denied. And it's most unfortunate that Dilara was forced to surrender Zehra to regain her freedom.'

'Fate is unfair as it made its plans Professor.'

'Destiny is an invisible thread which all of us hold the other end. Unconsciously we pull at this thread and by means of an enigmatic phenomenon it brings us together. Generally, I'm not prone to such illusory theories but when the inconceivable happens we take notice of the beliefs of those who've lived way before us. And destiny must have had something to do with Nilufer's encounter with Rifat that day he'd rescued her from being raped during the internal upheaval between our people. Had this event not occurred then she never would have found out what she did. And if Dilara hadn't crossed paths with the midwife that day in Lemnos as a homeless, unwed and pregnant girl chanting on the sidewalk then things might have worked out differently for her. But instead, she was preordained to become Spyros's mistress and mother to their son and to foster Despina and to renounce Zehra.

Like you said, she'd been deceived into thinking that the young woman Spyros kept in a niche under his house was his sister when all along it was his wife. The mother of Despina who'd never recovered from psychosis after childbirth.'

'I admire your fortitude and commitment to resolve this matter.'

'We all have a job to do Sister. Mine is to try and disentangle some of the clutter within one's mind. Once I've achieved to remove the turmoil within then I must guide them to a safe harbour. Similarly, to that of a captain at the helm that depends on his expertise to pilot his ship through turbulent waters to reach his destination. Now, you said Dilara sent a letter to a friend in the north prior to seeing you that morning! Do you know what it was about?'

'She didn't mention the letter at first because she was more interested to find out how Mr Jihan's wife died.'

'What was her interest, do you know?'

'I asked myself the same question. I thought that he would have told her. And it was only after she promised that she wouldn't tell him she'd found out from me that I told her that she'd died at childbirth.'

'What were the complications, did he say?'

328

'I think it was a ruptured blood vessel. After giving birth to a stillborn.'

'Then that's a justifiable reason.'

'Don't you trust me Professor!' She gave him a bold stare and when he returned her a frisky glare the holy nun's face softened.

'I didn't mean to insult you!' she added apologetically. 'Now where were we? Yes, I told Dilara the exact same thing I told you.'

'Sounds like she was trying to establish if Nilufer was adopted!'

'She'd already figured that out since Mr Jihan never married. What she hadn't figured out was how he'd come to adopt her. Though, she wanted proof that his wife died just the same. Or more factually, to support her belief that Nilufer was her daughter Zehra.

She was in two minds so to speak. Firstly, there was that snow dome she saw in her room. Dilara said it reminded her of those two children she'd met at the monastery of Apostolos Andreas not long before she came to the nunnery.'

'Before you go on, where was she in the intervening years? I imagine the second world war was in place. I was wondering how she survived!'

'She was a resilient and determined woman. Possibly this was due to all that she'd been through. She told me she worked as a farmhand in exchange for board and food. After the war, she bought cheap nick-nacks from the near east and sold them for a small profit. After all, Dilara came from a tribe of gypsies and was accustomed to this lifestyle. Though in hindsight the prospect of having a permanent home was the reason why she'd agreed to stay on with Spyros and nurture his newborn. Anyway, she was certain that the children she saw that day were Despina and Zehra.'

'Then why didn't she do something?' he declared.

'Surely, you can't be thinking straight Professor. You didn't expect her to abduct her daughter. Zehra wouldn't have even remembered who she was. By this time her mother had been absent from her life for almost five years.

Even if she told her who she was just imagine how confused a child of eight would be! And Despina! She couldn't have just taken one child and not the other. Besides, they believed they were sisters.'

'She was powerless to act. It must have been deeply hurtful. The irony here is that Nilufer recalls this encounter. And on the contrary would have been overcome with joy by the prospect of being reunited with her mother. Guess it wasn't meant to be. She and Despina called her the "camel lady." She recalled that she'd given them pasteli and a snow dome each. And had shown them her camel. Despina told her they'd run away to an orphanage. We can only assume that from an early age Despina had embraced the role as surrogate mother to Zehra. And she'd become an integral part of her life. Her decision to run away was a motherly response of duty to try and spare her sister from the ongoing mistreatment at the hands of their wicked father. Nilufer had described the self-pleasure she'd felt when the woman had embraced them both after they told her their mother had died. So, you see, these are the only joyful childhood memories she has before her amnesia. And as Nilufer's treating physician and after evaluating things I can understand her hostility towards Dilara that time she'd asked her where she'd gotten the snow dome from. You see, it was merely an unprompted reaction to try and preserve the memory of the woman who'd allowed her for the first time in her young life to experience what it felt like to be sincerely regarded and cherished. And afford her the maternal affection she'd desperately craved for. She wanted to preserve that memory to herself. Though the fateful absurdity here is that Nilufer couldn't have possibly known that Dilara, the woman she begrudged, was her biological mother. Apart from the figurine what else was it that raised her suspicions about Nilfuer?'

'The rice pudding was another thing that raised the alarm bells. You see, her milk child Despina was intolerant to milk…'

'Wait a minute!' he broke in anxiously. 'We are talking about Zehra, aren't we? I fail to understand how Despina's allergy to milk has got anything to do with Zehra.'

'I knew you'd be confused. I told you Dilara was in two minds about Nilufer. She wanted to believe in her heart that she was Zehra. But logic told her she was wrong.'

'Sometimes guilt can play on the mind and so one tends to be misled into inventing, if not even believing the things they want to believe to alleviate their conscience. Though generally people rely on instinct rather than reasoning. And so, there must have been something significant apart from the things she mentioned to deter her thoughts into sensing she was wrong.'

'Dilara wasn't aware of the underlying reason for Mr Jihan's decision to adopt her.'

'Then I gather you told her?'

'She became even more confused just the same. I can't blame her.

Nor will you after hearing what I have to say. As a physician Mr Jihan was summoned to attend to a child's life-threatening injuries. She was found in an orchard in the valley not far from here. One of the nuns saw her while cherry picking.'

'You don't say! How did she get there? Was it an accident?'

'That's the question on everybody's lips. Nobody knew who the young girl was or where she came from. Her age was estimated to be seven or eight. Dilara was adamant that the child was deliberately thrown off the mountain top. And that she must have been an unwanted burden in society. I told her there were such shelters like this one for such discarded children.'

'You mean she suspected that the child was her daughter Zehra? And that Spyros had something to do with it. '

'Especially after I told her what I knew. Something that I'd failed to even tell Mr Jihan over the past fifteen years. I'm sure after you hear what I have to say you will commend me and tell me that I only did what any other decent human being would do.'

'Well, go ahead! Tell me everything Sister!'

Professor Lambros sat quietly as the nun went on to explain everything Costa had told her that day.

'I could do with a stiff drink after hearing all of this!' He asserted soberly with a shake of the head. 'Trading a minor is an illegal offense! And in exchange for a couple of lousy hides! Why that psychopath should be hung, strung and quartered! Just like in Medieval times!'

'A prison sentence at least,' she scoffed.

'The child's situation was critical. She never would have recovered if not for Mr Jihan's enormous sacrifices. The authorities would have only notified Spyros. May God be pleased with you Sister! You did the right thing!'

'Ah, you see! I told you so!' she smiled.

His ears burned by the idea that he'd delighted her. Then in the true manner suggestive of an adept scholar he announced, 'Alright! Let's move on, shall we? Costa might have been right in his assumption that Spyros must have decided to come up here on a whim hoping he could persuade him into changing his mind. He was desperate to get rid of the child, wasn't he?

And just as desperate to avenge his mistress after she ran off with their son. So, Dilara's child became the ill-fated recipient of his seething reprisal. And it wouldn't have been any skin off Spyros's back if he could find pushovers like Costa to discharge him of the surplus burden.'

'It all makes sense to me. And Costa may have been right about the girl realising that she was being separated from her sister and somehow managed to escape!'

'Though we'd both agree in wondering how a child of eight could even manage to escape from the clutches of a brutal psychopath!'

'You're not wrong Professor. Even Dilara was powerless to defend herself.'

'There's a tortuous road at the topmost of the mountain. And obviously Spyros must have driven to get up here. And for the girl to have run off he would have had to stop the vehicle at some point or another. Considering the road is rough and narrow he would have parked very close to the perimeter of the overhead mountain. We can assume that at this point it was the child's only chance to flee. Spyros would have been hot on her trail which means the girl would have been terrified. In her haste to get away, it would have taken only a split second for her to lose balance and fall over the edge, thus tumbling down the steep slope and ending up in that orchard near the gorge below.'

'It's an excellent theory Professor. Even so, like I said, things didn't add up. You see, Dilara knew Zehra had brown eyes. And Costa claimed that the child Spyros tried to trade was a pretty girl with grey eyes. Nilufer has grey eyes. And so did Despina's mother.'

'You mean the sick woman she believed to be Spyros' sister?' He became disoriented at times by the interchanging events.

'That's right. Bebek, as she was called. Meaning child in both the Greek and Turkish language. Dilara described her grey eyes as being, "hauntingly sad." And Zehra wasn't intolerant to milk. She also had a distinguishable birthmark situated in her upper inner thigh. So, you can understand her great confusion.'

'Nilufer is Despina. Her milk child? Spyros's biological daughter? A case of mistaken identity!' He was utterly shocked by this sudden admission. 'Are you sure? What about the birthmark?'

'Mr Jihan had hired a nurse full time to care for the girl after she'd been discharged from the hospital and subsequent amnesia. Bathing and dressing the girl was part of her daily routine. She's retired but I told Dilara if she went up to the village it wouldn't be hard to find her if she asked around. She came back to say that the nurse hadn't seen such a mark on the girl's body. We must remember that the children were under the age of three when she left them and that frequently Spyros, was under the influence of alcohol and cannabis and wouldn't have known a "rat from a cat."

'What about the letter she sent to her friend in the north? Do you think it had something to do with her decision to leave?' He asked.

'Absolutely! She suspected Katina was Spyros's sister-in-law.'

'You mean his sick wife was her friend's sister?'

'That's what she'd figured out. It was too late, just the same.'

The elderly tolerantly listened on as she told him everything Dilara told her about the woman whom she'd considered to be her only best friend.

'Katina was the match that ignited the furnace then pushed both Dilara and Zehra into that hellhole to burn. Her mind was just as perverted as Spyros's. Both were depraved sociopaths.' He derided with a twitch of the neck.

'Dilara had felt bitterly betrayed! She'd thought that Katina might have cared for the children in some small way. Especially since she'd become substitute mother to her niece Despina and at a time when she believed the infant was orphaned of a mother. When all along Katina knew it wasn't true.'

'Perhaps there was an ongoing rivalry between Katina and her sister, like Dilara had said. Maybe they were both in love with the same man. Love is a powerful thing. Even known to cause wars! Some of these historical wars have been documented.'

He might have added that a single strand of a woman's pubic hair could sink a battleship. Though the elderly scholar knew such blasphemous commentaries in the presence of a religious nun would be indecent.

'I wouldn't know about such matters Professor. The only man I've ever worshipped is our Lord!' She asserted.

'Each to their own values Sister. Worshipping God in your opinion is probably the most unadulterated and satisfying kind of physical devotion there is. Because it's an unconditional love with no boundaries.'

She smiled by the thought that he'd understood the sentiments of that of a religious nun.

'I'm inclined to go along with Dilara's theory. Katina enticed Spyros with the field. Her sister was the bait that ended up in the putrid bowels of her catch,' he condemned.

'And disregarded Dilara's safety in the same way. Though where she got the field from remains a mystery. May God be witness to her sins and punish her accordingly. Like Dilara once said, people do desperate things in desperate situations. But to sacrifice one's own flesh and blood is pure evil.'

'It would be fair to say that Katina never did get back to Dilara after she sent her a letter. And since she'd figured out that she and Spyros were related she would have told him where she was. And had left the shelter in fear he'd come after her.'

'That's right. Several weeks had passed. And she was sure he'd retaliate after she ran off with the son he'd fathered.'

'Well, where is the boy? Don't tell me she gave him away?'

'What choice did she have in times of desperation and war Professor? The infant would have perished. On the night of her escape Dilara gave Omer to the village midwife who in turn gave the boy to the childless

Muslim couple in Rizo. The same couple I told you about that had first been promised by the midwife to raise Zehra.'

'It was a risk, don't you think? I mean the boy roaming around in the same village as his biological father.'

'Common sense would tell us that this couple who'd adopted the boy would have changed his name. Even Dilara was confident. And they are Muslim, which is even a more logical reason why he wouldn't have suspected. The boy would have been raised in accordance with Muslim customs and religious practices.'

'I'm not as optimistic! In view of both the past and present fluke events. And all of which superficially were influenced by the mysterious workings of that invisible thread of fate I spoke about and changing the boy's name won't guarantee this boy Omer won't find out! Small rural villages are notorious for gossiping. Particularly the women. This Rifat boy overheard his mother talking to their neighbour, didn't he? What if it had been Omer who'd overheard his mother tell their neighbour the circumstances in which he'd been adopted?'

He paused again to reflect, his downy lashes blinking with each passing theory, in the gold light that dusted the ancient stone walls of the modest room, until at last he let out an involuntary sigh.

'What is it?' She asked with equal sobriety.

'I'm thinking about that junior lieutenant Rifat. He told Nilufer he was from the village of Rizo. What are the chances of him being Spyros's son he believed Dilara ran off with? And what are the odds that this Despina he's in love with is the real Zehra whom Nilufer now believes she is! What a calamity it would be?'

'Good Lord! Sister Louisa crossed herself. 'You'd think there'd be more than one woman with the name Despina.'

'However, there'd only be one notorious psychopath named Spyros who'd have a daughter by the same name with a birthmark. Where's Dilara? She can't ignore this grave situation. This absurd bungled up mess! And to allow these two women to go on assuming they're somebody they're not! Nilufer has barely come to terms that she is Zehra. How will she cope with this next transition in her life?

CHAPTER TWENTY-SIX

Rizokarpaso – 12th January 1964

Their clothes and umbrellas were synonymous with the bleak, low drifting clouds that partly eclipsed the forest of red cedars. Their attitudes were of devastating grief where they stood alongside the freshly hollowed out earth that was to be Zehra's final resting place. There was a rumbling of clouds that was followed by a downpour of rain, washing channels of water between the ancient, leaning tombstones. Pater Christofis in his long ecclesiastical robe stood in a gesture of impatience for he had no wish to catch pneumonia. 'Shall we begin,' he abruptly asked, and then began censing with the censor and chanting,

Holy God, Holy Mighty, Holy Immortal.

Indeed, how awesome of death is a mystery! How the soul is forcibly severed from its harmonious union with the body.

What pleasure of life ever remains unmixed with grief? What glory endures immovable earth? All are feebler than shadows, all are illusive than dreams. In a single moment all are supplanted by death. But. Like a flower it withers, and like a dream it vanishes and dissolves away human

being. For you are the resurrection, the life and repose of your departed servant Zehra.

Rifat and Pandelis lifted the embalmed body out of the casket. And as it was lowered deep into the earth Pater Christofis recited the last prayer.

Sprinkle me with hyssop and I shall be cleansed, wash me and I shall be whiter than snow.

Rifat's eyes were so red from crying that it was as if the deep and raw wound within his soul had bled into them. His friend Yilmaz gathered him in his arms and said, 'take courage brother. I'm sure Allah has set aside a special place for your cherry!'

The word 'cherry,' prompted another deluge of tears.

'We'd joked about being two different fruits. Because she was a Greek Christian, and I was a Turkish Muslim. When all along we'd been propagated in the same tree and without even knowing it!' He revealed with a lump welling in his throat. Yilmaz tightened his arms around him and then thought to ask, 'brother is it true what you told me?'

'Hmm, about what!'

'About that shaitan being buried alive in that fake grave. Or was it a joke?'

'Shh, someone might hear,' Rifat warned, with a nudge of his arm.

'I saw a big black grow scuffing at the earth of the burial site as we'd entered the forest.'

'Shh, quiet brother,' Rifat elbowed him again.

'Huh, a devil knows where to find his other half!' Yilmaz whispered, then added, 'I reckon it's really a Christian saint in disguise bro. You know, come to do its duty on earth!'

'And what's that!'

'To stand guard just in case the evil spirit springs up from hades to haunt the people again!'

Rifat remained expressionless, even though it was hard to hold back his laughter. He'd always been drawn to his ex-army comrade's quirky humour.

'You always find a way to make light of a grave situation Yilmaz,' he murmured, then drew his attention back to Pater Christofis who was swivelling his censor in all directions above the burial site as he chanted the final prayers of intercession.

Pandelis, he too was burdened with immense grief as he watched on by Thea's side.

Jusuf and Zenep had come along to the service. It was their way of atonement.

'Allah, forgive us Jusuf. It's all our fault!' his wife wept.

'Zenep honey don't punish yourself. It's the way of Allah. Not the way we or Rifat or anybody wanted it to be! Now, best we go home before you catch a cold.'

Zenep now turned to her son, 'here, my brave lion!' She passed him over the long-stemmed white lilies. Rifat in turn placed the flowers atop the wet earth. Then collectively, Rifat and his family and Yilmaz offered their condolences to Pandelis and then departed the necropolis.

Pandelis turned to Thea and asked, 'are you ready to leave?'

She stared at him wide-eyed and said, 'all this grief has gotten to you Kyrio! Did you think I was at an amusement park? It's the middle of winter and I'm standing in a necropolis. And you ask if I'm ready to leave! I'll be as frozen as the dead soon if I don't!'

What she'd said brought a smile to his face, a smile that he'd thought would be forever lost.

Pater Christofis came over to him now and said, 'may the memory of Zehra live on. And may God grant you courage good Christian! He coughed, adding, 'winter is never a good time for a clergy.' The cleric stood there with his arms folded in front of him, bible in one hand, umbrella in the other, and with his eyes following the wealthy industrialist's hands pull out a bundle of liras from the pocket of his overcoat.

'Are you sure?' He announced with the attitude of being paid too much for his service, but rapidly pocketed the money between the slit of his robe just the same.

The cleric tipped his broad black hat and then trudged back through the necropolis, his umbrella turning upwards in the strong wind. Unexpectedly, his attention was drawn to an ominous black crow perched atop a familiar burial site. He pondered its purpose there when his conscience was alerted.

He shook his head, raised his eyes to the heavens, crossed himself and murmured, 'forgive me, God Almighty for I have committed a grave sin. I have offered prayers of intercession on behalf of a slain animal carcass. All for the sake of a piece of bread! One could only wonder what the pious man would have thought if he was aware of who was buried in that gravesite now.'

CHAPTER TWENTY-SEVEN

Lefkosia — 16th January 1964

Dilara found the Our House charity store at the end of the pedestrian street near the Green Line in the old town of Lefkosia. After the recent intercommunal conflict between Greek and Turkish Cypriots the Green Line acted as a buffer zone between the north and south. UN peace keeping forces had been dispatched to stand guard in the event of future outbreaks between the two ethnic groups. This was a strange new cosmos for Dilara after many years of confinement in an orderly institution of devout nuns at the Holy Trinity. She was akin to a bear outside of its biological surroundings of bird calls, mountains and waterfalls and leafy woodland. There was a thin mist of fog and the smell of freshly brewed Turkish coffee tempted her to dig into her pocket for some loose change, but upon reflection changed her mind when she thought about all those Afghan and Syrian refugees with young children back at the shelter. It was Sister Louisa's idea that she should work in the charity store. She'd told Sister Doula when she'd rang last week that it was important that Dilara interact with society to restore her self-belief and confidence.

Though Dilara was just as happy to help the nuns and other volunteer workers at the Our House shelter where she'd lodged over the past nine months. She adjusted the collar of her overcoat to cover her ears then hurried to the other side of the road. There she drew up the outside awning before she removed the key to the store from her coat pocket and opened the door. Once inside, she turned on the light, removed her coat and hung it up on a hook behind the door. Soon the destitute and homeless would come through the doors with coupons provided to them by the department of community services. The coupons were substituted for any essential second-hand item they should require.

No sooner had she took her place behind the counter when a tall man dressed in a fine tailored overcoat and long woollen scarf stepped into the store.

Dilara considered the anomaly of why such an imposing man would be browsing through a charity store in this part of town at such an early hour of the morning. Perhaps he was an office worker on his way to work. Curiously, she observed him as he calmly strolled around hand-picking out items to inspect. She watched him lift out a women's blue linen suit from off the makeshift clothes rack in the centre of the room. 'Nice suit. It is said that a rich man's trash is a poor man's treasure. I can understand why. This suit has hardly been worn. Probably one of my late mother's suits.' He revealed in a voice that Dilara accepted to be derisive.

'If it is, then may Allah be pleased with her. Countless people depend on such resources. What the fortunate regard as merely waste is the salvation of others.'

'Wisely spoken Miss. You must be a Turkish Cypriot!'

Dilara felt improperly slighted that he should be talking to her while his back was facing her. She guessed that just because a person was wealthy meant they had manners. The illiterate and poor were more polite.

She ignored his question and asked, 'is there anything you need help with? If you have a coupon, that is. Though you don't appear to be a man that should require such requisites. However, feel free to browse just the same.'

'How long have you been a volunteer worker for the Our House society Dilara?

Did he just call me Dilara? Who is this man! Allah! It can't be him!

Just then Dilara felt a forceful pounding within her chest that took her breath away. On impulse she turned, so that it was her back that faced him now, and she could neither speak nor turn, as if fearing if she did, she'd be deceived by her own eyes, and that the man she'd see before her was just an illusion and not the man she'd desperately loved and lost two and half decades ago. *Is it really you Pandelis?*

And as if he'd read her mind he said, 'yes, it's really me! Pandelis! Well, are you just going to stand there staring at the wall?' he asked pertly.

What else should I do? Fall into your arms? Tell you how lonely and lost I was in your absence?

'You've mistaken me for someone else Kyrio!' She disclosed weakly, then when she heard his footsteps drawing nearer added, 'go away! Tears had smudged the kohl at her eyes, the only make-up she ever wore.

'You expect me to believe you? Now that I've finally found you!' He was on her side of the counter now. And standing so close to her that she felt the point of his shoes on her heels.

Dilara was weakened to the core for she could feel the warmth of his body, and smell the masculine, pine-scented fragrance of his cologne, and she felt his dark eyes set upon her face, burning her cheeks and yet she felt as cold as a block of ice. *I'm going to faint! No Dilara you mustn't!*

When he saw that she was trembling like a bird that was afraid to fly he took her cold hands in his own warm hands, and then discreetly and pitifully considered her green, frayed woollen dress, her scuffed, second-hand ankle boots at her feet, and with the inconsolable thought that this wasn't the kind of life he'd envisioned for the only woman he'd ever loved.

'Why did you find me? It's way too late, don't you think? You never bothered to come back after you were discharged from the army! Or at least left me an address so I'd know where I could find you!'

'Please Dilara listen to me! You've got it all wrong. I did write you a letter just before I was discharged. I'd even written my address where you could contact me. I left it with Mehmet, you'd know who he is. He told me he was the son of one of the refugee tribes that raised you.'

'Mehmet! Well, I never got it.'

'He promised he'd pass it on to you. I'd also written that I wanted to marry you!'

'Well, I didn't get it and what makes you so sure I would've?' She defiantly broke in.

'Because you loved me. And because you were carrying my child! Zehra!' he frankly revealed.

Just then Dilara was shellshocked. 'Leave now! I never want to see you again. Go back to where you belong!'

He caught her arm, clasped her so tightly that she couldn't move.

'This is where I belong! Beside you. Did you think that the fire you'd lit in my heart twenty-five years ago would cease to burn? You deprived me of a life and a child! Why Dilara?' He stared longingly deep into her eyes, eyes that were reminiscent of the black pearls of the sea, read the torment and heartache within.

'What makes you think she's your child?'

'You haven't lost your performing talent Dilara! But now's not the time for play-acting. Sister Louisa told me everything.'

'What did she tell you?' she asked shaken.

'Everything! I know what happened to Zehra. And to Despina. After Despina's accident she was adopted by a Turkish Cypriot man called Jihan Akalay. He's a physician in the village of Kakopedria! You'd know him well, since you helped him in his clinic a few days a week. You might have married him if you hadn't found out the truth. That his adopted daughter Nilufer was Despina, your milk child. And that maniac Spyros had mistaken her for Zehra and planned on peddling her to a hide merchant just to get rid of his mistress's illegitimate child. Which happens to be my daughter too Dilara! My daughter, did you hear? You destroyed her life!'

Just then Dilara sensed that something had happened to Zehra. Had Sister Louisa lied to her when she told her that she'd found out that Zehra was studying literature and history? And that she'd moved

347

out of Spyros's house and was staying with a few college friends. And if he'd said that the nun had told him everything, then he would have passed on the good news by now.

'Where is Zehra!' She wasted no time to ask him.

'Now's not the time! Come,' he said, ushering her out from behind the counter.

'Let go of my arm! Where are you taking me? Let go of me or...'

'Or you'll what? Call the police? Tell them I'm abducting you after you abandoned our young daughter and left her in the hands of a psychopath! Ruined her life!'

He'd told Sister Louisa that it was imperative that she not disclose news to Dilara about Zehra's death. He wanted to break the news to her himself.

'Where are you taking me?' she demanded. 'I can't leave the store!'

'We need to talk! I've organised for someone else to replace you. Now come!'

Dilara felt the pressure of his hand firmly clenched to her arm, and she found it hard to keep up with his rapid strides as they walked back through the pedestrian street.

'Where are you taking me?' She repeated when she saw him open the front door of his vehicle parked by the curb.

'You'll find out,' he said as he waited for her to climb in. As retribution for what she'd done he might have told her that he was taking her back to where she deserved to be. Back to that hell hole where her nightmare had begun with Spyros. But of course, he knew it was beyond his gentle capacity to insult the woman he adored in such a harsh way.

Pandelis wasted no time climbing into the driver's seat, ensuring to lock all doors once she took up seat alongside of him. Dilara afforded him a questioning state and said, 'did you think I'd be foolish enough to jump out while you were driving?

'Nothing you did would surprise me Dilara!' He declared soberly as he pulled out of the curb.

He then added, 'you've made some reckless and unwise decisions in your life. And you've paid a heavy penalty as a result of those choices. We are the authors of our own novel. We can choose which way we want to go. And the outcome that we hope to achieve depends entirely on the decisions we make along the way. Did you honestly think when you left our young daughter with that psychopath Spyros that she'd be safe? Or did you just somehow assume that Katina would protect and raise our child in your absence? As you discovered for yourself the woman's a traitress.'

'I had to bury myself so Zehra could live. She wouldn't have survived otherwise.'

She didn't survive, just the same, he might have told her. And what about Rifat? Or Omer, as she'd named him prior to bequeathing him to Zenep and Jusuf. And what about his love affair with their daughter?

Zehra might have been able to accept the fact that she wasn't Despina. It wouldn't have happened overnight, but in time she would. After all, a name was just a name, it wouldn't have defined who she really was. It was the personality that reflected one's inner being. Regardless, of whether she was Despina or Zehra, it was the same person that Rifat had become acquainted with over the years. The only momentous bearing on their relationship was that they were siblings. And after building a lifetime of dreams for a brighter future together, and knowing she couldn't marry him, Zehra had nothing to live for anymore. Pandelis wondered had they not been siblings, would she have gone ahead and married Rifat? Or would she have believed that a tarnished soul couldn't rest in a wholesome heart after Spyros violated her womanhood! Would her cold and contorted body have ended up on the outcrop far below the cliff where she'd been found?

The vision of Zehra aroused him with untold grief. He had to force the tears back so she wouldn't see.

There was a long silence which was punctuated by the sound of Dilara's whimpering as she gulped back her own tears. Furtively, he rolled his eyes her way, saw that her tears had bled into the kohl at her eyes. He leaned sideways and retrieved his handkerchief from his coat pocket and passed it to her. 'Here, you've made an awful mess of your beautiful face. And your life Dilara!'

She recoiled when his fist struck the wheel with unrestrained anger.

The thought that she'd allowed herself to become her persecutor's mistress caused him unbearable anguish. After he lost her, for years he'd been plagued by the thought of her falling into the arms of another man, but he could never have imagined for one minute that it would be into the arms of a vile psychopath.

His mind was blown away, his stomach turned by the thought of that scumbag Spyros being intimate with Dilara. He could just imagine his boozy breath, his body dripping with foul odour, grunting and moaning like a wild boar with her pinned under him. His fist clenched the wheel, turned his knuckles white.

He'd have to get Pater Christofis to baptise her in holy water, cleanse the impurity of him from her body. *When lust has been conceived, it bringeth forth sin, and when sin is finished, it bringeth forth death.*

'You're scaring me,' she voiced quietly, with downcast eyes.

'If you could see inside my soul Dilara you'd also see me buried there. You'd find only a pile of grey ashes.'

'Forgive me. I know I can't change or repair the damage I've caused my children,' she said remorsefully.

'Your children? Zehra was also my daughter. The son you had with that dirtbag! He exclaimed with his eyes on her. Dilara let out a frightful squeal when she saw the vehicle swerve off course.

'You'll kill us both if you don't calm down!' she exclaimed panic-stricken.

Pandelis was quick to take control and pilot the vehicle to the side of the road's asphalt.

When the vehicle come to a complete halt, he glanced over at her and said, 'we both died a long time ago Dilara. So, how many times can a person die? He had the urge to kiss her, and when he did, Dilara felt her pulse quicken, as if all at once it was possible to be resurrected. In that moment of blissful trance, she could only hope that in time he would forgive her for all her transgressions, and that her own devotion in turn would be enough to restore his faith in her again. They had much to talk about over the ensuing few hours.

He told Dilara all that he'd found out about Katina and her sister. He also told her how he'd found out that he'd been born illegitimate as a result of his mother's affair with General Pappas.

'How did you find out? Did your mother finally confess?'

'I found out from our maid. Of all people. Thea was the keeper of our family's secrets for many years. It wasn't until recently she confessed everything to me. She'd said I deserved to know the truth. In fact, she'd even told my mother Sofia that she knew all the family's dirty laundry. Not long after mother had a stroke that left her partially paralysed. She's been confined to a wheelchair and has been placed in a nursing home because she needs high level care. In my opinion, there's nothing to say she wouldn't have had a stroke if she'd found out that I also knew about her and my late stepfather's secrets.'

'Ariana was the naïve casualty caught up in Katina's foul play. She was just a young maid in your family's household.'

'And I saw her as just that. In the same way as I did Katina. Besides, as you know my heart belonged only to you Dilara. Anyway, she bullied Ariana into marrying Spyros based on the promise that my stepfather would talk me into marrying her. You see, the field was in exchange for her silence, so she wouldn't report the rape. Losing a few stretches of land meant nothing to my stepfather compared to losing his chance at becoming the next mayor of Famagusta. Or even ending up in jail. Though he'd felt reassured for a while up until the time Katina broke the news to him that her sister was pregnant. Then Katina really did have him dancing in the palm of her hands. She knew that if news spread that he'd fathered an illegitimate child with a servant of his household his life really would be ruined. So, again in exchange for her silence she forced him to surrender the orchard house. She was just as obsessed with that house as she was with me.

352

She even went with him to the Department of Land and Surveys and had him transfer the title deeds in her name.'

'Really? Why, the traitress! What was she planning to do with the house?

'She must have worked out in that crazy mind of her that it was to be the matrimonial house after we wed,' he said with a touch of irony. He then added, 'that was just another thing mother found out about just before her stroke. The shock had been too much for her.'

'Well, you're not going to let her get away with it, are you? Give her the advantage of taking you for a dupe too!' Dilara complained.

'I've been to see her! She could hardly look me in the eyes.' Then he recalled what Thea had told him his mother had told Katina on the day she fired her. 'I'd say that she felt like a pathetic caterpillar that feeds in the earth.'

'That's a decent interpretation of who she is. Not even if you'd spat in her face would she have felt any differently. So, did you sort things out?'

'The title deeds have been transferred back into my name. I also want to tell you that I've organised to have Ariana institutionalised where she'd have proper care.

That shameless woman caused her sister to lose both her mind and child. Despina is her niece. But we'd have to say Spyros was just as much a culprit in all of this,' he condemned.

'God only knows what he did to his young wife! I found out that Despina's been seeing a psychiatrist for a few years. How will she come to terms knowing that her biological mother has been admitted to a mental asylum and knowing that her biological father had raped her mother? I was just thinking, do you think Spyros suspected that the child Ariana was carrying wasn't his after he married her?'

'What are you getting at Dilara?'

'He did collaborate with Katina, didn't he? And there's nothing to say that she didn't tell him.'

'I doubt that very much. I mean why would she? A cunning woman like her! Look Dilara, my late father Yiannis was a very rich and powerful man. If Spyros had known that the child Ariana was carrying was his, then he'd be the one with those title deeds to the orchard house in his hand. Not Katina! If anything, he would have blackmailed Yiannis for everything he just about had. Right down to the last drop of blood in his veins. He wouldn't have stayed on living in that hovel of his and toiling in the tobacco field.'

'In my opinion, what Katina felt for you wasn't love. It was nothing short of an unhealthy obsession that poisoned her mind and soul to commit traitorous acts of evil. May Allah punish her in whatever way He deems suitable.'

They stopped along the way to rest and have a warm meal at a roadside tavern. Since it was mid-winter, by the time they returned to the peninsula in the north, the sun had gone down. The scent of burning woodfire mingled in the veil of fog. It reminded Dilara of her time up in the mountains each winter when smoke rose in curls from the multitude of chimney tops atop the red terracotta roofed houses perched on the slopes of the surrounding villages.

Thea had lit her own crackling fire in the hearth of the living room in preparation for when Pandelis arrived home. She'd been kept busy during his absence over the last few days. She'd baked all kinds of traditional Cypriot pastries and cakes. This afternoon she'd made *drahana* soup, and a rabbit stew with plenty of onions, red wine, and dried coriander and cumin seeds for flavour, along with a side dish of pilaf.

Thea, as usual came out of the house to greet him, only this time, she came out with more enthusiasm. After all, why wouldn't she be eager to meet the stunning woman whose portrait she'd been staring at on a canvas for many years?

CHAPTER TWENTY-EIGHT

Lefkosia — 26th January 1964

Nilufer sat opposite Professor Lambros with the dreaded anticipation one has when expecting bad news. She'd received a phone call from him a few days ago asking her to come in and see him. She removed mastic from her bag, popped it into her mouth and watched him withdraw the familiar brown-leather covered notebook and place it atop the broad oak desk in front of him. 'I appreciate that you came! Would you like a glass of water before we start?'

'Water! It took fifteen minutes to get here, not four days.'

'How's your father?'

'I'm sure you didn't bring me here to talk about my father! You said it was important.'

'I see, you're still angry with him. You shouldn't be. Mr Jihan was the huge tree that shaded you throughout the years. You must be respectful of all his labour and dedication towards you.'

'You're right. But he could have at least been honest with me. Don't you think?'

'Sometimes we must be cruel to be kind. I'm sure he had your best interest at heart.'

'Well, his interest in me wore off the moment he met that woman! She was all that mattered to him!'

'You still hold a grudge against Dilara. You shouldn't. I'm sure she doesn't feel that way about you. I'm sure if you'd given her a chance then you both would have become friends.'

'Are you kidding me? She'd be the last person I'd want as a friend,' she criticised.

'Who would you regard as your best friend? Hmm!'

She gave him a questioning stare and said, 'are you trying to tell me that I'm unworthy of having friends? Or that I'd feel obligated to befriend that woman as a last resort so as to fulfill my lonely life?'

'That wasn't what I was implying. Besides, you've found a close companion in Rifat. How is he, by the way?' he cautiously probed.

'He's enlisted to go to flight school in Istanbul!' She revealed quietly, and he noticed the tone in her voice was that of regret.

Just then, the door swung open, and he got up to greet the couple that entered the room.

'Miss Dilara, Kyrie Pandelis. I'm glad you both could come. Please take a seat.'

'What are you doing here? What's this all about?'

'I can explain!' Dilara said.

'It's my father who needs an explanation for your heartless actions! I told him you couldn't be trusted! And I was right?'

'Your father is an exceptional and wise man. I admired him for his dedication towards the sick children at the orphanage. We both enjoyed each other's company.

We laughed a lot when we were together. I'll always hold him dear to my heart. But only as a special friend. I never once raised his hopes of marriage.'

Surreptitiously she considered Dilara's fine leather ankle boots, the dark woollen overcoat, and her curling, long reddish-brown hair that tumbled over the neckline. She'd done away with her habitual cotton headscarfs and dreary frocks.

The only thing that was in discord with everything else were the traces of purplish rings under her eyes. She wondered the reason behind this urbane transformation. She now set her eyes upon the well-attired man standing beside her.

'It appears you've substituted my father for a rich man to liberate you from the monotony of volunteer work Dilara. Perhaps you might like to introduce me to your new man!'

'You never did like me, did you? I can't blame you,' Dilara said warmly. 'That's because you didn't know me and that's why your treating physician has asked me to come here today. To give you a chance to find out who I really am.'

The elderly scholar was becoming restless. 'Please, we are all adults, and nothing is ever gained by bickering. Miss Dilara you might like to get straight to the point, or we'll all be here till dark.'

'I'm Zehra's mother,' she announced.

'Even your jokes are out of sorts Dilara. I'd always sensed a kind of shrewd, peculiarity about you!'

'Dilara is telling the truth. Please let her finish explaining,' Pandelis advised.

'There's nothing to explain! I know the truth! My mother was a gypsy whore who abandoned me with Despina's father. She was his mistress, and she ran off with the boy he'd fathered and left me with that monster. He tried to sell me.'

When Pandelis saw Dilara's distress he said, 'we are both aware of what he did to you.'

'Who are you? And what business have you got being here with this woman?'

'Pardon, I never got the chance to introduce myself. My name is Pandelis Gapsalis. Dilara and I met twenty-five-years ago. We were in love. I wanted to marry her. Something I should have told her before I was discharged from the army. And she never had the chance to tell me she was pregnant with my child. I'd written a letter with my contact details before I was cleared but unfortunately the letter was never passed onto her for some unknown reason. We both went our separate ways until I found her again.'

Dilara added, 'Sister Louisa asked me if the reason I didn't want to marry Mr Jihan was because I'd lived in the hope that I'd be reunited with the soldier boy one day. I told her that he'd never find me up in those mountains where I was. She said that only mountains never united, but people did. It turns out she was right! A wonder just the same.'

The elder nodded pensively then said, 'imagine the world with a network of invisible threads and every person at each end of a single thread. By some mysterious force we are lured to pull on it and are ultimately joined.'

'Well, Dilara you finally found your prince amongst men! And you Kyrie have found your princess bride in waiting! Why, it's the perfect fairy-tale ending. I've heard enough.'

She got up to leave when the elder said, 'sit down doctor Akalay! You came to me nearly three years ago wanting to find out the missing parts of your life. Now's your chance to find out the truth. So, you'd better think twice before you walk out that door. Otherwise, you'll go on existing in the shadow as somebody else's ghost without knowing who you really are.'

'He's right!' Dilara said, then added, 'that snow dome in your room. Do you remember who gave it to you?'

'You never give up, do you? I find your discourtesy and probing intolerable. I don't know what father saw in you!'

Dilara ignored the insult and said, 'I was the woman who gave it to you.'

'You don't know what you're talking about?'

'I took you to see the camel and you told me your mother had died! You told me you'd come on the school bus.'

'You're the camel lady! I don't believe it!'

'What about Bebek! Do you remember her?'

'You mean that anathemised woman who slept in a burrow under that man's house and ran around naked in the yard shouting profanities? How would you know her? And why are you asking if I remember her?'

'She's your biological mother. Her name is Ariana!'

'You're lying! I don't want to hear anymore! It can't be true! My mother was a gypsy whore. She was that man's mistress, and she ran off with the boy she had with him. So, it can't be true!'

'That boy she ran off with was Rifat! The junior lieutenant that rescued you! He was raised by a Turkish Muslim couple in Rizo. Their names are Jusuf and Zenep. Like I told you before, I'm Zehra's mother. Rifat and Zehra are siblings,' Dilara said.

'And I'm Zehra's father,' Pandelis offered. He then gave Dilara a meaningful stare and added, 'you might like to tell this young lady who she really is.'

'Your name is Despina. I was a young and unwed girl of eighteen with a newborn daughter I named Zehra. She was born just before Christmas in the year 1939. Your mother Ariana gave birth to you in the spring of that following year in 1940. I'd come to the village of Rizo that same day. I was going to give Zehra to that Muslim couple I just told you about. As things turned out I gave them my son Omer instead. This couple changed his name to Rifat, since he was to be raised in the same village as his biological father. Anyway, my plans were deflected when the village midwife found me that day and told me your mother had yielded to a strange illness after giving birth to you. Unlike anything she'd seen before. I agreed to become your milk mother. And that's how I met Spyros. He'd told me your mother had died and that your sick mother was his sister. I believed him and that's why I stayed on and became his mistress.'

'Why would my mother marry that maniac? And if he wasn't my real father then who is?'

'Your father is dead. And you wouldn't have wanted to know him.

Trust me. His utmost priority was wealth and power. Nobody would have been caught up in this whole perverted saga if not for his repulsive and immoral actions,' Pandelis explained.

'Then he must have raped her and left her pregnant with me then refused to marry her. Probably a proxy marriage to spare her honour. He maltreated her just like the rest of us and that's why she lost her sanity. Am I right? Tell me!'

'Something close to that! It's a complicated story. Perhaps one day I will explain,' Pandelis said.

'Where is my mother now?'

'She'll get the proper care where she is,' he advised.

'A mental asylum! Despina turned to Dilara and tempestuously said, 'it's all your fault! All of it! Do you hear? If you'd left that madman before you had Rifat then none of this would have happened. You brainless woman!'

'Please refrain from such offensive remarks!' the elderly cautioned. 'Or you'll regret it!'

'The only person who should have regrets is this woman! It was no wonder she took refuge in the orphanage of the Holy Trinity all these years. It was her way of penitence. Not even God would exonerate her for her wrongdoings! Wait till father hears about what a heartless char-latan she is! Why, he'll thank his good fortune that she left him and didn't agree to marry him!'

Dilara buried her tear-soaked face into the palms of her hands, her shoulders shook, her chest rising with each gasping sob. Pandelis tried to console her.

The elderly scholar considered her dejected demeanour then nodded with undecided emotions. He suddenly sprung from his chair and said, 'I'll get you a glass of water!'

He passed it over to her, took a seat behind his desk again, leaned back, folded his arms, and stared over at Despina guardedly, pondered a while before he said, 'I understand how hurt and upset you are. But Miss Dilara doesn't merit cruel insults just the same. It's unfair, don't you think? She'd assumed you were orphaned of a mother. In the same way Zehra was of a biological father. She told you she was only eighteen at the time.'

Dilara wiped her eyes and went on to explain, 'I was young and naïve. And I was in desperate need of a home for myself and that of my infant Zehra. As your milk mother Despina, I'd felt a strong maternal connection to you. But I couldn't have known that beneath the charm and courteous gestures Spyros was a deranged and evil man. He almost killed me. And he might have if I'd stayed on, and my children would have been orphaned of a mother. It was two years into the second war. I made the difficult and heartbreaking decision to surrender my children otherwise they would have perished of destitution.'

'They almost did, just the same, don't you think?' Despina asked.

'If I'd known what he was going to do, I would have sacrificed my own life.'

'Did you think a psychopath would take mercy on two small children? He was always drunk, and he smoked hashish, I remember. Zehra and I called it his snake pipe! Though we couldn't have known it was pot at the time.'

Just then the elderly scholar decided that he should be the one to clarify to Despina how she'd become who she is today. 'Seemingly a man in such a disoriented state of mind wouldn't have known a frog from a lizard, let alone who was who in the company of two toddlers. All it would take is just once to misidentify the child to be that of the other. So, in his neurotic and screwed up mind he'd just go on assuming her to be that child. He mistook you for Zehra.'

'Why that reckless, unhinged lunatic! He stole my childhood! My identity!' Despina cried. She felt like some nameless, wounded dog that had been rescued by a stranger and given a new name. Only to be returned to where it had originated.

'How can you be sure I'm Despina? You might be mistaken?'

Lambros readily said, 'Miss Dilara will confirm that you had a lactose intolerance when she took you off her breast. As you are yourself aware of. And you don't have a birthmark in your upper, inner thigh. That nurse that your father hired to look after you full time after you suffered amnesia after your accident also confirmed this. She bathed you each day.'

'And you have your mother's grey eyes Despina,' Dilara said, adding, 'Zehra has brown eyes. I hope you'll find a tiny space in your heart to forgive me. I'd loved you as my own daughter. My feelings haven't changed despite of what you think of me.' She wanted to fold her arms around her but feared her well-disposed deed would be met with condemnation.

She was unsure if she'd forgive her or not over time. However, either way, Dilara would respect her decision just the same.

'You mean Rifat fell in love with his own sister and thought it was me, Despina?'

Professor Lambros said, 'unfortunately, this appears to be the case.'

'O God! Why has this happened? Then that explains Rifat's random decision to go to flight school in Istanbul. He's running away! He's found out who his real parents are and that he was adopted and that Zehra is his sister! His heart must be torn into a thousand pieces. And what about Zehra. She might never recover. Well, where is she? Why aren't you with her?'

There was a long silence with momentary exchanged glances between them as if each were waiting for the other to break the sad news to her.

'My condolences. She was buried two weeks ago!' Pandelis quietly disclosed.

'She's dead! God no! A person can't die twice!' Despina's eyes welled with tears by the recollection of Zehra, the young girl whom she'd come to know as Despina. That smart, funny and compassionate girl who'd promised never to let go of her hand. Who'd always wanted to protect her from the evil fate of the man they believed to be their father.

Pandelis removed Zehra's diary from his coat pocket and passed it to her. 'You might like to read it! You were never blood sisters but bonded as such. You'll realise that Zehra never gave up on you! And she'd upheld a deep admiration for you up until the very end.'

Despina was genuinely moved by Zehra's unwavering adoration towards her all these years. Though unsurprised that she would want to document her life in a journal. Her soul must have been heavily saturated with undeclared grievances. She stroked the leather-bound diary ever so gently as if not to disturb the words of its author concealed within.

'Thank you. It means a lot to me.' She was soothed by the thought that while Zehra was sleeping her long sleep she would be just as much alive in her writings.

'I'm sorry for your loss.' Dilara said, adding 'I can't make you forgive me. But if there's a small chance that you'll find it in your heart to pardon me for my wrongdoing then this alone will be enough.'

Despina peered up at her, as if seeing her for the first time, and in that moment of silent reflection, observed how arresting her beauty was, and caught the absolute pathos within her dark eyes.

She gave her a meaningful smile and announced, 'I forgive you Miss Dilara.'

'All seems to have ended well! The elderly remarked as he walked around to their side of the room. He addressed his patient first, 'well young lady, doctor Akalay I couldn't have expected a better outcome, if I may say so.'

'Seems like you've finally gotten rid of me Professor! Despina teased.

'That was my intention all along,' he replied with equal irony.

Both Pandelis and Dilara chuckled by this interchange of humorous banter between them.

Then Pandelis said, 'Dilara and I are both indebted for all you've done. We'll keep in touch Professor.'

'I'll see you out,' then thought to ask, 'Miss Dilara, is it true that Sister Louisa likes a good drop of whiskey!

'Oh yes indeed. She says she only drinks on special occasions, though she always has a reserve hidden somewhere at the back of her closet in her office,' Dilara tittered.

'Is that right? Interesting lady. I think she and I would have been the best of friends had we met many a blue moon ago.'

Dilara was taken by surprise as she couldn't imagine a more unlikely combination. But it was said that opposites attract.

'You should visit her in the spring. It's cherry season. I know of a wonderful tavern that overlooks Morphu Bay. There's an ancient amphi-theatre just below the hill. Or you might consider a picnic in the open air.'

'You think the holy nun would be open to such a suggestion?' he asked.

'I'm sure she'd be delighted!' Dilara smiled.

'Well, now that's something to think about!' he chuckled, closing the door behind him.

CHAPTER TWENTY-NINE

Rizokarpaso-July 1964

Dilara was captivated when she drew back the curtain of the guest room upstairs and saw the spectacular vision in the mansion's garden below. It was a fashion parade of bejewelled women strutting in costly vibrant gowns and flared hats. And men in their dinner suits and bow ties appeared stifled in the mid-afternoon sun.

Maids offered the guests a variety of appetizers from oval silver trays while waiters poured champagne in glasses of crystal. Guests were entertained by a trio orchestra playing classical music positioned in a corner of the garden's high stone wall. To one side of the grass chairs were placed in long rows and which would be replaced by long tables after the ceremony when guests sat down to a feast of sumptuous food prepared by leading chefs.

'Oh my, what a grand affair it appears,' she quietly voiced as it all seemed surreal.

Pater Christofis was standing on the grass under an archway of palm leaves, gardenias, white sail-cloth lilies and pink and white roses. He was seemingly gratified that he'd been chosen to perform the marriage ceremony before so many distinguished and wealthy guests. He was even more pleased by the prospect of being well rewarded.

Dilara could see Rifat and his friend Yilmaz talking to the boy Nikos. Despina had told her that the boy was a Syrian fugitive who'd spent most of his time in a juvenile delinquent centre. She'd become fond of the boy with the carved earlobe during her counselling sessions with him.

And so, she'd organised with the appropriate government authorities to have him released on a good behaviour bond. Based on the condition he was placed in a good home. The government preferred these delinquents be rehabilitated rather than kept in detention centres.

Rifat had told her that his foster parents had agreed to let Nikos stay with them provided he worked alongside of Jusuf in his workshop to learn the trade of chair-weaving.

Despina was socialising with guests and whom was to be her maid of honour. She looked a vision of elegance dressed in a full skirted, strapless wine-red gown that Dilara had bought her for the special occasion. She even noticed Jusuf and Zenep admiring her from afar where they stood in the shade of a citrus tree. Rifat had been staying with his foster parents in Rizo since being discharged from the Turkish army.

Despina was on summer vacation for two weeks. When she had moved into the mansion, Despina had been staying as a guest at the orchard house. Lydia, the younger maid had been assigned to the house to tend to her needs. She'd been fascinated by the charming Mediterranean villa that was surrounded by vineyards and fruit orchards. Murat drove her back and forth each day. She'd told Dilara that she'd enjoyed her stay so much that she was reluctant to leave. Dilara felt the same way, however she knew that Despina had a bright career to pursue and that she'd always be dependent on the man who'd raised her as his own daughter. For that she was grateful. She also knew that her son had been spending a lot of time with Despina. She was always a tad breathless and excited to tell her about these day trips with Rifat. They explored ancient Byzantine ruins and cathedrals amongst the thistledowns and stunted fig trees and drove up to the headland to take in the breathtaking views of the Mediterranean Sea beyond the sea cliffs.

Pandelis had told them about the 'wishing tree,' he'd visited as a young boy, and so they'd picnicked there amidst the parcels of red poppies and wild herbs.

After they'd even left a coin under a stone at the foot of the tree and had tied a ribbon on its boughs and made a wish. Dilara wondered if her son and Despina had become more than just friends.

What a happenstance it would be if Despina became her future daughter-in-law. What about Jihan bey! Would he be mortified by the idea of Rifat being his son-in-law! Or would he adhere to his own philosophical evaluation and just be grateful for all the good things that had come his way in life?

She now pushed aside these speculative theories and thought about yesterday when both Despina and Rifat had gone to the forest of red cedars. It was to be her son's last tribute of affection for Zehra before leaving. Or for a while at least. An imposing tombstone of sandstone had replaced the mound of earth.

On the headstone, the inscription read: *Zehra Gapsalis 1939-1964. Dearly beloved daughter of Dilara and Pandelis and sister of Rifat.*

Thea had told her about the time Zehra had gone into Pandelis's art studio. And she'd seen the portrait of her that Pandelis had painted when she was eighteen before he'd been discharged from the Greek army.

She said it saddened her deeply knowing that Zehra went to the grave without ever knowing who her mother was. She'd said that if God had given her a sign, even if it had been in a dream, that Zehra was to tragically end her own life, then she would have told her that the portrait was of her mother when she'd asked who the girl was.

Dilara wiped a tear, mindful of the kohl at her eyes. She didn't want to ruin her make-up on her special day. Today was to be a day of celebration and she sensed that Zehra would want her to rejoice her life in as much the same way, not grieve it.

She could now see Sister Louisa and Professor Lambros chatting to Pater Christofis under the archway. She guessed affection had no boundaries, nor did it discriminate age or status. She would miss the religious nun who'd become her close confidant during her time at the children's orphanage.

Presently, Dilara moved away from the window and made her way across the imposing room. She stood before the mirror, deliberated a while, as if trying to reassure herself that the image of the woman dressed in a regal, long gown of ivory, embossed with a filigree of French lace was really her.

At that moment Thea came through the door of the guest room, and the aroma of frankincense wafted in the air, and so Dilara turned away from the mirror to see twirls of smoke rising from the tiny brass incense burner in her hand.

'Mashalla, even the most beautiful of goddesses would be envious of you!'

'Thanks for the flattery but I'm going on forty-four Thea, not twenty,' she laughed.

'Besides, I'm unaccustomed to such lavish attire. Give me a simple dress and flat shoes and a headscarf any day!'

'Kyria, it's your wedding day! And you are the lady of the mansion now. You can't walk around looking like a mud duck. So don't go asking me if that whopping diamond ring is suited to your finger!' she grumbled.

'It's magnificent I must confess. But I feel guilty when there are so many underprivileged children in shelters. I mean the cost of this ring alone could feed and clothe them for at least two years.'

'You're too sensitive and modest. You deserve such fineries. Besides, you're marrying one of the wealthiest bachelors in the country! Not only can he afford to clothe and feed these unfortunate children that you speak of but also give you the best of everything.' Then thoughtlessly added, 'Katina must have turned as green as a frog by now!'

She even had the unsettling thought that she might be lurking behind some dense shrub in the garden to get a glimpse of the bride. Thea imagined how distraught Katina would be at having laboured for many years at the expense of her lost dreams.

'Best I bless you before these coals turn to ash,' she advised.

She recited a prayer as she circled the burner a few times over Dilara's lowered head. Then spat a few times to ward off the evil eye, like this, ptou ptou! Satisfied, the elderly glanced at her watch.

'Good Lord! It's almost 1 p.m. You have twenty minutes to finish up here. And I'm needed in the kitchen!'

Thea didn't trust these modern-day caterers. They knew nothing about traditional Cypriot cuisine. They were used to what socialites considered to be fine dining as Sofia used to boast when she came home after luncheon with friends in town.

From what she described, to her, it sounded like a bit of caviar and a crab claw with a dribble of sauce on a fancy plate. *A waste of para*, she thought.

Just as Thea got to the door she looked back and said, 'by the way, don't forget to step on the groom's foot after the ceremony.'

It was Greek tradition that the woman step on her new husband's foot with her shoe so he would fear her in marriage. Though Dilara didn't need to be reminded as Muslims also followed this custom.

'And your bridal bouquet Kyria!'

'I won't forget!' Dilara was amused by the mature woman's tenacity. If only she wouldn't forget to simply call her *Dilara*, instead of addressing her in such a formal way.

It was beyond her nature to think herself superior to anybody else. It was apparent that the maid had been obliged to speak to the previous lady of the mansion this way. Thus, it had become force of habit that she spoke to her similarly. She realised there were many things she'd have to get used to as Pandelis's future wife.

Dilara was met by the proud groomsman Grigori Savvas in the

downstairs foyer.

When she stepped out into the garden with her arm threaded through his arm there was an eruption of animated applause and the women readily passed on their opinion of the bride amongst themselves.

'Oh, she's so beautiful. And the dress is magnificent,' one woman whispered.

'French lace, I believe! Must have cost a small fortune,' a second woman revealed.

'Shall we begin?' Pater Christofis asked with a great flap of his sleeves, seemingly unsure of what all the fuss was about as Dilara joined Pandelis under the archway.

The cleric began to chant the wedding vows in both elevated and mincing, low tones.

The ceremony concluded with the traditional Stefania being exchanged a few times over the bride and groom's head.

Then guests stood up and applauded and the trio orchestra struck up a lively Greek ballad.

The first to congratulate them was Despina and Grigori. Once all the guests had passed on their good wishes, everybody sat down to feast and drink. Tables were cleared and handkerchiefs came out, they joined hands and danced in circles.

'Am I allowed to smash a few plates?' Rifat asked, then left to find Nikos and Yilmaz.

Despina wandered off to find a waiter to refill her flute with champagne.

She rarely drank alcohol, save on the odd occasion when Mr Jihan insisted that a glass of red wine with the evening meal was both good for the heart and blood. Whether there was any truth in this, Despina didn't know. Though what she did know was that both the excitement of this ceremonious day and all the champagne she'd consumed had left her in a delightful state of merriment. Then again, it could just be that she was spellbound by Rifat's presence.

She knew that soon he would be leaving for Istanbul to attend flight school. It would take four years before he became a first flight officer. The thought momentarily dulled Despina's mood. She would miss him but would look forward to receiving his letters.

She could understand Zehra's deep and enduring adoration for Rifat. He was polite, informative and intelligent. The remembrance of her, even if it be elusive, brought tears to her eyes but the light of her spirit would glow eternally in her heart. Zehra was her heroine, friend and sister. But the sun always shined after the rain.

And if one died in spirit they would cease to exist. She peered over at Rifat and Yilmaz who were chatting by the fishpond. She suddenly saw Rifat burst into laughter, another one of Yilmaz's jokes, she assumed.

'So, you'll be flying planes, eh? Aren't you scared bro? I mean, flying up there so high in the air!'

'Anybody can fly a plane bro! It's what you can do in an emergency that counts. Besides, I'll be as close to heaven as anybody can get,' Rifat said.

'What if the plane came down? Nobody comes back from heaven!'

'I'd probably land on earth still seated in the cockpit with a smile on my face!' Rifat said.

'Why would you be smiling bro?' Yilmaz asked.

'A man can have an imagination, can't he?' Rifat jeered.

Yilmaz pondered a while but failed to grasp the ingenuity of his friend's mind. *Perhaps he'd meant that he'd seen his 'cherry' way up there in those fluffy clouds? Nah, he'd think him an utter screwball.*

'Well, did Zehra's father bury your father alive?' He now asked.

'Depends on which way you look at it!' Rifat replied.

'What do you mean!' Yilmaz asked.

'You can't have an empty grave bro. You've got to give the worms something to feed on!'

Despina was talking to Professor Lambros when she decided to join Rifat and Yilmaz. She excused herself then come towards them, a little wobbly on her heels. She then tapped Rifat on the shoulder. He turned, collided with her arm and the full glass of champagne in her hand splashed up, showering her face, and they burst into laughter. Then on a whim Rifat leaned over and kissed her wet cheek.

If Zehra had been staring down through the fountains of blue air and captured this playful moment between the two, she would recall a time and place where she'd been before. It was a long time ago, perhaps another era. But she was there now, but she would have to go way back to where it all began. A small lamp-lit room. A makeshift booth. School children huddled on a threadbare rug. A small, brown-eyed boy with coiling, longish dark hair squatting beside her. Both had cups of iced rosewater in their hands.

The curtain draws back, and the puppet drops just as the boy bursts into raucous laughter at its jaunty antics, splutters the iced rosewater all over her face then licks it off with his warm slippery tongue.

Made in United States
North Haven, CT
22 February 2023

32970258R00232